VAMP TOWN

BOOK ONE OF
THE MONSTER KEEPER SERIES

JEFF SEATS

SDPUBLISHING

Published by SD Publishing

Publisher's Note: This is a work of fiction. Names,
characters, places, and incidents are a product of the author's imagination.
Locales and public names are sometimes used for atmospheric purposes. Any
resemblance to actual people, living or dead, or to businesses, companies,
events, institutions, or locales is completely coincidental.

Vamp Town/Jeff Seats - 1st ed.

ISBN: 978-0-9983896-0-8

For my mother who wouldn't know a vampire from a zombie
but always believes in me.

Acknowledgments

Thanks to my daughter Elizabeth Seats and her friend Craig Riedler whose core idea of a bus load of people stumbling into a town populated by vampires led first to a screenplay and then to this novel. They provided me the rib with which I molded clay around to form the body and then breathed life into it.

Contents

Chapter 1

PROLOGUE

Russia 1792

A PAIR OF eyes stared hungrily out from the dark shadows. Through the brightly lit opening, the monk watched two boys run down the hill towards the ruins: his lair. He curled and stretched withered fingers in anticipation, skin milky white and almost translucent, like old vellum stretched over bone. His breath became shallow, and his pulse quickened. He could practically taste the sweet strength of the young blood flowing through their veins. He wanted to rush out to meet them, to sweep them up into his ancient arms, but the light was not his friend and had not been for a very long time, so he contained his urges. Patience was necessary if one was an immortal.

The intensity of the sunlight burned the ancient monk's eyes, and he had to close them for a moment or risk blinding. Typically, at this time of day, he would slumber in the dank, cold earth back inside the hill.

He had not always been immortal. He remembered himself, Grigory Lazar, as a child slopping pigs on his family's meager farm. Fleeing the life of a serf, he became a monk where he developed a reputation for the physical strength his years on the farm had brought him. Not long after, he was recruited into an obscure monastic order. Its sole vocation was to seek the undead and exterminate them. Father Lazar was known as a proficient hunter within the secret circles of the Russian Orthodox Church and his skills were notorious throughout the realm of immortals. He smiled to himself and let out an introspective sigh. He had liked that life.

The voices of the boys became louder as they approached. Lazar opened his eyes to observe their progress. Good, they were much closer now. Soon the wait would be over. He closed his eyes again to shield them from the glare of the relentless sun.

He could remember when he became an immortal with clarity, as though it had happened only a few days before, not 143 years ago.

Lured to the location of a nest, Lazar and his band of priests and monks—God's exterminators—were ambushed and eviscerated. All were killed except for Father Lazar, who was spared, and himself turned into the very thing he hated and had vowed to destroy; condemning him to an endless life filled with feeding off the blood of innocents. The irony of his last name being associated with that of the biblical Lazarus whom Christ brought back from the dead and Lazar being reborn as an immortal did not escape him and undoubtedly not his tormentors, either.

The hunter/monk could feel the changes occurring inside of him as he slowly transmuted over several weeks. Lazar prayed every day for the Almighty to save him. *Please spare me this burden! Take me into your arms like my brethren.* Each day, he felt the ever-growing urge to consume the blood of a living human. Each day, they force-fed him a mouthful of blood from one of the immortal's own cut wrists. Finally, the day of his total transformation had arrived. The door to his darkened cell opened, then closed. When he lifted his head, he saw a beautiful young woman standing before him.

The frightened girl saw the dirty cassock that he wore and, recognizing Lazar as a monk, desperately she rushed to him, landing on her knees, begging for his protection, seeking his blessing. "Save me, Father!" Those words rang in his ears for years.

There she was, looking to Lazar for help, even as he fought the uncontrollable urge to gorge on her pristine blood. Seeing such innocent purity brought tears to his eyes.

Lazar held out his hands, helping her to rise and stand before him. The scent of her fear filled his nostrils. His face flushed. He could feel his heart race as he reached out and touched her chin. Her mouth quivered. He could see that she was about to say words of thanks, but before she uttered a single one, he could no longer contain his new cravings. Acting on pure instinct, he opened his mouth and ripped into her neck with the fangs that had been growing over the past weeks.

He tore her throat apart, lapping up the blood as it gushed out and down the hollow of her neck and between her breasts, drenching her bodice with a bright crimson red. The sweet coppery taste of the blood was like honey on his palate. He wallowed in the gore that was once a perfect body. He became light-headed from the fresh, warm elixir. The blood gave him energy, a vibrancy that he had never felt before. He knew he could never go back; that he never would want to return to the life of a bleeder. He could feel immortality coursing through his veins, and he liked it.

The sound of the applause that broke out from the immortals who had turned him still echoed in his ears as they emerged from the shadows surrounding him, welcoming him to their exclusive club of the undead.

It was Easter Sunday, 1677, the day that he became a vampire.

"Wait, Vladimir!"

Father Lazar opened his eyes as he heard Alexei call out to his younger brother. They were so close now.

TWO BOYS RAN through the straw-colored grass towards the waiting, hungry eyes. Vladimir, the younger of the two, ran wildly ahead of his older brother, Alexei, as he made a beeline towards the bottom of the hill. His target was a dense cluster of gnarled old oaks growing out of piles of rock on the valley floor. Alexei stopped when he saw where they were headed.

"Vladimir!" Alexei yelled. "Mother said to stay away from this place. It is not safe!" Vladimir turned his head towards Alexei and laughed as he resumed his headlong run. Alexei continued the chase, and when he reached Vladimir, he grabbed his younger brother's shoulder, bringing him to a halt.

"When father returns to the dacha, he will be angry," Alexei said.

"Father is in Moscow with his regiment. He won't return for another week. Mother will have forgotten anything she may discover by then," Vladimir retorted.

"But it is never you he gets angry with. It is always with me, the oldest," Alexei responded with anger.

"You worry too much, brother," Vladimir said with a mischievous laugh and continued to run away.

At the bottom of the hill, Alexei finally caught up with Vladimir, but before he could catch his breath, Vladimir flashed a devilish smile and continued his headlong run deeper into the stand of the tangled oaks, leaving his brother behind.

Alexei looked around. The trees that surrounded him stood like guardians of the rubble that littered the valley floor: ashlar—block shaped stones cut by hand which had formed the walls of an old building.

He watched Vladimir run into the place where the trees stood thickest and toppled columns lay on the ground. Further on from there, an overgrown arch stood, framing an entrance that appeared to lead directly into the depths of the hillside.

"Vladimir! Stop. It is not safe here. Please stop!" Alexei called.

Just before Vladimir continued through the arch, he stopped and turned to his brother, waiting for him to catch up.

When the boys were together, Alexei said, a bit breathlessly, "Mother told us not to go in there. It is cursed. Bad things happen to those who do not heed the warnings."

In a mocking tone, Vladimir responded to his brother. "What bad things? Monsters? The Devil? I tell you nothing bad happens in there."

"And how can you be so sure?"

"I have been in there many times."

Alexei stood with his mouth agape.

"There is nothing scary at all. In fact, a nice old monk lives through the arch."

"Have you seen him? Talked to him?" Alexei asked.

"Yes, I have spoken with him, but I have not seen him out here in the sun. The monk always stays in the darkness of the shadows. He says that the light is bad for his aged skin. He just wants us to be his friends. Today, he wanted me to bring you to visit with him," with a change of attitude Vladimir continued. "I know mother counts on you to watch over me. I do not want you to get into trouble, so come in with me and protect me from a frail old man. Please?" Vladimir reached up to grasp Alexei's shoulders and gave him the best penitent face he could muster.

Alexei weakened, "Well, you do what I say, and if I say we leave, we leave. Yes?"

"Certainly, *dear* brother. I will do as you say, always," Vladimir let out a vexing laugh, turned, and continued his headlong run through the arched opening and into the blackness beyond.

Alexei started after him, stopped, picked up a hefty branch as a weapon, and continued after his brother into the ruins. He had never been this far down the hillside before, but Vladimir seemed more than familiar with this place. Alexei called out, "Vladimir, where are we going?"

His younger brother turned back and shushed him. In a soft voice, he urged, "Quiet! You might scare him away." Slowly

Vladimir continued to inch further into the darkening shadows of the opening.

Alexei cautiously followed through the arch and into a large, rubble-strewn space and stopped. All around him, he saw the remains of an old Russian Orthodox church, the roof long since collapsed to the floor. He looked up and saw that the leafy canopy of the ancient oaks obscured the sky.

Vladimir turned and waved, his gesture urging his brother to catch up. Alexei carefully walked further into the shadowy space, picking his steps deliberately, not wanting to trip on the debris that littered the tile floor. Beneath his feet were images of saints whose faces and halos had been chipped away. On the surface of the remaining walls, icons were visible, but they too were damaged, their saintly faces having also been chiseled off.

Vladimir stopped and peered into the darkness. He called out, "Father Lazar?" His voice echoed off the crumbling stone. "I brought my brother as you asked."

There was a rustling noise. From the ominous shadows in front of them, a hunched old man appeared to materialize from wisps of the blackest smoke. He wore a threadbare monk's cassock and stroked a long and stringy beard with bony fingers. His skin was white as snow, lips cracked and red. His eyes glazed, alabaster orbs, pupils of onyx.

Splotchy patches of sun filtered through the broad oak leaves, falling across the decaying roof and onto the floor, creating a definite line where the dappled light did not reach any further. Father Lazar stood, just on the other side of the line, in the dark, studying the two boys. He could not recall the last good meal that he had had. His isolation and the superstitions of the peasants had ensured that most mortals stayed away from his lair, leaving his only source of sustenance coming from rodents and birds. Without the blood of humans, his vitality had ebbed, and powers faded. His body aged, deteriorating incrementally, as though he were a mortal again.

The fragrance of the boys' sweet blood was like that of a heavily perfumed woman. The warm fluid pulsing through their veins gave off such an irresistible scent that his mouth salivated as he contemplated the tangy copper flavor of their blood. The urge to drink them dry was overwhelming, and he all but forgot the larger purpose that he had for these two. No, he would only drink from them sparingly and slowly turn them into immortals while molding them into tools for his vengeance.

Father Lazar spoke in a weak, scratchy voice, "Such a good boy you are, Vladimir. Step closer, the bright sun is hard on these tired eyes of mine. Come."

Vladimir made a hesitant move towards the old monk with Alexei right beside him, branch in hand, ready to use.

As they stepped out of the light, the monk's withered hands darted out from the shadows. His bony fingers wrapped around the boys' throats. Alexei was no longer in control of his muscles. His hand opened, letting go of the branch and the weapon clattered upon the broken tiles, unused.

Lazar lifted them up and pulled them into the opaque darkness, feet dangling above the floor. Their screams were stifled by the firm grip of the monk's hands.

"Thank you, my son. You have proven yourself to be an excellent friend."

Chapter 2

THE BUS DRIVER

T HE BUS RATTLED its way up an empty stretch of forgotten highway, one of a fleet of ten buses owned by Cascade Stage Lines. The company had gotten a good deal on it and on all their other vehicles, too. This one, *Number Seven*, had a former life toiling away for Trailways and was retired in '99. To say that the owner of Cascade was cheap might be a bit of an exaggeration. Sure, he never painted over the original Trailways or Greyhound colors, but he always tacked on a brand-new Cascade Stage Lines sign and rechristened each coach with a city's name. This one was the *Pride of Ontario*. There were others named after Bend, Baker City, The Tri-Cities, Klamath Falls, and so forth, all towns serviced by the company.

The *Pride of Ontario* was on its weekly run from Reno to K Falls, Bend, east to Baker City, and then on to Ontario, ending up in Boise. A milk-run as they said in the trade. Straight up north on US97; a route that Eddie had been driving for the last ten years. Aside from some challenging winter weather and the occasional forest fire burning across the highway, not a bad gig. And the scenery never disappointed, even after all these years.

Baker City was his destination tonight. Another driver would take over there and continue the remainder of the run into Boise.

Traveling north, the volcanic ranges of the Sierras and then the Cascades were visible out the left side of the bus, with deceptively wide-open stretches reaching to the horizon out the right side. Most of this bus's route covered the area of Eastern Oregon that geologists called The Columbia Plateau, but regular people called it the High Desert. It wasn't flat how picture books depicted deserts, however. Anyone who had traveled the area could see that the earth had been chiseled over the eons by receding glaciers, floods, volcanic activity, and rivers carving distinct paths into the red earth. This expansive land concealed hidden valleys and deep gorges and then rose into hills that turned into mountain ranges. And, yes, there were flat areas, lots of them.

Eastern Oregon was a hard country and not to be trifled with. Its sparse population was mostly ranchers or those who wanted to hide away from a busy world. It was a wild, empty, beautiful place with surprises around every bend and at the bottom of every dip in the road, where new things could be discovered, and almost anything could happen.

Edward Conner, Eddie, was the driver of the *Pride of Ontario*. Despite being sixty-five years old and a retired Marine, he wore his thinning, long gray hair pulled back in a neat ponytail as a sign that he wasn't ready to roll over and play dead. Eddie felt that there was some youth still left in him, which was why he wore the slightly too tight Hawaiian shirt, not one of those faggy, overly floral ones. This one was a classic with an ocean blue background, surfers riding white breakers, and clumps of green palm tree islands dotting the ocean. Eddie was expected to wear a company issued jacket with the Cascade patch on the shoulder and company cap, like what cops or airline pilots wore, but the shirt passed muster for some reason, which he wasn't about to question. He resisted wearing those gray pants, the ones with the black stripes on the sides, mostly because they didn't come in big and tall sizes and while there was some play from the elastic sewn into the waistband, it only helped so much, but he rarely got to win that argument. All things considered, though, Eddie was lucky to be working for such a loose organization that allowed him the long hair and his comfortable shirt. Couldn't complain much about that.

After over twenty years of living in Eastern Oregon he still only really knew the major roads and highways and that long stretch off the county road to his house that some called his driveway, which was the reason he found himself and a busload of people, lost.

Damn! He yelled inside his head. Just trying to get home the fastest way. He was tired of hearing his wife rag at him for missing another family birthday. This one would be his grandson's fifteenth. Fifteen years. Where the hell did the time go? At least the boy was too young to have gotten caught up in those godawful wars in Iraq and Afghanistan. His grandson would never have to see the shit that he saw in Nam. No. He would never have to do the shit that he did. Knock on wood.

Snapping out of his thoughts, Eddie came back to his present situation. *Damn it! I'm lost. How the hell . . .? I've been driving this route for ten fucking years. Shit!* Too much in a hurry not to piss off her royal highness, he took a shortcut he had been told about years before by that driver . . . *What was his name? Shit.* It really didn't matter now. He wasn't the one here having to deal with this problem. *My problem. I'm in so much trouble.*

Eddie drove on over the unfamiliar stretch of highway, trying to put the situation into perspective. Even though getting lost was undoubtedly the result of a wrong choice *he* had made, nothing could be worse than the trouble thrust upon him because of his decision to join the Marines.

Fresh out of recruit training at Camp Pendleton, he stepped off a Pan Am 707 and onto the tarmac at Tan Son Nhat Air Force Base near Saigon on January 30th of 1968, just in time to help usher in the Vietnamese Year of the Monkey. Within twelve hours he was in the fight of his life as the Viet Cong launched their surprise Tet Offensive catching the United States off guard.

Charlie eventually lost that battle, but not before taking the lives of a lot of guys during those frantic days; guys who might have become Eddie's friends—if they hadn't, mostly, died. The shit he saw.

Now that was trouble. He could have died. And if dying wasn't at the top of the list of "being in trouble," then Eddie didn't know what would be. At least all he was right now was lost. Bad? Yes. Life-threatening? No.

On the other hand, the immediate trouble he was facing was spelled with a capital "T." While death was not imminent, he was going to feel some pain because of his decision to take an unknown route. Trouble from home. Trouble from work. And, most immediately, trouble right here on *Ol' Number Seven.*

As the bus continued up the highway, Eddie peered out the windshield looking for road signs or anything that he might recognize so he could get this group to its intended destination and he could get home in time for his wife. He looked at his watch and sighed. The big hand and the little hand were telling him that the schedule would be a bit off tonight. Eddie chuckled to himself and thought, *Those that live by the schedule die by the schedule.* Well, as bad as this was, at least no one was going to die over it.

The sun was setting to the left and rear of the bus, which was a good sign, meaning he was heading in the right direction, sort of. As Eddie continued driving up the road, still looking for anything telling him where he might be, he noticed the needle on the gas gauge was bobbing around the *"E." Mother fu . . . Am I ever going to catch any breaks today?* He kept on driving until the needle took one last bump before it settled and moved no more. The bus was out of fuel.

Eddie slowly put his foot on the brake pedal and brought the bus to a stop. He laid his forehead down on the steering wheel and banged on it a couple of times. He knew how fucked he was in oh so many ways. Eddie raised his head and looked back at the passengers in the mirror just above his head.

Nine passengers to give him grief. Eddie took in a deep breath as he looked back at each of them.

Which one would be the first?

Slowly, he surveyed each of the passengers and did a tactical assessment of who might be his tormentor; a holdover from his years in the corps. Old habits die hard.

The family in row three didn't seem to be capable of giving him too much grief. He reached for the passenger manifest and checked for their names. O'Neil. The little girl? Cindra.

Of course not. The father? Eddie looked at the seating chart. Wilson seemed too kicked down by whatever had happened to him to complain about anything, though there might have been a time. The wife? Marion. When she got on the bus, she fussed and harrumphed over the soiled seats; dramatically dusting off the cushions before letting her daughter sit. Even made a few overly loud comments about the cleaning standards. Maybe her.

How about that quiet guy in row five? Paul Mathews. No way. He's military. Eddie could spot them a mile away. When he climbed onto the bus with a slight limp, Eddie asked him if he could assist in any way. They both locked eyes and knew the other for what he was.

The guy smiled and said, "Not unless you got any extra ibuprofen."

Eddie opened his bag and fished around in it, shifting a 9mm handgun at the top, and pulled out a small bottle and offered it to him. "800mg from the VA. None of that pansy, over-the-counter, 200mg stuff."

When Eddie handed Paul the bottle of pills, he could see that the guy was checking out the gun. "Beretta, for emergencies."

"Nice piece. Name's Paul. Guessing Nam."

"How did you guess that? The gray hair?"

"The ponytail."

Eddie smiled at that one. "Yep. Marines retired. I'm Eddie."

"You look like life's treating you well. For an old Jarhead, that is. Thanks for the drugs. Can I pay you?

"Nah. The least I can do for a grunt."

"Rangers."

"You guys have always been touchy about your labels. Welcome aboard the *Pride of Ontario,*" Eddie smiled.

"Oh, and nice shirt," Paul said as he moved on through the bus.

Nope. Not going to be him.

So, how about that weird couple back in the seventh row? A lesbian and a gay guy. At least that's how Eddie read the two. He knew it wasn't the best of character traits that he judged books by their covers, but after working around people for as long as he had, it was hard not to. Looking at the manifest, he read their names: Jenna Johansson and Kelvin Jarrett. Kelvin? One thing for sure was that they had a sense of humor, always cracking jokes; like they were performing for an audience, but the only ones paying attention to them were each other. No other others required. They'd been at it since they boarded in Reno.

Looking back into the mirror, he watched the two carrying on; oblivious to the fact that the bus had stopped moving. Well, he could also scratch them off the list of potential threats.

Eddie's focus moved further back into the bus, and he stopped with the beautiful girl in row eight. When she boarded in Reno, every guy was looking at her, and she knew it; probably could tell if a pair of eyes weren't staring at her. You wear clothes like that and in that way and, well, you'll get looked at. Not that she wasn't attractive. Hell, she was stunning, but her choice of outfits broadcast something else entirely. Too bad. She could easily stand with the top models in New York or Paris.

Glancing down at his clipboard, he saw her name, Stephanie Siaskowski. That last name sure was a mouthful.

When she walked past Eddie down the aisle to her seat, she saw he had noticed. He was sorry to admit he was a flawed human, but it didn't stop him from following her using the mirror, just like he was now. No man could honestly say that they wouldn't turn their heads to look when she walked by; medium height, dark straight hair cut at the shoulders, a perfect figure with what he considered was the ideal breast size, not too large and not too small. Other than whiplash, however, she wasn't going to cause him any problems.

The woman and man sitting in the back of the bus were the last two passengers he needed to consider. He'd seen these two before in the same situation, but with different names and faces. The woman, Ellie Struthers, was her name this time. Attractive but clinging to her man for some ungodly reason, probably too convinced that she was in love with this guy. This one had slight bruising around her neck like she had been grabbed, but makeup and a scarf covered it well. Some of the women he had seen were far less lucky with visible black and blue marks that just couldn't be hidden.

The woman? Not a chance. Too passive.

That just left the guy. Richard Conroy. The loud, belligerent, arrogant, and just a plain mean type of person who would have gotten at least one sock party in boot camp. A fuckin' jock type who thought his weightlifting physique could intimidate anyone, but when challenged, he'd back down. They called these guys paper lions. Eddie studied him, watching how he hemmed in his girlfriend up against the window to keep her under his control. God knows what they've been doing there in the back seat this whole time, but Eddie was happy that he wouldn't be the one cleaning up the coach after this run.

Yep, that's the guy who is going to go off. Richard Conroy in 10B.

Eddie looked down at the bag sitting at his feet, making sure that the gun was within reach. *Just in case,* he thought. *Just in case.*

Chapter 3

CRAIG

"HELLO. THIS IS Dr. Gwen. You're on the air. How can I help you?"

"Yes, thank you. My name is Jerry."

"Your question, Jerry?"

"Uh, um . . . My mother won't stop telling me what to do. You know? She says stuff like, 'Where's your raincoat?' or 'You need a haircut.' or 'Eat more fruit. It's good for you.' You know, things that you would tell a little kid."

"Okay, so your question is?"

"So, how do I get her to stop?"

"First of all, she's a mother and mothers are the way they are. How old are you, Jerry?"

"Sixty."

"Wow! It seems at age sixty you shouldn't need to be asking me how—"

A sudden rap on the glass snapped Craig Wright awake, causing him almost to fall out of his chair. The late-night radio talk show hadn't worked at helping him stay awake.

Craig turned off the internet radio stream and shifted his chair, acting like he hadn't nodded off, before turning back to the window where the banging was coming from. He focused his sleep-clouded eyes on the person standing behind the glass. It was Ben Saunders holding up two cups of coffee.

Saunders motioned with the cups towards the door. His lips moved, forming the words, "Open the fucking door." Craig couldn't hear Saunders' voice, but his ESP training told him from the raised cups he should open the door so he could get the caffeine fix he so desperately required.

Reaching under the desktop, Craig pushed an unseen button. The electric lock buzzed, and the door opened. Saunders entered, walked down the steps to their workstation, and set the cups of coffee on the desktop before sitting down next to Craig. "And that, my friend, is why the boss makes two people watch the control room during the night shift," he nudged one cup closer to Craig. "Anything happen while I was gone? Not that you would know."

Craig reached for the cup eagerly. "Oh, sweet Jesus! I am bored out of my mind."

"I take that to mean no."

Craig grabbed the large cup with a hand-written note on the side: dark, two shots, extra sugar. The steaming aroma hit his nose and gave him a momentary lift. He tipped the cup to his mouth, but only a dribble came out.

"God, I hate these plastic lids, tiny damned holes! How the hell are you supposed to drink through that?" Craig popped off the cover, letting a bit of the dark elixir splash out, and took a drink. "Tastes better with the lid off, at any rate, even this crap," he took a second sip, and the warm, bitter liquid flowed over his tongue and down his throat. He savored the moment and felt the artificial pickup kicking in.

"You must have fallen asleep right after I left for the coffee. Your wide open mouth made a great target."

Craig looked at Saunders, "Whatever, dude. I thought I saw a big-ass horse fly and followed it around the room as it flew up to the ceiling, which was when you made me lose it with all your banging on the glass."

"Yeah, right. Were you trying to catch it with your pie hole? By the way, you might want to wipe that drool coming from the side of your mouth." Craig bit and raised his hand to the left side of his face. "No, the other side." He shifted his hand, but stopped in mid-motion.

"God damn you! Can't you cut a guy a break? I've been at it since zero-dark-thirty this morning."

"Yesterday morning. And it's we. We've been at it since yesterday morning," Saunders interjected.

"Yeah, yeah. Yesterday . . . Yesterday? Shit, this isn't what I signed up for," Craig's eyes glazed over as he paused and let this sink in. Then he shook his head in somber acceptance. "Another weekend lost to the gods of preparedness." Craig lifted his cup, toasting the invisible powers that liked to mess with his life. He took another slow drag out of his cup and rubbed his red eyes.

"Point taken, my friend, but the boss wants us all to be able to manage Control no matter what happens. I hate to admit it, but with what we're dealing with it isn't a bad idea. Besides, it's what she wants and what she wants . . .,"

"She gets."

"Exactly."

The two sat back in their chairs with their coffees. The empty, mostly dark control room surrounded them. Directly in front sat their workstation with a couple of monitors and keyboards, telephone, notepads, and scant few personal items. Several other workstations surrounded them: chairs empty, monitors asleep, task lights off.

This is Control-West. One of three such control centers located across the country for the CSC to monitor their various reservations. Con-West was responsible for the area west of the Rockies; located at Mountain Home Air Force Base in Idaho because of its central location to all CSC reservations in the region. Con-West's placement within an air base provided it with the appropriate government/military cover it needed to maintain operational secrecy. Also, an air force base had the facilities to support the CSC's drone monitoring program and house the military personnel and equipment necessary for prompt deployment should it ever be required.

The control room itself stairstepped, like rice patties, down from the observation window in the room's rear towards a wall in front with one over-sized screen mounted on it. All the workstations faced this screen, and right now it showed two maps, one of the entire United States and a more detailed map of the Western States. The same images were on their desktop monitors. Scattered across the vastness of the country, multiple dots appeared. All were emitting solid green lights. Everything looked to be good.

Craig took another drink. "Ah. Nothing like a cup of Joe to help a guy through the rough spots." he closed his eyes, losing himself in the moment, then snapped them back open. "Who the fuck keeps messing with my duck?"

"What duck?"

"This duck," Craig reached for the yellow bathtub duck sitting on the surface in front of them. A Boise State Broncos toy horse was posed to appear to be trampling it. Craig took the horse and tossed it into the garbage. "Fucking blue turf."

"What is it with you and your stupid school rivalries?" Saunders asked.

"School rivalry? I just don't like anyone messing with my stuff. This duck is something of a lucky charm for me."

"Right," Saunders responded with disbelief dripping from his voice.

"My mom gave it to me as a gag gift when I got the job working for the senator."

"That's what you told her you were doing?"

"Well, yeah, or I could have told her a real whopper like 'Hey Mom, I got this position working in a secret government organization. It's one of those "off the books" groups. Very hush, hush. So please don't tell anyone.' What else should I have told her?"

"I suppose the first lie is better than the second."

"What did you tell your wife?"

"Oh, that I'm an FBI agent. More plausible and easier to explain the weird hours."

"Weren't you in the FBI before you joined the CSC?" Craig asked.

"Makes the lie easier to tell."

For a moment, they just sat back in their chairs and quietly drank their coffee.

Then Saunders deliberately turned to Craig. "So. You ready for tadpole indoctrination?"

Craig sat up with eyes wide open in panic. Then he rested his forehead on the desktop. "Oh, God! Not again. Already?"

"Who's going to do it this time, I wonder?" Saunders fished around in his jacket pocket, pulled out his hand, and produced two match sticks. In a very business-like tone, Saunders said, "We do it the same as before." He offered his hand to Craig. "Pick."

"Ah, shit. I did it last time. I shouldn't have to do it this."

Pushing the matchsticks closer to Craig's face, Saunders insisted, "You know the deal. Pick."

Craig put down his coffee cup and took a deep breath. He closed his eyes and removed a stick from Saunders' hand. He slowly opened one eyelid just a crack and saw Saunders with a wide grin on his face. Craig's focus shifted to the object between his fingers, where he was holding an obviously shorter matchstick. "Crap! Not fair. Just not fair. I hate giving the welcome speech to the new recruits. God, I hate it!"

Suddenly the room filled with the blare of an alarm. Craig stopped and looked up at the big screen. One of the green dots had turned into a flashing red alert strobe, its rhythmic throbbing keeping tempo with the clangor of the warning buzzer.

Saunders stood and looked at the big screen. "That's Site-Delta. Who's Rez is that? Dawson's?"

Craig dialed the phone, then answered Saunders, "Yup." Speaking into the handset, "Dawson, you got another runner . . . Yeah, well, you shouldn't be all that surprised, seeing as it's a full moon." Craig pushed a red button on the desktop. "I just sent the Action Team the notice . . . Yes, uh huh . . . Why, you're more than welcome." He hung up the phone. "Putz."

Saunders typed into the keyboard. The big screen in front showed a FLIR image. Text at the bottom of the screen read: *RES SITE-DELTA. Camera 1.* Through the grainy, green glow of the night-vision camera, they saw a fence along with trees and other vegetation. Saunders scrolled through the various camera angles. "Isn't this the second month in a row that Dawson has had a runner?"

"Yeah, fortunately, no one got the chomp last time," he rapped his knuckles on the fake wood grain of the desktop. "Here's to the same dumb luck again tonight."

Saunders abruptly stopped scrolling through the various camera options. On the screen, they could see the image of a dark green figure running away from the fence. As the figure moved, it alternated between running on its hind legs much like a human, then hunching over in an unnatural awkwardness to use its arms as a set of forelegs. The general impression was that of a human trying to run like an animal, an ape, or a dog.

The night vision technology did not show facial features very well from this camera's angle, but they could see that the creature had shaggy hair or fur covering its head and face, as well as the rest of its exposed body. There appeared to be remnants of fabric clinging to its body.

Then, from behind a tree emerged another dark green figure whose silhouette showed it to be a man wearing tactical gear and holding up a weapon, which he pointed at the runner.

Craig's eyes were glued to the large monitor. "Here we go. At least Dawson had sense enough to place armed guards around the perimeter after last time."

"Wonder what slush fund they reached in to pay for that OT?" Saunders asked.

The image on the screen showed the two figures stopping and confronting each other.

Saunders sipped at his coffee absentmindedly. "Some poor Schmo getting chomped or not; Dawson has some serious explaining to do about these two incidents."

"He sure as shit does. Wouldn't be surprised if they transferred him up to Crack-O-My-Ass Alaska—"

On the screen, they saw the creature quickly move towards the man with the gun. A bright green flash erupted from the muzzle of the rifle, but the creature moved with incredible speed and was on top of the gunman before he could fire again.

Saunders spit out his coffee. "Oh, fuck!"

The creature started ripping into the gunman's body with his teeth and claws. Grainy, dark green spurts erupted from the downed man. Craig and Saunders could only watch helplessly as he was torn apart on the big screen in front of them.

Craig frantically began hammering on the keyboard as though the energy he placed in the act could somehow erase what had already happened. Instead, all he could do was change the view of the vibrant green horror playing out on the monitor in front of them, zooming in on the carnage; virtually bringing the gruesome scene directly into the control room. He slowly stood and watched the man's guts being torn out and chewed on as the creature fed on its kill. *He has to be dead by this point. Right? God, I hope so,* he thought.

Craig picked up the phone and dialed. "Dawson? The shit just hit the fan . . . One of your men just went down . . . No, I don't know . . . Yeah . . . An Action Team was doing some insertion exercises with an Osprey not too far from there. They should be on site in . . .," he checked his watch, ". . . twenty. You think the other guards can hold him?"

As Craig talked with Dawson, the screen showed other armed men arriving and surrounding the creature as it feasted. First, one gun went off, then two. Then every weapon was unloaded into it.

Craig zoomed the camera in on the creature as he crumbled to the ground. The grainy, green torso of the dead creature filled the entire screen at the front of the room. A close-up image of its face revealed that this was once a human male in the process of mutating into an animal. The man's entire head and face were covered with fur. His nose, a snout, and long lethal looking teeth protruded from his mouth and were smeared with dark green liquid, the blood of the dead man. His hands were also covered in dark green, blood-matted fur. Another fusillade of bullets from the guards made the corpse jerk as they emptied their magazines into it.

Still, on the phone to Dawson, Craig exhaled, "Well, looks like you were right. Situation contained. I don't envy you the paperwork . . . Yeah, you too. Have fun in Alaska."

On the screen, the creature was splayed out on the ground, dead. The guards approached it. One stepped up and poked the body with the barrel of his M4. No movement. He put an extra round into the head of the corpse, then he looked up into the camera and gave a thumbs up sign.

"Can you get a close-up of the dead guard?" Craig asked.

Saunders scrolled through the cameras and found one angle that could work. He pulled up the image and zoomed in on the dead man. "I'm not sure. Is that—"

"Swanson. Shit!" Craig hung his head in dismay.

"He was a good guy . . . Any family?"

Craig shook his head. "I have no idea. Don't know much about him, actually. Now I wish I did."

A few moments of silence passed between the two men. All they could do was watch the camera feed as the guards zipped Swanson's remains into a bio-containment bag and loaded it into a Humvee and then it drove out of frame.

"Well, I guess that's it," Saunders said in a subdued tone. He typed a few commands into the keyboard. Another guard had fired up a flamethrower and moved to the dead creature. Then, with a click of a mouse, Saunders disconnected the feed from Site-Delta. The monitor switched from FLIR green back to the original status, showing two maps. All the dots had returned to a steady green.

Deflated from watching a member of the team getting killed, someone he knew, Craig flopped down into his chair. Then he commented callously, showing that he had erected a hard wall around his emotions; a thing he learned to do long ago as the fat kid who lived with the hurt of insensitive ribbing from his peers. (Emotions that had been rubbed very raw with the loss of his partner a couple of months earlier.) "I wouldn't want to be in Dawson's shoes right now. Letting anyone off your Rez, not good, not good at all, but having one of your men butchered? Definitely at the top of the not good list." He took a drink of coffee and let out a long sigh. "We just watched one of ours get . . . eaten. Damn!"

Saunders rubbed his tired eyes. "I can't remember a time in the twelve years that I have worked with the CSC that I've been this close to witnessing one of our own get it. Not a memory one wants to carry with him."

Craig let the comment pass, not hearing it. He was too stunned by what he had just witnessed via the satellite feed of Swanson's horrific death, made even more heinous by the unnatural, grainy green of the night vision camera.

The last time he saw death up close, it was in vivid living color. Katherine—Kathie went on ahead without him. Craig had yelled at her to wait, but he was too involved in subduing, more like fending off, his attacker to do much more than yell. She didn't even turn or acknowledge his warning. She just bolted off after the other predator that they had been after. By the time he had staked his assailant, it was too late.

Craig found her on the floor, bleeding her life away through the opening in her neck that was more of a tear than a bite. Kathie's wound was a hemorrhaging gash that could not be treated. No amount of his field first-aid training could have helped. Not even a combat surgeon could do anything about such a wound.

But it wasn't as though saving her life was now a priority. They both knew this. Craig clenched his eyelids tighter as he remembered looking into his partner's green eyes, made greener by the contrasting red that continued to spurt out of her neck. She was asking him to end it. The expression on her face pleaded with him to do the necessary thing, but her eyes showed forgiveness.

Craig raised his arm, pointing the barrel of his automatic directly at her heart. The moment before he pulled the trigger, he suddenly realized that he was in love with Katherine. An emotion that had escaped him for most of his life and now . . .? The calm smile on her face was what he concentrated on. Just the face; no catastrophic wound to the neck, only her beautiful face, sharp green eyes, and Celtic red hair. Then he pulled the trigger.

"I said, are you going to make the call, or should I?" Saunders asked, "Hello? Anyone home?"

And then Craig was back.

"What was that? Sorry . . . I was someplace else."

"Are you going to make the call? You are the Officer of the Watch."

Craig reached for the phone and punched in the number for the Con-West commander.

"Sorry to wake you, ma'am . . . Yes. It was another attempted breakout from Site-Delta. That's right . . . Last month too, almost to the day . . . Sorry to report that a casualty . . . Sergeant Swanson . . . No, the lycan was taken down . . . Yes, I'm sure that Dawson knows the procedures . . . Okay. Good night, ma'am."

"Any yelling?"

"No, but Dawson is in one deep pile of dog poop."

"Wolf poop."

"Dog, wolf all the same to me." Craig took another pull off his cooling coffee. "Wish this had some whiskey in it."

Saunders held up the long matchstick. "Now, where were we?"

"Ah, hell."

Chapter 4

OUT OF GAS

ORN BRAKES SCREECHED, and the bus jerked as Eddie brought the vehicle to a complete stop, sending a cloud of the High Desert's red, volcanic dust swirling around the tires.

The battered metallic skin of the bus glowed, bathed in the heavenly orange light of the setting sun. A high overcast was quickly rolling in from the Northeast, throwing a blanket across the red-tinged blue sky, causing the dissipating light to reflect off the underside of the clouds, creating a halo that outlined the peaks of the Cascade Mountains. The view was breathtaking, yet strange to Eddie. The mountains should be a lot closer. Normally at this point on the route, he always imagined that he could reach out the window and touch them, feeling the icy cold of their glaciers on his fingers. Now they seemed so distant and two-dimensional, like a painted stage set propped up behind the bus, more like bumps on the horizon than mountains.

But this was not the regular route. *This* was the fucking shortcut he had never tried before. "Shit!" he said, almost too loudly. He glanced up at the mirror to see if any of the passengers had heard his outburst, but saw nothing to worry about.

Eddie looked out the windshield at the unmistakable landscape of the High Desert, yet he saw nothing familiar. If you live in an area long enough, you become well-acquainted with every rock and tree. You recognize them like faces of friends, and they become signposts showing you're heading in the right direction on your journey between here and there. The signs that he now saw said he was utterly lost. He shook his head and cautiously looked up into the mirror again to study the passengers behind him.

As expected, there was general, surprised unhappiness emanating from the passengers caused by his stopping the bus in the middle of the road. He looked back down to the gas gauge and tapped it a couple of times, then again, harder. Tapping never helped, of course, it was just a thing to do to but empty was still empty or close enough. The extra mile or two he may have been abele to go with what was left in the tank would make no difference. He glanced up into the mirror one more time. The irritated passengers were still irritated and getting more so.

He sighed and pictured his wife with the grandson's birthday cake; candles burned almost into the frosting, looking up to the wall clock. Oh, Holy Mother of God, he would never hear the end of this! He reached into his bag, pulled out a map, and unfolded it across the top of the steering wheel. Eddie put a finger down on a spot that he supposed was their location. He looked out and tried to make some visual connection between the image on the paper and the landscape in front of him. Nothing jibed.

The dark of night was asserting itself as the last sliver of sun retreated behind the distant mountains. The overcast would make this night darker still. Motionless, the bus sat while the gathering clouds came fully together, completely covering the sky in a billowy, charcoal colored blanket which crowded out the last of the diminishing light and would successfully block the moon and the stars.

Eddie looked out the window and shook his head, then switched on the light over his seat to help read the map. Several of the passengers also reached up and switched on overhead reading lights, turning the windows into black mirrors that reflected the interior back in on itself.

Suddenly realizing that he had stopped the bus in the middle of the road, Eddie put it back into drive and coasted off onto the gravel of the shoulder. He took off his cap and rested his head on the steering wheel again in frustration and slowly banged on the hard plastic. When Eddie opened his eyes, he was staring down at his feet, looking at the dirty floor and the worn pads of the pedals. "Crap," he said almost too loudly.

From the back of the bus, an angry voice shouted out, "Hey! Why are you stopping here, old man?"

Eddie looked up into the mirror. Great. He had called it correctly. It was the jerk sitting in the back with his girlfriend. He was only slightly surprised that it took him so long to make a scene. He hated people like this, and right now he was glad that he lived out here in the desert, far away from most humans; not that he wasn't a patient man, but his fuse was only so long.

The jerk stood and took a step up the aisle. "I've gotta be in Boise tomorrow." He bent to look out the window in a dramatic move to emphasize his point. "And by the way I see things outside, it looks like it's night already."

Eddie turned in his seat and looked down the aisle at the guy from 10B. "Sir, please remain seated."

The guy took another step towards the front. "Don't you speak English?" Then he repeated his earlier comment very slowly as if he was an ugly American speaking to a foreigner. "*I said*, I-have-to-be-in-Boise-*tomorrow!*"

Eddie saw Paul shift in his seat to position himself for quick action if needed. The strange pair in row seven stopped messing around and looked up to watch the impending train wreck. Marion O'Neil leaned across the aisle and spoke to her husband in a loud stage whisper.

"Wilson, do something."

Wilson turned to look at the angry guy. What he saw was a tense wad of muscles ready to unwind. Looking back at the bus driver, Wilson saw a tired old man clearly trying to keep his cool. This was not the type of situation that Wilson found familiar. In his long gone tech business, he fought his battles over phones and computer screens. Those were the kinds of confrontations he understood.

But as an up-and-coming tech entrepreneur in Bend with the next big social media app, he also had to fight to convince several high-profile investors to back him. The begging for start-up capital was not an easy thing for him to do, and then when the economy tanked the last thing anyone wanted to invest their money in was yet another social media app. Wilson found himself bailing water out of his sinking business, which was a whole new battleground that he was also unprepared to fight in.

First came the cold shoulders from his investors, then the late paychecks to his employees, then the landlord locking the doors. Finally, the creditors came with their court orders and cleaned out his bank accounts and the mortgage company foreclosed on their home.

In retrospect, he should have stayed in San Diego, where he came up with the app, but he wanted a simpler life for his daughter, and Marion was all for the move. God, who wouldn't want to live near the Cascade Mountains? Waking up every day, looking west across the Deschutes River at the Three Sisters glowing from the rising sun. There was a good reason so many from California had migrated to the small Central Oregon town, and its striking beauty was a potent factor.

The failure of his company was a predictable event. It was only a matter of time before the market was oversaturated with similar products. Wilson had foreseen that but had bet he could finish development and get the product out before the market imploded. So had his investors. But when the bubble burst, he was the one who got washed away, along with the many others trying to cash in on the same bonanza.

Cindra was born in 2008. While this event brought tremendous joy to their home, it still did not improve their overall situation. The following year, people were openly calling the economic crisis a depression, and all hope of fulfilling his ambitious dreams disappeared like wisps of early morning fog on the river. At least it was a comfort to know that the world economy had a minor role to play in the demise of his company. It wasn't totally on him alone.

Knowing that he no longer wanted to swim in the shark tank of investors, Wilson sold the license to his app and used the money to pay off the remaining creditors and finance their move to Baker City where he found a job as a marketing manager with a start-up brewery. In reality, the job would be nine parts bartending and one-part marketing, but this opportunity meant that things were on the upswing. In the small town of Baker City, he believed he could establish a more peaceful life for his family in a stress-free environment.

Wilson O'Neil was tired of the fight, at least for now. He looked again at the two men standing in the aisle and shook his head. "There's nothing I can do. This isn't my fight."

"You're not even going to protect your wife and daughter?"

"From what? Loud voices?"

Marion's face turned to ice as she abruptly leaned back into her seat and folded her arms, no longer wanting to talk to her husband. Even Eddie felt the intensity of the action.

Pulling the name from the manifest, he looked at Marion. "Mrs. O'Neil, this is my problem. There is nothing your husband can do to help me, but thank you for trying." Then he looked at Wilson and gave him a look that said, "I did my best pal, you're on your own."

Marion's eyelids turned to thin slits through which she shot red hot laser beams at the driver, giving him her silent response. Her frustration level was rising, but she knew she had no hope of controlling the situation. She wasn't usually the type who sought such things; controlling wasn't in her nature.

Marion met Wilson in college at UC Santa Barbara, a notorious party school, where living in a dorm would seem like a resort vacation to most of America. They were a handsome and popular couple, and many considered them to be the most likely to get married and be successful. Wilson could keep up a good GPA even while being president of the Delta Tau Delta fraternity and while Wilson was there, the Deltas did everything that they could to live up to the reputation set forth for all frats known as "Deltas" by John Belushi and *Animal House.*

She wasn't much of a party girl, though she wasn't a recluse either. Marion's only desire was to find a good man to marry and be the best mother and wife she could, which was a role modeled by her mother, but she was no pushover.

She never considered herself to be a "feminist," though her beliefs and politics leaned strongly in that direction. Marion just knew that her best contribution to her husband's success would be in helping form and maintain a supportive and loving home for her family. She didn't blame Wilson for the economic downturn that helped speed the demise of his company, but she wasn't blind to the mistakes he made that weakened the foundations of the business, making it vulnerable. Early in the company's troubles, Marion found that if she didn't at least take control of their home life, then Wilson was sure to experience a meltdown, and that wouldn't have done any of them any good.

"Hey!" 10B yelled.

Marion placed an arm around her daughter's shoulder and pulled her close. Something was going to happen between that loudmouth and the bus driver, and she wished they weren't there to have to witness it.

"I'm still here," Dick yelled louder.

I can see that, asshole, Eddie thought and slowly closed his eyes, trying to control his anger. He was a pot ready to boil over, but like his wife liked to remind him, it wasn't always necessary to be right, especially if you're about to burst a vein in the side of your head. He could see her in his mind's eye and acknowledged her caution. Besides, Eddie knew this situation was his own damned fault, no matter how much of an ass 10B was being. He took a deep calming breath, opened his eyes, stood, and turned to the passengers.

Eddie took one step into the bus and addressed the troublemaker. "Sir, if you will just return to your seat, I will resolve this issue and get us back on the road shortly."

"What issue, man?"

Eddie could feel the passengers watching him; eyes peeking over the seat backs and he knew what they were saying. He fucked up.

"Sir, uh, I'm sorry. I don't recall your name."

"Dick."

Of course. "Uh, Dick, it appears that we are . . . lost. That is, I'm not quite sure exactly where we are."

This admission made the other passenges' whispers turn into loud protests.

"And we're almost out of gas."

"What the . . .?" Dick took a menacing step towards the bus driver.

Paul rose out of his seat and moved closer to the aisle.

Eddie gave Paul a quick wave off and redirected his attention back to Dick. The other passengers quieted down and turned their eyes towards the confrontation in the aisle.

"Sir, I said I would handle this, so please sit down."

Ellie quietly came up behind Dick and touched him. She tugged on his shirt to get him back to his seat. "Come on back to our seats, Richard, and let the driver do his job."

Dick turned on Ellie and yelled into her face, "That's just it! If he did his job, we wouldn't be in this situation right now!"

Ellie placed her hand on Dick's shoulder and slightly pulled him in the back to the rear of the bus. She murmured, "Come on, sweetie . . .."

He yanked his shoulder away from Ellie's grasp and shoved her away from him. This sent her falling into the row where Paul was now standing and into his arms, catching her before momentum drove her onto the floor. They stood face to face. For a moment, Paul held onto her, keeping her on her feet. He stared into her eyes. She looked back into his, and for a split second, Paul felt a jolt of electricity.

"What do you think you're doing, pal?" Dick asked Paul.

Connection broken. Ellie freed herself from Paul's steady grasp and slid out into the aisle, where Dick pushed her back towards their seats. This time, when she stumbled, she fell heavily to the floor. Stunned by the fall, Ellie picked herself up and slunk back to her seat, not making eye contact with anyone.

Dick and Paul locked eyes, sizing each other up. There was a pregnant pause as each man waited for the other to do something. Then Dick broke out into a huge, fake grin. With the wave of his hand, Dick blew off the incident like he had nothing to do with it and joined Ellie in the back of the bus.

Thus, ended the first "battle" of the *Pride of Ontario*.

Paul watched Dick make his way back to the rear of the bus and sit. When Paul felt confident there would not be any further outbursts, he turned and slowly lowered himself into his seat, hoping that was the end of the excitement for this trip, but he was trained for such things and awaited the next incident. It was the realist in him.

Paul Mathews was traveling to gather his thoughts about what he should do next with his life. He never thought too much about it, his life, that is. Ever since 9/11, at fourteen, the only thing that Paul could think about was joining the Army and go off to defend his country. Well, maybe he also had an unyielding desire to get away from his stifling mother. To be fair, she became more protective of her only child after Paul's father died. She hovered over him with such a heavy hand that it kept him from forming any genuine and lasting friendships.

His high school years were a nightmare. His mother wouldn't let him do anything that might get him hurt. When Paul tried out for the football team in secret and got accepted, she marched him down to the coach's office, where she made him tell Coach Parsons, to his face, that he was quitting the team. The coach could see the anguish in Paul's eyes at having to do this, and Paul appreciated how the coach handled the incident, but that didn't stop the guys from giving him crap. "Puss Boy," or PB for short, was his nickname for the rest of his days at Stadium High School in Tacoma, Washington.

He smiled at the thought of Coach Parsons. The man knew the score when it came to understanding Paul's situation. He even convinced Paul's mother to let him be the team manager since nothing "harmful" could happen in that position.

Nothing damaging to the body, but the ribbing he received from the team could have been detrimental to his psyche had he been a weaker person. Instead, the taunting and towel snapping taught Paul how to behave and banter around men. He crossed over into full-on acceptance when he struck back at his tormentors.

That one day, before practice, when he got into their lockers early and applied a thick layer of the heat rub to all their jocks was sweet revenge indeed. After about thirty minutes, the entire team had to make haste into the showers, pulling off gear and jocks to wash away the burn. Instead of beating the crap out of Paul, the team bowed down to PB, honoring his assault, and from that point, he was one of them. His memory of catching the coach's smile while the players were madly washing away the burn was the best since before the death of his father.

The day after he graduated from high school, Paul walked straight into the recruiting office and joined the Army as his father had, finally doing something in which his mother had no say. The Army was a good place for him to grow up. He never realized just how much his mother had shielded him from the world and the life choices that others make just in the everyday act of being a human. The Army taught him to take the initiative and to achieve and grow as a man.

What Paul saw and experienced in Afghanistan began this process of self-reflection. Three deployments under his belt had placed a heavy burden on his soul. He loved the Army, and he wholeheartedly believed in its mission to protect the United States, but the destruction and death he witnessed and caused were always going to be a part of him. He needed to put things into perspective and rest his injured body after that IED blasted a Humvee out from under him.

This long-deserved leave would help him, hopefully, decide on staying in the Army and taking the career path or setting out on fresh adventures. By his standards, he had all the time in the world to think on this since he didn't have to report back to Joint Base Lewis-McChord until the end of the week.

Paul looked up to the front of the bus and nodded to Eddie, signaling that he had his back.

Eddie nodded back at Paul, signaling his thanks, then wiped his brow and returned to his seat, where he reached into his jacket pocket and brought out his cell phone. He swiped at the screen a few times. No signal. He turned around and held it at a different angle and still nothing. Under his breath, Eddie said, "Shit." He turned back to the passengers.

<hr />

AS EDDIE STOOD and turned his back away from the front of the bus to address the passengers, Kelvin saw something dark fly past the windshield outside, moving too fast for him to identify. It could have been a bird, maybe a bat. Perhaps the wind had picked up some leaves. Then it returned and flitted behind the driver, past the windshield again from the opposite direction.

Kelvin looked around to see if anyone else saw what he did. No one seemed to have noticed. He nudged Jenna in the ribs and said to her under his breath, "Did you see that?

"The bus driver? The 'all-American family?' I can't see much with these seatbacks blocking my view."

"Something weird flew by the front of the bus."

"It was a bird."

"No. It wasn't solid. It was . . . .." He tried to show her with his fingers wiggling, intertwined, as he moved his hands apart and together in front of her face, "Like smoke coming off a campfire. See?"

Jenna brushed Kelvin's hands away from her face. "No. I don't see, and neither did you."

"I saw it! It was like black strings. No, like that Halloween, cobweb stuff you have to pull apart."

"Shut up. You're high."

"No, I'm not. I told you I'm not doing that stuff anymore."

———◦———

EDDIE LOOKED BACK towards the passengers and saw that the comedy team was still at it. He shook his head, not understanding how they could keep up their routine even in the face of bad news. Then he raised his voice slightly to address all the passengers. Holding up his phone, Eddie announced, "Okay. I'm not getting any signal out here. Any of you have a better service than me?"

Wilson O'Neil shrugged his shoulders apologetically and his wife, looking at her phone, shook her head "no" as she returned it to her bag. Paul looked at his phone and gave a "no go" head shake. Eddie saw that pretty girl, Stephanie—funny how he remembered her name—in 8A, searching her bag for her phone.

Kelvin called out, "I have one of those pay-as-you-go Walmart specials, but I'm sure I wouldn't get a signal out here even if I *did* have any minutes left to use. Besides, my phone needs charging." Jenna gave him a punch in the shoulder. Kelvin responded with a melodramatic silent "Ouch" and gave her one of those over exaggerated limp wrist slaps back at her, "Bitch." Then they hugged, giggling to themselves.

Eddie gave the odd couple a sideways stare as they continued to carry on in their never-ending show, and then an excited squeal slipped out of Stephanie's mouth. "Found it!" She turned it on. "Hey! It looks like I have a signal." She stepped into the aisle with her phone held out. The light from the screen highlighted the underside of her chin and nose, giving her face an almost angelic glow.

Eddie stepped towards Stephanie, but Dick hopped up and reached her first. He grabbed her hand seductively and looked at the screen. "Sorry, beautiful, but you ain't got nothin' too." He moved his eyes from the phone to Stephanie's body and gave her a quick once-over. "Signal that is." She smiled at the compliment. Dick gave her a wink and got a coy look back in response.

"Say, what's your name?"

"Steph."

"I'm Richard. Pleased to meet you."

"Same." Steph returned to her seat, unaware or not caring that everyone had just watched the guy use one of the sleaziest of pickup lines in the history of man and right in front of his girlfriend.

FROM THE REAR of the bus, Ellie watched Dick go through the motions she had seen countless times before. She was used to it. Dick needed to feel wanted, and this was just a little game for him, only a flirtation like all the others. He always came back to her. That had to mean something. Right?

So, Ellie sat with her eyes closed, waiting for her boyfriend to return to his seat after he finished playing his little game. He always chose the back near the restroom because it's secluded and far from prying eyes so he could "pass the time."

Ellie Struthers grew up, allowing others to take advantage of her, thinking that she couldn't stand up for herself. Her dad treated her mother and, at times, her like they were undeserving of decency and respect. And that continued into her mother's second marriage with yet another poor choice of life partners.

Ellie's stepfather liked to say she reminded him of Sally Struthers, that ditsy blond actress on that seventies TV show *All in the Family*. He always would refer to that actress whenever he was making a point about her appearance, like the way she wore her hair or her choice of clothes. It certainly didn't help matters that her last name was Struthers, an ironic coincidence when combined with her blonde hair and good looks.

Ellie never understood what his fascination was with that old show, except that maybe he had a crush on Sally Struthers in his early teens. She could almost envision him hiding in his bedroom, door locked, drapes drawn, and looking through a fan magazine with pictures of her. It made Ellie shiver with disgust, especially when he stared at her breasts as he commented on her clothing selection. "That old Archie

Bunker wouldn't allow his daughter out of the house in that tight of a blouse."

These she considered the "good" memories of living with mom and that perv.

The terrible stuff came when he entered her room after beating her mother. Ellie could hear her sobbing away from down the hall as Mr. Shitburger—Dwayne—would throw open her door. No, these were not good memories. Dwayne would open her closet and pull out the tight blouse and shorts that really seemed to get him going. He'd toss them onto her bed.

"Change." He'd always say in a matter-of-fact tone.

She would always resist, always. And he'd always reach out and slap her across the face. She would hesitate, and then he would get furious. Ellie had seen mad like that with her real father and knew when to do what she had been told.

"Change. Now!"

Shaking, Ellie would undress and put on the clothes. Dwayne's breath would turn into quick panting as he watched. She always tried not to show him too much, but it was hard in her small room. Besides, Dwayne wanted to see her dressed as his fantasy from *All in the Family*.

When she had put on the "ungodly" clothes as Dwayne called them and then combed out her long blonde hair just so, he would lick his lips and then slowly close her door. She could hear her mother sob out, "*NO!*" And then it would be just her and him in the room.

"Move around slowly. Unbutton the top of your shirt. Bend over a bit." He would watch her performance. It never took long before he would unzip his pants. If you could bleach out a memory, that would be the one, but no amount of bleach could remove that image from her head.

Aside from the initial slap or two to get his point across, Dwayne never touched her sexually. He was a watcher and boy did he enjoy watching. She could feel his eyes on her, even if they weren't in the same room. She could never find it, but she was confident that there was a peephole in the bathroom, and that enabled him to watch her while she showered. But if she said anything about her suspicions, it would bring about the beating of both her and her mother. Ellie was so tired of getting hit. She would do almost anything to keep that from happening again.

Despite her home environment, Ellie did well in school. It was the least she could do for her mom. She had so little to grab onto, and Ellie was determined to give her as much as she could. Getting good grades wasn't all. Ellie was on the debate team. She edited the yearbook and volunteered at a woman's shelter. The irony was not lost on Ellie as she helped women who were not unlike her mother and her.

Not long after she started volunteering, Ellie began taking a self-defense class where she learned the basics and was rather impressed with herself with how well she picked it up. She believed that one day, this knowledge would save her mother from another horrific beating and maybe even keep her from having to see Dwayne's wiener yet another time.

She knew that there would be no way she would ever hook up with an abuser like both her father and stepdad had been. No way.

Meeting Richard Conroy was a flotation device tossed to her sinking life. Perhaps a bit rough around the edges, but he was from working-class stock, and rough is what you would expect. Not quite the captain of the football team, but a talented player who got a minor scholarship to a junior college down south of the Bay Area. That was enough for Ellie, so she kissed her mother goodbye and gave Dwayne the finger as she closed the door behind her.

Ellie's life was just starting, and she wasn't going to look back. Except that she did. Her crying mother was looking out the window and cautiously giving her daughter a wave goodbye.

She opened her eyes and found that she was looking directly at that handsome man who held her a few rows up. And he was looking at her. Ellie quickly turned her gaze back to Richard.

Too late. He caught her looking at the guy. In a fury, Dick stomped back to their seats and shoved Ellie into the side of the bus. The pain wasn't as bad as the humiliation, but Ellie held in a whimper, not wanting anything further to happen. It was a hard lesson learned from years of abuse.

Dick then turned his attention to Paul and gave him a stern stare, a warning to not be looking at his girl. *His* property. Paul stood and stared back, not intimidated in the least. After a moment of an intense stare-down, Dick again cracked a slight smile and waved his hand as if nothing had happened. With his eyes still looking at Paul, Dick deliberately moved in even tighter with Ellie and started whispering in her ear and kissing her lovingly on the cheek.

Apparently, the second "battle" of the *Pride of Ontario* had ended in another draw. Paul lowered himself back into his seat. He folded his arms and tried to act nonchalant but was ready for the real smackdown that was brewing.

"OKAY, SO I guess that means that no one has any phone service out here," Eddie announced from the front of the bus. He paused in thought, then said, "It's too dark out there now to make it worthwhile to be roaming around. It's safe and relatively warm inside the bus. At first light, I'll go find some help."

Dick jumped up again, enraged. "First light!" He took a step back into the aisle to make himself seen. "I told you I gotta be in Boise!"

Ellie stood, took in a deep breath, and walked up the aisle to Dick, again, then gently tugged on his sleeve to get him to come back to their seats. Dick turned forcefully and pushed her away from him, causing Ellie to stagger backward and land on the floor in the middle of the aisle, smashing her elbow on an armrest as she went down. Climbing to her feet, she brought her hand up to the sore elbow but stayed standing where she fell.

When Dick pushed Ellie to the floor, the others stood in alarm, ready to do something, but what to do was the question. Paul knew and jumped out into the aisle, standing between Eddie and Dick. Paul was finished with this blowhard, and he had the skill set to put an end to him and his loudmouth skills that he wasn't afraid to use on this guy.

Dick now stood face to face with Paul. Usually, he could out-bluster most people, but this guy was a potential threat. Looking over Paul's shoulder at the driver Dick could see that even the old hippie seemed emboldened by his presence, and as if those two weren't enough to take on, he saw by the expressions on the other passengers' faces that he had crossed a line in public that he should not have. No one could have accused Dick of being highly educated but, in the mathematics of personal confrontation, he held a PhD and knew when he held the weakest hand.

This time, when Dick felt the tug on his sleeve, he gave Paul one last menacing stare before turning and forcing his way past Ellie, moving back down the aisle to his seat where he would be out of sight of the rest of the passengers. Dropping himself into the seat next to the window, Dick rested his head on the cold dark glass and tried to look outside at the desert, away from his problems, but all he saw was the reflection of his own sulking eyes staring back at him in the black mirror the window had become.

Ellie looked up at the passengers who were still standing and staring at the loser of a human she was traveling with or were they looking at her in judgment? Either way, she had stopped caring about what others thought long ago. With her eyes, she pleaded for them to mind their own business. After a moment, each sat back down. A tense silence fell throughout the bus.

Paul remained standing, however, and kept looking back at Ellie, who was embarrassed by his scrutiny. Looking now directly into Paul's eyes, she could feel heat rise from her neck and into her cheeks with a flush of shyness. He gave her a warm, friendly smile, and then she abruptly shook her head, a silent signal for him to stay out of it. Ellie dropped her eyes. What was she feeling? Shame? Attraction?

Ellie turned back towards the man who hurt her and gently sat next to him. She combed her fingers through Dick's hair and cooed soothing words of comfort into his ear, but she could still feel Paul's eyes burning into her.

Eddie returned to his driver's seat when Dick sat down. All this tension exhausted him. That Ranger guy had helped him three times in less than thirty minutes. He needed to thank him. He glanced down at the open bag sitting next to him on the floor. The Beretta 9mm lay within easy reach; a little something "just in case." For a few fleeting seconds, he thought that he might have been about to experience his first "just in case" moment. Nam gave Eddie a healthy respect for guns and when to or when not to use them. He wondered if he could have used it if Dick had been more aggressive. He looked towards the rear of the bus where the two huddled together. At this moment, the blonde stroking Dick's hair seemed to him more like a little lost girl than the girlfriend of an asshole.

Relieved that tonight wasn't the time for him to learn whether he would have used his piece, Eddie turned back to the front of the bus and opened the map again to see if he could make sense of where they were. He yawned and conceded that, without daylight, he could do nothing more. Time for some shuteye.

Eddie looked back at his passengers. "I can leave the lights on, but with no fuel, the batteries will last only so long. If you all don't mind, I'll shut things down and wait 'till morning."

Getting no objections or comments at all, not even a whispered grumble from Dick, Eddie shrugged his shoulders and shut off the switches that controlled everything. The interior of the bus fell into darkness except for the glow of cell phones being checked one last time.

From behind him, Eddie could make out the voice of the little girl traveling with her parents. She had been a real trooper throughout all this and now, having to sleep in a broken-down bus, well, a little whine from her would be acceptable.

The voice of her mother broke the silence if just by a whisper. "You are such a brave girl, my darling. This is not quite the adventure that we told you about, but just think of the memories and the stories you will be able to tell your new friends in Baker City."

Cindra listened to her mother try to make lemonade out of the lemons that this day had brought. Her mother always tried to find the silver lining in any dark cloud, and when it came to her daughter's life, her mother was overly protective, trying to shield Cindra from the big evil world; like she couldn't see what was going on. She may have been only eight years old, but she wasn't stupid.

Cindra was the apple of the O'Neils' collective eye. She was outgoing, creative, and her life force could only be described as infectious. A good student, Cindra excelled at everything she touched. The tensions of the past several years should have affected her more than they appeared to have, hearing her parents argue the way they did sometimes would have had an effect on anyone, but the adventure of moving to a new town had overshadowed the family's financial demons.

Now the only stress on her parents came with leaving one life behind and starting a new one. Of course, an eight-year-old can only know and understand so much, but she could distinguish between the types of "conversations" before the decision to move, "How are we going to make the car payments?", with after, "Do you think the schools will be good in Baker City?" She knew the difference between the angry voice and the concerned one. The latter was far more tolerable. She hoped that what her parents said would be true, that she would have fun in their new home and that she would make new friends. Cindra closed her eyes, imagining her new life as sleep caught up with her.

————◆○◆————

WITH THE COMMOTION finished—he hoped—Eddie listened as the passengers settled in for the evening. From the back, he could barely hear the girl make soothing sounds, trying to keep that dick under control. Humph. Good luck with that. Other voices drifted up to Eddie's ears. He heard the woman's voice from that weird couple, "Mom and Dad, a funny thing happened to me on my way to Portland. First, I got on the wrong bus and wound up in Reno, and then I got on the wrong bus again and wound up heading for Boise. Kelvin? Kelvin's just a friend. I'm a lesbian, remember? And he's a . . . just what are you, Kel?"

Kelvin burst out in a guffaw, "Oh, you are so bad!"

Good thing they're headed to Portland. The wine and cheese crowd will eat those two up, Eddie mused.

The snickering continued from the strange pair, but soon faded out and, aside from the whispered words of comfort from mother to daughter, he could hear no other sounds. Everyone else was lost in thoughts or had fallen asleep.

Eddie yawned again, stretched, and draped himself over the steering wheel to get comfortable. Finally, after the light from the last of the cell phones winked off, the bus descended into complete darkness.

Ah, some peace and quiet, Eddie thought. He squirmed to find a comfortable spot for his butt and folded his arms across the steering wheel, forming a pillow of sorts. He lowered his head onto his crossed arms and looked out to the left side of the bus. Eddie closed his eyes. Ouch! His back screamed at him, and he knew it would yell even louder in the morning, along with everyone else. Still trying to get comfortable, he sat up again and adjusted his body.

Out through the windshield, he saw that the night wasn't all that dark now that the artificial lights were off and his night vision had kicked in even on this overcast, moonless night. Before he set his head down one more time in another attempt to get to sleep, something caught Eddie's eyes . . . Something . . . Black. It flew past the bus like threads being swirled around in the wind or wisps of smoke; something darker than the night, a blackness that he could see against the blackest shadows of the landscape.

Wait! Did the black filaments just converge into a shape, the form of a man? Eddie rubbed his eyes and peered into the night, straining to see what it was, but saw nothing. *Tired old man's eyes are playing a trick on me,* Eddie thought and shrugged, resting his head back onto the wheel. Since his days "in-country" back in Nam, he had not had such an F-ed up day as this one, bar none. Oh yeah, he was so fucked!

If a place is quiet enough, the silence can be so oppressive it can almost have a sound unto itself. The silence of this Eastern Oregon night permeated the bus. As Eddie listened, his eyes glanced up into the gray clouds where he knew there was a star field so massive that it almost would have outshone the full moon. He sighed, knowing that he was missing one of the joys of being so far from the light pollution of the cities. He yawned again and felt the weight of his eyelids as they lowered and then shut, and Eddie was asleep.

FIBROUS THREADS OF black danced around in front of the bus, intertwining like fingers of smoke caught up in the currents of heat rising from a fire. They spiraled in a whirlpool of murky vapor and came together to form into the shape of a shadow of a man standing on the other side of the glass from the sleeping driver.

Eddie dreamed that a ghostly figure with blood-red eyes and pupils of empty desolation was studying him through the windshield as though he were a specimen on display. The Shadow Man peered through the windshield, past Eddie into the interior of the bus at the passengers. He floated down the exterior and paused at each of their windows, studying each.

In this dream, Eddie wanted to yell out to everyone, to warn them about the man whose feet did not touch the ground, but his throat felt constricted, voice stifled, as if controlled by an outside force.

The Shadow Man first scrutinized the O'Neils, then moved on and stopped, taking a long look at the Army Ranger. Next, he floated down to Steph's window, where he lingered and ran his fingers across the glass as though he were stroking her hair. At the end of the bus, the Shadow Man saw Dick's face smashed up against the glass. He paused, then flicked out his tongue in a licking gesture a ravenous man might at the sight of a thanksgiving dinner he could not touch. He then crossed to the opposite side of the bus, where he found Jenna and Kelvin and gave them a studious once over.

"Wake up!" Eddie wanted to yell. Then the Shadow Man was standing, looking straight into his eyes, making him freeze with fear.

The Shadow Man smiled. Sharp, dagger-like white fangs protruded from his mouth.

Eddie woke with a start, heart beating like a drum, sounding an alarm, a call to arms. He stared out into the night, rubbed his eyes to clear them, but saw nothing. Unconvinced, he turned on the headlights of the bus. There, threads of blackness swirled about but dissolved before his brain could register their existence. Eddie shook his head and thought to himself, *What a silly thing, being spooked by what? The dark?*

A bit of wind kicked up the dust, swirling it around in the lights. See? Nothing. He turned off the lights and attempted to get to sleep again. The wisps of blackness swirled over the top of the *Pride of Ontario*, then vanished into the night.

———————◆◇◆———————

LIGHT FROM THE rising sun slowly crept across the scrub as it inched westward towards Cascade Stage Lines, bus number seven. The overcast of the night before had lifted, and the brightness of the sunrise reflected off the windows of the bus. Golden colored light climbed its metallic surface, peeking inside and waking each of the passengers as it fell upon their faces.

When the sunlight splashed across Eddie's closed eyes, he knew it was time to wake up and come to grips with his situation. Damn! First things first, however, right now his bladder was urgently telling him to get the hell up and empty it! He never listened to his dad when he complained about this part of the aging process. But who listened to old guys whine about their bodily functions? Eddie sighed, opened his eyes, and sat up. Oh, God! His back reminded him they were going to have issues today.

Eddie sat up straight and stretched, first twisting his back to the left, then to the right, and felt a pop or two as his vertebrae realigned themselves. The vivid dream of the Shadow Man had faded—erased from his memory. He opened the door but, before he exited the bus, he reached into his bag and rooted his hand around the bottom, then stopped and brought out a rattling bottle of ibuprofen. He looked at the bottle. 200mg. Ugh. He popped the cap off and poured out the last two tabs into his hand. He was momentarily sorry for his over generosity earlier, giving his extra bottle to the Ranger, and the stronger ones at that, but the guy had been a great help and the way he favored that knee he would need them more. Eddie shrugged and tossed the brown pills straight into his mouth, swallowing them dry with a slight grimace. He placed the bottle back in the bag, saw the Beretta, and grabbed it.

When he stood, he looked back to make sure that none of the passengers were looking at him. He didn't see that Paul was feigning sleep and watching him through his barely open eyelids. Confident everyone was still asleep, he slipped the gun into the waistband of his pants at the small of his back, adjusted his jacket to make sure that it covered the handle of the gun and climbed down out of his office and into the new day.

The morning was sunny, which was a far cry from the overcast sky of the night before. Eddie stepped away from the bus, wasting no time enjoying the sweet air. He had business to attend to and made his way to the nearest wall of scrub and stepped behind it, unzipping his pants. Relief.

Eddie could hear the other passengers exiting the bus, but paid no attention to them until he finished. This was probably going to be his last private moment for a while, and he chose to enjoy it. When finished, Eddie zipped up, tucked in his shirt, smoothed his pants, straightened his jacket, and double checked the gun was easily within reach. Then he placed his Cascade Stage Lines cap on his head as though he was still that young Marine back in Nam getting ready for battle. Ready, he walked back to the bus, attempting to look as official as possible.

The O'Neils exited the bus first and huddled a bit away from the door. Wilson stretched. Marion was trying to comb Cindra's hair and straighten her clothes. She pulled a handkerchief out of her bag and licked it to wipe off the corner of her daughter's mouth. Cindra did her best at resisting her mother's fawning, but with little success.

As Marion wet her handkerchief again with her tongue, Cindra cringed. She hated it when her mother tried to clean her face like this. Yet, she stood there and took it, believing that one day, her mom would relax and let a kid be a kid. She understood what the term "little trooper" meant when her parents called her that and, frankly, she was getting tired of hearing it. Cindra could tell that her cooperation helped, and she could see the love they had for her in their faces, but did her mom have to wash her face with spit? She was getting tired of that too!

EDDIE ARRIVED BACK at the bus just as Marion finished giving her daughter a spit bath and was in the process of vigorously brushing lint off Cindra's back, which appeared to be less of a cleaning ritual and more of a spanking. When Marion spotted Eddie, she asked in a tone that foreshadowed how the rest of Eddie's morning was going to go, "Don't you ever clean the interior of these things?" Wilson yawned and discovered that he had more urgent needs than to listen to his wife complain to the driver, so he moved to the other side of the bus for a little "personal" time.

A noise from the interior of the bus drew their attention to Steph, who stood at the top of the stairs. She yawned and stomped down to the ground. Now that she was standing in the full light of day, Eddie really got a better picture of this lone traveler. What he saw confirmed his assessment of her when she boarded the bus in Reno.

Steph was one well-packaged woman, and Eddie could understand why she was the center of the ruckus between Dick and his girlfriend: jeans too tight, a loose tank top that flopped open in all the right places, and an excess of costume jewelry. When she stretched, her shortcut shirt rose and revealed the bottom of her breasts. "And to think I was trying to avoid sleeping on a bus when I booked this trip. Ha!" Steph said to whoever was listening.

"I like your fashion sense, sweetie. Seeing anyone?" Jenna asked Steph as she stepped down off the bus. Steph abruptly stopped stretching and consciously pulled the bottom of her shirt down, covering as much of her exposed skin as possible and then, as an exclamation point, she put her coat on and buttoned it up. Without saying a word or looking at Jenna, Steph moved away, pretending she was checking out the scenery.

Kelvin, Jenna's companion/sidekick/straight man, followed her off the bus. He snickered at Jenna's comment and joined her a few feet away from the door, where they huddled and continued their private joke-fest.

Next in line to exit the bus was Paul, who stepped down in a fit, ready-for-the-day fashion.

"You always this bright-eyed in the mornings?" Kelvin wondered.

"Yep. Force of habit. Greet the day with a good attitude 'cause who knows how shitty it could end up being. I think those were Custer's last words." Paul winked at Kelvin.

Kelvin blushed a little, and Jenna gave him a slap on the arm to snap him out of his stupor.

Eddie only smiled at the fake historical reference. Everyone knew Custer's last words were, "Ah, shit."

Paul walked away from the door opening, limping slightly—his knee stiff from sleeping on the bus in an awkward position. When he stepped out of the shadow of the bus and into the direct morning sun, he turned towards the light and closed his eyes to absorb as much of the warmth as he could—like he was charging his solar cells for the day to come.

Ellie and Dick came out of the bus last. They paused at the top of the stairs in a quiet argument. Then, as they descended, Dick grabbed Ellie's elbow to keep her close.

This commotion drew the attention of the other passengers, who turned to see what was going on. Embarrassed, Ellie yanked free of Dick's grip, jumped the last two steps off the bus, and stumbled, nearly falling to the ground. The momentum of this action sent her on a collision course with Paul, but she recovered from her graceless exit coming up short of landing in Paul's arms. Ellie caught Paul's eye and gave him a brief, awkward smile, then promptly disengaged, not wanting to rile up Dick any further. But instead of rejoining her boyfriend Ellie stayed where she was and hovered in Paul's general area.

Having nothing more to see regarding Ellie, everyone turned to watch the drama king make his entrance.

Dick stomped down off the bus, giving Ellie and Paul the evil eye.

"Hey, I slept like crap. Sorry! Okay?" Dick said defensively to everyone.

Marion threw Dick a glare. The fire that seemed to emanate from her eyes was intense enough to bubble paint. She drew Cindra back away from the bus and the source of the offensive language and fumed at Dick, "There are children present!"

Dick made an overly dramatic visual scan of the area, then looked at Marion. "I only see one." He laughed at his attempt at humor. He got nothing but blank stares in return. "Get it? There's only one child. Not *children*." Still, he got no acknowledgment of his joke and waved his hand towards the group as he turned away from them. "Fuck you all too!" he said under his breath as he walked away from the unappreciative audience.

Then Dick noticed Steph and checked her out as she stood in the morning light. He nodded his head in appreciation. Dick looked back around at the group and saw that Ellie had turned away from him, so he strolled over in Steph's direction.

To distract themselves from the uncomfortable situation with Dick, the passengers pulled out their cell phones. They spent a bit of time holding them up in different directions and at weird positions, trying to find the perfect spot to locate a signal. An outside observer might imagine them as a flock of plastic yard flamingos preening in the morning sun. None had any luck, and they each turned off their phones in frustration.

Eddie also rechecked his phone and pocketed it after he saw no signal. The start of this new day was going to be just a continuation of the night before; all shit-show all the time. He looked at the passengers, adjusted his cap, again, and cleared his throat, "Well, as a representative of Cascade Stage Lines I guess I'll head on down the road a bit and see if I can find a house or someplace with a landline. You all sit tight. No point in all of us getting lost any further."

Hearing this, Dick turned from Steph and charged towards Eddie and aggressively poked the driver in the chest with his finger, causing him to fall back a few paces. "Look, old man. We wouldn't be here, lost, in the first place if you didn't get off the main highway."

Eddie straightened and stepped back towards the group. "We were running behind. Thought I would try this shortcut I heard about . . . Look, I'm sorry. I must have taken a wrong turn because we should have been in Baker City by last night. Stay here. The company will be looking. Until then, I'll go see what I can find."

Approaching Eddie again, Dick said, "That don't help much. I should just . . ." He clenched his fist, getting ready to strike.

Paul took a slight step forward when he saw the bus driver reach behind his back, going for the 9mm. But then he stopped as he watched the driver think twice about that move and brought his right hand around and stabbed a finger in Dick's chest.

"Look, Dick!" Eddie stepped right up to Dick and stuck his finger in the guy's chest. "It was my grandson's birthday yesterday, and I was supposed to be home last night, not here. I'm more scared of what my wife is thinking right now than I will ever be of you! So back the Fu—" Eddie saw Marion's face scrunch up and then quickly glanced down at Cindra. "So back the hell off."

Dick, kowtowed by Eddie's powerful reaction, raised both hands up, palms outward, as he backed up and slunk off towards the scrub line and pretended to relieve himself.

Eddie straightened his jacket and went into the bus, emerging with a small cooler and a thermos. "It ain't much, but my wife packs me a few things to eat on these runs, just some crackers, and stuff. Help yourselves." Eddie adjusted his ponytail and pulled his cap down on his balding head. "You all just relax as best you can. I'm sure help will be here soon."

With that, Eddie started walking down the road.

Chapter 5

LIZ

L IZ TURNED THE knob and pushed the door of her dorm room open. She entered the compact unit and turned up the AC. Even though it was only 9am, Southeastern Arizona could get hot quickly. As she let the frigid air washed over her body, she wondered why Fort Huachuca had been selected for her enhanced training—sometimes it was just too damn hot to concentrate on her classes—not to speak of the effect the heat had when it came to the physical exercises. Then the proverbial light bulb went on in her head—*unless*, any negative reaction she had to things such as temperature or the quality of the food or the meanness of the instructors could be used in evaluating her status, affecting her future assignment, or reassignment back behind a desk.

Sufficiently cooled down, Liz collapsed onto her bunk, exhausted but feeling alive after the ten-mile run. Outside her window, she could hear others going through training. The almost melodic voice of a drill instructor calling cadence drowned out the other sounds.

"Birdie, Birdie, in the sky

You drop whitewash in my eye,

I don't sigh. I don't cry,

I'm just glad that cows don't fly!

Sound off!"

"One, Two."

"Sound off . . .."

As the impromptu serenade from the marching trainees faded, Liz hopped up from her bunk, kicked off her running shoes, and started removing her T-shirt. She was ready for a nice cool shower to wash away the sweat and grime.

A solid knock on the door made her pause. Liz pulled her shirt back on, then opened the door. Standing outside her room was her drill instructor, Master Sergeant Terry, a tall African American man, in his early 40s, built for action. "Looks like you went and got yourself noticed, Adams." Liz gave him a questioning look. The DI continued, "You've been slotted for a unit. By the looks of this envelope, it's for one of those elite secret outfits." Terry held out a manila envelope.

Liz did a fist pump. "Yes!" She had been working for this moment these past weeks—hell, the previous year. First, she had to get through boot camp and prove that she could swim in the deep end with the boys. She knew she could best most of them. So, it didn't sit well with her when she was assigned desk detail at one of the many military installations outside DC.

Barely a month into that assignment, Liz got another similar-looking envelope—without all the secret stamps—informing her she had been selected to go through another form of basic training for evaluation of both her physical and mental skills. Passing would mean assignment to some unspecified, "important" duty anywhere the government deemed necessary. Failing would, more than likely, land her back behind a desk. And she did not want to go back to a desk job. Though, by accepting that last offer the military had made, she ended here, in this oven, 15 miles from Mexico for enhanced training.

Now Master Sergeant Terry was standing at her door with *another*, similar envelope in his hand.

"It looks like they assigned you to something important and . . . secret," Terry said, with a bit of sarcasm in his voice. He turned the envelope over, displaying the *SECRET* word stamped in red on the front and back.

Never having been one to contain her emotions, the excitement of the moment overwhelmed her, and Liz gave the hard man a hug before he could fend off the assault. The master sergeant stiffened at the embrace and frowned at the display. Liz backed away from him as quickly as she could.

"I thought I had drilled that exuberant shit out of your system, Adams," Terry said sternly. "It's what got you assigned to 'guarding' that keyboard in DC in the first place."

"Sorry, Master Sergeant."

"Don't be sorry." He reached up and nailed his finger into her forehead. "Use that head of yours."

Liz swallowed hard and looked down at the envelope in his hand.

"One of my many functions is to identify candidates for this enhanced training program. I've been following your progress since your first week in basic when your DI flagged you as a potential. You didn't get assigned to a desk because you can't shoot a weapon or because you aren't fearless. What got you sitting at a computer is that often, when presented with new input, you tend to lose focus."

Liz looked up again and into that imposing face.

"When something catches you off-guard you've gotta soldier up and concentrate. Take a moment to understand your situation. Then, with knowledge, you can take the appropriate action. In our business, a lack of focus can get people killed. Come on. You know this." The master sergeant stared intently into Liz's eyes.

"I know Master Sergeant. It's just that . . .,"

"You get nervous. You project all the ways you can screw things up, which makes you get flustered and instead of acting, you react and end up doing stupid shit that makes you look foolish."

"Like hugging a master sergeant."

"Yes. When you react like you just did, you play into the stereotype of an emotional female, and you have worked too hard to let others' ideas influence your life's path."

Liz stood ridged, listening, wanting to defend herself, to counter what the master sergeant had been saying but knowing full well that he was right.

Terry looked at Liz, frozen by what he had been saying, and let his stone face crack a slight grin. "Listen . . . You will make a damned fine addition to whichever outfit has tagged you. But, because this world ain't fair, even in the twenty-first century, you, as a woman, have to work twice as hard to prove that you are capable of anything asked of you." He held up the envelope. "Now you have an assignment where the skills you have honed are needed. So, remember what I have been telling you. Your training days are over. Out there it's real life. Your life and others."

Sensing that Master Sergeant Terry had come to the end of his lecture, she lifted her head and smiled hesitantly. Pointing at the envelope, Liz asked, "Um, which one wants me? CIA, FBI, Army Intel?"

Terry's face returned to its hard-as-stone facade. "Well, private, if I knew it wouldn't be much of a secret, now would it? But I can tell you that if I *knew* and told you, I would find myself serving out the rest of my career on the dark side of the moon and maybe my retirement as well." He held out the manila envelope again, offering it to her.

Liz accepted the envelope and looked at it. There was her name, *Elizabeth Adams*, printed on the front and in boldface, red type, *SECRET* and then, *Eyes Only*. Master Sergeant Terry looked at her and watched the blood drain from her face. "I can't say that I have seen many top-secret envelopes in my time, but I do know that this is no shit to mess with. You are instructed to open and read the contents in private."

Liz just stood staring at the envelope, not sure what to do, afraid of what she might find inside.

"Uh, look Adams..." Terry's voice softened, and he dropped his facade for a moment.

Liz looked up into his eyes. *There, those unnaturally blue eyes do have some humanity*. At this moment, she could almost see her father in those eyes. Her dad had that same look when she graduated from high school, reassuring her that going off to college was the first of many grand adventures.

"You shouldn't be surprised at any assignment they offer. You accepted the invitation to come to this enhanced training program just for such an opportunity."

Liz lowered her head, listening to the fatherly voice.

"You have earned this. No one let you slip past some glass ceiling. This is all you. Now your hard work has gotten you a posting, and I would guess that it has nothing to do with desks. Unless that's what you want?"

Liz backed into her room, head swimming, and sat on the edge of the bunk. "I . . . I know, it's just that, at the end, after so much work . . . I, I . . .," She placed the envelope on the bed beside her.

Back into character as the perfect drill instructor, Master Sergeant Terry belted out, "Soldier, come to attention!" Shocked, Liz popped up, as she had been programmed to do. Terry leaned into her with his all too familiar hard face. "I did not train you to be a puss! And neither did my brother and sister DIs while you were in boot camp! Are you trying to malign our credibility?"

"Yes, Master Sergeant."

"What?"

Louder, "Yes, Master Sergeant! I mean, no Master Sergeant!"

"You will not second-guess yourself. Second-guessing yourself implies you are questioning my training. You wouldn't be second-guessing me, would you?"

"No, Master Sergeant!"

Terry grabbed Liz by the shoulders and looked into her eyes, smiling. "Good." Liz relaxed, feeling the strength and confidence of the drill instructor flow into her through his powerful hands. He let her go and backed into the door opening. "Now read your secret message and find out your assignment." He smiled. "Unless you lost your decoder ring." He closed the door slowly, but before it completely shut, he popped it back open and poked his head in with a warm, fatherly look. "Make me proud, Adams."

"I will, Master Sergeant. Thank you." Liz gave him a smile as the door clicked closed, leaving her alone.

Turning back to her bunk, she looked across at the envelope, which was waiting for her patiently to open it. Liz took a hesitant step, then another, reaching the edge of the bunk. Slowly, she reached down for the envelope and picked it up. Her heart was beating a cadence inside her chest more aggressively than that of any DI.

"Hidy hidy hidy ho.

Willie willie willie wo.

Lift your eyes up to the sky.

See Liz Adams walking by!"

Liz looked again at the envelope. She stared at the front of it with her name clearly typed and the red stamps declaring that this was a *SECRET* communication. The powerful and encouraging words from Master Sergeant Terry still rang in her ears, but she just looked at the unopened envelope and wondered what she had gotten herself into. Sure, it was one thing to get herself off to school when dad was still sleeping from pulling an all-nighter at the theatre, but it was a whole other thing when it came to opening a manila envelope which could mean a serious, life-altering change.

The voice of her dad came to her. "Come on, slowpoke! Gotta go. Hop to it." Then her mother would add, "Ready, Freddie?"

Liz's life played out like a movie projected across the empty wall of her dorm room. There she was at age six, standing in front of a drawer full of clothes. Her father was becoming increasingly frustrated that she couldn't choose what to wear, even though it was time to be getting out the door and off to school. After he made a few suggestions, which she rejected, he just started pulling clothes on her—not caring if anything matched. The comparison of trying to put a cat in a bag had been used to describe how difficult she made it for her dad. Then her mother appeared on screen, reminding Liz of the mantra she applied to just about everything: "I can do it myself!"

Both of her parents had told her often over the years that they would've rather had a strong-willed girl than a pansy. But, honestly, Liz believed a child like her would drive anyone nuts.

From the moment she was born, Liz functioned as an autonomous creature within the family. Her parents used to joke that she was a little alien living in her mother, ready to spring forth and wreak havoc on the world.

As it turned out, having an independent streak was a good thing when her family broke apart. It wasn't one of those *Lifetime* made-for-TV films. No melodramatics. Mostly, it was unmet expectations that ended it all.

Liz's dad worked in the theatre. Scenic design was his passion, or so he believed. He was a good guy but worked way harder and longer than the paycheck justified. Something about art. When her mother could no longer take the uncertainty of his income, she went looking for a more stable life.

The divorce happened when she was twelve. Her parents made it as painless as possible for her. Liz wasn't used as a pawn and had it quite easy, but she missed the familiarity of a home with two parents, even with the tension and unexpressed emotions.

Her mother did find stability in a job that she excelled in, but from a personal point of view, she was always searching for a spiritual place that was elusive for her to grasp. The earth goddess may have had some calming effects on her mother, but those benefits did not translate over to Liz's life.

So, whether she was at her mom's or dad's, she still had to make things happen the "Liz way." But that independent streak slowly morphed into a defensive barricade, masking her more anxious feelings. Being a tough, go-your-own-way little girl gave her parents the misguided reassurance that they weren't ignoring their daughter. They believed they were giving her space to be a free spirit, but, in reality, she found herself increasingly craving a more stable, structured environment within which to live. Not finding one, she raised herself as she shuffled between two houses, never being comfortable in either and falling into the habit of making things happen the "Liz way." But the lack of adult guidance nagged at her.

Not surprisingly, she found herself drawn to parental types and continuously sought their approval. This desire to be accepted frequently led to over-zealous behavior with the potential of disastrously embarrassing consequences. Take hugging a master sergeant as an example. So not in good form. When nerves and adrenaline kicked in simultaneously, her overwhelming desire to please could make her look more like the bumbling fool and not the sharp, intelligent person who she usually displayed, and was.

Now, despite her years of fighting it and believing that she could only count on herself to get things done, she longed to belong to a cohesive family. The military attracted her because of the possibility of finding that connection and a place where she could direct her abilities. In Master Sergeant Terry, she found the guiding force of a mother and father that she didn't have growing up. She appreciated him for that and now was worried that in taking this new assignment, she would forever lose the connection she had formed here.

The momentary daydream seemed to put Liz's life into perspective. She grabbed the envelope with her left hand and used her right to tear it open. Even so, she cautiously peered inside, looking for any hidden surprises. Finding none, she pulled out the letter slowly, unfolded it, and read:

Elizabeth Bernadette Adams: You are to report to Mountain Home AFB 5th, July, 0800 hours for introductory session and assignment.

Liz glanced at the calendar on the wall. Not that she didn't know that it was July, but the shock of how soon she had to report hit her. Today was the third. She'd have to get moving to make the travel arrangements from Fort Huachuca, almost on the border of Mexico, all the way north to Idaho. What the hell was there in Idaho? Suddenly Liz thought that her career just got sidetracked to the lower fifty's version of Antarctica, the middle of Spudville, Idaho. Great! She looked back at the travel orders.

You have been chosen to become a member of a very select organization, the nature of which will not be revealed to you until such a time when you are instructed as to the vital service you will be asked to perform for the safety of your nation and humanity. Your understanding of the importance of the mission must be acknowledged before you are allowed fully into the unit.

To even reveal this much information to anyone will be considered an act of treason.

Well, they didn't mess around when it came to secrets. Maybe the middle of a spud field was the perfect spot for this "mysterious" organization. But first things first. A shower was in order, then she would begin packing her gear. Now, Liz found herself excited by the whole cloak and dagger, feeling her orders imparted. *Safety of humanity?* It sounded like an evil organization needed stopping, and she was just the person who could do it.

Chapter 6

ALEX

A S THE EXPANSE of stars faded away in the light of the rising sun, Alexei Rurik took one last look around the mountaintop and breathed in the last of the early dawn air. He was tempted to watch the sunrise. He longed for the warmth that he remembered from his youth, but the burning heat that the rising sun would bring to him was more than he wanted. He liked living far better.

Alexei appeared to be in his late twenties, or possibly 30, though he was pushing almost 200 years old—according to the way mortals figured time. He was strikingly handsome with sharp features—red hair shot through with blond streaks and pale skin.

With the sun creeping over the top of the eastern ridge, it was time. He walked to the trailer that was attached to the back of his jeep and opened the lid of a long rectangular box and climbed in. Then he laid back into the container that served as his bed when he went out camping and closed the lid. Comforting darkness surrounded him. Alexei turned the latches and sealed himself in from the harsh morning sun and other dangers that might lurk about, trying to catch him in his slumber.

The cool, slightly damp soil lining the box felt good on his back. The low hum of the generator that kept his coffin/trailer comfortable while he slept was barely audible through the insulation used to surround it. From the outside, the box looked like an overly long metal ice chest. But this box was designed to keep him safe during the daylight hours, not keep beer cold, though it could be used for that too. One of the many marvels of the twenty-first century, courtesy of the United States Government.

The thrum of the generator always lulled Alexei to sleep. There was something about the rhythmic quality that must remind him of being in his mother's womb—a safer place, and time, far from where he now lay.

As Alexei felt sleep embrace him, his thoughts went to a time when he was a mere human boy and to the day when Vladimir had tricked him into going down into that ruin of a church. Mother had warned them, and she was correct. But she had no idea. It was just some idle superstitious talk from the local peasants that she repeated, but the talk of ghosts and supernatural occurrences was nothing compared to what lay in wait amidst the gnarled old oaks. What people should have been afraid of were vampires.

The first time Alexei had seen that mad monk Lazar, he felt such a chill—like the summer had disappeared and they were standing in an ice palace. He should have listened to his mother. More importantly, he should have listened to his inner voice and the alarms that were sounding. Instead, he had to protect his younger brother, his brother who had already been visiting Lazar, his brother who had been bitten and then drunk of the vampire's blood starting the process of turning him. His brother, who had been under the monk's control the whole time and lured him to the ruins and into this so-called "life."

Not that he had been able to turn and flee if he wanted to. There was no choice. He was doomed from the moment that the monk gazed into his eyes. Alexei lost all control and awareness of everything. His brother was nowhere around, and the rocks of the ruined building were just a gray blur. All he could see was Lazar. All he could do was what the monk willed him to do. Lazar's mouth did not move as he spoke, but Alexei heard the words, not through his ears but inside his head, one mind communicating with another. *"You have nothing to fear, my son. I offer you a life that is far more vast and exciting than anything you could hope to see as a simple human."* Then the monk's mouth *did* move. As it opened, sharp, white fangs extended down from his upper jaw. What Alexei felt as the Lazar bit into his neck was not quite painful. Though the pain was present, there was something else his young mind could not process for lack of experience. Was it pleasure?

Father Lazar did not consume the brothers as he would have done with common bleeders. He kept them like flies caught in his spider web and drank of their youth only sparingly. Lazar had a grand plan for Alexei and Vladimir, which required their turning to be a slow, methodical process.

He taught them the ancient ways of the vampire realm and shared with them his accumulated wisdom as it flowed from the cuts in his wrists and into the boys' eager mouths, one drop at a time. Lazar was grooming them, taking his time, turning them to be used later.

Alexei remembered the days back in Moscow, away from the life force Lazar offered through his veins, and how he longed for the family's return to the country come summer and the sweet warmth of the old monk's blood.

It went on like that for years. The daylight hours gradually became harder to take. Both brothers gradually became night people. His years at university were hard to endure as their classes took place when the sun was still out, so he would bundle up with long flowing coats, scarves, and floppy hats whenever he had to venture outside. Alexei took to wearing dark glasses to keep the glare of the sun from giving him a headache. He waited in anticipation for the night when he could peel off the layers of protective fabric and breathe freely. All the while, his thirst grew, which he tried to quench with animal blood purchased from the local butcher. It served a purpose. The cow's blood kept him from feeling like he was starving. But his genuine desire was for human blood.

The more complete his transition from human to vampire became, the more he stopped looking at people as potential friends and started seeing them as walking sacks of nourishment. He would wonder what their blood tasted like based on appearance or attitude. Women no longer were targets for his sexual desires. All he wanted to do was stroke their lovely necks, then slowly sink his growing canines into them, puncturing the primary artery between heart and brain. Those were the torturous days before his total change.

He never asked Vladimir if stray cats and dogs were enough to satisfy his cravings. Alexei and his brother had been growing apart throughout the years of their university education, so they rarely spoke to one another.

But he was afraid that Vladimir was moving beyond the blood of animals and seeking that of humans. He saw more than one female at the school, walking around with a medical dressing wrapped around her neck. The reason for their wounds Alexei could only surmise. And there were ever increasing rumors revolving around the disappearances of some students. Their absence from classes was no surprise, after all, not everyone could withstand the rigors of academic pursuits, and many returned home. However, when it was discovered that each of the missing had also up and left their lodgings unattended, and with all their belongings still in place, well, that pointed at something possibly nefarious going on. And Alexei had his suspicions.

Their last summer at the family dacha was the end of their lives as humans, at least as bleeding mortal humans. By now, they were visiting the monk almost every night, and on this visit, Lazar spoke to them as though this was their graduation.

"My sons," the monk said. "Tonight, you will fully transition from that of a mortal bleeder and join the ranks of the chosen. I selected you to be immortals, but not ordinary ones. I have been educating you through my blood, instilling in you the qualities and knowledge to be great leaders. Through you, I will vanquish those that have made me such as this. You will be my revenge and in so doing come to command the allegiance of all the vampire houses." Then he reached out his ancient hand and tenderly caressed Alexei's cheek. "And you, Alexei, you are destined to be Khan, the absolute leader of all immortals."

The shock and devastation etched on Vladimir's face were the most memorable parts of all that took place that night. Alexei could tell that his younger brother felt betrayed by their blood father. It was Vladimir who discovered the old vampire. It should have been he who would ascend to the highest heights of the immortals. "Why not me?" He demanded.

"You are strong, my son, but," the monk placed his hand on the young man's shoulder as he spoke, but Vladimir angrily shook it off, "Alexei is cautious. He thinks before he acts," he continued. "He can focus his power, which makes him the one to lead, but with you by his side, there will be no immortal that can stop the two of you. You will remove my enemies—the ones who condemned me to this life—and seize control of the chosen. It is your destiny!"

There was more than just anger in Vladimir's eyes that night. Alexei could see the beginnings of jealousy and a raging hatred that would one day be his downfall or Alexei's.

"Now it is time for you to bring your strength to full fruition." Father Lazar led them around a corner of the old ruin. Standing there, waiting for them, were two peasant girls held motionless by Lazar's mental control. These girls had terror in their eyes. They knew something terrible was about to happen, but they were helpless to do anything about it. "Tonight, you will be reborn into the life of the undead. Drink deeply, my sons. Soon the day will be upon us, and you will need to be safe in the dark; otherwise, the light will destroy you."

The brothers approached the girls. Alexei slowly stroked the neck of one, making her feel as much at ease with her destiny as possible. He did not desire to take her life to sustain his own, but the urge to consume her blood was all but overpowering him—horrified by what he had become, but even more horrified by the way Vladimir approached the other girl.

Vladimir grabbed her long hair and pulled her head back, exposing her throat. He took his anger out on this poor girl, not just biting her but tearing into her neck with such savage power he severed her head from her shoulders. Alexei watched as Vladimir lapped up the gushing blood, bite after bite. It was as if he were eating her whole. When he got to her heart, Vladimir took it into his hands. How it was still beating Alexei would never know.

Vladimir licked the still pulsing organ, tenderly caressing it, studying it, and only then did he slowly bite into it, expecting to savor the last drop of the girl.

Father Lazar, now in the role of kindly mentor, chuckled and said, "I made the same error. The heart is a tough organ. The head is where you find the most and sweetest blood. We bite the neck because the blood flows through it on the way to the brain. It is the brain that demands the most blood. Drink from the head."

And drink he did. Alexei remembered how intoxicated his brother became from emptying the skull of the young woman. Vladimir stood holding the severed head high in the air with his mouth wide unsuccessfully catching the last drops of the red fluid which dripped down onto his blood-soaked shirt and added to the pool that formed at his feet. He looked like an inebriated Kazakh who had celebrated too much after a victory. When finished, he collapsed to his knees in a drunken stupor, awash in her blood.

There was so much blood that Alexei became distracted from his own innocent. She looked into his eyes with an unspoken prayer. He stroked her cheek, and she smiled weakly, hoping. Then, without hesitation, Alexei crossed over and entered the ranks of the immortals.

So many years had passed and now this life of . . . What? Alexei knew his vampire family felt like kept animals. It was because of his agreement, his promise to Theodore to end the life of wanton killing, but what choice did he really have? Let the vampire hunters exterminate them all? At the time the original treaty was signed, vampire numbers had dwindled to mere thousands. The death of his blood father signaled the end even before Alexei ascended to the high seat of the council.

Alone in the crumbling shell of the church that was his lair, Lazar was found by vampire hunters led by an Orthodox priest. They had entered the ruin during the day, finding Lazar asleep, and then the killing began. The hunters drove a stake through his heart and into the earth beneath him. They hammered a stone wedge into his open mouth, keeping his fangs from use even in death, and then they torched his body and sprinkled its glowing embers with holy water. Alexei discovered Lazar's remains days later.

From that moment on, Alexei made his play to ascend to the top of the council, to take control of all the disparate vampire families. He made Vladimir his second, sharing with his brother the power which was now theirs. Vladimir never challenged Alexei's rule. Together they continued the practices the ancient ones had established before them, siding with despots and tyrants and trading protection from the vampire hunters during the daylight hours for access to the bleeding hearts of the rulers' troublemakers in the dark of night.

And why not? What had worked for centuries was bound to continue to work. Right?

Now, locked away from the devastating light of day, Alexei considered the deal he had struck. It was much the same deal that vampires made with tyrants—protection from the hunters in exchange for blood. The same, except this was different. A vampire's nature is to roam freely, picking its prey, not hidden away in the middle of nowhere, kept from the hunt and the treaty deprived them of that.

How many more years could this deal stand? And was the agreement still valid when the other principal signatory had died almost 100 years earlier?

Alexei closed his eyes, ready for sleep. There were always many questions and few answers. One thing was indisputable, however. Vladimir was restless, as were several others, with the most disturbing question of them all hanging over his head. Did Alexei have the strength to hold off a rebellion?

Chapter 7

ROADSIDE ATTRACTION

T HE EARLY AFTERNOON sun beat down on Eddie's back. Like most of the weather in Oregon, Eastern Oregon especially, you never really got the weather you liked or needed. Take, for instance, the previous night. The clouds had built up overhead in such a thick blanket that the moon and stars could not cut through. A little light might have helped him then, maybe even kept him from taking that, oh so wrong turn. Who the heck was he kidding? The sky was relatively clear, and the sun was still up when he took the shortcut. He would have to come up with a better story than that.

Eddie took off his hat and wiped a wrist across his sweaty brow, sorry that he didn't have any water with him. What was his wife always saying? A human needs eight, twelve-ounce glasses of water a day, give or take. He placed his hat back on his head and wet his lips with a swipe of his tongue.

This was probably the worst situation he had found himself in since he left the Marines. Certainly not as bad as Tet or the shit his dad had been through during the Second World War, taking part in some of the nastiest of the island hopping, and then finding himself in Korea smack dab in front of the Red Chinese Army at the Chosin Reservoir. His dad always loved to quote his commander's line whenever adversity struck. "Retreat hell! We're just advancing in a different direction."

Eddie wished he had some catchy quote to fall back on from his days in Nam. He'd sure be using it right now. For the moment, however, he would settle on the tried-and-true SNAFU—Situation Normal All Fucked Up.

He looked around and surveyed the area. There was nothing but the endless sagebrush and scrub juniper of the High Desert. Odd, he typically would have thought that this was the most beautiful place he had ever seen, but being lost with an out-of-gas bus and nine angry passengers, not to mention the thirst, he now found this part of the world bleak and inhospitable. He smiled at the weirdness of life and how perceptions could change so quickly.

The truly weird thing, though, was that he just now noticed a chain-link fence running along one side of the road topped with razor wire, something he should have seen if he hadn't been feeling sorry for himself. Eddie shook his head. *Stupid!* he thought. How long had he been walking alongside it? What else had he missed? He looked back in the direction he had just come from, and there it was—the fence going as far as he could see. Turning back, he now saw that the fence continued along next to the road in the direction he was headed until it disappeared in the distance.

Eddie wondered what was being kept in behind the fence or, for that matter, who or what was being kept out, and why? He chuckled, *Jackrabbits, that's what.*

Through the thick wire links, he saw nothing but the same nothing he had been seeing for some time now. Stepping closer, he grabbed onto the fence and hung onto it while he tried to see any sign of life on the other side.

A rusted metal sign hung near his left hand, black letters on a yellow background. He stepped back to read it:

No Trespassing.

Dept. of Interior, Bureau of Indian Affairs.

In smaller letters at the bottom:

RES SITE-ALPHA.

Eddie looked up and down the fence line. He saw the same sign hanging every fifty feet or so, regularly spaced like those old Burma Shave ads on the side of the roads he saw when he was a kid:

DON'T LOSE

YOUR HEAD

TO GAIN A MINUTE

YOU NEED YOUR HEAD

YOUR BRAINS ARE IN IT

BURMA SHAVE

Eddie took a closer look at the sign, hoping to find a phone number in tiny print somewhere. No such luck with that, but he still rechecked his phone for a signal. Still no luck there either. Pocketing his phone, Eddie proceeded with the long walk up the road.

Maybe, at least, the fence suggested he might find some help. At the top of a slight rise, Eddie stopped and looked around, hoping that the height might give him some extra help in scouting out the area. He scanned left, then right. Nothing, again.

Just as he was about to traipse on, he stopped and looked through the fence one more time. Off in the distance, there was a structure. The building was hard to make out, obscured by overgrown scrub, but it was there all right; on the other side of the fence topped with razor wire

He now studied the barrier for a way to get to the building. The razor wire was intact all along the top for as far as he could see in both directions. The fence was sound. Aside from the weathered metal, it looked like it was doing a reasonably good job of keeping him out. Eddie placed his hands on his hips and backed up to get a better look at the problem.

How in the hell was he going to get past this fence and over to that building? He saw no breaks and climbing was out considering the concertina wire and his physical shape. He slowly thought through all aspects of his dilemma. Well, if going over or through the fence was out, maybe he could get under it somehow.

However, from what he saw, the chain appeared to be sunk into the ground, leaving no possibility of a gap for him to use. He looked back in the direction he had come from and could see no way under it either. So, all Eddie could do was continue following his current heading and hope he could find an opportunity to get under before venturing too far away from that building. He resumed walking and in relatively short order came upon a dip in the ground along the fence line. Eddie stepped over to the dip. Several tumbleweeds had gathered there and hid the bottom of the fence, but as he pulled the dried branch balls away, he exposed a gap between the bottom of the chain link and the ground. He smiled at an example of how erosion could be your friend.

The opening looked to be somewhere around nine inches, which was large enough for some people to squeeze through but was too narrow for Eddie, even on his best day. He bent over and grabbed the chain link to see if he could push or pull it to make the opening larger, but nothing moved. He turned and looked around to see if there was anything he could use to help widen the opening. Behind him, across the road, was a jumble of decayed wood from an old structure that had collapsed onto itself, so he extracted a couple of pieces of wood that looked like strong possibilities to use for excavation.

With tools in hand, he knelt at the fence and began digging to widen the gap. The work was not as easy as one would think. In this desert, the ground was hard, compacted from centuries of weather, and full of rocks, not at all sandy like the Sahara.

As Eddie slowly dug and scratched his way into the hard ground, his mind wandered. He thought about Charles Bronson digging his way out of the stalag in *The Great Escape*. That scene where the tunnel collapsed always gave him chills. Tunnel rat he was not. With that thought, he pushed the dirt further away from the opening than was necessary. After about twenty minutes, he stopped and studied his work.

The opening now looked large enough for his spare tire—a.k.a. fat gut—to make it. Eddie got onto his hands and knees and crawled under the fence. He stuck his head through and, almost immediately, the collar of his jacket got caught on the rough bottom edge of the chain-link.

He pulled back out and remembered his days in boot camp. Eddie took off his hat and set it to the side and gave the rubber band holding his gray ponytail one more loop, making sure that his hair would not get caught up. Then he rolled over onto his back with his face, looking up at the sky. Immediately, Eddie felt a sharp pain in the middle of his back, sat up, and turned to look for the rock that had just tried to attack him. He brushed his hand along the ground, looking for the offending stone. Nothing. Eddie laid back down to try again, and the stone poked at his back even harder. *Damn! Fuck!* He shot up and tried to spot the boulder that had to be there. This time, when he turned, he felt a tug on the back of his belt and reached to check it out. *Oh yeah. Duh!* He grabbed the gun he had tucked in there earlier and set it on top of his hat. Feeling stupid, he lay down on his back for the third time and slowly shimmied under the fence.

This time, his head and shoulders cleared the ragged metal fingers that reached down to catch his clothing. Then it was his stomach's turn to squeeze through. He sucked it in as if he were showing off during ladies' night at the Elks Lodge. With his gut clear of the teeth on the chain-link monster, it was easy to pull his legs and feet through. And then he was on the other side; easy as that. Eddie stood up on his creaky knees and looked through the fence at the road he had just trudged down and then turned towards the building; intent on finding help.

With a long-ingrained habit, he reached up to adjust his hat, but it wasn't there. He'd taken it off to dig and set it on the ground next to him, on the other side of the fence, along with the gun. He wondered where his brain had gone. He wasn't going anywhere without his hat or 9mm, so he knelt back down at the gap and reached his arm under the fence.

He stretched and strained. He shmushed his face against the sturdy wire and extended his arm as far as he could, willing his fingers to grow just a hair more, and touched the brim of the cap with the very tip of his middle finger. He grunted and pressed his face even more against the fence and felt the hat move just enough for him to snag it with two fingers in a tweezers-like move and pull it closer to him. He grabbed the gun first, brought it under the fence, and then repeated the process to rescue the hat.

A bit winded, Eddie stood and tucked his gun back into its home behind his back. He rubbed his face where he could still feel the wire pushing into his skin, imagining the diamond-patterned red marks that his effort would leave. Then Eddie brushed the hat off, placed it on his head, and adjusted his clothes. *Now* he was ready.

The target of his exertion stood about a hundred yards away. It appeared to be an old, weathered storage building or barn. When Eddie got closer to the structure, he saw no windows, but at one end was a set of large double doors. One was partially open. Carefully, he approached and peered inside. All he could see were dust particles flitting about in the beam of light created by the open door and his cast shadow falling across a planked floor, making him look taller and slightly thinner than what reality had established. Aside from this, the rest of the interior was a yawning, dark void.

"He . . . Hello?" Eddie called out into the barn. There was no response. Eddie called out again, a bit louder. "Hello?" Still nothing. He scratched the back of his head, shrugged, and proceeded into the barn, following the beam of light on the floor. Inside he announced loudly to the person who obviously was not there, "Um, my bus has run out of gas a few miles back. Got lost somehow."

Eddie stopped a few feet inside the barn. His body was silhouetted by the early afternoon light as he stood framed in the door opening. The interior was too dark for him to see anything. Stepping even further into the barn, he called out again, "Anybody here? I could use a phone. Hello?"

Black, smoke-like wisps flitted through the air, darker than the darkest corner of the barn. Eddie took another step, then another, and a third stopping where the beam of light ended, and the impenetrable shadows of the interior began.

He squinted his eyes and peered into the darkness. Eddie couldn't see a darned thing but he could feel something. The skin on his face and hands felt like he had stepped through cobwebs as the ebony wisps brushed against his cheeks and moved through his ponytail. He rubbed at his face and hair to wipe away the sticky silk and shivered at the thought of how giant the spider was whose home he had just disturbed.

Peering more intently into the dark expanse of the barn, Eddie thought he saw the outlines of various objects: a ladder against the wall, an oil drum, and perhaps a stack of tires. With his eyes finally adjusting to the dark, Eddie now saw the black tendrils dancing around him. He watched, amazed, as the shadowy wisps split apart, wiggled around, then come to rest right in front of him, merging into a black, formless shadow. Then the apparition materialized into a large, dark shape of a human body. The Shadow Man!

"What the hell . . .?" Eddie reached for the Beretta and pointed it at the Shadow Man. "Stay back." He almost pleaded, backing up towards the open door.

The figure remained motionless.

"I, I won't hesitate to use this if I have to."

The Shadow Man took a step towards Eddie but stopped at the line, delineating the wedge of sunlight from the dark gloom of the barn.

"Seriously. Move again, and I *will* shoot." Eddie was close to panicking. The gun shook in his hand.

The Shadow Man solidified and took on weight and definition. As Eddie watched in frightened, amazed curiosity, a human emerged before his eyes. It only took an instant. Now standing in front of Eddie was a handsome man with strawberry-blond hair and pale skin, but his eyes . . . his eyes were ivory white with pupils so black as to be a gateway to hell itself.

Eddie continued to back up to the door, keeping his eye on the Shadow Man. The man didn't advance beyond the dark shadows, but Eddie could feel his eyes fixed on him. Then he heard a voice coming from inside his head. "I can help you." The sound of the voice was so soothing that it unnerved Eddie. He fired his gun once, a miss, and the bullet buried itself into the floor harmlessly.

The Shadow Man did not move or flinch. Eddie could feel the man probing the inside of his brain. He fired again. This time, it was a direct hit to the chest, and the man's body jerked with the impact, yet he still stood.

Eddie fired again and again with the same result.

"Relax Edward. You are already mine."

The voice filled his head. He had to make him stop. Eddie fired more shots into the Shadow Man.

Blam! Blam! Blam!

Five bullets into the man's chest, nothing fazed him. "Shit!"

Eddie threw the gun at his tormentor. It missed and skidded off into the dark. He turned to flee, but something was wrong. He was frozen, unable to move. The Shadow Man was reaching into his mind, controlling his very core. Eddie's body was no longer his. Then he heard that voice in his head again. *"You are mine. Do not fight. Fighting makes it painful, and I do not wish to cause you pain. I only want your blood."*

Eyes open wide with terror, Eddie tried to move, to run for the door, but he was held where he stood. *"You will now walk to me into the dark,"* the voice instructed, and his legs moved. *"Yes, come to me."*

Like an automaton, Eddie walked the few feet toward the Shadow Man. When he stepped out of the light and into the dark, the Shadow Man dissolved back into wisp-like black tendrils and enveloped Eddie. The sticky silken threads attached to Eddie's body and formed a type of cocoon around his torso which then lifted him up into the rafters. The bus driver's hat fell to the floor as he still vainly struggled to get free.

His kicking feet flashed through the wedge of light that streamed in from the door as he tried to save himself. Gradually, Eddie's resistance slowed, and then stopped; the fight had ended, and his body hung limp; red liquid oozed down onto his black shoes and into the upside-down Cascade Stage Lines hat, which now served as a basin for his dripping blood.

Chapter 8

INVESTITURE

CRAIG WRIGHT AND Ben Saunders paused by a door. Both men wore gray business suits, one darker than the other. Their skin tones took on an unhealthy, green tinge because of the cool-white fluorescent tubes used to light the hallway they were standing in. Their voices echoed off the hard surfaces of the flat white cinderblock walls and institutional green linoleum tile floor. The door had a sign screwed onto the surface. It read: *Lecture Hall.*

These men were agents with the CSC, holding positions in an organization that no one knows exists and wouldn't believe it if they did. Not even their closest relations could be told what they did, so they were required to live dual lives. That meant to the outside world that they appeared to be every day, ordinary Joes (or Josephines). No complaining about their bosses when they got home, at least not their real bosses.

Craig's mom thought he worked in a senator's office as a staffer. Not quite the position in which she had pictured him. Not that it was any of her business, but shouldn't he have been promoted or something after all these years? He seemed a bit old to be just a staffer. After his stint in the army, she thought he might find something more exciting, like maybe a job in the State Department, or that he might even join the police—something she could brag about to her friends. Not that she wasn't proud of her boy, but after almost getting himself killed in the Middle East, shouldn't he cash in on the experience? Was there anything wrong with a parent wanting the best for a child? But she knew her son, and he wasn't the type to get himself noticed.

Growing up, being known as the "fat kid" taught Craig how to keep a low profile and not draw attention to himself. Still, he had friends even though they were the other "losers" in the school and, despite it all, managed to have a self-confidence level of about a five on a scale of ten. Which, when you thought about it, was not too bad for someone who would be picked last on a softball team and only then to be the backstop. Oh, how the kids had fun with that joke.

The middle child of three boys, Craig, never seemed to fit in with his siblings either.

His oldest brother Tom wasn't a blood brother but adopted by his dad in an earlier marriage and then brought along when he married his mother. For whatever the reasons, Tom wore a discontent with his life on his sleeve making it hard for the two to be entirely comfortable with one another, though as the years passed an uneasy truce had been established between the two, which eventually developed into a kind of brotherly bond.

And his younger brother, Peter, saw that keeping to himself was probably the better part of valor in a household made volatile by Tom's occasional acting out, so he escaped into a world where he had control, playing alone or drawing at his desk or sorting his baseball cards.

The three boys never really found a common bond, and while they all loved each other, they were never close.

The thing that brought Craig out of his shell was the Boy Scouts. There was a great group of fathers connected to his troop who saw his potential and nurtured it, motivating him from one leadership role to the next highest until he became senior patrol leader and was the kid running the entire troop.

The self-confidence he gained after seven years of scouting gave him a portal to look through, showing him the path to a place where he had a role other than being a target of ridicule from ignorant bullies. The fat had faded from his body during his years in scouts but the scorn he experienced and the lack of self-esteem which he felt as a result never entirely vanished. They languished in the back of his mind and challenged him his entire life. At his most introspective moments, he knew he had overcompensated for these feelings by a gruff, and sometimes unforgiving, approach to others.

When he got out of college, he found his studies gave him a well-rounded liberal arts education but no clear path to employment. Something about the military seemed to attract him. Within days of getting his BA, Craig enlisted in the Army. After basic, he found himself fast-tracked through the ranks as one commander after another saw his potential and kept moving him forward.

Operation Desert Storm was the deal breaker. He came upon the aftermath of the Highway of Death, the six-lane ribbon of pavement in the desert leading out of Kuwait to Iraq. Before the defeated Iraqi army fled, it plundered Kuwait—commandeering any vehicle they could to haul their spoils—and then crowded onto Highway 80, creating a miles-long traffic jam. The U.S. forces had discovered this retreating horde and initiated an air assault, raining death down upon the heads of mostly ignorant and impoverished conscripted soldiers. It had been estimated that as few as several hundred and possibly as many as 10,000 were killed in this shooting gallery. Lieutenant Wright and his unit came across the horrid aftermath of the burned-out hulks of vehicles. He remembered the one charred body of a driver sitting behind the wheel with a look of surprise and then understanding of his fate still visible on his face—frozen in time, as if sculpted by the devil. At that moment, Craig decided that this probably was not the avenue of service that he thought he was looking for and chose not to re-up.

Within weeks after his discharge, Craig's father was diagnosed with Parkinson's. His availability came in handy as he became his dad's caregiver, helping keep him at home until the last possible moment. Upon his father's death, Craig began looking for a new role for himself in the world. But it found him in the form of a former commanding officer and an offer to put his training to the service of humanity.

Which was the reason he now found himself standing in front of this door.

"Come on, Benji! I've done the last five of these things."

Saunders held up a broken matchstick in front of Craig's face. "The matches don't lie, brother."

"You cheat."

Saunders patted Craig on his shoulder sympathetically. "And you are a sore loser." He grabbed the handle and swung the door open into the room. "Remember, as you look at them, just imagine that they're all wearing only underwear. Or is it always open with a joke? Hell, do both."

"Thanks. Asshole."

Saunders gave Craig a wink and a quick shove through the door and slowly closed it behind him.

Craig turned to the door when he heard the latch click into place. Trapped. He swallowed slowly. Accepting his fate, he turned back and looked up and into the same lecture hall he fondly remembered from the last several times he was manipulated into "hosting" these proceedings. At the front of the room was a simple desk. Behind the desk, a projection screen had been pulled down, covering wall mounted chalkboards. The desk faced risers with those chair/desk things that stair-stepped up to the back wall where a glassed-in projection booth was. The lecture hall was small, as these places went. It sat forty, but only the bottom two rows of chairs were populated with ten bodies—men and women.

Craig looked up to the booth where Saunders was now standing at the window, giving him a thumbs up sign with a big grin. *Fucker!* Craig thought and then stepped up to the front of the desk to address the waiting audience.

Nerves were about to overcome Craig as he tried to find his voice. He wished he had taken a couple of those drama classes when he was in high school. Being cast in a role or two may have helped prepare him for standing in front of a group of people. Then again, maybe not. Wasn't it Olivier who confessed to having thrown up every time before he went on stage? Someone else for sure, but that didn't matter.

Clearing his throat, Craig began, "Welcome to the CSC. I am Agent Craig Wright. You have all volunteered to . . . to. . ." He grabbed the glass of water off the desk and took a drink. He closed his eyes to collect himself, inhaled deeply, exhale and opened his eyes. The men and women sitting before him now appeared to be sitting in their underwear. The men he looked at were all wearing a mix of tee shirts and jockey shorts. Then his gaze fell onto one woman who sat wearing a white slip. Then he looked at another who was wearing a no-nonsense bra and waist-high panties.

Craig turned his head towards the last woman who was sitting in the front row. She was gazing at him. He looked into her eyes, but then his gaze dipped to her bare shoulders and lacy black bra. He felt the heat of his cheeks flushing from embarrassment. Flustered, he gave a gulp and turned back to the desk to "organize" some papers. He took another drink of water and cleared his throat. When he turned back around, everyone was fully dressed. He looked at the woman in front, now wearing a blouse, jeans, and jacket. He read the name on her ID badge: *Adams, Elizabeth.*

"So . . . I'm not a public speaker, and I don't play one on TV."

Nervous chuckles came from several in the room. The one woman who had the lacy bra, Adams, had a broad grin on her face.

"Damn it. I'm not good at this but . . . Sorry. . . please bear with me."

Craig closed his eyes, opened them, and looked up into the booth. Saunders was standing in the window dressed in underwear: a wife beater riding up over a beer gut, boxers with teddy bears, and black socks with garters. Saunders grinned with a thumb up sign. Craig smiled back and relaxed.

Now in control, Craig addressed the gathered inductees. "Good morning, ladies and gentlemen, and welcome to the CSC. All of you have volunteered to work for an agency in the United States Government that none of you knows anything about. And by 'volunteered,' I mean that you accepted this invitation to be here today." Craig held up a manila envelope with *SECRET* stamped in red on the face.

Craig paced across the front of the room. "In fact, very few people know of this agency's existence except as a budgetary line item.

"You were all told upon graduation from your respective enhanced training programs to report to Mountain Home where your assignments would be revealed. All you know is that it is something highly secret and vital to this country and humanity." Craig paused for dramatic effect. Maybe he was an actor after all. "You were all selected for your advanced skills in various areas that were observed and noted during training."

Craig stopped his pacing dead center of the room with an ominous look on his face. "Now, before I tell you more, I am obligated to ask if any of you wish to withdraw because once I proceed with your indoctrination, and you learn about the CSC's mission, there will be *NO* turning back. The government will own you."

Craig took a deliberate pause and scanned each of the ten faces before him. "Anyone?"

No one made a sound. Their faces were all set, but there were flickers of—something—in some of their eyes. Excitement? Fear? There always was a bit of both when presented with the option to flee the unknown or stay and learn what possibly could be so secret.

"Alright. Good. Let's start with the name of this agency. The CSC. We are the Center for Specter Control."

Some of the recruits stared at him questioningly. A few had shocked expressions. The woman from the front row, Adams, raised her hand.

"Yes?"

"Aren't specters ghosts?"

"Well, yes, that's true, but the word specter implies a lot more than just ghosts."

Liz continued her questioning, "You mean, like, pod people, and zombies and stuff?"

"No," Craig answered, then thought a bit. "Well, yes, in a way."

Craig waved up at the booth. The room lights began to dim.

"The best way to describe our mission is for you to watch this short film the CSC had produced for this moment. Please bear with the production quality as they made this in the '50s. You'd think that some highly secret government agency would have all the black money in the world to produce a better version, but the pencil pushers say that enough was spent on its initial production. To them, it's still perfectly good. I find it kind of quaint, but it does tell the story. You'll be glad to know, however, that they have provided us with only the best projection system that money could buy . . . in 1990." This got a few smiles from his audience.

Craig looked up at the booth, and the lights finished dimming. Before the room went totally dark, Craig added, "Don't let all this talk of no money and hand-me-down equipment fool you. Where it counts, we have only the best state-of-the-art tools to help us do our jobs." As the room lights went out, a colored light show began shooting out of the projector, which danced across Craig and the screen behind him.

The film's opening titles ran accompanied by official-sounding music. The credits ended and a menacing-looking notice materialized.

This is a TOP SECRET communication.

If you are watching this without explicit permission from a designated representative of the United States Government, you are in violation of US Codes: 50, Section 3341 and 18, Section 798, and subject to the punishments listed therein.

The warning dissolved, and the image of an army general appeared. He was standing in front of a wall with an American flag just off his right shoulder, and a framed photo of Ronald Reagan hung off to his left. "Hello. I'm General Lee Thompson, Commander of the CSC. This is usually the moment in your indoctrination where we try to tell you some extremely sensitive information concerning the nature of our organization. Before my time, some brainiac determined that showing you all a dramatization would be less . . . Shocking. I have seen lots of people like yourselves come through here. And I tend to agree that this film is a good way to break the ice on the subject. But if I had my way, we would have re-shot the whole darned thing with Steven Seagal."

The general showed a broad smile and waited for his unseen audience to laugh at his joke. (Which they didn't.) "But budgets and bean counters being what they are, I have to show you a brief history of the CSC as filmed in 1955. It's a little hokey in places, but it gets the point across. As a side note, I left the original introduction by General Arnold

Trapper intact. He was the commander when I was a mere recruit, like yourselves." He paused dramatically. "Welcome to the Center for Specter Control."

The color image of General Thompson faded out, and the black-and-white image of another army general faded in. He was sitting behind a desk, reading some papers. There were framed photos of Presidents Eisenhower and Theodore Roosevelt on the wall behind him. An American flag prominently stood next to the pictures.

The general looked up from the papers as though he was interrupted while doing some important work and glared sternly into the camera. "Hello, gentlemen. I am General McQueen. You are now a member of the most secret agency in the United States. What you will learn today will rock your belief system to its very core. But do not let that sway you from your sworn duty."

The general stood and walked to the front of the desk, perching on its edge. "No words can adequately tell you what the CSC is or how our organization came into existence. The following dramatization of the events that led up to the formation of the CSC should help. I will address you further after the presentation."

The general stepped over to a projector and turned it on, the lights of the office/movie set dimmed, and a black-and-white photo of Theodore Roosevelt appeared on the screen and slowly dissolved into a sepia-toned scene from the Spanish-American War. A narrator's voice came on, "In 1898, the United States went to war with the Spanish Empire. A dark secret exposed during the height of the conflict overshadowed the actual cause of the war."

Herky-jerky, old film stock showed Roosevelt chatting with his men, mouth moving at an unnaturally high rate of speed. He paused, grinned at the camera, and quickly turned back to his men. The next scene was obviously staged footage shot for this film. An actor who was now playing Roosevelt seemed convincing with his classic grin, mustache, and pince-nez resting on the bridge of his nose and strongly resembled James Cagney.

The narrator continued, "The Spanish held the high ground, San Juan Hill. Theodore Roosevelt and the Rough Riders had to take that hill, but they had no idea that the Spanish had allies or who they were."

A poorly faked night scene showed another actor playing a Spanish general, looking over a map on a table. Several other extras/officers stood next to him. The camera focused on the pale face of another, obvious actor—Ricardo Montalban?—dressed in civilian garb. When he smiled into the lens, a pair of fangs flashed menacingly from his lips.

The narrator went on, "This person is Alexei Rurik, the leader of the Spanish allies and the patriarch of all the houses of the vampire realm." The narrator of the film took a dramatic pause. The image of Alexei Rurik froze, and the camera zoomed in so that his face filled the screen with fangs visible. A montage of old prints and illustrations of vampires attacking humans ran through the following narration.

This line elicited a general reaction in the lecture hall from the audience. Some were quite appalled, while others outright laughed. A few were speechless. Liz turned around from her seat in the front row and hushed everyone with a forceful, "Shh!"

"For hundreds of years, vampires had aligned themselves with the most despicable of mortal leaders trading their services as assassins—eliminating political opposition—in exchange for unfettered access to their underclass' blood and protection during the daylight hours.

"However, the accumulated losses from fighting as mercenaries for human tyrants combined with the world's great religions' determined efforts to exterminate all vampires had taken its toll on their population to the point where it was possible to see the inevitable end of the vampire race.

"In 1890, Alexei Rurik responded to a call from elements within the Spanish Royalty to help Spain defeat the United States in Cuba. He gambled that by assisting Spain, a Catholic country, they might discourage the Church in its hunt for immortals with an additional bonus of open access to the blood supply of the oppressed Cuban peasants.

"This turned into a costly, strategic error. The U.S. Army, having learned to kill on an industrial scale in the Civil War, was unlike any human force that the vampires had encountered up to this point. And when faced with Theodore Roosevelt and his Rough Riders, Rurik could see the eventual defeat of the Spanish in Cuba, leaving no one to protect his people during the day, their most vulnerable time leading to their eventual, complete destruction.

"In a bold move to save his people from extinction, Alexei Rurik made contact with Theodore Roosevelt on the night before the charge up San Juan Hill."

More reenacted footage showed Rurik and Roosevelt in a tent at night surrounded by American soldiers.

"Rurik negotiated a deal with Roosevelt to ensure the safety of humans and the longevity of his race. Theodore Roosevelt agreed to create a permanent home for the vampires and supply the necessary blood to keep them fed in exchange for a cessation of vampires' nightly feasting on the innocent."

The staged scene showed Theodore Roosevelt and Alexei Rurik signing a document and shaking hands. This scene was cut short, and the lights of the movie set/office came up to full, revealing General McQueen perching on the front edge of his desk looking into the camera.

"Admittedly, it took a few years to implement this agreement, but with the elevation of Roosevelt to the presidency after the assassination of McKinley, he persuaded Congress to establish the Center for Specter Control." The general stood.

"The CSC was hidden within the Department of the Interior under the Bureau of Indian Affairs. Initially, its purpose was to establish a reservation where vampires could live in peace without fear of being hunted, and humans could live without fear of the night. Site-Alpha was the first such reservation.

"Back then, the word 'specter' referred to ghosts and other seen and unseen things that were scary and unexplained. We might call them monsters today."

The general moved to the back of the desk and sat in the chair so that the photo of Theodore Roosevelt was in the frame. He picked up a pipe and held it, ready to light.

"Over the years, the CSC's mission has expanded to find and contain all specters that roam this earth. Whatever your assigned duties, your active participation with this organization begins today, right now."

The general relaxed and cracked a slight smile. "Welcome to the CSC. Thank you, men, and good luck out there."

The general leaned back in his chair and lit his pipe as the scene faded.

The closing credits with patriotic sounding music rolled and then ended. The projector was switched off, and the room went dark. The only light was the green glow emanating from the *EXIT* sign over the door. Not a sound could be heard except for nervous coughing. Lots of nervous coughing.

Chapter 9

THE CENTER

A GENT CRAIG WRIGHT surveyed the stunned faces of the rookies. They had just watched a movie, produced by their government, telling them that the things which they had believed to be just the stuff of scary stories were, in fact, real. He had seen those looks many times before—incomprehension, panic, terror. Not all faces looked surprised, however. Adams was smiling and bursting with excitement. *What's up with her?* Craig wondered.

"Well, sorry about the dated material. As I said, they made the film in the '50s, and no women worked for the CSC at that time, other than secretaries, of course."

Another agent entered the room, a tall, shaved head, wearing the same boring suit as Craig. He had a stack of folders under his arm. "The talented and lovely agent Dave Hamilton—" Agent Hamilton shot Craig a not-so-nice glare. "—is handing out folders that have further material regarding the vamps. Memorize it. It could save your life, and as in all things at CSC, the information in these folders is highly secret."

While Hamilton handed out the folders, Craig continued with his briefing.

"Now the Cliffs Notes version."

Everyone in the room had grown more attentive. Adams sat so far forward on the edge of her seat; it appeared that the slightest tap would send her to the floor.

"Humans have been telling stories about vampires for thousands of years. The ancient Sumerians and Egyptians had legends about blood drinkers. The Chinese called their version Corpse Hoppers. During the plague in Europe, they believed vampires fed off the dead bodies. They even thought female vampires spread the disease.

"In the Middle Ages, Eastern Europeans would go to great lengths to keep a vampire from rising out of the grave once interred. Suspected vampires would have iron stakes driven through them and into the ground to hold the bodies in place. They rammed rocks and bricks into the mouths of the dead to keep them from chewing their way out of their burial shrouds.

"Red hair was once believed to be an indication that an individual was a vampire or might become one. In some biblical accounts, Judas Iscariot was said to have had red hair."

Liz suddenly became aware that all the eyes in the room were focused on her red hair. She remained sitting upright and didn't move, but she imagined herself dissolving and merging her molecular structure with that of the chair she was on, thus removing herself as the target of the moment. Her only reaction to the attention was the uncontrolled flush that ran up her neck and colored her cheeks.

Craig brought everyone back to him as he continued, "Of course, a lot of these legends are fables, old wives' tales. Many, however, have proved true." Jokingly, he looked at Liz and continued, "Red hair, for example—" Liz tensed up. "—not true." Liz relaxed some. "Mostly." Everyone laughed at that.

Liz wanted to say something smart, something intelligent, as a retort like, "Fuck you," but she bit her tongue and looked into Craig's eyes and gave him a thin, tight-lipped smile.

For a second, they locked eyes and Craig thought he could hear her swear at him. *She's got spunk*, he thought. *I'm not sure if that's good or not.* Then he broke out into a broad grin. "Frankly, I've never met anyone with red hair who became a vampire. Ever. So, I think you're safe, Adams . . . though I *do* know one or two vamps, who are gingers."

Then Craig continued to address all the recruits. "You can find more of this popular culture stuff online. The relevant info that you'll need for working at the CSC can be found in the folders you just were issued and our library.

"You just saw that Theodore Roosevelt signed a peace treaty between humans and vampires. But that wasn't the first time that he had had experience with them. At the age of 36, Roosevelt became the commissioner of the New York City police department. At the time, the city was experiencing some ghastly murders. These deaths made the Ripper's work in London appear to be the work of a child.

"In all cases, the killings took place at night, and the victims' throats had two large puncture marks, or their throats were just torn away. The bodies were found drained of blood. The press called them the "Night Stalker Murders." In reality, the city was infested with vampires."

A hand shot up from the second row. "Excuse me, sir. I, um, I like to read true-crime novels—Capote, Ann Rule—anyway,

I've read about Richard Ramirez. He was the Night Stalker in California, not New York, and that was in the 1980s."

Craig nodded his head in agreement, "And in 1974 there was a *Night Stalker* TV series about a reporter who uncovered stories dealing with the supernatural. It's a cult classic around the CSC. So, what you have here is an example of someone borrowing from someone who borrowed from the tabloid headlines of 1895. There's no keeping good sensationalism in the closet. Someone will always plagiarize a good sounding label.

"Okay. Where was I? Oh, yeah. With help from a vampire hunter sent from the Vatican . . .," Craig saw Liz was about to interrupt and stopped her. "It's in your folders." He said as he threw a cautionary glance in her direction. Liz relaxed back into her chair and opened the folder, looking for and finding the section that Craig had referenced. Keeping a wary eye on her, Craig continued, "With help from experienced vampire hunters, Roosevelt established a special detective unit within the NYPD tasked to track down the vampires and their nests. Later, when Roosevelt became president, he asked these same investigators to form the CSC." Craig paused, letting this sink in.

"We supply the blood . . .," Craig saw Liz raise her hand at this. So, he looked in her direction again and answered her before the words could leave her mouth. "*We* do this," he said, staring at Liz, "using several methods. The first is blood collected at donation centers, which we run in many cities. We also provide livestock that can be consumed within the borders of the Rez. This satisfies the vampire's need to rip into live, warm flesh. And now and then, we provide fresh cadavers; unclaimed bodies from the morgue, which I admit is rather disgusting." Then, pointedly, he added, "You can find all the sordid details in the folders."

Craig looked over to Adams, expecting some outburst, but her face remained calm. She had opened her folder and was casually looking at it, apparently reading the section Craig had called out, but her body language revealed how interested she was as she sat on the edge of her chair, wanting more.

"The first reservation was an abandoned mining town in Montana in 1901. The CSC didn't have very much experience with keeping humans and vampires away from one another and thought an isolated, empty town was just the ticket, except that people would wander in from time to time.

"Once in a while, things didn't work out well for those folks." Craig used two fingers in a biting motion against his neck. "Most of the time, those that found themselves in this seemingly abandoned town would experience what anyone of us might call 'supernatural occurrences' such as hearing voices in their heads or seeing human bodies materializing before their eyes. These were usually enough to send them running with their tails between their legs. In turn, they would spread stories about the impossibly weird shit they had seen." He could hear some chuckling at that. "Hence the term, 'Ghost Town.'"

It was his favorite line, especially when recruits had an "ah-ha!" moment of learning about the origins of a term.

"Not that the CSC didn't make use of the fear generated by the label 'Ghost Town.' You could call it an early disinformation campaign." Now there was some outright laughter. Even Adams was smiling again. "But it became quite clear that we had to do more in the way of keeping unintentional blood donors away from the vampires."

Agent Hamilton walked up to the movie screen and raised it, revealing a map of Oregon. A red arrow pointed to a spot in Eastern Oregon roughly centered in that part of the state.

"Today, the vamps live in a replica of an American town from the 1960s, built in an isolated valley, ostensibly as an A-bomb test site."

A hand popped up from one man in the back row.

"Yes. Question?"

"Yes, sir. I grew up in Seattle. I studied Northwest history. I don't recall reading anything about atomic test sites anywhere in Oregon. Aside from Hanford, Washington, where they process uranium for nukes and the Idaho National Lab where the government does all sorts of nuclear research projects. The only other likely spot is the Boardman bombing range on the Columbia River, and that's for Navy pilot's target practice."

Craig looked up to Saunders, who was still watching from the projection room. Saunders gave an approving smile and a nod to the question.

"You make a good point. All tests for nukes take place in Nevada. Always have—except for a few atolls in the Pacific that got erased. At the time, there were no more ghost towns left to turn into an appropriate reservation for the vampires. All the ones that could have worked were becoming tourist destinations like Virginia City in Nevada. We had to abandon plans for its use because of that exact reason. The early sixties TV show, *Bonanza*, popularized Virginia City, and it suddenly became a tourist destination. So, with a little bureaucratic sleight-of-hand, we had Site-Alpha built using funds from the Department of Defense as one of their test sites, though you won't find it on any of their books."

Craig looked around and could see that more than one face registered a question, so he added, "This is no cardboard, pretend town. They built these towns like the real thing, with actual bricks, concrete, and steel. The buildings were stocked with actual items—canned food, furniture, books, and other stuff, as well as mannequins dressed in different types and colors of fabric. They did this to study the effects of a bomb blast on structures and the effects of radiation on any surviving things and people."

Agent Hamilton stepped up to the wall behind Craig and grabbed the line hanging from the bottom of the map. He gave it a good hard yank, and the map snapped up, revealing an aerial photo of a small, isolated valley.

Craig picked up a long pointing stick and traced a line around the valley. "Until five years ago, we had armed guards patrolling the perimeter, but the effects of a bad economy play hell on nonexistent secret government agencies. God only knows what the new administration will do to decimate our budget further . . .," Craig heard a small cough come from Hamilton, who was still behind him, and he saw Saunders slowly shaking his head up in the booth. ". . . but I've been told that I sometimes bring a bit too much politics into these little chats." He smiled apologetically. "So, now we rely totally on technology to monitor the reservation: sensors to detect a breached fence, drones, and satellite fly-overs."

A hand shot up in the front row. "Yes?"

"Sir. My only knowledge of vampires comes from popular fiction."

"Which can be quite accurate."

"Well, then I'm kind of wondering . . . Aren't vampires supposed to fly? How can a fence keep them in, really?"

Craig stopped to consider the answer. "The main reason the vamps stay where they are is their mayor."

Liz blurted out, "What? They have elections?"

Annoyed, Craig responded. "No." He paused. But he had opened the door for the question by mentioning the mayor. *Damn it!* "It's a title we use for the strongest of the vampires. Alexei Rurik. You saw him in that film. He is the one who 'convinced' the others to go along with Roosevelt's deal. He is their leader. Their Khan. And make no mistake, he is the most powerful vampire of them all and can enforce the agreement. So, it's our little in-house joke, but, yeah, Alex is the mayor of Vamp Town."

Liz was about to ask another question, but the door opened, and three agents walked into the room, followed by Saunders. They stopped and stood behind Craig. Like Craig, they all seemed to have shopped at the same uniform outlet store—their suits all of various shades of gray.

Craig became still and looked at each of the newbies in their eyes. Then, seriously, he spoke, "We are not the *Men in Black*. There are no Maulders or Scullys. No *X-Files*. And there are no aliens in Area 51. But there are actual monsters out there that have been terrorizing humans for centuries. We have successfully kept this reality from the public for well over 100 years. And we plan to keep it that way. No one who has made it this far in the process can walk away.

There is no quitting. You are now the property of the Federal Government. One loose tongue will land you in the blackest hole for an extremely long time."

Craig surveyed the recruits to make sure his last words had set in.

"Ladies and gentlemen, we are The Monster Keepers. Welcome to the CSC."

He picked a folder up from the desk. "You probably noticed that the folders you received have different colors. The colors show the area you have been assigned to—technology, analysis, action team, and fieldwork."

The recruits nervously shifted in their chairs. The tension was thick in the air. Liz was about to bust with exuberance. *Please let mine be fieldwork. Or action team. Either work*, she thought.

Craig nodded to the guy from Seattle in the back row. "Blue signifies you have been slated for analysis. If you have a blue folder, step on down and join Agent Hamilton." Along with the amateur NW historian, another guy with a blue folder stood up and, together, they made their way to stand near the agent.

"Yellow folders mean that you have been recognized as a technical genius and will work in the control room monitoring the reservations. I see three yellow folders, right? Good. Please join the blues down with Dave." They stood and joined the others.

The door opened, and another person, dressed in a black ACU and combat boots, joined them. "This is Captain Smith. He is the commander of our Action Teams. When the shit hits the fan, it's one of his teams that is sent to mix it up." Craig nodded to a woman with a green folder. "You have been assigned to work with Smith. Listen to him. He will keep you alive. Please come on down."

There were four recruits left sitting in the room. All had red folders on their desks. Craig addressed them. "You four have been selected for field work."

Liz couldn't keep from grinning. *Yes!*

"Those with the red folders will remain while all of you . . .," Craig indicated those who were standing at the front of the room, ". . . will follow Dave and Captain Smith out and into your new lives. Again, welcome to you all."

Agent Hamilton opened the door, and the new agents exited, followed by Captain Smith. That left Craig along with Saunders, the three other agents standing behind him, and the four recruits with red folders.

Liz held onto her red file folder like it was the map to the lost gold of the Incas. Her energy was hard to contain as she remained at attention in her chair, all nerves. Craig gave her another once-over look. *This one has trouble.* He shook his head again, then turned to watch the last of the six leave the room, with Hamilton taking up the rear and closing the door behind him.

Now Craig addressed the remaining four. "On the inside cover of your folder, there is a name attached. That person is one of us standing before you now and will be your new partner. I do not know of who has been assigned to whom. Others with higher pay grades have made these determinations based upon your skills and mental compatibility. The agent they assigned you to will be your teacher, coach, and parent in this new life of yours with the

CSC. Take what they say as if they are the words of God himself. Listen to them and follow their instructions." He hesitated for a moment, then added, "Your *life* depends on listening and learning all that you can from your partner. I know . . .."

Craig's voice trailed off as he momentarily got caught in a memory loop recalling the death of his last partner. He shook his head, wishing that she hadn't gone off into the building alone after he had told her to wait for the Action Team to arrive. Saunders placed a hand on his friend's shoulder, bringing him back into the present.

"Sorry," Craig said. Then he cleared his throat and looked at a man. "You, in the back row, please say your name and read the name of your new partner."

"Matt Jones." Then he looked down at his folder. "Agent Mendez."

"New Agent Jones, please come down and join Agent Mendez." Mendez stepped forward and shook Jones' hand.

Craig looked at the woman three desks to the right of where Jones had been sitting. "And you next."

"Sara Washington and my new partner is, uh, Agent Fowler." Agent Brad Fowler stepped up to greet Washington. He shook her hand and gave her a slight slap on the back, just like the good old boy that he was.

That left one man and Adams without assignments. Craig paused as he looked at them both. Then he turned to Saunders and gave him a weak smile.

Craig gestured towards the man. "And you?"

"Van Wilson. Umm." He fumbled with his folder as he tried to open it. "Agent Garnet."

"Wilson, come on down and meet Agent Bob Garnet." Van Wilson walked over to Bob Garnet who greeted him in a stiff, professional manner.

Liz waited for Craig to ask her to read who her partner was. Craig, again, turned to Saunders, who had a grim look on his face and was shaking his head slowly.

Craig took a deep breath and slowly released it, taking as long as possible to keep the inevitable from happening. Finally, he looked at Liz. "And you?

"My name is Elizabeth Adams. Liz." Looking at her folder, she stood up and announced her new partner's name. "Agent Craig Wright!"

Craig grimaced and gave her a weak smile. A quick glance at Saunders confirmed what he thought. The ass hole had a massive grin on his face, and he was nodding his head in amused approval.

Liz trotted down to stand with Craig, clutching her file to her chest with a beaming smile on her face and looked right into Craig's eyes. "I am very excited to be here, sir!" Liz held out her hand to shake with her new partner.

He looked down at her outstretched hand and shook it with little enthusiasm.

I hate my job.

Chapter 10

INCURSION

A FEW HOURS after Eddie had gone off in his search for help, the passengers grew weary of just sitting around and waiting. Jenna and Kelvin seemed to be having the best time sitting under the shade of a juniper tree. Every so often, Jenna would rise to her feet, face her audience, Kelvin, and deliver one of her stand-up comedy routines. At the end of her monologue, Kelvin would laugh and clap wildly. Then Jenna would collapse into laughter and hug him. They had been carrying on like that since the driver had walked out of sight and seemed that they could carry on like that for days.

To say that Jenna and Kelvin were good friends would be an understatement. They had met only a couple of years earlier in Chicago and instantly became inseparable companions. Perhaps it was that they found themselves at opposite ends of the same life story and the one complimented the other.

Jenna grew up doted on as the blessed child to a couple who had been trying to have children. By the time her parents had all but exhausted their financial ability to continue with the various fertility treatments, the miracle baby, Jenna, was born.

At an early age, Jenna felt she was slightly different from the other kids she played with, but it wasn't until middle school that she discovered her attraction to girls. When she was asked to the school dance by Daren, she said yes, but spent the entire time with Whitney and some of the other girls. Daren didn't seem to mind since boys of that age hadn't any clue at all about how to be around girls. To them, these first dances were just a way to get out of the house and hang out with the guys and continue their grab-assing from earlier in the day. She felt an attraction to Whitney that she couldn't explain, but it was there, a kind of lightheartedness when she was with her. Whatever it was, it was a feeling that she never wanted to end.

In high school, Jenna found herself hanging out with the theatre geeks. Drama class taught her how to channel her spunky nature. Improvisational acting exercises helped her to hone her abilities at clever wordplay into solo performances, which opened the door to stand-up comedy. Oddly, she found that standing up in front of an audience, she could be herself, talk about her shit and get laughs. The more she realized she was indeed drawn to women, romantically, the more comedy became a safe place. She could explain herself to the world without fear of recrimination.

Of course, she didn't need to explain herself to her parents, not the golden child. She could bring home a gorilla and introduce him as her husband, and her parents would have taken them to the fanciest dinner in town and shown the happy couple off to all their friends. By the time Jenna graduated from college, she had no doubts about which side of the fence she had fallen on. She was a lesbian. And, while not strident, she was not bashful about letting the world know about it.

Now, she was going to visit her parents in Portland after a couple of years of learning the comedy ropes in Chicago. Chi-Town was a happening place for new comedy talent, but she was due for a change, and Portland was a new "In" spot and definitely diversity friendly.

However, she obviously had no pressing need to get there anytime soon. Choosing to book her trip cross-country using the cheapest of cheap bus lines may have saved her money, but this was the second time that the direction she thought she was going in was not taking her closer to her end destination. The first was when she wound up in Reno. Close to Portland by about 500 miles or so to the south. Nevertheless, she was making progress. At any rate, this would make great material for her act. And besides, she had Kelvin to share it all.

Kelvin Jarrett had the aisle seat next to Jenna, where he always sat, on trains, planes, buses, and even on the "L." Jenna wanted the window seat so she could look out at the view and Kelvin let her do just about anything she wanted. Not that he minded, though it could kind of hurt when she used him as her verbal punching bag in her stand-up routine. Kelvin was to Jenna what Fang was to Phyllis Diller or Edgar to Joan Rivers. He could almost hear Jenna paraphrasing the old Henny Youngman bit, "Take my Kelvin. Please!" But he took it all in good stride despite some minor hurt feelings. Jenna needed him. He's her sounding board, and she's his family. Not that he grew up without a family, but in rural Prue, Oklahoma, guys like him were not readily accepted, and parents were inclined to reject their children who did not act like "normal" kids.

In his high school years, Kelvin was an outsider and hung out with the small group that did not fit into the social norms of his age group. His "group" wore outlandish outfits: cub scout shirts under black dusters, orange-colored hair, black nail polish, Doc Martin boots, etc. Kelvin was known as a "Dork" and did his best to reinforce that perception. He saw himself as a sort of Ferris Bueller type only without the popularity.

On his sixteenth birthday, his father had gotten tickets to a RedHawks game in Oklahoma City. His dad had never paid attention to whether or not Kelvin liked baseball, and telling him otherwise would spoil this real father/son outing. He could still remember the warmth of his father's arm around his shoulder. This rare, outward sign of affection weakened Kelvin, who lowered his guard, thinking that they had achieved some new level in their relationship.

To Kelvin, going to a baseball game had to be the most tiresome thing to do next to watching paint dry, but he felt excited to be sitting with his dad like he could tell him anything and his father seemed to show interest in his son for the first time in years. It started with small talk.

Dad asked him how school was going.

Kelvin responded.

"Ball!"

Dad asked about what subjects he liked most.

Kelvin responded.

"Safe!"

Dad asked about college and his aspirations.

Kelvin responded.

"Take me out to the ballgame. Take me out . . .,"

Dad asked if he was interested in any girls at school.

Kelvin responded. "Well, I, um . . . I'm not sure there are any girls that I'm interested in."

Dad's surprised expression. In retrospect, his dad's line of questioning was a setup, a trap that Kelvin fell right into. "I'm not sure I like girls. In that sort of way."

"Strike three!"

"You mean you like boys?" his father asked.

"Um, no, sir. I . . . Not boys either. I don't know what I like."

"You're outa there!"

The two-hour ride from Bricktown back to Prue was in total silence. Kelvin went to bed and listened to at least another hour's worth of his father yelling to his mother about "fags, queers, and perverts living in his house."

That night, Kelvin began planning for the day he would leave that house and that town. Maybe head somewhere, anywhere big enough where he might fit in better. They met in Chicago. He was waiting tables at a small comedy club where Jenna was the warmup act. Kelvin could tell that she was nervous and needed to calm down, so he slipped her a couple of cocktails, which she downed appreciatively. It was the beginning of an unbreakable partnership.

So here he was, following her to the coast. Of course, he couldn't say no. Jenna was/is the first girl he was ever close to. Her being a lesbian made their bond seem safe with none of the sexual expectations that hovered around intimate relationships. He had a feeling that this trip would not be just a "visit" to Jenna's parents. He felt she was going to stay in Portland, at least for the foreseeable future. Kelvin was okay with that. Portland seemed like a place where he could find more of his kind.

Kelvin turned and gave Jenna a smile, then hugged her.

"What's that for?" Jenna asked at the hug that came out of the blue.

"I just love you is all."

"Oh, if that's all . . .. I love you too, Kel," she said, returning the hug.

Marion O'Neil sat nearby idly fussing over Cindra, picking off bits of lint from her sweater and brushing her hair. She smiled at the sincere affection she saw in Jenna and Kelvin's hug. It was apparent that they shared a loving bond that superseded sex, and she felt a twinge of jealousy at seeing that type of relationship. Looking over to Wilson, Marion wondered, *Were we ever that close?* And if we were, what happened? Redirecting her attention, she continued to fawn over her daughter, which was what she did when the thoughts in her head became too much to handle.

Wilson sat staring off into the distance with a blank face. His thoughts were unreadable to the rest, but when things slowed down, and he had time to think, he always would find himself back at the office, second-guessing his choices. The business was not just a victim of market circumstances. He knew his decisions had driven the company into the ground. He blamed himself for that and for putting his family in this awkward position. So here they were on the side of a dusty road heading to a tiny town where he would pour beer and clean grease traps.

Usually, Marion could distract him, but this bus thing was so out of the ordinary that she found herself at a loss. Wilson would have to fight his demons all on his own this time. She only hoped that he would not descend to that dark place he sometimes found himself. It scared her and, worst of all, it scared Cindra.

Steph spent a lot of the time just roaming the area. She strolled quite a distance from the bus but was never out of view of it. She turned back to look at the bus and saw that guy, who couldn't mind his own business, get up and walk in her direction, probably to hit on her. All guys hit on her after a certain point, and now it was his turn. He was good looking enough but too nice. Steph liked the bad boys, just more fun. And she liked having fun.

As far back as she could remember, Steph was comfortable with her sexuality. She was the first of her friends to go all the way with a boy back in middle school. In a complete role reversal from contemporary narratives, Steph made the first move on the boy. She smiled as she saw, again, the boy in her mind's eye.

He was cute in a fly caught by a spider sort of way. She was curious about the things she heard her older sister talking about and wanted to see if what she heard was true. The poor boy hadn't quite reached puberty, and while he got an erection, it was more cute than exciting and the more she touched it, the more she understood that she would have to pick older targets to experiment on. Come to think of it, that wasn't her first time having sex since nothing *came* of it. She smiled at her pun. No, that was more like an extended version of playing doctor.

Her real first time was when she was a freshman in high school. She picked her target, a senior, and then let him think he was making all the moves. Now that was a more satisfying encounter, if rough and rushed, but she knew that sex was something she liked and wanted more of it.

Steph's mother could tell that her daughter was maturing and becoming sexual. Though she did not know the extent of Steph's experimentation, she knew that there would be no stopping this train.

Her mom would make attempts at moderating Steph. Like the time, she had this "almost" tank top on that revealed a bit of her tummy and a lot of her cleavage. "Sweetheart, don't you think it's a bit too cold to be wearing that top?" Her mom asked. To which she responded by draining her OJ and giving her mom a peck on the cheek as she went out the door. "Love you too, Mom."

At least she listened when it came to Mom's insistence on protection. Steph liked having sex, but the thought of a disease or having a baby scared the hell out of her.

An image of her mother materialized, standing out amid the scrub and rocks. She had been reliving her experiences with her mother ever since she got the call from Dad telling her that Mom had lost her battle with cancer. Now she wondered if her mom would have cared about Steph's activities if she had known that she wouldn't live to see the age of fifty. She touched her mother's locket at her neck and watched her image fade into the landscape. "I love you, Mom."

"You should be careful of rattlesnakes. They tend to blend into the ground." A voice said from behind her.

Startled, Steph quickly turned to look at Paul. "What?"

"I said you should be careful of rattlesnakes. There're lots of them out here."

"Well, I don't like people sneaking up on me," she said, surprised at this only slightly more sophisticated ploy to get into her pants. Or was it? "Besides, I'm not afraid of snakes," she said, giving him an icy stare.

"Didn't say you were. It's just that, around here, a rattler can look like a weathered stick."

"Like I said . . .."

"Okay, suit yourself," Paul said, raising his hands in the air as he backed off. He walked back to the bus and sat down in its shadow, leaning against one of the large black tires.

Steph turned away and walked towards where a few juniper trees were growing. As she did, she looked back and saw that Dick was obviously checking her out. He seemed like a jerk, but close enough on the scale to her tastes. With a pretended air of indifference, she continued towards the trees.

Ellie and Dick were sitting on a couple of large rocks off to the side of the road. Ellie had her eyes closed and her earbuds in listening to music on her phone. The warmth of the morning sun felt good, so she was content with getting lost in her music and allowing the heat to wash over her body.

Dick was at a loss. All this sitting around and doing nothing was grating on his nerves. He saw that dude talking with Steph, and he got a bit bothered by it. She wouldn't be the type to be interested in a gimp. Couldn't he tell she was way more interested in him, Dick? After watching them exchange a few words, they parted ways, and Dick watched her wiggle her shapely ass over to the trees. Did she kind of signal with her head that he should join her? Not the type to be told twice, Dick stood and brushed off his pants.

Ellie opened her eyes when she felt him stand up. Taking her earbuds out, she began to say something, but Dick cut her off. "Uh, just gotta take a piss. You sit here and relax."

Ellie deliberately closed her eyes and replaced her earbuds. In a practiced exercise of self-control, she took in a slow, deep breath and turned up the volume, using Taylor Swift to drown out the words that she wanted to say. Opening her eyes, she saw Dick's shadow on the ground moving away; then she raised her head enough to see him follow that girl towards the stand of trees. Ellie shook her head and turned away, pretending not to have just witnessed what everyone else had.

As Ellie pivoted her head, she made brief eye contact with that guy who had helped her the previous night. He nodded, but she continued turning as though she never even saw him. Needing something better to distract herself from what she knew Dick was doing, she selected Rihanna's Cold Case Love from her playlist, turned up the volume, fished a book out of her bag, opened it, and tried to read.

Paul watched as the whole drama between Ellie and that dickwad unfolded. *I thought I heard his name was Dick, right?* How appropriate. Shifting his eyes from Ellie to Dick and back, he saw one sick man follow that hot-looking girl to the other side of the trees. Then he looked back at Ellie and watched her pretend to read a book. Paul hated what he saw, so he stood and walked over to Ellie. He had no idea what Dick intended on doing, but he felt an unexplainable attraction to the woman and, at the very least, believed that she could use a friend right about now.

Sitting on the rock, pretending to read, Ellie was painfully aware that the others were looking at her. That her head was tilted down to the open book didn't mean that she was reading, however. Her eyes were scanning everywhere around except the page of the book; taking in as much as her limited field of vision would allow, which was mostly the ground. Then she saw something move across the gravel up to her left. At first, all Ellie could see was the shadow of a head then, shoulders, and finally, a whole body moving, limping, towards her. When a pair of male shoes stopped in front of her, she knew she had to engage. Ellie took a deep breath, deliberately placing a mark in the book, removed her earbuds, and looked up.

"You hurt yourself?"

Paul sat down next to Ellie. "What? The limp? Just a little something that happened in Afghanistan. They tell me I should be good as new in a few months, so can't complain too much." He paused a moment to gather his nerves. "Look, I'll just come out with it. You don't have to stay with that creep."

"That creep's name is Richard, and he's been my boyfriend since high school. We take care of each other. You don't know him, or what he's meant to me. He just has a short fuse. I don't know why I'm telling you this. It's none of your business. Right?" Ellie said, rather snippily.

Paul got the message and quickly stood. He held up his hands in a "sorry I said anything" signal and backed away from Ellie as though he had almost stepped on one of those hidden rattlesnakes he warned Steph about. He walked back to the same spot next to the bus, shaking his head. So, he'd pissed off two women in fifteen minutes. A new personal best. And all because he was trying to be a good guy. He believed he had learned to understand the Taliban fighters to a certain degree, but women, now that was a different insurgency altogether. He sat down and leaned his head back against the tire. With little prompting, his eyelids closed, and he fell asleep.

———— ◆◇◆ ————

THE SCREECH OF a red-tailed hawk penetrated Paul's ears, and his eyes snapped open. He checked his watch to see how long he'd been asleep. Almost an hour. Wow! He had had no idea he was that tired. The first thing he saw when he looked up from his watch was Dick and Steph emerging from the trees and walking back to rejoin the other passengers.

After an awkward silence, Dick stepped out in front of the small group. He raised his hand and cleared his throat to get everyone's attention. "Hey! Everyone. It's almost two. That driver should have found help by now and come back for us, or the fucked-up bus company should have found us. I say we get the hell out of here. Anyone else?"

Dick looked around at everyone and got no response.

"Well, fine, but *we're* getting the fuck out of here."

He reached down for his coat and bag and then grabbed Ellie by the sleeve and jerked her up and onto her feet. Ellie barely had time to grab her stuff before Dick guided her brusquely towards the road. He gave her another small push when she stopped in front of Paul, fumbling with her belongings. Paul got up and moved in between them, preventing Dick from pushing her again, buying Ellie a bit of time to gather her things.

The two men stood face to face in a glaring match; both ready to throw down, but Dick broke first and said to Paul, "Hey, asshole. Get out of the way." He stepped around Paul and grabbed Ellie, pulling her down the road. "Come on! Let's go."

Barely turning back to the rest of the passengers, Dick yelled, "Last time, you guys can stay here with no food and freeze your asses off tonight or follow me!"

With that, Dick marched off with Ellie in tow. Ellie looked back at Paul and mouthed a silent "thank you."

After a pause, Steph grabbed her things and ran down the road after Dick and Ellie.

Jenna, Kelvin, and the O'Neils looked at Paul.

"You gonna go with them?" Jenna asked Paul.

Paul thought for a moment and looked down the road at Dick, giving Ellie another push. "Sure, why not?"

With that, the remaining passengers picked up their bags and coats and headed off down the road after Dick and company.

Paul was not sure that what they were doing was the right move, but since he had first seen Ellie boarding the bus, he felt drawn to her and the thought of her out in the middle of nowhere with that, asshole, made him uncomfortable.

His army shrink would be proud of the restraint he had been exhibiting ever since Dick started raising a fuss the night before. Well, fuck the doctors and their diagnoses. He wasn't going to let a few letters of the alphabet identify him. *PTSD, screw it*. Besides, following this crazy train with Dick as both the engineer and conductor could be amusing. Grabbing his coat, Paul followed the pathetic group of lost passengers, taking up the rear like he always did in the Stan.

After a few paces, Paul stopped and rubbed his knee. This walk would be bad for his injury. He reached into his pants pocket and removed two ibuprofen tablets, and dry swallowed them. Then he continued following the group as they walked down the empty blacktop.

—◆—

FEELING FULL OF himself as the assumed leader, Dick paused at the top of a rise, arms akimbo, looking like a scout exploring out ahead of a wagon train. He struck this commanding pose for everyone to see, positioning himself so that the clear blue sky behind him silhouetted his chiseled physique, pretending to search out ahead of the group but watched from the corner of his eye as the rest of the passengers trudged up the rise to join him. Then he saw that son of a bitch limp up behind everyone else. *Shit!* he thought. Why didn't he just stay back with the bus?

As a distraction, Dick decided to do the job he appointed himself to do and check out the area. To the left was that chain linked fence they'd been following. To the right, there was a whole lot of empty ground broken up by scrub, tumbleweed, and juniper. There was no sign of people anywhere—no fingers of smoke rising from a chimney, power lines, or telephone poles. No cell towers. There wasn't even a rusted hulk of an old abandoned car, nothing except for the chain-link fence topped with razor wire they had been following along the side of the road. There had also been no sign of the bus driver on the way to this spot, and from this vantage point, he saw nothing that would suggest anything different up ahead. He thought for sure they would find that old hippie sitting along the side of the road collapsed from exhaustion.

Wilson dared to step close to Dick and asked, "See anything?"

"Does it look like there's anything to see? In case you hadn't been paying attention for the last hour, take a look. Do you see anything?"

"I, um . . . It just looked like you may have spotted something the way you were staring out into the distance. Couldn't tell, sorry."

From over by the fence, Kelvin called out. "Hey, check out this sign!" He was referring to a yellow rusted metal sign hanging on it. "No Trespassing. Department of Interior, Bureau of Indian Affairs. Hey, an Indian reservation. What's a RES SITE-ALPHA?"

While the others focused on Kelvin and the sign, Cindra O'Neil had followed the fence for a few more yards. She stumbled over a piece of weathered wood, looked down, and discovered the hole that the bus driver had excavated under the chain link.

"Hey, Daddy! Look at this."

Everyone walked over to her position and looked at the opening, scooped out under the fence.

Ellie asked, "You think a coyote could have done that?"

Kelvin feigned a child's reaction. "I hope not; coyotes creep me out. All that howling that they do; they're freaky."

Jenna gave up a coyote-like yelp from behind Kelvin, who turned and laughed, giving her a slight slap on the arm.

"Hey! Look over there." Steph pointed to the barn hidden by shrubs and trees.

Marion said, "It's a building. Might be someone there who can help. Maybe the bus driver is there."

Paul added, "If the bus driver saw it, then he may have dug this hole himself."

Again, it was time for some real leadership, and Dick offered it up. "Well, no reason for us not to check it out." He stepped back from the hole and waved his arm towards the gap under the fence, pointing the way for someone to make the first move. The passengers all looked at each other to see who would be the first to crawl under the fence. No one stepped forward.

"No one?" Dick asked. "Okay, then. You first sweetheart." He said to Ellie, giving her a bit of a push into the hole. Ellie, who was standing on the edge, lost her balance and slid down the loose dirt, almost falling on her face, but she reached out and caught the links of the fence, saving her from total embarrassment. She looked back at Dick, still standing on the edge of the hole.

"Come on, what're you waiting for?" Dick asked impatiently.

Ellie replied with a look that could have been caused by her squinting from the bright sunlight or by the growing number of questions that were forming regarding her boyfriend. Whichever the reason, she lowered herself to crawl under the fence and shimmied through the opening.

Halfway through, she felt a foot pushing down on her butt. "Hey!" She let out.

"Your pants were going to get caught on the wires," Dick said with mock concern. "Sorry. Just helping."

Under her breath, Ellie responded, "Right," then finished crawling through the gap, and stood up on the other side.

"See, that was easy," Dick said to everyone.

As she brushed herself off, Ellie asked, "Are you going to stand over there and help the others like you did me, or are you coming next?" This came out louder than she expected and could see Dick was none-to-thrilled by the comment, but it was too late to take it back. She saw Paul, standing at the back of the group, smiling, and nodding his head—obviously enjoying the exchange. Dick gave Ellie a dark glare, then instantly he grinned and turned to the others.

"Okay, now my turn," Dick said while shooting daggers with his eyes towards Ellie. He hopped down and expertly got through the opening without the jagged fingers of wire touching him as though it were a drill he had run on the practice field a million times. On the other side, he stood next to Ellie and put his arm around her shoulder in a seemingly loving embrace, but his fingers dug into her arm, transmitting his anger, all the while still grinning. "Come on, you all. Let's do this!"

Hesitantly, the rest followed. First went Jenna and Kelvin, making quite the production out of it. Halfway under the fence, Kelvin pretended to get caught and launched into a film scenario of a killer about to get him. "I'm stuck! Go on without me."

"No, damn it. Your life means something. You can't give up," Jenna said in return.

Steph interrupted, "Give it up, you two, and get a move on."

"I don't think girlfriend likes the show, Jen."

"No accounting for taste, Kel. Come on, give me your hand." Jenna reached out and helped Kelvin through.

Steph followed, trying not to get her pants dirty.

Kelvin loudly whispered to Jenna, "Saw more dirt on her clothes after she and Dick came back from behind the trees." Jenna punched him for his naughty comment and laughed.

Steph turned a cold shoulder to both as she walked by. The message to them was, "Think what you like."

Wilson went through before his family, then paused on the other side of the fence to help them as they passed under it. Cindra crawled under with no problem, even though Marion fussed about her getting her clothes snagged.

Marion took her turn and hesitated, afraid that she was going to get hung up. Paul stepped down and grabbed the bottom of the fence in an unsuccessful attempt at making the opening larger. He moved nothing, but Marion seemed to think he did, and she passed under without a hitch. The placebo effect in action.

The O'Neils hugged and moved off to join the rest who were heading towards the barn, leaving Paul alone, still on the other side of the fence. *Hey, thanks*, he thought. *Crippled war vet here*. Well, crippled might be working it a bit, but he stood on one side of the fence with a bum knee, and they were walking away from him like he didn't exist on the other.

What had his shrink told him? "At times like these, take a moment to calm yourself. Breathe in and slowly exhale. Let the frustration out. You do yourself and others no good if you dwell on perceived slights." Breath in. Out. Ah, okay, now he was back—sort of.

Paul bent down and moved under the fence with some difficulty. This type of obstacle would have been a breeze for him back in basic, but with his knee not cooperating; it was a slow, painful exercise clearing the jagged wire. Awkwardly, he got under, back to his feet, and moved to join the others when he noticed Dick had turned to check on his progress. The frown he saw showed that Dick was not happy to see that Paul had made it under the fence. He bent to rub his knee. The pain pills were wearing off. He saw Dick turn back with a smile, apparently satisfied with Paul's handicap. He reached for the bottle but thought he should wait before taking any more. Who knew how long they would be out here? Instead, he gave the knee a good rub and walked/limped his way over to the barn, joining the others who stood outside of it, not moving.

The passengers had stopped at the open door of the building, not making a move. Dick stepped up to the threshold and peered inside. All he could see was the shaft of light that illuminated the planked floor and the outline of his cast shadow. Outside the area of the floor, delineated by the sunlight, there was nothing but darkness. "I can't see a God damned thing." Without hesitating, Dick pushed the door open wider and stepped through and into the barn.

Dick blinked to adjust his eyesight to the dark interior, but all he could see was the bright V shape cast onto the floor from the door opening and the complete blackness surrounding it.

Steph pushed the door open wider still, and the cast light on the floor reached further into the barn. At that moment, Dick thought he saw a dark form, a shadow, blacker than the surrounding darkness, dart out of the way of the growing beam of light.

Dick turned back to Ellie. "Did you see that?" Fear was clear in his voice.

The others had been inching into the barn but stopped when they heard what Dick said. No one acknowledged that they had seen anything, but they remained frozen in their tracks, afraid to advance or retreat.

From the rear of the group, Paul stepped forward, following the beam of light. He walked past Dick and stopped at an object on the floor that the expanded area of illumination had revealed. It was the bus driver's hat. "Looks like the driver came in here. Where do you think he is?"

Snapping out of his stupor, Dick pushed Paul aside, bent down, and put the hat on his head. Turning to show off, as if he were just crowned king of the lost passengers, he announced, "Hey, now I'm officially the boss."

Everyone stared at Dick in horror.

"What?"

Ellie stammered and pointed. "There's bl . . . blood coming out of the hat!"

Dick touched his forehead and felt dampness. He looked at his fingers and saw blood on them. "What the fuck!" He threw the hat to the ground. A ring of dripping blood circled Dick's forehead and clung to his hair.

Then they heard a rustling sound coming from the rafters above. Followed by a quick movement that peripheral vision could only see. Threads of a shadow, black against the darkness, flitted over their heads. It flitted from one side of the group to the other, at once here, encircling them, and then over there. The passengers could feel a presence with them in the barn like a tingling surge of electricity charging through the atmosphere.

Several tried to focus their eyes on the flitting black tendrils, but they could see nothing. When they stopped straining to see it, however, their peripheral vision caught it again darting about in the dark shadows, staying away from the beam of light streaming in from the open door.

Dick didn't hesitate. He quickly turned and elbowed his way to the door in a mad dash to be the first to leave. The others followed in various forms of panic. Ellie stood in the beam of light, not sure what caused the stampede, and not sure how to feel about Richard leaving her alone. No, not alone. Paul was still there, too.

Paul crouched down to look at the hat, grimacing as he forced his knee into compliance. Like a detective studying a crime scene, he looked around the interior of the barn. He could see nothing, but he had felt the same "presence" as the rest of them. Looking back at the bloody hat, he shook his head and said somberly, "Doesn't seem like the driver will make any more birthday parties." Reaching out with an extended arm to the floor, he pushed up from a crouch and stood unsteadily. As he did so, his foot kicked something hidden in the shadows. He stooped to see what it was and picked up the bus driver's 9mm.

"What's that?" Ellie asked him.

"It was the driver's," showing Ellie the pistol as he checked the magazine, which appeared to be about half full. "Looks like he fired it a few times. I wonder if it helped." He replaced the magazine and put the gun into the waistband at the back of his pants. "Bad shot?" Ellie suggested.

"No, I think he knew how to use this. Something else had to have been going on." He looked around the barn. "Where is he? Weird." He kicked the bloody hat out of the way. "All of it. Damned weird."

He turned to leave. "Come on, let's get the hell out of here." Together, they walked out of the barn as the black tendrils continued dancing around them in the shadows.

Outside the barn, the group had scattered in all directions. Their sole motivation was to get away from that creepy place and as far as possible. The driver's bloody hat was one thing, and a bad one at that, but what was it they had just seen, felt—experienced? A black shadow darker than the surrounding darkness of the unlit room. More than a shadow. A very black form that moved with a speed that made one question reality.

There was something, someone in the barn with them, and it most likely had killed the driver.

The passengers circled the barn, looking back with heightened caution; their animal instincts for self-preservation dialed up to ten. Paul and Ellie were about to crawl back under the fence when they heard Jenna. She was waving and yelling.

"Hey! Come over here! I think we're saved!"

Jenna continued waving, and Kelvin jumped up and down excitedly. The others soon joined them and found themselves at the top of a hill, looking down at a small town sitting on the valley floor.

Having regained his composure and reasserting his command status, Dick smiled and gave Steph a pull on her arm. "What are we waiting for? Come on. Let's go!" Together they ran down the hill towards the town and the end of their nightmare.

———◦◦◦———

A TECH SAT at a workstation in Con-West, several monitors were in front of him. A red warning icon was madly flashing on the screens. Eyes wide with surprise, the technician grabbed a phone and punched in a number.

Con-West Commander Samantha Cole put down the report she had been reading and picked up her ringing phone. "Yes?"

"Ah, ma'am. I think you should know that there is an alarm coming from Site-Alpha."

Cole looked up from her desk and through the glass wall of her office that provided her a panorama of the command center. With the phone pressed up to her ear, she stood and looked at the big screen in front of the room. A large map of the western United States showed a series of scattered dots representing the various CSC reservations in the region, all showing a solid green light. All except for the flashing red dot in Eastern Oregon.

"Ah, Fuck!"

"Ma'am?"

"You heard me. Keep watch on matters while I call Agent Wright and the Action Team."

The commander of Con-West drew in a deep breath. This was *not* one of the things Cole wanted to deal with today. She reached down to the phone and punched in Craig's number.

Chapter 11

SMALL TOWN U.S.A.

A T THE TOP of the hill, Paul stood in a fog, unaware of the others running past him. He could only focus on the bloody cap. Clearly, the driver, Eddie, had been murdered. But aside from the cap, there was no other indication that he was dead.

He mentally reviewed the interior of the barn. There was no sign of blood other than what was in the upside-down cap. While it seemed to hold an enormous amount—an average adult male has ten or so pints coursing through his body—the cap contained nowhere near a pint, let alone ten. Where was the rest of his blood?

For that matter, where was the driver? If his body were still in the barn, it should have been easily found, but Paul couldn't remember seeing any drag marks across the dusty floorboards. So, had the body been moved? Carried out? Not easily, there was a lot of man underneath that cap. So where was Eddie's body? And why would anyone kill him in the first place?

Paul just shook his head. Nothing about what he had seen in that barn made any sense. What was that thing that seemed to hover around in the shadows that spooked everyone? It appeared to be thick cobwebs, or dust caught up in a swirl of wind—even though the air was still. At any rate, cobwebs and dust don't kill a man, but who or what did? Aside from the driver's footprints in the thick layer of dust, the barn showed no sign of any other human having been inside. God! This hurt his head. The situation required experienced Army CID investigators, but he wasn't sure that even they could figure this one out.

He watched as the others made their way towards the town. Paul couldn't blame them for running ahead for help, not after what they had just seen—witnessed? Frankly, it was all too creepy, even after what he had experienced in Afghanistan. He reached behind his back and felt for the 9mm. At least he had the old Marine's Beretta. Just in case. *Thanks for that brother.*

The voices of the others brought his focus back to the top of the hill where he was looking down at Dick and Steph acting like they were in a race to beat the others to the bottom of the hill. Jenna and Kelvin held hands, like first graders during recess, skipping down the slope. The O'Neils slowly picked their way through the knee-high grass, avoiding any holes or hidden rocks that might trip them up, careful of where their daughter stepped.

"Watch out for that hole sweetie," Marion fretted.

"Let me lift you over this rock," Wilson urged.

Paul watched and wondered what kind of childhood that little girl possibly could have when fawned over as she was, living in a protective bubble. But, then, he didn't know them. Who was he to judge? Maybe she had hemophilia or something bad like that. It wouldn't be good to get an injury that could drain you of your blood in their current situation.

And speaking of not judging, there was Ellie off to his right by several paces. What was going on with her? What was going on with him? He chose to follow the group because of her instead of staying with the bus, which was the only smart thing to have done.

After the others had gone far enough ahead, Ellie started moving down the hill on her own. Paul observed her slow progress as she stepped around objects in the unfamiliar terrain. He thought that she might be moving slowly, not just for safety but also trying to be careful not to catch up with the rest of the group—possibly she even had wanted to go down into the town with him. He shook his head. *That's wrong-think, my friend*, he thought. *She's not interested in guys like you.*

Speaking of which, that boyfriend of hers was a real piece of work. Rubbing her nose in his shit was the height of meanness. Paul couldn't think of ever having witnessed such psychological torture as he had in just these past twenty-four hours. Not even the cruelest of drill instructors could do what Dick was doing to Ellie, but at least DIs had the intention of teaching you to keep your head down and to fight back. Dick, on the other hand, seemed to be trying to teach Ellie to keep her head down and be subservient. Still, she didn't appear to him to be the type to continue to put up with the crap that Dick was dishing out.

Paul decided to remain at the top of the hill and study the layout of the town for a while longer. There was something, a bit too—not right with this place which bothered him. From this perspective, he could see that the town was small and highly contained consisting of a grid of only four blocks, each surrounded by pavement. Its overall perimeter defined by streets which encircled the four blocks. On one side of this boundary, or "city limits," were buildings and on the other was the vast open high desert.

The whole place had a dropped-from-the-sky quality to it like someone had planted seeds in the middle of nowhere, then watered them, and up sprouted this town. This little out of place burg, combined with the mysterious death of the bus driver created a conundrum that filled Paul's head to the point of bursting; not to mention the slight issue of being lost in the middle of Eastern Oregon.

Right now, however, his focus was being redirected towards his throbbing knee, which was stiffening up. He'd been standing too long and needed to move, so he started to walk down to join the others. Even though the incline was gradual, it still gave him difficulty. Seeing a dried-out branch, he bent to pick it up for use as a walking stick. Just as he touched it, he heard a cautionary rattle coming from a nearby rock. Paul froze. *What was my warning to Steph?* he asked himself rhetorically.

Then he wondered how the hell everyone else could traipse down this hill without disturbing a rattler themselves. Then again, how the hell did he get to be the only one who got injured when his Humvee got exploded by that IED? Dumb fucking luck, that's how.

Still grasping the branch, Paul slowly rose and got a bead on exactly where the snake was. Keeping a close eye on it, he backed cautiously away as the rattling continued.

At the bottom of the hill, Ellie finally turned around to see where Paul was. She saw him standing still, almost frozen, holding a stick over his head and then he began doing some sort of slow-motion moonwalk. *What is he doing?* She had pegged him as being a bit more firmly planted on the ground.

Is he having some kind of PTSD attack? He did say he was in Afghanistan, she thought. *Maybe I should go up and see if he was okay?*

Paul slowly turned away from the snake, and as he cleared its territory, the rattling stopped. He mopped his brow with the sleeve of his jacket and put the tip of the branch into the ground and leaned on it to relieve the pressure on his bum knee. At the bottom of the hill, he could see that Ellie was staring up at him. *Is that a good or a bad thing?* Paul asked himself. He chose "good" and gave her a wave. He raised the branch and pantomimed that he was going to use it as a walking stick and then began to hobble in her direction.

Ellie watched Paul do some more weird dance moves holding the stick in the air. She waved back at him. *What did PTSD do to people? Should I be worried?* she wondered. Not just because the bus driver appeared to have been killed, but should she be concerned by a potentially crazy soldier? No, she decided, she should be worried by her boyfriend. Richard was the only one that had harmed her in any way. What was she thinking? This guy, Paul, he'd been nothing but friendly and he'd even gotten in Richard's face twice to protect her.

Paul finished limping down the hill and joined Ellie. "Thanks for waiting for the gimp," Paul said weakly.

Ellie smiled. "I was mesmerized by your interpretive dance performance back up there."

He looked at her quizzically.

"You know, picking up that branch and swinging it around in the air."

"Oh! That. That was me trying not to get bitten by a rattlesnake. Was I any good?"

She laughed. "No, not very. But you pulled off crazy really well."

"One of my shrinks would like to talk with you later," Paul said, smiling.

Then they both heard an airplane engine high above them. Ellie looked up and started to wave frantically, like they were going to be rescued, finally, from this desert island. "Hey! Down here!" She yelled, uselessly.

Paul just watched her with bemused appreciation. "You know, you're not so bad with the interpretive dance moves either."

"What?" Slightly embarrassed, Ellie lowered her arms. "But how are they going to see—"

"First, it's too high up, and if it had pilots, they would have to be looking for us specifically with binoculars to be able to spot your waving arms."

"And second, that's a drone. It's unmanned which means no eyeballs, at least not on board and again, they'd have to be searching for us to know where to look. It's probably BLM or some university program flying that thing, but nice try."

"Oh," Ellie flatly said as she watched the drone fly away to the east. "Well, come on then, Richard will be chomping at the bit for me to join him."

"Even with her?"

"Yes. Especially with her."

"Then you lead, and I'll follow at a safe distance. It's not like I have much of a choice," Paul said as he limped into town. Ellie gave him a warm smile of encouragement and took off in front of him.

———◆———

ON THE BORDERLINE dividing the natural terrain of the desert and the man-built environment, the small band of lost bus passengers stood, not quite ready to cross over from the wilderness and into this oasis of civilization. Dick had continued to charge headlong into the town, assuming that they were still following his lead until he turned back and saw that no one was behind him, not even Steph. He stomped back to the hesitant group and asked angrily, "Why the hell have you stopped?"

"Um, those two." Kelvin pointed to Ellie and Paul as they approached.

Ellie reached the others first with Paul limping his way a few paces behind her.

"What the fuck were you two talking about?" Dick asked Ellie accusingly.

Marion shot Dick an icy look as she tried to cover Cindra's ears.

Giving Steph an evil eye, Ellie answered, "He was telling me about the rattlesnake he almost grabbed instead of that branch."

Kelvin jumped up in an overly animated fashion. "Rattlesnake? I walked that way, and I could have been . . .."

"Oh, stop with the drama queen routine," Jenna told her friend.

Kelvin shot her an overly harsh look. "Oh, you stop you lesbo from planet Femtron." Then he broke his fake indignation and laughed. Jenna slapped his shoulder and laughed with him.

As Paul limped up and joined the group, Dick gave him the stink eye. Paul returned the look, unafraid of the implied warning he had just been given then asked, "You gonna keep wearing the bus driver's blood like some trophy?"

Dick rubbed his sweaty face and looked at the redness on the tips of his fingers. Alarmed, he grabbed Ellie's bag, pulled out a white blouse, and then wiped his face with a terrified frenzy.

Out! Out damned spot! Paul chuckled to himself as he watched Dick wipe down his head.

Marion removed a bottle of water from her bag. She started to offer to pour a little on the blouse but, Dick, being the "dick" that he was, grabbed the bottle out of Marion's hand and drained most of it onto the fabric. With the damp blouse, he vigorously wiped the red stain from his face then poured the remainder of the bottle on his head giving his hair an agitated once-over attempting to remove the remains of the bus driver. The others just stood by and watched this self-centered clod of a man do his thing—resigned not to do anything that could further agitate him.

"I was saving that water for my daughter."

"Huh? What?" Dick asked as he finished turning Ellie's white blouse pink. "Oh, yeah, well I'm sure there's more water in town." He tossed Ellie her blood-tinged blouse and joined Steph. The two headed into the town with the others following.

Stunned by her boyfriend grabbing her shirt without asking, using all the O'Neils' water, and by his bullshit pairing up with Steph, Ellie silently stood and looked down at her ruined blouse. Very deliberately, she rolled up the sullied garment, as if it were worth saving, stuffed it into her bag, and zipped it closed. Dick had outdone himself this time. When she looked up, she saw that Paul was watching, gave him a weak smile, wiped her nose, and proceeded on into the town.

Paul rubbed his knee again and swallowed a couple more of the painkillers before he followed. I hope there's a drugstore around here. Some more ibuprofen would be good. He thought. I may go through the rest of this bottle before morning. Then he continued to walk into the town, taking up the rear of the group—his uncontested position.

As Paul had noted from the top of the hill, this was a perfect-looking, small American town. It was the kind of place where you could see Andy and Opie walking back from the pond with a couple of fish that Aunt Bea would fry up for dinner, but this town was only so big—four square blocks, to be exact. As far as the eye could see, there was no sprawl of any type. No strip mall. No gas station or convenience store. There wasn't even a visible road leading into or out of it.

The passengers walked up a street between two blocks that had several suburban residences to their right and a park on the block to the left. The neat, tidy houses he saw from a distance, upon closer viewing, showed years' worth of weather damage and neglect, siding and trim paint peeling, and missing shingles from roofs. Yards were overgrown, and the grass was brown and dying.

Cars at curbs and in driveways appeared to have all been parked at the same time, considering the similar layers of dirt which had accumulated on them. The debris that was trapped between deflated tires and pavement answered any questions regarding how often these cars had been driven and how long they had been sitting idle. This observation applied to all the vehicles that they saw. And anyone who paid the slightest bit of attention to automobiles would notice that not one was manufactured later than the 1960s. Car enthusiasts would peg the newest at around 1963 and, aside from the dirt and tires, these cars were mostly in mint condition. At the very least, this town was a car collector's paradise.

As if all this wasn't odd enough, there were no signs of people whatsoever. They saw no indicators that anyone lived in these homes, walked these streets, or even was breathing the same air. No clothes were left out to dry on laundry lines. No toys were strewn about in mad abandon. There weren't any newspapers on porches or overflowing mailboxes. Not even a yard gnome could be seen peeking out from its protective hiding place in a shrub. This was a seemingly soulless place, devoid of life.

The park to their left showed the same lack of care. The patches of grass that were visible appeared to be dry, burned-out islands in an ocean of red/brown dirt. The trees were in various stages of death for lack of water. Playground equipment sat idle and rusting. If a picnic had ever been held there, it had to have been an awfully long time ago. A gazebo had seen better days, its shingled roof all but disintegrated from years of neglect.

No one said a word as they walked through this dead zone. The weirdness of the place was palpable, yet the passengers continued moving further into the town, hoping that they would find assistance.

Coming to the end of the residential block, they stopped at an intersection. The street signs indicated that they were standing on the corner of A Street and B Street.

"Not very original around here, are they?" Jenna observed. Not even Kelvin could muster up a laugh at that line, the creep factor being as overwhelming as it was.

"I noticed from the top of the hill that these two streets cut the town into quarters, forming four blocks. There are also four streets surrounding all the blocks which seem to constitute the city limits," Paul said.

"I saw a sign when we crossed that street and entered the town." Wilson injected. "That sign said First Avenue. So, maybe the other streets that surround the town are Second, Third, and Fourth Avenues."

"Makes sense," Paul said approvingly.

"Okay, so they have a small, ordered life around here. So what?" Dick spouted off, obviously getting irritated with the situation.

They stopped in the middle of the intersection and looked around; behind them was the residential neighborhood and park. Ahead of them was a block on the left that seemed to have commercial buildings and to their right was a block with office buildings and official-looking types of structures.

"See anything? Anyone?" Paul asked as he turned around, looking at this strangely laid out community. "Because I sure don't."

"Not even any traffic," Ellie stated.

"Or anything living, not even cats or dogs," Kelvin added.

"Maybe it's a town holiday, or they're at church," Marion suggested.

Dick was starting to get fidgety. "Well, they gotta be somewhere." He took off to the right down B Street. The others followed, lacking any other helpful ideas.

They passed a post office on the corner. A bank was next to it, and then there was a three story post-war style-glass office building of three stories.

Marching ahead, Dick took a left around the corner and onto Second Avenue. Most of the others trailed him like sheep; joining his quest to find some evidence of life.

Paul didn't follow but stayed put, in the middle of the intersection, and turned in a circle, taking a panoramic picture of the town with his mind's camera. As he finished his slow 360 turn, his lens caught Ellie standing next to him.

"What're you thinking?" she asked.

"Well, it's like there's. . . It's just so odd. Look at these buildings. There seems to be one of each kind of structure that would be in small-town America. But it's like they were placed here all at once, not built over a period of years. You know?"

Ellie looked at the buildings and shook her head, not quite sure where Paul was going with his thoughts. "Nope, you lost me."

"Alright. Let's say that you are constructing a model town for a toy train set. There are these plastic kits that you assemble and put on the spot where you have decided the town should be. Look." Paul pointed across to a building. "There's the kit model of a post office. And one for a bank next to it and an office building. Really? An all glass facade building in the heart of cattle country?"

She had never really noticed buildings much before, but Paul seemed to have a point.

"And look at those houses. See, a two-story Victorian next to a fifties ranch which is next to a Cape Cod." He continued to point out the differences in the buildings. "And the materials they used. That one there is all brick, and over there the building is stone, and of course, there's that glass-encased office building."

Ellie thought that she was starting to understand his line of thinking. "Yeah, like someone had a checklist, and they ticked it off. Check, one post office. Check, one bank. Check, one farmhouse."

"Exactly."

She gave Paul a studied look. "You an architect?"

"Naw, military. Doesn't the haircut give it away?" he said, brushing his hand along the short-cropped side of his head. "I just have always been interested in buildings. A hobby, I guess.

Kelvin jogged around the corner from Second Avenue. "Hey, you two! We found a city hall or a police station. Both I guess."

They moved to join Kelvin, but he stopped Ellie at the corner. "It might be good if your boyfriend doesn't see you two walking together. You know? He's been asking where you are and not in a nice way."

"Thank you." She said to Kelvin and gave Paul a hesitant look. "How's your knee?"

"Hey, I'm fine. You should get going. You don't want Richard to have an aneurysm, do you?"

Ellie smiled mischievously at that thought.

"Go. I'll hang back with Kelvin here and tell him my thoughts."

Ellie gave a wave and disappeared around the corner.

"What thoughts you want to tell me, Mr. Man?"

"First of all, I want to thank you for diffusing the situation back there."

"Me? What situation?" Kelvin said, feigning a lack of understanding.

"You know when Dick almost had a cow as Ellie and I caught up with you all."

Kelvin gave Paul an overly dramatized questioning look. "You mean about the snakes? I hate snakes!"

Paul smiled perceptively. "Well, thanks anyway. I didn't have the energy to fight that asshole."

This time, it was Kelvin's turn to smile knowingly. "Just doing what I do."

"Something tells me that there is more going on inside that head of yours than what you let on," Paul said.

Suddenly feeling awkward that someone had seen through his wall, a flush of red spread across Kelvin's cheeks. He cleared his throat. "So . . . anything else you wanted to tell me other than how fucked up this weird town seems to be?" Kelvin asked.

"Took the words out of my mouth." Paul put his hand on Kelvin's shoulder. "Come on, and let's catch up."

———————◆O◆———————

THE POLICE STATION was in the middle of the block. City hall was there too, right next door. Kelvin ran ahead and waited for Paul at the top of the stairs before entering the building. Paul gritted his teeth and climbed the short flight, joining Kelvin, who held the door open for him.

"Thanks," Paul said appreciatively.

"Age before beauty."

Paul gave Kelvin a little poke with his walking stick as he passed.

"Hey! I could learn to like that."

Paul smacked Kelvin a bit harder.

"Ouch! I've changed my mind," Kelvin said with a smile and proceeded into the building.

Inside, the group had stopped in front of a tall desk. The rest of the station was visible beyond, separated by a low wooden railing with a gate built into it as you might find in a courtroom. The interior of the police station had a feeling like it was right out of a Perry Mason episode; one of those where Perry goes to the small town to save a friend from a murder conviction.

Dick stood at the desk and rang the bell. "Where the hell are the cops?" He pounded on the bell a bit harder.

Ellie took a seat next to Jenna on a bench along a window wall. "This is a bit spooky, isn't it? I mean, where is everyone?"

"Yeah, I'm starting to get a little wigged out." Jenna looked out of the window behind them. "It's just so strange not seeing anyone. You know?"

"Yeah, like some end of the world story," Kelvin said. "Bus breaks down in the middle of nowhere and while the passengers wait for help a plague sweeps across the land, leaving this rag-tag group as the last survivors of civilization left to repopulate the earth . . .," He looked at Dick, "Ewww!"

"Just shut the fuck up," Dick said to Kelvin. He was obviously a bit freaked out by all this as well. "There must be a festival or town meeting is all. We'll find someone."

Kelvin added just one more example. "Or Wicker Man ceremony."

"Enough of this." Paul pushed his way through the gate. "I'm going to see if I can find anything that can help."

Since Paul gave them permission, the others crowded through the gate behind him and entered the office area.

Paul went from one desk to the next. Mostly all he saw were office items scattered about; papers, pens, staplers; the usual types of things but nothing like personal effects. There were no family photos, no greeting cards, no post-it notes, and no computers, but plenty of manual typewriters. He spotted a desk calendar, blew off a thick layer of dust, and held it up. "Hey look at this. 1961. Strange . . .."

Steph pointed to a framed picture of JFK hanging next to a flag. "Isn't that Kennedy? Like Bobby, I think?"

"Close," Wilson said in a dry tone.

Jenna looked through some notepads, blowing the dust off as she paged through them. "And all the paperwork is blank. No printing or anything."

Marion closed the door of a file cabinet. "Same with all the files. The folders have no labels on them and the papers inside have no writing. They're all blank like they're just space-fillers, and there's no trash in the garbage cans either."

Paul picked up a handset from a rotary desk phone. He dialed, heard nothing, and tapped on the button in the cradle several times.

"What are you doing?" asked Ellie.

"Saw this in a movie. It's supposed to reconnect to the phone line or wake someone up or something, but it doesn't matter, seems to be dead." Paul held the receiver out for others to hear. "No dial tone."

Frustrated, Dick slammed back through the gate and headed to the front door of the police station. "Come on, let's get outa here. We gotta look around some more. Someone in this town has to have a phone that works."

"Um, anyone check their cell phone yet?" Jenna asked as she pulled hers out and turned it on. The others did so as well, but they all returned them to their pockets with the same No Service message. "Just thought it was worth a try."

Cindra tugged on Marion's wrist. "I'm hungry, Mommy."

"We all are sweetheart." Marion looked to the others. "Let's find a place to eat. They'll have a phone too."

Wilson stepped toward his family. "That sounds like a good idea."

"Are we just going to bump around the rest of this town until we stumble on something or does anyone have any idea of how we're going to find this food joint?" Jenna asked.

Paul grabbed a yellow pad and pencil off a desk. He blew away the dust and drew a square then divided it into four squares. "This is the town. It's laid out as a big square with A and B Streets bisecting it into four quarters or blocks and four avenues forming the boundary." And then he drew an arrow. "This is north. These bottom two blocks . . .," Paul circled them. ". . . we walked by the park, here, in the southwest and this residential area in the southeast. The top two blocks appear to be stores and businesses in the northwest." Paul pointed the pencil at the top left square. "And governmental and official-type buildings in the northeast block, which is where we are standing now, here, on Second Avenue." He marked an X on the map to represent the police station.

"To save time I suggest we split into two groups. One group will continue up Second Avenue to the north with Dick and check out the backside of the town along Third and then down Fourth."

Dick puffed out his chest for seemingly being validated as a leader, even though he was chosen by the one person he really wanted to punch out.

Paul continued, "I'll take the second group back the way we came and check out the stores up this portion of A Street we haven't seen yet. Then continue along B and then up north on Fourth. Both groups should converge somewhere along Fourth. If what I'm thinking is right, there should be at least one cafe and a grocery store in this town somewhere and this commercial block in the northwest quarter is the most likely location."

Paul put the pencil down and surveyed the passenger's faces for questions. "Okay, we good with this?"

"Who goes with who?" Kelvin asked.

"Oh, um Steph . . .," Paul began.

"She comes with me." Dick asserted.

"Okay, and Ellie . . .,"

"She's with me too."

Kelvin whispered to Jenna, "The cock of the walk." Dick heard the comment and gave Kelvin a menacing look. And much to his own surprise, Kelvin returned a look, telling Dick that he wasn't afraid of him. Even though Kelvin had gotten used to bullies a long time ago and knew how to deal with them, it didn't mean that he liked confrontations.

Ellie nodded to Paul that she would be alright as she moved to join Dick's team.

"Alright then. Jenna and Kelvin come with me. Wilson, why don't you go with Dick. Marion and Cindra can be with me." Paul winked and smiled at Cindra. She bashfully stepped behind her mom. "This town isn't all that big, so we should be able to see everything that there is left to see in fairly short order. Good luck."

With that, they left the police station heading out to find some evidence of life and, perhaps, along with it a place to make a phone call and maybe grab a bite to eat.

Once outside, Dick led his team up Second Avenue. He stopped and turned and, not seeing his group directly behind him, gave a whistle and a wave for them to catch on up, like a general ordering his troops forward into battle. Then, to put an exclamation point on it, Dick clapped his hands, yelling, "Come on, people. Snap it up!"

Kelvin said to Jenna, "What a d.i.c.k."

"What gave you that impression?" She fired back.

"Hey, you guys," Paul chided them as he nodded his head back towards Cindra

"Ooo. Sorry captain!" Kelvin saluted.

Paul smiled. "Stow it, soldier."

"Yes sir, Mr. Man!"

Paul shook his head and limped around the corner. At the post office, he looked up the portion of A Street that they had not yet explored. The standard architectural types from his train set analogy were laid out in front of him. The next building was a fire station and then a school and then possibly a courthouse. Across A Street was the commercial block where he believed they might find a living, breathing human being along with food and a phone.

"Let's go this way," he suggested as he hobbled across the street from the post office. On this corner, they found themselves in front of a shoe store.

Kelvin chimed in. "Unless we do some serious boiling, I don't think there's any food in here." He tried the doorknob and found it locked. "Besides, it looks like they're closed for business. I guess our money is no good to them."

Jenna gave him an affirming nod.

Up the street, they saw Dick and his group cross the north end of A Street as they worked their way along Third Avenue. Paul waved and yelled, "See anything?"

"Not a fucking thing," Dick yelled back.

Marion sent Dick an angry look as though he cared what she thought.

"Kelvin, you and Jenna finish going up A Street and check out all these storefronts." Paul directed them. "And if you find a drugstore, I could use some more ibuprofen." He winced as he rubbed at his bum knee. "Marion, Cindra, and I will continue along B Street. Find us when you're done."

Jenna and Kelvin took off and stopped at the first storefront. They peered in through the dirty glass and tried the door. It was locked and wouldn't budge. They looked back at Paul signaling that the store was locked. Paul waved them to continue, turned to go, and saw that Cindra was crying, refusing to move. Marion was doing her best to calm her to no effect.

Paul took a knee in front of Cindra, grimacing from the pain. "Listen, honey. If we are going to find any help, we all need to act as a team. You are as important as I am or your mother. Maybe you're more important because you are a bright kid, perhaps one of the most observant girls I have ever met."

Cindra sniffed.

"I mean it. And you've also been acting very bravely in a rough situation."

Not having been around children very much, at least those who spoke English, he had a hard time judging, but at this very moment, she was wiping away her tears and started to walk towards the next storefront. Marion smiled and wiped moisture from her eyes as well.

At the door, Cindra tried the handle and found it locked. She shook her head indicating a "no go" and moved on to the next. Three doors away hung a sign stating that it was a grocery store. Cindra ran to it excitedly and gave the door a try. Marion joined her daughter as she entered. Paul caught up with them as they walked out with their heads hanging a bit low. Through the open door, Paul saw a store full of nothing. Another empty model kit building.

They continued with a few more storefronts and found the same thing; either locked doors or empty rooms filled with dust and unused furnishings. Jenna and Kelvin came back from their survey and rejoined Paul, Cindra, and Marion. "No luck Cap," Kelvin reported with a salute.

"You know." Paul said, "You can be a tad annoying."

"A tad?" Jenna chimed in.

"Sorry. Just giving the man here the respect he deserves."

—◦—

THEY FINISHED CHECKING the remaining stores and stopped at the end of the block. Looking up Fourth Avenue, they saw the other group at the north end of the block and waved. Then Wilson became agitated. He waved and shouted, almost jumping up and down. He was pointing at something that was between the two groups and ran towards it.

All the passengers hurried to join Wilson where he was standing.

"What is it, Wilson?" Dick asked, a bit out of breath.

The storefront that he brought everyone to had its windows painted black and looked as dead as all the other buildings. Perhaps more so.

"Don't you see?" Wilson asked.

"No," Paul responded.

Wilson pointed up to the sign over the door which read: *Bucket of Blood, Bar & Grill.* The neon sign in the window was glowing *OPEN.*

How did he see that when no one else had? Frustration, fatigue? Whatever. The neon light screamed electricity, which was the first they had seen in use all day, which implied that someone might be home.

Wilson hugged his wife and daughter and looked up at the sign. "It's just like in that ghost town, Virginia City, in Nevada! Remember last year? You know, where all the cowboys died in shoot-outs?"

Marion nodded and hugged her husband back.

Dick went up to the door and gave the knob a turn. It moved. A bell tinkled a "welcome" as the door swung open. Music from a jukebox flowed out to greet them. They could see lights on inside. It looked like their problems were on the way to being fixed.

Dick led the way inside with the others behind him.

Paul paused. Before entering, he turned back and looked across Fourth Avenue and out at the empty expanse of the high desert stretching west, away from the town. The sky was transitioning from a warm reddish-orange of the sunset into a deep purple as evening was slowly pushing the light of day out of its way to make room for the darkness of night.

This is one damned strange place. Paul thought, then walked through the door.

Chapter 12

DUTY CALLS

T HE SUN WAS just rising as Liz completed her run. She stopped to catch her breath and take in the magnificent countryside. Southern Arizona had its attractions, but to appreciate the Southwest you had to kind of really like the heat. Not here in Idaho. From where she was standing, Liz could see the Snake River Valley cradled by the Sawtooth and Bitterroot Mountains to the north and the Owyhee Mountains to the south. Not visible to her, but to the east, sat Pocatello and Idaho Falls at the foothills of the Grand Tetons. The morning sun was starting to spread its warmth over Mountain Home. This country was beautiful, and she was excited to discover everything about it.

Liz looked at her watch and hustled back to her new apartment—military living at its finest. As she jogged to her quarters, she passed some others that she recognized from the lecture hall. They acknowledged one another but did not stop to talk. They were forbidden to discuss their work outside the CSC facility, which was a tightly controlled thirty-acre compound carved out of the 122,000 acre base. The regular military and civilian contractors called it the "Asylum," because of all the crazy shit that had to be going on in a fenced and restricted area within a fenced and restricted area.

Weird stuff going down within the CSC compound or not, to everyone at Mountain Home, those who entered and left the "Asylum" were all assumed to be civilian contractors working on top-secret projects. No one questioned further, at least not in public. It wasn't the military way, but that didn't keep rumors from proliferating. One rumor was that the CSC compound housed all sorts of alien remains. Others said it was a high-tech tracking station for satellite surveillance, or a secondary command center for NORAD when the shit *really* hit the fan. And there were one or two who knew a guy, who knew a guy, who had been inside and saw that they were flying secret, illegal hunt and kill drone missions over friendly countries.

After a quick shower, Liz headed to the commissary for breakfast. She bypassed the serving line and went instead for a bowl of granola, some fresh fruit, and coffee. Balancing a tray of food with a full bag of paperwork, she found an out-of-the-way spot in the dining area where she could sit, read, and observe, getting a feel for the place she now called home. Setting her tray down, Liz opened her bag and removed the red folder along with a stack of other material she had dug up in the CSC library, then she set her phone on top and opened the folder to a marked page.

As she read, she absentmindedly took a scoop of granola into her mouth and dribbled milk onto some of her paperwork. "Shit!" She paused to wipe it up and then looked around the room. From this vantage point, Liz saw one of the other new field agents sitting with his partner. She wondered how he was faring so far. Probably a bit disoriented, just like her. Their body language suggested that they were talking shop; leaning in close to one another so no one could hear. At least that was how it appeared to Liz, especially when the veteran agent stopped talking and looked up as a random airman walked by. He gave her the evil eye until she was safely beyond earshot, then the agents resumed their huddle and, presumably, their secret discussion.

Just as Liz was going to continue her studies, the front door opened and she saw Agent Wright enter. He was half reading a newspaper while walking, seemingly aware of obstacles in his path as he swerved around one contractor, veered to the left of a chair, through the turnstile, and straight to the coffee urn without looking up. She stood and waved, but Craig was too focused on the paper and the coffee. She watched him fold the paper under his arm before he poured coffee into a cup, emptied three sugars into it, and then gave it a good stir. Coffee and paper in hand, Agent Wright looked up and around, probably looking for a place to sit.

Liz decided that this was as good a time as any to get started with her new partner, so she stood and waved, trying to get his attention.

———◆———

WHEN HE GOT his mug filled, Craig surveyed the room looking for a quiet spot to enjoy the drink and read the paper before going to work.

In the corner of his vision, Craig caught the motion of a waving arm. It was Adams. Talking with her wasn't the way he wanted to kick off the day, so he pretended not to notice, but she continued signaling, not getting his subtle message. "Leave me alone." And now all eyes in the hall were drawn to the animated redhead.

"Over here, Agent Wright!" Liz was almost shouting, which pretty much made it impossible for him to do anything but join her. Craig walked over to Liz and sat down.

Leaning in close to her, Craig spoke in a hushed voice, "When we're out, and in the general mix of the population, I am just Craig. We're civilians here. Right?"

"Sorry, sir . . . Craig. This covert stuff is new to me. Won't happen again."

"You'll get the hang of it." Craig surveyed the dining hall and saw the other agent with his new partner, sitting discretely away from the general population. They seemed to be chatting up a storm. Well, Craig had been a newbie to some old fart of an agent too, at one time. So, this was what he was supposed to be doing. He might as well start now.

Still standing Liz asked awkwardly, "Join me?"

Craig smiled and nodded as he took a chair and then looked for a spot to set his coffee down on the crowded tabletop.

"Oh! Just a minute." Liz said as she took one pile of paper and stacked it on top of another, making some room for his cup. "There."

"Thank you." Craig set his cup down and asked, "So how was your first night here at Mountain Home?"

"Not bad, but no drill instructors calling cadence or yelling at enlistees like at Huachuca. The jets taking off and landing will take a bit of getting used to, though."

"No. No DIs. By now everyone here should have had all the stupid yelled out of 'em."

Liz smiled at the joke. Perhaps there was hope for her.

"As for the jet engines . . . Think of it as white noise. After a bit, you'll not even notice it."

"Sir. I mean Craig."

Liz leaned into Craig as he took a sip of his coffee. The grimace on his face said that she might have gotten too close to him, that or the coffee was bitter. She decided it was the coffee.

"So, I'm curious about a few things. First, the information in the folder seemed thorough, though I'm sure that there's plenty that it didn't cover."

Eying her extra reading material, he replied, "Well, it looks like you're going to make up for that."

Liz tried to consolidate the papers on the table. "I like to be informed. You said it could save my life."

"That I did."

"And now I have a couple of questions."

"Yes?" Craig answered in a tone, suggesting that she should start asking.

"I'm curious about the Catholic Church's involvement. You mentioned the Vatican yesterday, and the historical overview—" Liz began to open the red folder. "—also stated that the Pope knew . . . I guess, still knows, about the existence of vampires."

"Yes?"

"So, what's up with that?"

"Former Catholic?"

"No, well, I'm not the best one ever, but I still feel like I am one."

"Me too. So, tell me why you have a problem with the Pope knowing?"

Liz leaned in closer to Craig and lowered her voice a few notches. "Because we're talking about vampires. Until two days ago I didn't think vampires really existed. Why would the Pope—"

"You checked out the stories of the vampire myth online?"

"Yes." Liz thumbed through a stack of papers and grabbed a sheet she downloaded from Wikipedia and showed it to Craig.

"Then you know that the legends go way back in time, even before there was a Catholic Church," he asked, urging Liz to seek answers beyond what was printed on the paper in front of her.

"Okay, I understand that but—"

"The Church is almost 2000 years old. You haven't considered that it would have encountered vampires at some point?"

"Okay. It's just that it's so hard for me to wrap my head around the whole idea, especially after watching so many Dracula movies."

"Understandable. Erase all that you think you know. You're here because vampires exist. The CSC is here because vampires exist. Vampires made an agreement for protection because the Pope knew, as did other religions, and was working to eradicate vampires from the face of the earth."

"So . . . other religions worked with the Catholics? How well did that work?" Liz asked incredulously.

"Not too well at first, but all religions had a vested interest in cooperating. Vampires don't discriminate. They're equal opportunity suckers." Craig smiled at that one, but Liz didn't crack—too intent on learning more. "Years ago, the major organized religions formed a secret council to coordinate their efforts. Since the Roman Catholic Church had the largest global footprint, still does, by the way, it was agreed that the bulk of the responsibility of hunting vampires landed on the Vatican."

"Are the other religions still involved?"

"In hunting vampires? Not like before the treaty, but they still have hunters out there looking for the free radicals."

"The what?"

"The free radicals are what we call the vampires who refused to join in with the treaty. They're burrowed deep underground and keep an extremely low profile. We go after them too. Stop me if I'm overloading you with this stuff."

"Oh, no. This is interesting. We?"

"Yep, field agents like us."

Liz grinned, not entirely comprehending what Craig meant by what he just told her. But she pressed on. "Okay. One more question."

"Shoot."

"The mayor of Vamp Town. Alexei. What's his story? Can you tell me?"

Her line of questioning impressed Craig. He figured she would want to know some of his more harrowing experiences, the exciting bits. Instead, she was reading up on the history of the agency, and now she was asking about Alex, who was the key to the whole success or failure of containing the vamps.

"From what he's told me, Alex and his younger brother Vladimir were turned when they were children, not all at once, mind you, but over the course of many years. Their 'blood father' . . .," Craig drew air quotes around the term, "was a Russian monk and a vampire hunter who, himself, had been turned."

Liz drew in a short breath at that little tidbit.

"Alex's story started in 1792 when he was 12; his brother was 10. They would visit the monk's lair a few times each summer when their family lived out in the country, away from Moscow. During each visit, the monk drank small quantities of their blood, and at the same time, he fed them small amounts of his from cuts on his wrists. They became, um, addicted I guess is the right word, to drinking his blood while, at the same time, the freshness of their blood invigorated him. There was something of a symbiotic relationship between him and them.

"The turning process took years. Gradually the boys became increasingly light sensitive and eventually started sleeping only during the days; their need for blood steadily grew until the need turned to a driving thirst and then pure lust."

"So why did this monk not just turn them right away? I mean, or just drink them dry. Sounds like a lot of time to wait for just a taste only a couple of times a year for, how long?"

"For something like ten years. He fed on animals and other humans for sustenance, but Alexei and Vladimir were special to him. He could taste potential in their blood, and through his blood, he passed on all his knowledge. He was mentoring them to become leaders of the entire vampire realm. And Alex was groomed to be so powerful as to be able to command respect and subservience from even the oldest of the undead."

Liz could only say, "Wow." It was the age-old story of innocence lost.

Then she stopped and thought a bit about what she was just told. "Wait a minute. Alex's brother is named Vladimir?"

"Yes."

"Vlad."

"Yep."

"As in Vlad the Impaler? Dracula?"

"Yeah."

"Fuck you! Damn. You sucked me in, and I fell for it. Ha. Ha. Ha. You got the new kid. Very funny. I'm sure you and the others will get a good laugh over this at the Agent's Club or wherever you get together for a drink." Liz sat back in her chair and crossed her arms; angry at herself for falling for the hazing.

Craig smiled. No one had yet caught that weird coincidence. "Vladimir is a popular name in the Northern Slavic countries." Liz gave him a skeptical look. "Hey, you asked, and this is the story." He got no response. "Okay, I've met

Vlad. He doesn't look like Bella Lugosi or Christopher Lee. In fact, he has red hair. Like you."

Liz looked up and smiled weakly. "Yeah, right."

"Well, not as intense as yours, but it sure is red, and like I said yesterday, it isn't always true."

Liz scrunched her face in, still not willing to believe him.

"Alex is the strongest vampire on earth. Vlad pulls up a close second. But it's Alex's strength that got the vamps to agree to the treaty and his continued power keeps them all in line. I hope nothing happens to Alex. I trust Vlad for about as long as we can go for a walk, hand in hand, on a bright summer's day." He gave Liz a wink. "Which wouldn't make for a very long walk."

Liz laughed despite her accusation at being taken for a fool. "One more question. At investiture yesterday, someone behind me asked why the vamps don't just fly over the fence and escape. And you answered that Alex is too strong, which you just repeated." For dramatic effect, Liz flipped through the papers scattered in front of her. "But I have not found anything in my reading so far that explains what that means. How can Alex keep them from leaving the reservation?"

Craig brushed his hand over the research papers that Liz had spread out in front of her. "So, you say you've read through all this?"

"Well, yeah, most of it."

"And you've read through everything in your folder here," Craig asked, pulling the red folder out from amongst the papers.

Hesitantly, Liz answered, "Yes. At least I thought so."

Craig opened the folder and flipped through several pages and stopped. With a finger, he pointed to an article. "Did you happen to read this?"

Liz took the folder and read the heading of the article. *The Nature of Vampires.* With a sheepish look on her face, she confessed, "I, uh, I think that the pages must have stuck together. This one completely slipped by me. Sorry, I—"

"Nothing to be sorry about. I think this will answer that question. Mostly." With that, Craig picked up his coffee and unfolded the paper, and prepared to enjoy this morning the way he liked, in silence and with hot caffeine.

Liz looked down at the open folder and began to read.

She looked up and saw that Craig had a smile of satisfaction on his face. Shaking her head slightly, she resumed reading.

The Nature of Vampires

by Craig Wright

Ethologists disagree on the exact nature of vampires. Research on the subject is, understandably, challenging both from the highly secret aspect of the topic and the danger involved to the researcher. The volume of information on the question, after thousands of years of study, could fit on an old-school three-and-a-half-inch floppy disc, with room to spare.

There is, nevertheless, an overwhelming agreement that once a person becomes a vampire, he/she is no longer a human and cannot be considered "alive" in the standard definition of the term. However, there is some argument about whether there exist any elements of humanity in a vampire after its transition, such as a carryover of human traits. It has been documented that those who have been turned do, for example, show vestiges of their former human selves through their expression of emotions such as love, hate, generosity, greed, pity, jealousy, and lust.

While some similarities exist between species, it is not to say that the two are the same in any substantial measure. Vampires are dissimilar to the humans which they once were and any other creature on the earth in several ways, primarily in how a vampire sustains life. The drinking of blood, preferably human, as its sole means of sustenance, is, perhaps, the main difference. Many disagree on whether a vampire can physically ingest human food and drink. Some maintain that if a vampire takes in "normal food," it would become violently ill and find itself close to death. Others dismiss this as merely an old wife's tale.

It should be noted here that over the centuries, there have been more old wives' tales on the subject than solid research. And increasingly, the myths and legends about vampires are proving to be more in line with reality than expected. At any rate, there is no disagreement about the vampire's need to consume blood to survive. Any blood, but human above all else, and the fresher, the better. Without human blood regularly, a vampire will grow weak. After a prolonged period, it will go through an aging process; though there are no recorded instances of a vampire dying of old age, old wives' tales included.

Another significant difference is that one isn't born into the race. In fact, vampires are sterile. They cannot procreate. Vampires do not have a sex drive as other living beings, and some say that their sexual organs no longer even exist or have devolved through lack of need. This is not to imply that they do not have "urges," but their form of sexual release occurs by biting the neck of a victim and consuming his/her blood.

Simply stated, a vampire is added to the population when a human is bitten and then made to drink that vampire's own blood. Thus, for a vampire to be created, a person dies, forfeiting his/her previous life, and then is "born" again as an "immortal."

When a person is turned, it is not a random occurrence. Vampires are very picky when it comes to whom they will share eternity. Most often, the victim/candidate is preselected and submitted to a rigorous vetting process before being brought into the fold. Something about the candidate catches the eye of a vampire who will then study the target to determine whether he/she could be a compatible addition to the family.

Sometimes a victim, who is in the process of being consumed for dinner, has a specific taste in his/her blood. An undefinable quality—a je ne sais quoi as the French say—that saves them from consumption and death. They are selected to join the "family" on the spot, with no further vetting required.

The process of turning can take hours, days, or longer, depending upon the amount of the vampire's blood the chosen one has consumed. The longer the turning process takes, the more knowledge and insight are passed on through the "parent's" blood. The longer it takes to become a full-fledged vampire, the higher in status and stronger one becomes within the social structure.

However, no matter how much blood is consumed during the process, once started, it cannot be reversed. If the bitten is cut off from drinking more of a vampire's blood, his human body will go into a type of shock. This usually leads to death. Vampires view this as a form of miscarriage or abortion—an infant not reaching full term occurring either through random chance or as an actual decision.

The behavior of vampires is most closely associated with a pack of animals, dogs, or wolves. When they are "born" a vampire knows from its first breath what they are and how they are supposed to behave. Animal behaviorists call this "instinct." Instinct is the innate part of behavior that emerges in the beast without any training or education.

Through instinct, the vampire knows its place within the "pack" and the rules which guide the entire race. They know, through this imprinted instinct, for example, that sunlight is dangerous, that they can't enter the house of their prey without being invited in by a human, that garlic is offensive, that holy water is hazardous, and that silver is deadly.

All this knowledge is engraved onto the core of the vampire and is passed on through ingesting the blood of their "blood parent," who received the same imprinted information from their "blood parent," who received it from theirs, and so on stretching back through time. These innate behaviors are rigid and predictable. And, as in pack animals, there is stamped a mentality of extreme loyalty and devotion to the leader. The vampire has an innate understanding that all defer to their leaders, thus establishing a dominance hierarchy within the race.

The vampire hierarchy resembles the human pyramid governance model. There is the Alpha, the Khan; the ultimate ruler at the top—the president. The Betas represent the heads of the families and sit on the grand council—the Congress. And the Omegas who make up the general vampire population—the electorate.

The Khan can either be elected by the heads of the houses or become such through exhibiting his/her dominance over the council. In some extremely rare situations, a Beta will challenge the Alpha's position. This attempt to unseat the leader occurs when the Beta believes that it has acquired the strength to take on the Alpha—which it will need because, without the ability to defeat the Alpha, death is the only reward.

Not much is understood as to what exactly makes a vampire stronger than another. Physical strength can be measured, yes. But what gives the Alpha mental dominance over an entire race? We do know that this mental capability is obtained through selectively feeding off of the choicest blood donors to which the Alpha has first selection rights. The fresher and younger the blood, the more of these qualities of "strength" seem to be imparted.

The how of it remains a mystery. Perhaps there are enzymes in the fresh young blood of a human that combine with the vital body chemistry of a vampire to enable the mind control required to tame a race. All vampires have these mental capabilities which they use to varying degrees in subduing their victims, and all signs

point to a connection with the consumption of fresh
young blood—both in quantity and frequency—to how
powerful a vampire can become. However, due to the
nature of how a vampire dies, no postmortem has been
possible, so these studies remain open-ended.

LIZ CLOSED THE folder and looked up.

Still smiling, Craig put down his paper. "Not too bad for someone without a Ph.D., huh?"

"Well, I—"

"Don't answer that," Craig said, cutting her off. "I'm not going to tell you that article answers all the questions you still have, but at this point in time, this is all we've got. Maybe someday you'll get to write the addendum."

Liz shook her head and was about to say some self-deprecating thing when a cell phone rang.

The ring tone was the *X-Files* theme, and of course, it was on the loudest setting. Heads around the commissary turned in their direction. Liz held up her hands, indicating it wasn't hers. Craig acted like he didn't hear anything at all. Finally, after the third ring, Craig, a bit embarrassed, pulled out his phone and answered it. Liz stifled a laugh as Craig spoke into it.

"Hello?"

"Agent Wright. There's been an incident."

"Ah, shit, not another one. It's morning, so it can't be Dawson's."

"It's not Site-Delta. It's Site-Alpha, Vamp Town. There's been an incursion."

"An incursion? Sweet Jesus! I'll be right over."

Craig stood and shoved the phone into his pocket. "Well, Adams looks like trial by fire for you. There's been an incursion at Vamp Town. That's our beat."

"Wait. An incursion? Someone is breaking into Vamp Town?"

"At this point, that's all I know. Something or someone has gotten into the reservation. Come on, we need to get to Control for more intel. Let's hope that the incursion was just a couple of coyotes or jackrabbits. Humans stumbling into a town full of vampires could get very messy. And neither of us wants to be on the clean-up crew."

Without saying another word, Craig turned and took off. Liz looked down and saw all the items on the table that were laid out to continue her research into the CSC, then she looked back up to see Craig making a beeline to the door. *So much for a low-key first morning on the job*, she thought. Instantly Liz gathered everything—printouts, phone, ID, keys, and the red folder—and haphazardly shove it all into her bag. Rushing to catch up, she fumbled with pulling on her coat while keeping the open bag from spilling its contents and made it to the door just as it closed in her face. In a Jerry Lewis flick her character would have gone sailing backward, bag flying into the air, papers fluttering throughout the room like falling snow, her landing on her ass, and coat coming to a rest on top of her head in a most unflattering way. But this was no comedy.

Undaunted, Liz placed her hand on the crash bar, but before opening the door, she caught the reflection of the other two agents in the glass panel, watching with concerned faces. She turned briefly, and the veteran gave Liz a nod and thumbs up signal along with a small, supportive smile. Then, with a grim look on his face, he turned back and, shaking his head, whispered something to his new partner. Liz processed that moment. *He knows that something bad is happening*, then hammered her hand against the crash bar, slammed the door open, and sprinted off after Craig, who was almost to the Asylum's gate where she joined him.

Craig had impatiently stopped and turned back to see where Liz was, thinking that she was far behind him, but when he turned, she was right on his heels. He nodded, face as cold as stone, and slid his security card through the reader. She followed, a little winded, beads of sweat on her brow. As she passed through the gate, it caught the strap of her bag. *Really?* she thought with exasperation. It took a moment to wrestle the bag free without spilling its contents. Craig turned and saw the tail end of that battle, shook his head, and moved on towards the command center.

"Sorry," Liz called after him. *What the fuck, man?* What was I supposed to do? Let secret shit fly all over the place?

Still shaking his head, Craig kept moving toward the command center. On the surface, he was disturbed that Liz was in no way ready for this job, but just a bit further down, his thoughts went back to his last partner. *I don't know if I can handle losing another.* Holding open the door to the control building, Craig kept up his gruff exterior. "Come on, Adams!" he said impatiently and started mothering her down the hall as she passed him.

Christ, why me? Liz thought as she heard the door close behind them.

———◆———

CON-WEST COMMANDER Samantha Cole had moved down from her glassed-in office that overlooked the beating heart of Control-West and was now standing in the control room next to a tech who was switching camera feeds, trying to get as clear an image as possible. On one side of the large screen that dominated the wall in front of them was a satellite image of the reservation, RES SITE-ALPHA. On the opposite side was a closer visual from a drone flyover. A smaller screen inset in the bottom right corner showed a map of the other reservations in the Western United States. All were indicated by steady, glowing green dots. All but the flashing red spot in Eastern Oregon.

The entire edge of the screen was pulsing red, which framed all the images they were looking at, emphasizing that there was, indeed, something serious was going down, and just in case no one had noticed, other alarms filled the control room with a mad cacophony of blaring noise and flashing lights as a reminder.

Commander Cole pinched the bridge of her nose, trying to rub out the beginnings of a significant headache. "Can someone please turn off all these alarms?"

"Sorry, ma'am." The tech responded as he clicked on the keyboard and moused over some digital sliders on his screen. The throbbing—*Arnt! Arnt! Arnt!*—of the klaxon faded and the swirling "fire-engine" red lights stopped their rotations and went dark.

"And the big screen, too."

"Yes, ma'am." The tech moved the mouse a bit, made a couple of clicks, and very quickly the red-throbbing frame around the big screen just turned to a steady red light.

"All the way, William, if you please."

The glowing red frame winked out totally when the tech moved the cursor over a button on his screen.

Craig entered the control room and walked down to the same desk he had manned the other night. The blue bronco was back, and the duck had been flattened and painted blue as though the horse had trampled it into the blue field of Boise State. Craig looked at the tech, who glanced back at him. Their eyes locked, each knowing that this was just the first battle of a larger war.

Liz was right behind Craig as he entered the command center, still concentrating more on keeping the errant papers in the bag than on the path she was walking and didn't quite see that the floor stair-stepped down from the door. The abrupt step down caught her by surprise, and she felt like she was going to take a tumble. With Master Sergeant Terry's voice playing in her inner ear, she made a quick assessment of her situation and dropped the bag which stopped her forward motion and allowed her to stay upright and on her feet.

"I see you have a newbie Craig." The commander didn't look back at Craig but addressed him like she had eyes in the back of her head.

As if she didn't know. "Yes, ma'am. This is Li—"

Commander Cole turned and offered her hand to Liz. "Elizabeth Adams. Welcome to the CSC."

"Thank you, sir. Ma'am . . . Commander."

Craig gave her a nudge to shut up and cut her losses.

"Master Sergeant Terry was my drill instructor, too." Commander Cole gave Liz a quick, knowing smile. "He told me that you have the makings of a good agent. Don't let him down."

"No, sir. I mean yes, ma—" *Damn it!*

"Hell of a first full day on the job, Adams," Cole commented as she returned her attention back to the large screen.

"So, what do we have? Coyote?" Asked Craig.

"I wish." She pointed up to the screen. "This was shot an hour ago from a satellite fly-over." Cole nodded to the half of the screen that showed an enhanced aerial image of Vamp Town and the surrounding countryside. "Caught the shot just as it was going out of range. But you can clearly see why the auto alarm sounded. And this—" Now she indicated the left side of the screen. "—was taken from a surveillance drone that we tasked to the Rez when the alarm sounded."

Video images showed the nine bus passengers walking/running down the hill into the town below. One woman, standing with a man, turned up to the drone and waved to it.

Liz offered an observation, "It looks like one of them is signaling for help."

Another tech, a row of computers down from where they were standing, turned and spoke up. "I found a post online that Cascade Stage Lines is missing one of their buses. It services the eastern side of Oregon. The bus should have made Baker City early last evening but was a no-show. Its route wasn't supposed to be near the Rez. The manifest says . . . That . . . it had nine passengers as well as a driver."

"Which would make ten total . . .." Commander Cole said, staring at the screen. "William, reverse the video. Now freeze it."

"Well, there's only nine people visible." Craig counted. "Which could mean that we already lost one. Holy shi—"

"Language, Agent Wright." Cole cut him off.

"Sorry, ma'am."

"So, no input from the fence sensors?" Cole asked the tech.

"No, ma'am. Everything indicates that the fence is intact, no cuts, no tampering."

Craig asked the tech to zoom out of the picture a bit more. The top of the hill was now visible as well as the barn and the perimeter fence. "Then those people had to fly over or . . .,"

"Dig under it," Liz said, finishing Craig's thought. "There!" She pointed to a spot at the fence line where the bus driver had dug.

Commander Cole smiled, appreciating that Liz had a brain underneath that mop of red hair.

"God damn it! F' Congress and their sequester. This shit would not be happening if we still had humans patrolling the perimeter."

"Spilt milk, Craig, spilt milk." Commander Cole lamented.

"Have you made the call?" Craig asked.

"No. I waited for you. You're his contact."

Craig picked up the phone and punched a button.

"This is Agent Craig Wright. CSC50782 . . . Yeah. Get me the mayor of Vamp Town. Now!"

The line clicked over to some recorded music. Craig had been put on hold, to which he rolled his eyes and sighed deeply. *Fucking budget cuts.*

"Agent Wrigh . . .,"

"Yes, Alex, we ha . . .,"

"Sir, this is Rendel. I'm the operator. The mayor doesn't respond to our call."

"Shit. Okay, keep trying and patch his call through when he does."

"Will do, sir."

Commander Cole's eyes were fixed on the screen, trying to will the figures to change into a herd of sheep running downhill to their slaughter instead of humans. "Keep me informed, Agent Wright."

"You know it, ma'am."

Grabbing Liz's arm, Craig turned and headed up the terraced floor of Control to the door. "Come on, Adams. We gotta gear up."

"Gear up?"

Chapter 13

HUNGER

T HE DOOR OF the Bucket of Blood swung open with little resistance when Dick gave it a push. A bell at the top of the door tinkled, welcoming the new customers. As Dick inched the door open wider, a beam of light from the setting sun snuck into the dimly light bar, casting itself into a place that it had not been allowed to visit in ages.

The bartender barely had time to hold a tray up to shield his face when Dick abruptly exposed the shadowy interior to the waning light of the setting sun. Two old regulars, seated at the far corner of the counter, hastily ducked behind the wood structure to hide from the sudden exposure to the daylight.

"Hey! What gives?" One of the old guys complained.

"Shut the fucking door!" The other yelled. "You want to cook us?"

The bartender peeked over the top of the tray at the intruder and saw the limited intensity of the light invading his bar. There wasn't enough oomph remaining in that ray of diminishing sun to burn his skin or cause any noticeable vapor to rise off of his exposed skin, so he lowered the tray, then looked with surprise at the bus passengers crowding their way through the door. "Well, get yourselves inside and close the damned door. The flies like it in here too!" The bartender barked at them.

Startled, Dick moved out of the tiny vestibule and further into the bar, making room for the others to enter. Paul limped in last and closed the door as requested. No, ordered. The bell merrily tinkled as the door banged shut.

The lost and now wary passengers stood in a tight, defensive cluster as though they were the 300 Spartans ready to take on Xerxes at Thermopylae. This bit of life, discovered in the last building they checked, was disquieting. After what they had seen of this empty town, to be standing in a perfectly preserved 1960s-era cocktail lounge was another non sequitur in a day full of them.

They were in a 60s retro heaven. Satellite-style light fixtures orbited over the bar; the front of which was covered in tufted black vinyl. The low back stools were similarly upholstered and tufted but in red upholstery. The same red vinyl could be seen in booths that lined the back wall. Sparkling, red-orange lamps hung like rough-cut plastic jewels over these comfortable cubbies, emanating a dim, warm glow while directing a soft beam of light directly down onto the tabletops, giving them the illusion of self-levitation. An interesting mix of Tiki and Space-age looking decorations adorned the walls. The dark ceiling was bespeckled with tiny bits of reflective glitter, allowing for the feeling of a star-studded galaxy.

The room was dark even with the table lighting and the strings of colored Christmas lights which were festooned from the ceiling. The effect was that of a very secluded hideaway. With the door closed, there was no way of knowing if it was night or day since the windows had been painted black.

The air was stale, and there was a smell; an odor of something funky that attacked their noses. Funky wasn't correct. Malodorous was more the word as though this room had within it the decaying remains of something ancient. It wasn't quite the acrid stink of death, nothing that intense, but there was an underlying fetid scent that was impossible to ignore. Maybe it was just that the door was always kept closed, and no fresh air was ever allowed to enter this atmospheric joint.

The doorbell tinkling behind Paul signaled to the old regulars that the last offensive ray of sunlight had receded from the interior and that the blessed gloom had returned. They cautiously raised their heads above the bar top. What they saw was an interesting surprise, indeed. One gave the other a nudge with his elbow while he licked his lips.

Dick stepped further into the bar. "Hey, what gives around this town? Where is everyone?"

The O'Neils stepped from behind the group and came forward. Marion spoke up, "Our daughter is starving. Are you still serving lunch?"

The bartender leaned over the bar top, getting closer to the passengers. He inhaled deeply and savored the smell of the warm bodies standing in front of him. He spoke with a slight but noticeable Irish accent. "Can't say when the last lunch was served in here or dinner or even the last time we had guests join us for a meal." He shot the regulars a wink and a grin. "It looks like that's about to change in a hurry."

The bartender and the regulars laughed at this, likely, inside joke, then he turned back to Marion. "Food that you would eat? I think I may have something in the back . . . but drinks that I have plenty of." He picked up a bottle of whiskey and set it on the bar top. "How's about I pour something for you to enjoy while I see what I can scare up?"

"We'll pass on the booze, but water and food would be great," Paul said, stepping from the back of the group. "And since it's getting dark, we sure could use a motel. Can you tell us where to find one?"

"Name's Sean," the bartender said, giving Paul a visual appraisal. *He's a tough one, but the limp makes him easy prey,* he judged. "Since it's almost dark out, you won't have to wait too long before the innkeep shows up and she can take you there herself." He turned with a smirk towards the regulars, who were laughing with him at yet another joke.

"We've walked all around your town and didn't see a motel. Where was it?" Wilson asked.

"Oh, I'm sorry. Motel, hotel. The difference means nothing to me. The hotel is around the corner on Third."

"We walked that side of the block and didn't see any hotel sign. Right?" Dick said dubiously.

"You're right. No hotels." Wilson agreed.

Steph and Ellie both nodded in agreement with that, too.

The bartender lowered his voice like someone was listening. "Ah, look, this is a small town, as you have discovered. There isn't a lot going on here that brings in money. The hotel isn't quite legal. Off the books, if you know what I mean? So there aren't any signs. You pay cash, and you've got a room." He gave the group a pleading look. "I know we're avoidin' taxes, but it's the only way to make it out here."

Dick stepped up to the bar so that he and the bartender were almost face to face and said to him sympathetically, "Hey, I get it, dude. We all do. Right?" He turned back to the others, who smiled and nodded. "We're just tired and hungry. First thing in the morning, we're out of here. Okay? No trouble."

The bartender broke into a big smile. "Okay. But leaving won't be necessary."

"Or possible." One regular said under his breath to the other. His buddy gave him a visible elbow to the ribs.

Paul had been watching and listening to these "private jokes" and was becoming uncomfortable with the whole situation. "You know, maybe we should get back to the bus. Someone is probably looking for us right now."

"Why?" Steph protested. "They have rooms for us to use. Sleeping on that bus sucked."

Not as much as it's going to suck here, lassie, thought the regular with a sinister smirk.

"Yeah, if you could call it sleeping," Kelvin said. "I spent more time trying to get comfortable than I spent sleeping. My back deserves a soft bed."

"My poor baby." Jenna stroked Kelvin's head in mock empathy.

"Mommy." Cindra pulled on Marion's arm again. "I'm hungry!"

"And I had the weirdest dreams... A man... Red eyes," Ellie added, losing herself for a moment as images of her dream returned.

"Yeah, me too," Steph said, surprised that she shared a similar experience. A vivid memory of a dark man touching the window she had rested her head against trying to sleep. She could feel the sensation of her hair being stroked. The recollection sent a chill down her spine.

The bartender gave Cindra a lecherous smile; eyes filled with restrained desire. Feeling the strange energy emanating from him, Cindra retreated behind Marion. "And how can we let the little princess not have any dinner? Let me check out what I have hiding in the back room and get you fed. We can figure out how to serve the rest of you later." He turned and brushed through some curtains that hung across the door opening.

The bus passengers were left standing with the two regulars staring at them. The whites of their eyes were yellowed and cloudy with age. Within them floated islands of black pupils that drilled into each of the travelers, sizing them up. Studying them. One whispered to the other, and they giggled like schoolgirls. Then the other had something to add, and the giggling continued.

———◦◦◦———

THE BARTENDER DREW the curtains closed behind him as he entered the superfluous back room—built as a kitchen with a sink, fridge, stove, and other items used for food prep. All were covered with a thick layer of dust, not having seen any service in years, if ever at all. Cobwebs showed that the only living things in here were spiders.

Floor-to-ceiling shelves stood along two of the walls holding pots, pans, dishes, and other utensils. There were also stacks of canned food. The bartender moved over to one shelf. He pulled down a couple of cans and looked at them. All were of a uniformly olive drab color with plain, black stamped lettering. He placed several cans on a tray and wiped the accumulated dust off with his towel to read the contents stamped on the tops. *Ham and Lima Beans In Juices. B-2 Unit Crackers and Cheese Spread. Peanut Butter.* Oh, *Pound Cake.* Now the little one should like that. He pulled a couple more cans down and placed them with the others. *Beef Hash. Pork and Scalloped Potatoes.*

Honestly. How could humans stand to eat this stuff? The last army food he had eaten was as a soldier in His Majesty's 60th Foot fighting Napoleon. At least that food wasn't canned, though canned was probably better than the rotting horse he had to eat. No matter, he was reasonably confident that they wouldn't have much of a chance to eat any of it anyway or complain to the "chef." Besides, he was just going through the motions of accommodating the bleeders until the others arrived. *Then let the games begin!*

The bartender stacked a few plates on top of the cans and grabbed a random handful of silverware. Stopping to ponder the irony of giving silver to a bleeder, he chuckled. *Good thing it's stainless.* Then he lifted the tray and took it out to the front of the house, where he deposited it onto the countertop in front of the passengers. The silverware fell off and scattered, clattering onto the hard surface. "Sorry, no can opener."

The regulars laughed with gusto.

Steph stepped up to the bar. "I'll take that drink if you don't mind." She pointed to a bottle on the shelf. "That a Merlot?"

Without looking back at it, the bartender responded, "No, darlin'. It's kind of a local specialty that takes some gettin' used to if you're not so inclined. You look more like a whiskey kind of gal, anyway." He poured her a shot. "On the house."

❖

OUTSIDE THE BUCKET of Blood, the sun had almost entirely set. Darkness was quickly moving in from the east, bullying the last of the sun away until there was only a slight glow of orange hugging the top of the western hills, then it too was gone, and the cloak of the night covered Fox Valley yet again.

As if there were a chime sounding simultaneously on a hundred different alarm clocks, the residents of this tiny burg began to emerge from the empty buildings. They filtered out the doorways of the vacant shops, empty offices, and deserted houses filling the streets while they took in the fresh evening air. They stretched and loosened their limbs after a long day of repose. Some twirled and danced around in joyous freedom from having been cooped up in stuffy quarters. Others stood clustered together in groups or sat alone, watching the stars appear in the sky.

Several stainless-steel hospital carts were rolled out onto the street. On them were trays full of flat plastic IV bags: tubes from the tops flopping over the sides. The bags contained a thick red liquid and were lined up like CDs in a music store: easy to flip through to find the right selection. White labels applied to the bags had large black printed letters identifying types: *O, A, B,* and so forth.

One man stood and flipped through the bags at one cart and then the next, clearly frustrated. "Who keeps taking the AB positive?"

A woman waltzed up to him, a tube running into her mouth from a bag labeled *AB+*. She sucked in the blood, smiled coyly, and then sashayed away, revealing another AB+ bag concealed behind her back, and gave it a little flip, teasing the man to join her. He hurriedly grabbed one of the other bags from the cart and followed her.

Another man leaned against a mailbox and drained a bag, letting the contents ooze out of his mouth. He closed his eyes in near ecstasy as the sweet coppery elixir slowly trickled over his chin and down his neck, attracting a woman who came up to him and began licking the red syrup from his throat. She then unbuttoned his shirt and licked the blood from his chest, which was rising and lowering in excited anticipation as her tongue followed the stream back up his neck and then to his lips. Red, dripping tongues swirled around one another, darting in and out of their mouths in a lusty tango. Long canines flashed in the darkening evening as the licking developed into a biting game reminiscent of puppies at play.

Around the town, other such dramas were transpiring, reenacting this nightly ritual of coming together, feeding, and sexual release. After "mealtime," the locals drifted off in search of other pursuits. Some preferred isolation and wandered away alone. Others stood around in groups of twos and threes, idly chatting. One couple walked, hand in hand, down the street; passing a red bag back and forth as if they were sharing a malted milk at a soda fountain. Still, others sat down with leather-bound books and read.

Vladimir watched these scenes of life play out around him while he finished licking the sweet red liquid off the lips of the countess. He gently sank his fangs into the side of her exposed neck, puncturing the skin ever so slightly, sucking in a small amount of her blood. The bite caused her to make a sharp intake of breath and then let out a moan of desire. He stroked her golden hair and then cupped her breast in his hand. He kissed her passionately, releasing her own blood back into her mouth. She swallowed, and he licked the remains from her lips.

"Until tomorrow, my lovely," Vladimir said in a soft, enticing tone.

"Yes." The countess responded as she dreamily sauntered over to a small group who had gathered nearby.

Vladimir straightened his shirt and tidied up a bit before he, too, walked over and joined them. These were his people; his hardcore supporters who believed, along with him, that the treaty his brother signed with that bombastic blood sack was not in the race's best interests.

These were the malcontents. They resented living in this depressing, fake town, this prison. The so-called life they experienced here went against the very nature of a vampire. Roaming the earth and freely choosing their prey, stalking it and deciding when to pounce and feed, then languishing in the satisfyingly warm aftermath, was what a vampire was born to do—not slurping blood out of a plastic bag through a straw at preordained hours like a frail human on life support.

These malcontents held the other inhabitants in disdain as they tried, sadly, to act like the humans they no longer were. Holding hands! Reading? Staring at the stars. Romantic claptrap! Those were the weak ones, blindly following whatever Alexei wanted. To be sure, these iconoclasts also, lamentably, felt the uncontrollable urge to do the Khan's bidding. The cursed imprint of thousands of years of shared species memory was impossible to shake off. In this, they conceded Alexei had the strength of will to hold them here and keep them from flying off, but he couldn't control their desires which were always focused on leaving, escaping the confines of this valley, and the mental grip of Alexei's will.

They held together as a group based on this focused goal and waited for Vladimir to challenge his brother and free them all from their confinement. Right at this moment, they watched their master walking toward them; each sensing that something was different about him tonight. He seemed to hold himself taller. His body was less tense and more relaxed. The closer he got, the more they could read a confidence in his demeanor that wasn't always present. Vladimir seemed to radiate an aura of strength and power that sent chills down their spines. When he finally stepped into their little circle, they surrounded him, wanting to absorb what he was exuding.

"My friends," Vladimir said, looking into each of his follower's eyes. "Let us proceed on to that lively night spot we call the Bucket, shall we? I feel like celebrating." There was general agreement. Vladimir turned to a huge Samoan fellow and grabbed his arm in a sign of brotherly affection. "What say you, Apelu?"

"I say, lead on my master."

"We go together as brothers," Vladimir responded, draping his arm around the large man's shoulders. The two stepped across the street as one. The others of the group excitedly followed, leaving the losers, Alexei's "lemmings," to their pathetic, make-believe lives.

When they rounded the corner, Vladimir stopped abruptly. He inhaled, catching a scent on the wind, then drew in another, deeper, breath and turned towards the Bucket of Blood. One more satisfying intake of the aroma of fresh warm blood, and he smiled with satisfaction. "Do you smell that, my friends?" The others mimicked Vladimir. "That is the redolence of a special treat. I had hoped that they would join us tonight, and here they are just in time for dessert, too. Come!"

IN AN ATYPICAL reaction, Wilson slammed his hand down on the bar top. "What the hell do you call this?" He held up one of the cans. "And even if this was still edible, you didn't bring a can opener. My daughter is hungry and wants some actual food!"

"Don't we all, brother." A regular spouted off.

Paul stepped to the bar and looked at the canned food. "Where did you get this stuff? An army surplus store?" He looked at the bartender. "You guys, a bunch of survivalists?" He held up a can, showing it back to the rest of the passengers. "This is a U.S. Army issue ration." He looked closely at the can. "I'm no military history buff, but this shit isn't anything like what they feed us grunts in the field today. This looks like something from the fifties or sixties. Maybe even World War Two."

Dick pushed forward, getting into the bartender's face. "Trying to poison us, are you?"

"Now, why would I want to taint your blood like that?" the bartender answered.

Paul reached to his belt and pulled a Leatherman multi-tool out of its sheath. He handed it to Wilson. "You know how to use the can opener on this thing?"

"Like the ones on a pocketknife. Right?"

"Yep, the same. I think that the cheese spread and crackers would be the safest to try. Maybe the pound cake. At least stay clear of the meat products, but that could be true even if this stuff had been canned yesterday." Wilson took the tool and the cans of food with his family over to a table and opened them for his daughter.

The little bell jingled its welcoming tune as the front door opened and the group with Vladimir began to filter into the Bucket of Blood. With every bump of the door, the bell would merrily dance and tinkle again. As they entered, the locals found the tiny vestibule blocked by the bus passengers, whose intoxicating bouquet of fresh, warm blood permeated the vampire sanctuary.

They deliberately walked through the knot of passengers, savoring the moment, eyeing each one as though they were buying cattle at auction: mentally assessing the stock, noting body types, health status, and temperament of each animal, determining which would fetch the highest price. Having made their appraisals, they moved to the back of the room and clustered at the end of the bar with the old regulars where they compared notes, excitedly speaking with one another in subdued tones, pointing and nodding towards the bewildered passengers. The charged atmosphere in the bar was palpable.

The new arrivals crowded the counter, giving their orders to the bartender. Eyes darted back and forth to the passengers; trying to figure out why so many humans were standing in their bar. Several shots of the local favorite were poured and downed. By the third round, loud, inebriated chatter filled the air, which none of the passengers could make out. However, by the way they were being studied, it was undeniable that they were the chief topic of the conversation as first one pair of eyes would turn back towards the passengers and then another. At one point, all the locals suddenly stopped talking and silently stared at the stranded group.

"I don't think that they get many visitors here?" Jenna said under her breath to no one in particular.

"Kind of obvious," Paul replied.

"Well, my Spidey senses are tingling. I can tell you that." Kelvin chimed in nervously.

The bell on the door dinged happily as it swung open again. The Samoan, Apelu, entered and joined the blabbering group of vampires at the back of the bar. A few steps behind Apelu, Vladimir entered, exuding an air of commanding confidence that all in the room could feel.

Vladimir appeared to be in his late twenties. He was an extremely handsome man, fit with flawless pale skin, strawberry-blond hair, and eyes of ivory surrounding deep black obsidian pupils. He walked past the passengers, giving them no attention, and joined the locals at the end of the bar. He grinned and nodded to his people as though he was saying, "See what I brought you?"

He purposely looked across the room at Steph. When their eyes connected, Steph had an overwhelming feeling of déjà vu. *Was this the man I dreamed was studying me through the bus window last night?* She wondered. The man with red eyes and piercing black pupils. How could that be? It had to have been just a dream; that man was floating, hovering over the ground. But she could still feel his fingers running through her hair, imploring her to let him into the bus. It was so real.

As Vladimir turned towards the bar, the locals stepped aside, making space for him, acknowledging his status. He leaned against the counter and ordered a shot of the house specialty. The bartender poured the thick, dark red-looking liquid into a glass. He slammed it down, asking for another. Again, the glass was filled. With drink in hand, he turned around, leaned back against the bar, and gave all the passengers a slow and steady once-over, focusing on Steph, who had not stopped looking at him since he had arrived. Vladimir gave the glass a vigorous swirl, held it up to the light, and looked through the liquid as it clung to the side, appreciating its legs. He put his nose down into the opening and inhaled sharply, taking in the bouquet.

Then he placed the glass against his lips and tipped it ever so slightly, letting the thick red liquid just barely touch them. His tongue slid out of his mouth, and he tasted what was on his lips, smiling as he appreciated the vintage.

Satisfied that it was a drink worthy of his attention, Vladimir let the remainder flow into his mouth, rolling it over his tongue and allowing it to slowly drain down his throat.

Setting the glass down, he tilted his head over towards the bus passengers and asked, "When did these tasty morsels arrive?"

One of the bar regulars reported, "Just got here as the sun was setting. Say they're off of a broken-down bus up the highway a bit."

Vladimir smiled. "Yes, the ones I saw last night. Has anyone informed Alexei?"

"Nope. Wanted to wait till you arrived. Didn't want a perfectly good social activity to be spoiled by your brother," the bartender responded.

"Excellent. Let us keep this party to ourselves, then, shall we?"

Vladimir gave a nod to Apelu. The giant Samoan finished his drink and gave the passengers a knowing smile as he walked past them, heading for the entrance. At the door, the bell tinkled as he opened it to check outside to see if Alexei or one of his "people" were about to enter. Satisfied, he closed it, reaching up to silence the annoyingly happy little bell. Then Apelu threw the lock with a solid thunk and turned his imposing figure back towards the room and crossed his arms guarding the door. The look on his face dared anyone to challenge him.

Paul gave Apelu a hard stare and turned to Wilson. "You recognize that guy?"

"That big Asian? No. Why?"

"He's a Samoan. I think he used to play in the NFL. Rams maybe. I know for a fact he went to Cal, no, UCLA."

Wilson shook his head. "Sorry, football isn't my thing."

"Why do you think he's living out in the middle of nowhere, Oregon?"

Wilson shook his head again and shrugged.

—◦—

VLADIMIR SLOWLY SURVEYED the passengers. Yes, these were the humans that he had observed on the bus. He could not taste them last night since they were so rudely shut up in that contraption and no one had the manners enough to invite him in. Thoughtless people. The world today was so much different from that of the past, so impersonal.

They were all here, well, not all. Vladimir had gotten acquainted with the driver earlier. He still felt energized by the infusion of the fresh blood, though it was a little on the sour side. Older donors tasted a bit "off," not like the warm sweetness of youth. Vladimir's gaze drifted back to Steph, and he smiled, imagining biting into her smooth skin.

Vladimir reflected on what a fortuitous gift these mobile blood repositories were. After tonight, he knew nothing would remain the same, as long as Alexei didn't arrive and spoil things, that is.

He studied the unsuspecting humans, determining their fates, and decided that he would distribute them to a few of his favorites.

The typical American family with the little one. He watched the husband fumble with opening a can. Yes, they should go to the Wainwrights. That would be fitting. Vladimir looked at Charles and Amanda and gave them the nod that the family was theirs.

The capable man? Vladimir draped his arm around the countess' shoulders and whispered in her ear. She smiled as she looked over at Paul and licked her lips in anticipation.

The lesbian and the odd man were a matched pair and should be appreciated as a matched pair. Vladimir gave Helena and Kurt silent permission to pursue their needs with those two.

The troubled one and his girlfriend. These two would be shared among the rest of his people.

That left the attractive one. She was reserved for himself. Vladimir had decided the first time that he saw her head leaning against the bus window, that she would not be a mere dining experience. No, the past night, when he watched her sleep, he delved into her mind roaming at will. He learned she was ready to change her life, which was the ideal ingredient for someone whom he could turn and mold to become a member of his immortal family. His gaze stayed on Steph. *Ah, yes, my prize.*

———◆———

STEPH COULD FEEL Vladimir's eyes on her, and she looked through the room to him as if summoned to do so. Their eyes locked. Steph's heart beat harder than ever before. It felt like it was going to burst out of her chest.

She watched Vladimir walk over to the jukebox and make a selection.

The sleek lines and soft, seductive lighting of the classic 1956 Wurlitzer 2000 invited touching. The library of 45s rotated until the chosen song was located and pulled up to the tonearm, and then it played.

Steph's breath became shallow. Her cheeks flushed as Vladimir sauntered up to her. In a slight Eastern European accent, he introduced himself. "I am Vladimir. Would you care to dance?"

Vladimir held out his hand, and Steph reached up and grabbed it. She stood as if hypnotized.

Steph could feel Vladimir's eyes drilling into the core of her very being, accessing the hard drive of her soul while he moved her across the floor with erotic, fluid motions.

His voice filled her head. *"Stephanie, do not fear me. I want you. And I know you want me too."*

Music from the jukebox filled the air. A song from the 1950s. It was familiar. Maybe she'd heard it on the oldies station or in a movie, but it had only been background music. A pleasant piece, but nothing to draw her attention. Now it was being used as a tool to seduce her, and it was working. Steph gazed up into Vladimir's eyes. She couldn't see anyone else. *"My love must be a kind of blind lo . . .,"* but the rest of the words and tune were lost in a blur of wild sensations. She could no longer tell if she was inside or out in some garden or on a busy street. *"Sha bop sha bop."* She lost track of time and did not know if it was day or night. Were there stars out? Were they visible or covered by clouds? She didn't care. *"Sha bop sha bop."* All Steph knew was that she was alone with Vladimir. And that was all she wanted.

His presence was instantaneously all-consuming. When Steph opened her eyes, the room was swirling around her. The colors and the lights merged into an Andy Warholesque psychedelic motion picture; objects and bodies blurred and melded together, making it impossible for her to stay focused on her perception of reality. Weren't there others with her?

Vladimir was all that she could see. He was her everything. Steph saw glimpses of her childhood, images of growing up, her mother, father. Someone else, recent. An image of Dick washed through her and dissolved as Vladimir's overpowering presence erased all that was there. It no longer mattered what had happened in her past. She was a different person now. She felt like a baby being born into a new life—a life that would never end. One meant to be spent with Vladimir.

Steph could feel him inside of her, caressing her mind, but she didn't feel violated. Instead, she felt the warmth of being wanted and loved, and that was all she desired now and forever.

———◆———

THE PASSENGERS WATCHED, mesmerized by Vladimir, smoothly swirling Steph across the floor. They could tell he totally captivated her. He moved her around the room in graceful, fluid motions. They danced as though they had been partners forever, being able to anticipate the other's moves.

The locals were also spellbound by what was playing out before them. It had been many long years since they had witnessed the artistry of Vladimir sweeping a human off her feet. They became increasingly intoxicated, watching the seduction ritual playing out in front of them as the couple danced by them again and again with Steph, the marionette, and Vladimir, the puppeteer. As he and Steph glided past the locals one more time, he looked at them and licked his lips, smiled, and revealed a set of nasty looking sharp fangs.

Steph rested her head on Vladimir's shoulder, and all that she could think about was the sound of the music and the beautiful mix of colors that filled her eyes. She looked up into his face. Everything else had disappeared from view. He sent her into a spin and then drew her back into his embrace. The music had stopped, but the pair continued to dance. Steph was now under Vladimir's complete control.

The passengers had remained huddled at a couple of tables, not quite knowing what to make of the bizarre ritual they had been watching unfold before their eyes with Steph and this Vladimir.

With all attention focused on the dancers, a local woman spoke to a man standing next to her. She then gave him a peck on the cheek, finished her drink in one swallow, and walked towards the huddled passengers. With a warm, friendly smile, she touched a chair at the O'Neils' table.

"May I join you?" she asked, her voice revealing a Midwestern accent.

Wilson looked at her and then at Marion, who nodded yes. "Please," he responded.

The woman moved the chair between Wilson and Cindra, sat, and introduced herself. "My name is Amanda." She said, looking at Cindra admiringly. "You have such a charming daughter. My husband, Charles, and I could never have children." She nodded to the man she was standing with by the bar, giving him a smile and a wave. He raised his glass and acknowledged the attention. "Oh, we would do just about anything to have a lovely little girl like yours." She reached out her hand to touch Cindra's hair and combed her fingers through it. "Such beautiful hair . . .." She said wistfully, her fingers lingering as she caressed the little girl's silky-smooth hair. Cindra remained still as stone, afraid to move.

Marion reached under her daughter's chair and drew Cindra closer to her in a protective move. The woman reluctantly withdrew her hand. "Yes." Marion said, "Having children is a blessing from God."

Amanda pondered the comment for a moment. "I guess that must be it, then. God has not seen fit to bless us for quite some time." She stood and smiled down at Cindra and reached out to touch her hair one more time, but, changing her mind, she retracted her hand and strolled back to her husband. They both ordered a house special, then leaned in to chat with the bartender looking towards the O'Neils.

Marion got a brush from her bag and pulled it through her daughter's hair as though she were combing out the touch of the woman's fingers.

This time, Charles, the husband, walked over to the O'Neils' table. He looked down at the open cans of crackers and cheese spread, lids bent back. "Sean tells us you haven't eaten and are looking for something other than these old containers of who knows what. My wife, whom you just met, and I would be honored if you came home with us for dinner and you could spend the night too."

Cindra reached her fingers into a can to fish out another cracker. "Ouch!" She winced and drew her hand away from the rough edge of the lid. Blood sprouted from the cut.

"Oh, honey, I'm sorry I didn't tell you to be careful about the sharp edge," Wilson said, fussing over the cut finger.

The room went deadly still. All eyes were fixed on the nectar that was welling up from the wound. Cindra put the finger into her mouth and sucked at the blood. Charles looked at Cindra's finger longingly. His nostrils flared with the intoxicating aroma of fresh blood and licked his lips with hunger. A band-aid materialized out of Marion's bag. With a tissue, Marion wiped off the blood and set it down before covering the wound.

Charles watched Marion going through the motions of first aid like a mark following a shell game, determined not to let his eyes off of the ball: the cut, the blood, the finger in the mouth, the tissue, the band-aid.

In an instant of unrestrained desire, Charles snatched the bloody piece of tissue off the table and held it up to his nose, then noticed the surprised looks the O'Neils were giving him. After an awkward moment, Charles attempted to regain his composure and stammered, "I'll, ah, just take care of this for you." He turned to the other locals and displayed the red-tinted tissue, flaunting his prize. Then, as one more little tease, he put it to his nose, inhaled deeply, and flashed a triumphant smile.

After making sure his daughter's hand was alright, Wilson looked up to Charles, who suddenly stopped displaying the bloody tissue and had successfully pasted a look of feigned concern on his face. "Thank you, but we don't want to impose. This food will suffice." Wilson said, spinning the can of hash reluctantly around on the table. "And I'm sure we can stay at the hotel."

"Well, if we can't offer you food, I have to tell you we have no hotel here. So perhaps a room might be attractive?"

"But the bartender said the hotel manager would be by soon. Well, not for a proper hotel but the off-the-books one. We totally understand the legal and tax implications and won't say a word."

"Sean? He told you that?" Charles looked over at the bartender, who just shrugged his shoulders and gave a weak grin. "Sean's such a kidder. Irish humor. Please consider the offer. We would love to spend a bit more time with your daughter and have you both for dinner."

Cindra's eyes grew wide. She shook her head and spoke to her mother in a loud whisper. "No, mommy. I don't want to go. Can't we go back to the bus?"

Marion smoothed Cindra's hair in a consoling way. "Honey, I think meeting new people would be good for us, and I have to admit, a bite and a bed sound awfully tempting."

Taking Marion's statement as the word from on high, Wilson looked at Charles. "Well, you heard from the boss. We'd love to."

Charles waved over to Amanda, letting her know the deal was set. She raised her glass in acknowledgment and came back to the table to join them all.

"Great! We just live down the street."

Marion and Wilson started gathering their belongings. Marion looked at Cindra, who had not moved. "Come on, sweetie. We're going to the . . .." She looked at Charles.

"Oh, my apologies. We're the Wainwrights. I'm Charles, but you already know that, and the missus is Amanda." Amanda had joined them and offered her hand to shake.

"Pleasure to meet you," Marion said while shaking Amanda's hand. Marion arched her eyebrow when she touched Amanda. "Oh, your hand is like ice. Look, if you aren't feeling well, we can . . .,"

Charles held out his hand to Wilson, who took it. "Nonsense. Amanda always runs a little cold-blooded after the sun goes down." He said, grinning.

"And what would your excuse be?" Asked Wilson upon noticing the chilled skin of the hand he was shaking.

"Oh, a heart condition. Runs in the family."

Wilson nodded understandingly. "And of course, you've already met our daughter Cindra."

"Oh, we have. My wife has taken a shine to her. It's strange, but Cindra is so much like our daughter."

Marion stopped putting on her coat with a puzzled look and said to Amanda. "Didn't I hear you say that you didn't have any children?"

Amanda stood tongue-tied. "Well, yes, I, I'm, um . . .."

Her husband put his arm around her and held her close. "Amanda has trouble acknowledging things that have happened to us in the past. We lost a daughter to cholera. She was so young and vulnerable. It affected us deeply. Amanda pretends that we never had a daughter to lose," he said sadly and hung his head low. There was an uncomfortable pause.

Wilson broke the dark moment with fake cheeriness, clapped his hands together and said, "Well, then, I'm looking forward to a good night's sleep, not to mention whatever specialty you will serve up for dinner. Marion?"

"Oh, yes. Come on, Cindra, let's get going." She helped her daughter with getting on her coat and then followed Wilson and the Wainwrights as they made for the exit.

Before the Samoan unlocked the door, Paul stopped Wilson and pulled him aside. "I heard him mention something about cholera. My history is foggy, especially on medical issues, but I think that the last significant cholera epidemics in the United States occurred in the nineteenth century."

Wilson gave Paul a blank stare.

"Think about it, Wilson. These people can't be older than in their late twenties. And look at Steph." The song on the jukebox had finished, and Vladimir had left her to replenish his drink, but she remained in the middle of the room, swaying to music that no one else could hear. "Don't tell me there isn't something strange going on here."

Wilson brushed Paul's hand off his arm. "Look, my family is hungry and tired. There is no place to spend the night other than accepting the kindness that is being offered. I can't give them much more, but this I can give them, so stay out of our business. Okay?" he said, handing back Paul's Leatherman.

Paul tried one more time. "Why do you think that big Samoan goon is standing by a locked front door? Is that to keep someone out or us in?"

Irritated with Paul, Wilson broke away and rejoined his family. Apelu unlocked the door and swung it open. The bell dinged its merry tune, wishing the O'Neils a good night.

Paul called out to the O'Neils before they cleared the opening. "Hey, let's meet back at the police station at 8 a.m. Okay? We can figure things out fresh in the morning."

Charles led the O'Neils out the door with Amanda taking up the rear of the group, ushering them outside. Amanda turned to Paul. "Oh, don't worry about them. We're night people, but we'll make sure that they're put down early." She turned back to the other locals, winked, and smiled. Her lips parted slightly, revealing her fangs as she prodded the O'Neils out the door.

Again, the bell dinged its little tune when the door closed. Then Apelu reset the lock and stood with his arms crossed, making it clear that the other passengers were staying inside.

With that, the locals at the end of the room resumed their chatter. Laughter erupted as the occasional eye sneaked a peek at the stranded and, now apparently, imprisoned passengers.

Paul sat down in a chair with his back against a wall; the room laid out before him. Without knowing the threat, he sensed that nothing good was going to be happening tonight, and he didn't want to be caught off-guard. He reached around his back and felt for the driver's 9mm. Paul hoped he wouldn't have to use it, but the signs were pointing to the potential need. *Just in case.*

Chapter 14

ACTION TEAM

C SC AGENT CRAIG Wright busted out the front entrance of Control-West. He was a man on a mission. His Rez was now the center of trouble, and Craig had no intention of freezing his butt off in Northern Alaska or Antarctica even if global warming was melting it down to the rock of a continent that it was. He just hoped that not too many people would have to die before he could contain this problem; though he knew that at least one had already and that more probably would too.

The door Craig just slammed open quickly closed before newly minted agent Liz Adams could slip through it. *Thanks*, she thought sarcastically. Adjusting the bag which had been handy for carrying all the reading material had now become a liability: one she was going to have to jettison soon. She didn't believe that gearing up included any part of this bag or its contents.

Liz hit the crash bar hard and hurried to catch up with her new partner as he made straight for the entrance of the concrete structure that stood several yards ahead of them. He had a head of steam built up and was moving at full tilt. The whole idea of going out on an action on her first day was messing with her equilibrium. What was she being thrown into? Did she have to go up against vampires, actual vampires today, right now?

Totally distracted by these thoughts, Liz felt something slip from the open bag. She stopped in time to grab some errant papers which were making a disorderly escape and be distributed by the wind throughout the base. Now would be a good time just to unload the bag right here, but these were secret documents. *Shit!*

Liz saw Craig getting further away from her with each determined step, but she paused. The voice of Master Sergeant Terry was close to the surface of her consciousness. She put the bag down and made sure that all the documents were inside and that the flap was secure. She wondered what Agent Wright must be thinking when two feet appeared on the ground in front of her. Looking up, Liz saw Wright looking at her. His expression gave the answer to that question.

Craig stood over Liz and watched her finish securing that damned bag. He thought again of his last partner, Katherine—her death, and she had been experienced. The urgency of the moment became dulled by the thought that Liz was an untried agent going out into the field for the first time; a situation that wasn't good for the action team, for him, and most of all, potentially, for her. He took in a calming breath, but the concern and frustration in Craig's voice could still be heard as he spoke to her. "Listen, you gotta stow that stuff and pay attention to the task at hand. I don't have time to teach you all you will need to know right now, but this one thing I will tell you. If you don't focus and stick with me, you may very well be experiencing your first and *last* day with the CSC. And I'm not talking about getting sent back to a desk."

Liz stood up straight when she heard that.

"Are you catching my drift, Agent?"

Liz picked up the bag and shouldered it.

"Yes, I am." He just called me an agent!

"Good. We're going to the armory where we will join the Action Team. From there, we will board an Osprey and head to Vamp Town. I will brief you more when we are en route. So, stay frosty. Watch me. Do what I do. Copy?"

"Loud and clear, sir." *He called me an agent!*

Craig turned and rushed towards the armory door. Liz followed him right on his heels, bag under control, and hanging over her shoulder.

Directly inside the armory, they stopped in a vestibule where Craig passed his security card against a box next to a door. The light on the lock shifted from red to green. He opened the door, allowing Liz to pass through first. On the other side was a reception area of sorts. A desk, occupied by an armed guard, served as interference before the open hall behind it. The guard looked at Craig and let him pass as he headed down the hall towards another door. Liz followed Craig, but the guard stood, placed a hand on his sidearm, and stopped her.

"Sorry. ID?"

Liz's eyes flashed wide open. When Agent Wright had gotten the phone alert, he ran out of the commissary just saying that she should follow. Dazed, all she could do was cram everything that was on the table into her bag without thinking, and chase after him as fast as she could. Now she was being asked to produce her security card that was deep somewhere inside the mess that was her bag. She huffed as she dropped the bag down on the desk and started fishing.

Craig stopped halfway down the hall. He turned and looked at Liz. "Come on!"

Feeling around inside the bag, Liz was having no luck at locating her ID. She looked down the hall to Craig, as she ran her hand through the bag one more time. Still finding nothing, Liz gave him big round eyes of frustration and shook her head as she desperately dug through it, again, deeper this time.

"Oh, for the love of . . .." Craig jogged back to the security desk. "Hey Edwards, she's my new partner. Agent Adams meet gent Tyler Edwards. Okay, let's go." Craig turned to leave, expecting Liz to follow.

"Sorry, Craig. You know the rules. Hell, you wrote a bunch of them."

"We have an Action Order. Protocol can wait."

"Sorry man. No card, no pass through."

Craig looked at Liz. "Find it. Fast!"

"Roger." Liz dropped her coat onto the floor, then turned the bag over on top of the security desk and emptied it out. The red folder fell out along with all the other reading material, scattering onto the desktop and floor in a flurry of paper, followed by her phone, keys, and a wallet. She gave it another shake, and a small notepad dropped out followed by a half dozen other odds and ends, and finally, a paperback dropped onto the pile, the last item to flee the satchel's crowded confines.

Craig picked up the book. *Twilight*. He grunted and tossed it back onto the pile.

Holding the open bag over the desk, Liz shook it vigorously one more time, making absolutely sure it was empty. A few coins fell out along with a breath mint. Then she rifled through the pile of stuff on Edwards' desk and stopped. From under the notepad, she pulled out the ID card dangling from a lanyard and slipped it over her head. Then Liz held her ID up to Edwards' face.

"Does this work?" she asked him in a voice tinged with sarcasm.

Edwards looked at it and then at Liz. Defeated, he nodded. "Yes. Now go save the world."

Craig was mostly down the hall when he yelled back at Liz. "Agent!"

"Coming!" Liz looked down at the collection of items scattered all over the desk. The red folder full of secret information which she had received yesterday screamed at her to grab and protect it. She looked towards the end of the hall where Craig was at the door waiting, then she looked down at her disheveled belongings and then up at Edwards. The entire process took only a few seconds, though it seemed to Liz like she was taking a physics final. Well, why wasn't this the place to be rid of the troubling bag and its secret contents? Edwards was an agent too. Right? "Nice to have met you." She said to Edwards as she turned and ran after Craig. Turning back to the desk, she called out to Edwards, "Will you watch my stuff for me? Thanks!"

Liz was already at the door that Craig was holding open before Edwards could respond. He watched the door close behind the new agents. "Yeah, sure . . . I guess." Then he looked down at the heap that Liz had left and put the items into her bag. *Tell me that's not a dirty tissue.*

━━━◦◆◦━━━

ON THE OTHER side of the door, Liz found herself in a hive of activity. Men and women were rushing to fulfill their assigned tasks. Some of the personnel were serving support functions, filling containers, going over checklists, and carrying gear to a group who were preparing to head out on the mission. Obviously, they were the Action Team.

This room was a combination of a ready room and an armory. A series of lockers lined opposite walls of the space. In the middle were long tables lined with a few benches and stools. There were seven Action Team members standing in front of their lockers changing into black ACUs, the type that SWAT or Special Ops might wear.

Liz took a moment and studied the team as they prepped for, what, battle? There was a quiet intensity about all of them as they geared up. Professionals, getting ready to go to work.

Above each locker was a small chalkboard. The first locker was empty. The black surface had been wiped in a smear of white dust. The next locker was labeled - *Sergeant Okada*. At least the three stacked upside-down Vs which were drawn next to his printed name implied he was a sergeant. A quick scan down the line of lockers showed that all the team members were sergeants.

There were two more empty lockers. The next one was identified as belonging to - *Sergeant Timmons*, followed by one for - *Sergeant Ortega*. Next to Ortega's locker, the chalkboard read - *Sergeant Ellingson*. She was already dressed and checking the edge of a katana for sharpness.

At an empty locker next to Ellingson, Liz stopped. The name of Swanson was written in white chalk as all the others, but there was a piece of black ribbon applied diagonally across it. A photo, apparently of Swanson, was on the top shelf of the locker. Inside the main alcove below the shelf where his ACU and belts would hang sat an empty pair of combat boots with an upside-down rifle. On top of the rifle butt was a helmet facing out into the room. A fallen warrior memorial. A folded U.S. flag rested solemnly on the toes of the boots. A rosary, along with a set of dog tags, hung from the grip of the rifle.

After another empty locker, she saw Sergeant St. Jean checking himself out in a mirror getting ready to head into Boise and paint the town red. At the locker next to St. Jean, Susan Todd gave him a poke in the arm. "What the fuck? Do you think some cute vampire's going to go for an asshole like you who's just going to kiss her and ram a clove of garlic down her throat? Really?"

St. Jean finished combing his hair and checking himself before he turned to respond. "Darlin', I take it when and where I can. Want some?"

"As if. Your hands are too small," said Todd, and turned back to her locker and finished her prep.

Standing at the next locker, Sergeant Matt Ortega chimed in, "Hey St. Jean! You told me I was your one and only. What gives?"

At the end was Sergeant Evers. He saw Liz standing frozen in front of Swanson's locker and walked over to her. Quietly he said to Liz, "Swanson. Lost him a couple of nights ago at Site-Delta." Then he returned to his locker.

Liz had a passing thought that she wished she had met the Action Team before an emergency. Maybe even had time to work out with them. You know, just to learn how they operated and perhaps not get in their way while doing it. At least not drop her shit all over when it was time to act. Jeez, what a mess she had made already. Maybe she could buy the first round when they got back.

Many weapons covered the wall at the end of the elongated room. The hand-painted sign above designated it the "Wall O' Hurt." Every type seemed represented, from tactical assault rifles to small arms to nasty looking mini RPGs. A caged cabinet revealed shelves with a variety of gas canisters of unknown chemical agents. There was one portion of the wall devoted to "old school" weapons, which included swords, battleaxes, maces, longbows, and compound crossbows.

The team members were in various stages of zipping up their ACUs, lacing boots, and putting on body armor. They all had sidearms, some more than one, and were checking the magazines for full loads. Several were also selecting more substantial weapons from the wall. Some chose standard looking M4s; standard, except for the add-on's that must have some unique vampire fighting attributes. Others seemed to prefer old school for this work, reaching for the medieval-looking weapons available, a battle axe, spiked mace, and short-bladed broad sword.

Everyone was focused and moving with extreme efficiency. Aside from Evers, no one noticed the new person in their midst as they checked and double-checked their gear and that of their teammates standing next to them.

Liz stood in the middle of the room, watching all the activity, listening to the banter, and completely, utterly lost as to what she was supposed to do.

Craig had headed straight for his locker, completely focused on the job, shedding his jacket and tossing it onto the stool in front of it. All the lockers were an open front style like you might find in a locker room for baseball or football players, with no doors to get in the way, making for quicker changes. He grabbed his tactical vest and started strapping it on. Then he saw Liz unmoving, transfixed by the activity of the team preparing to earn their paychecks.

"Ah shit, Adams, I'm sorry. Forgot about you for a second." He motioned to the locker next to his. "This is your locker." He pulled out the vest that was hanging inside and handed it to her. "We'll sort out the details when we get back."

Liz moved in stunned silence. Her first full day as an agent and she was going straight into action. Whatever that might mean with no warm-ups or test scenarios and certainly no virtual gaming. She looked up at the chalkboard where a name had been poorly erased. *K . . . Rumsbi* or *Ramsby*? It was hard to read.

Craig noticed her lack of movement. "My last partner used this locker. I'm pretty sure that vest will fit. You look the same size as her . . .." For a brief second, Craig was looking at his last partner, Katherine, not Liz. Was it the red hair? Then he blinked, and Adams was commanding his full view. "Now come on. We've got to go do some world saving." He cracked a weak smile, but all this overwhelmed Liz to the point of inaction. He snapped his fingers. "Hey, wake up. We have work to do. I'll help you with the collar on the bird."

Craig went to the small arms section of the wall and pulled down a .357 Magnum and an HK 9mm. He set the HK and a couple of extra magazines on the table in front of her. She looked at it and the magazines, still in a daze. "It's the gun you qualified on, right? I read your file."

Liz picked up the gun, holding it close to her body. Turning slightly away from Craig, she gripped the slide and pulled it to the rear, checking the chamber. The weight of the weapon in her hand gave her a feeling of confidence, and the familiarity of the gun reminded her of the hours she had spent on various target ranges. A clarity rolled over her. She'd trained for this—well, not this, but for similar situations. Why should vampires make any difference? Confidently, she holstered the weapon. "Ready," she said.

Sliding extra magazines over to Liz, Craig pointed out, "The slugs are silver. Gotta get 'em in the heart or brain. Anywhere else will just make 'em hurt a hell of a lot, slow them down some and make them extremely angry, think wounded Grizzly bear angry."

"Copy."

The swirl of activity around Liz continued as the other members of the Action Team finished their prep: loading weapons, checking tension settings on crossbows, and making sure that the sword edges were nicely honed. Sergeant Evers was loading canisters into a Milkor, an M-32 six-shot 40mm grenade launcher. She looked at it with appreciation. She had never seen one up close but recognized it. The markings on the canisters he was loading puzzled her, though.

Evers looked up and saw Liz with the question on her face. "Aerosolized garlic, stuns 'em long enough to detain or kill."

Craig handed Liz a knife. The weight surprised her. It was light compared to the blades she had practiced with. Looking closer, she saw it was a beautiful piece of sculpted hardwood.

"Wooden stake. If a vamp gets too close, and nothing else has worked, shove it into its heart good and hard."

The surreal nature of going into a potential battle with vampires sank in and become a tangible fact to Liz. Wooden stakes? Garlic? Silver bullets? *Holy shit!*

Craig addressed the entire group. "I'm not happy that we have to do this. Vamp Town has been the one model reservation, but I guess all good things must end sometime. If we're lucky, we can get there in time to do some good. Okay, mount up!"

Support personnel opened a set of double doors. Framed in the opening was an Osprey warming up on the tarmac.

The Action Team streamed out towards the plane and then on to Vamp Town.

Chapter 15

DINNER TIME

I NSIDE THE BUCKET of Blood, Vladimir continued to dance with Steph in his seductively charming way. In fact, he had been dancing with her for almost an hour. During that time, he had repeatedly returned to the bar for another hit of the local specialty, leaving Steph to move across the floor, swaying to her internal music. Whatever was playing out inside her head was locked away from all, except the one who, by all appearances, was manipulating her.

Vladimir downed another drink and wiped the red off his lips as he looked in the direction of the bus passengers. He smiled a knowing smile that said, "Be patient, your time is coming." His confidence was infectious with his people and worrisome to Paul. Ever since the O'Neils left with that couple, he had felt that the ill-fated group of passengers was like grazing bison being stalked by wolves. The weakest would be culled from the herd first. Then the pack would move in to get at the stronger animals, the ones that gave the most fight were a more satisfying kill.

A man and woman stepped away from the jukebox. They moved in a slow, alluring manner to the song that they had chosen. *Strangers in the Night*, but it wasn't Frank Sinatra's voice singing. The silky voice plus lilting piano and strings of the Connie Francis version gave a buoyancy to the couple's steps as they walked towards Jenna and Kelvin.

The general din of the room increased with the addition of the music to the loud, intoxicated voices and exaggerated laughter of the locals, adding to the party-like atmosphere that had been developing. A party that the bus passengers felt, oddly, like they were both crashing and the guests of honor.

Jenna first felt the focused eyes of the approaching vampires drilling into her. Their smiles were inviting her to wonder about the possibility of an exciting night. Kelvin watched his friend falling under a spell cast by the approaching strangers. Then he felt their sights focusing on him, too. He resisted looking. Kelvin wanted to get Mr. Man's help, but he could no longer control himself. Powerless, he was compelled to look up at the approaching couple. Without asking, the woman sat down next to Jenna, and the man joined Kelvin. A force was holding the two friends that neither of them could explain or evade.

The woman said in an enticing voice to Jenna, "I'm Helena." She reached out for Jenna's hand and caressed it softly. Jenna's last ounce of resistance fell away, and she became lost in Helena's longing gaze.

"My name is Kurt." The man almost whispered into Kelvin's ear. His soft voice and warm breath sent Kelvin into a spin of acceptance and desire.

Paul watched this ritual unfold, not sure what exactly it was that he was seeing, but convinced that the next pair from his adopted herd was about to be harvested.

Helena slid her chair close to Jenna, keeping her eyes locked onto her prey. Words could not form in Jenna's mouth as the woman moved into her personal space and then, intimately, she lowered her head in the act of submission against Jenna's shoulder and nuzzled her neck. Jenna could feel her pulse pounding against the walls of her neck; blood banging to get out. She tried to move, but nothing happened. Her brain had lost the ability to command her limbs and her voice as well. Panic and excitement welled up inside of her. She heard her voice screaming, but couldn't feel her lips move. No one heard her. She felt like the trapped prey to the spider. Yet, she wanted to know more about this woman, this woman who, without a word, seemed to know all about her. Helena gazed into Jenna's eyes and stroked her hair, spreading a feeling of warmth through her. Awareness of the world around dissolved. Right now, it was only Jenna and her new love, Helena. Maybe this one would last for the rest of her life.

Kurt's gaze was entirely directed at Kelvin with an unwavering intensity that turned Kelvin into a puddle of jumbled-up feelings. Perhaps, he thought, he had found his chance at happiness at last. Kurt touched his knee ever so slightly, which sent an electrifying surge through his body.

Jenna and Kelvin sat next to each other, back touching back, but they were miles apart from one another. To them, the world was full of endless possibilities, and their new friends would lead them in their explorations. As with Steph swaying on the dance floor, they became fixated on personal desires, no longer in control of what happened to them next. Nor did they care.

Paul had been sitting at the closest table to the exit as was possible. The door was still being guarded by that UCLA linebacker. Saluni! That was his name. Apelu Saluni.

Paul smiled at the minor victory, remembering the obscure football player's full name. Saluni, linebacker for UCLA and was drafted in the second round by the Los Angeles Rams in '89. But why was he here? And why did he look so young? He should be pushing fifty by now. Standing there guarding the door, he didn't look any older than twenty-five. Perhaps it was the dim lighting. This guy couldn't be Saluni. No way.

The large guard caught Paul studying him and gave a knowing grin. He pulled up his short sleeve, revealing a blue and yellow Cal Bears tattoo on his impressively broad shoulder, and gave Paul a wink. Paul flashed a nervous smile at the Samoan. *Oops!* Cal, UCLA, whatever. At least he was in the same neighborhood. With that mystery solved, he turned back to the room where strange things were continuing.

To Paul's right, Jenna and Kelvin were entwined in their own worlds of intimate conversation with their new acquaintances. At least he thought that there was some conversation going on between them, though he didn't see any mouths moving; only the dreamy smiles of his friends and the knowing looks shared between the locals as though they were feeding off of each other, voyeurs to the other's conquest.

Distracted, Paul was surprised by the presence of a beautiful local woman. She sat next to him, moving in extremely close. Paul scanned the room, looking for hidden cameras. There was something just too weird going on, what with the O'Neils' departure, Steph dancing under the apparent control of Vladimir, and Jenna and Kelvin lost in their fantasy romances. Now this woman putting her impressive assets on the line to ensnare another of the flock.

She leaned into Paul, allowing him to get a good look down at her open blouse. He couldn't help himself and got an eyeful of some lovely scenery. She leaned in and whispered into his ear. "My name is Countess Marietta von Strozzi, but I prefer Marie. So much more informal. Yes?" Paul shifted uncomfortably in his chair. "Please forgive me for being so forward, but I find you to be incredibly fascinating. Are you a military man?"

He felt himself slipping into a stupor, but he couldn't stop it. The countess spoke softly into Paul's ear. Her soft breath sent a chill cascading down his spine. She swirled her fingers around his neck, loosening his collar. Paul's heart raced and his cheeks flushed. Blood was being pumped through his body at full throttle.

Then, abruptly, the countess stopped touching Paul as though she discovered he had the plague. She pushed her chair back and stood, tipping it over. Without looking back, she stormed over to the bar and drained a drink. Angrily she told the others standing near her about that jerk at the table over there, like he had said something, done something, wrong.

Paul regained his composure the instant that the countess stormed away. More importantly, he was regaining his sense of self-control. He bent down to pick up the chair, and a chain slipped out from his unbuttoned collar. Paul sat back and looked at all the locals who were giving him the stink eye. Paul touched the chain as he awkwardly tried to ignore the bar full of locals glaring at him now like he was a weirdo. Idly fingering the silver chain and the crucifix that hung from it, he stared back at them, unafraid.

Ellie had left the table where she and Dick were sitting when it became apparent that he was more concerned about

Steph's dancing partner than his girlfriend. Since then, she had been standing out of the way in a corner, leaning against the wall.

She watched Jenna and Kelvin meet their new "friends" and saw that attractive woman sitting with Paul. Ellie was surprised by how forward she was with him, almost falling out of her blouse as she did. Ellie had to admit that the woman possessed a very nice set of breasts, but *really*? Did she need to be that flagrant about showing them off? Ellie knew she was naïve concerning men, but, as far as she knew, they didn't need that much bait to get hooked. And that dumbass was letting her rub up against him and unbutton his shirt! *I had a different opinion of that one*, she thought with disappointment.

Suddenly, the local woman stood and slammed her chair to the ground; like it was a definitive statement with an exclamation point. Then she stormed away from Paul as if he were a perv.

Perhaps out of boredom, but more likely to make Richard jealous—as if anything could at this point—she wandered over to where Paul was staring blankly, playing with the chain around his neck.

"Wow, she's hot," Ellie said to Paul, sitting down next to him. "What did you say to turn her off?"

Holding the crucifix between his thumb and forefinger, Paul still stared after the woman. "Shit, I didn't say squat."

Paul focused on Ellie. "Have you noticed anything, oh, strange going on?"

"You mean before or after we found the bus driver's bloody hat?"

"After we crawled under that fence, nothing has seemed right. The way this town is laid out, finding no one until after sunset, and then the old army rations. And look at those two lovesick idiots." Paul nodded toward Jenna and Kelvin. "Those two locals sashayed up to them and have had them eating out of their hands ever since."

"Yeah, and what about that hottie who seemed to have your number?"

Paul continued to touch the crucifix, feeling the smoothness of the silver. "Yeah, what about that? It was like I had no control. Like she was manipulating me. I couldn't move or speak. I couldn't break free . . .,"

"And I saw the orbs she used to hypnotize you with."

"No, it wasn't like that," Paul said defensively.

Ellie smiled at him. "Really?" They were now facing each other.

"And Steph? That tall dude, Vlad? From the first moment he came in, he targeted her, and she hasn't been off the dance floor ever since. She even dances when there's no music. I swear it looks like he wills her to move one way and then another without talking or even touching her."

Ellie looked out onto the floor where Steph and Vladimir continued to dance. Steph's eyes were closed. Her face was unreadable, yet she seemed lost in a state of bliss, just like Jenna and Kelvin. Then she shifted her eyes over to Dick. There was no bliss on his face, only anger and jealousy as he watched Vladimir and Steph dance like Astaire and Rodgers around the room.

"He really is a good boyfriend," Ellie said when she saw Paul was looking at Dick, too.

"Save it. You just keep making up reasons not to dump him." Paul exhaled a calming breath before perusing the next words. "You seem so much better and smarter than that. I'm sorry, but it's true."

Ellie blushed and started to speak. "Well . . . I . . ."

Then Dick stood abruptly, pushing his chair back violently, and walked over to the dancing couple. He tapped Vladimir on the shoulder.

"Hey, pal. Mind if I cut in?"

Vladimir stopped dancing. Steph continued moving, circling around the two men.

Vladimir held out his hand to shake. "I do not believe we have met. I am Vladimir. And you are . . .?"

"I'm . . ."

"An annoyance." Vladimir sneered, "Now go on over to your girlfriend Mister 'Officially the Boss.'"

For a moment, Dick was back in the barn, picking up the bus driver's hat and putting it on. Blood oozed out around his forehead. In the shadows, there was motion. Tendrils of black vapor intertwined and laced together, forming a human shape, and then out of the fog, a face materialized. Dick's eyes opened wide in horrifying recognition. It was Vladimir. Impossible! *He's fucking with me*, Dick thought.

The momentary shock of this realization sent the blood rushing down from his head to his feet. He became dizzy and light-headed. He staggered back and connected with the bar, holding onto it for support. His mind was swimming with the image of the black vapor forming into Vlad's face. Dick turned away from Vladimir and Steph, trying to clear his head. As he faced the bar, the bartender arrived with a glass and a bottle of vodka.

"You're lookin' a bit peeked, lad. A shot o' this should set you straight." The bartender poured Dick a healthy amount of the clear booze, which he downed without difficulty. A second shot was poured and downed. Now Dick could feel the flush of warmth return to his cheeks, and he felt more like his old self. Dick was poured a third shot, which he grabbed and turned back to watch Steph still cavorting with that guy.

He slugged down the drink and stepped away from the bar. That additional drink inflamed a desire not to let this yokel get the best of him. He puffed up like a strutting cock flaunting his plumage, projecting a willingness to do battle with his usurper. He was going to do something about that Vlad guy; *really* do something. Now, however, wasn't the right time to act. There were too many locals in the bar to come to his defense. He'd bide his time and wait for the appropriate moment.

Dick turned to go back to his table but stopped and swung around and pointed a menacing finger at Vladimir. "I'm not done with you!"

Vladimir flashed Dick a condescending smile. "Nor I you." Then he spun Steph across the floor and continued in his dance of seduction.

Ellie gave Paul a weak, apologetic smile. She stood and moved to do her job, one she had been doing for years, and went over to join Dick, who sat fuming at how Vladimir brushed him aside as if he were a nobody. She took up her usual position next to him and sat quietly, whispering, trying to calm him down.

Paul sat back in his chair, disappointed. He thought that maybe she was listening to him. Obviously not. Nothing more to do now than watch this slowly evolving situation. Something just wasn't right around here and all this activity revolving around nine lost bus passengers could not be considered ordinary, even for the middle of Eastern Oregon. Especially here.

Ellie put her hand on Dick's knee, softly stroking it as she continued to speak soothing platitudes into his ear. He abruptly pulled away from her. "Leave me the fuck alone!" She tried again. Dick gave her a shove, and she tipped over backward in her chair. Ignoring Ellie on the floor, he stomped to the bar and ordered another drink.

Dick's sudden, explosive reaction to Ellie's attempt at calming him down surprised Paul, though it really shouldn't have. He jumped up and limped the few paces over to her, holding out his hand to help Ellie to her feet. She accepted, and they returned to his table.

As he sat, Paul scanned the room. After such a major public blowup, all eyes should have been on Ellie, but no one was paying attention. The locals were partying or watching Vladimir, and the remaining passengers, other than Ellie and himself, were lost in la-la land.

Then the two locals sitting with Jenna and Kelvin stood and extended their hands to their conquests. The next two to be culled from the group accepted the offered hands and rose out of their chairs. Then Helena put her arm around Jenna's shoulder and walked her to the door. Kurt whispered something into Kelvin's ear. They giggled and followed.

Paul quickly jumped up and reached out, putting his hand on Kelvin's shoulder, stopping him. Kelvin looked down at it like a fly had just landed there. Paul tried to say something to keep them from leaving, but the Samoan placed a finger in the middle of his chest and stopped him, shaking his head. "Not you. Just them." Paul attempted to step around the obstacle, but Apelu had several pounds on him, and it was all muscle.

Paul watched the four walk out of the bar; the bell jingled as Apelu closed it. The loud click of the lock emphasized the fact that the remaining passengers were being held captive.

By now, Dick had knocked back a couple more vodkas. Primed, he took a deep breath and stormed onto the dance floor.

Dick tapped Vladimir on the shoulder again. "Hey! Vladdy. I don't know what you're doing or what's going on around here, but it stops now! Da?"

Vladimir flashed his fangs. "Oh, very much, *da*!" Vladimir lunged. In one swift, smooth motion, he grabbed Dick by the shoulders and flopped his head back to expose his throat. Opening his mouth wide, Vladimir bit into Dick's neck and tore a sizeable chunk out, painting his lips and chin in a shiny coat of dark red blood.

Stunned, in shock, and not sure what had just happened, Dick grabbed his neck and felt the bleeding gash. He looked at Vladimir, who still held him up by the shoulders, gloating over his kill.

As he looked around the room, perhaps for the last time, Dick saw the shocked face of Ellie. Even that fuck-wad Paul was staring at him, mouth almost to his knees. The locals stood frozen, worked up into a frenzy but trying to hold back their bloody urges, waiting until they were given permission to let loose.

Dick felt the life drain out of him but, aside from the initial chunk of neck being torn out, he was surprised that there was no pain. In fact, he was light-headed and couldn't remember the last time he felt so good. In his final survey of the bar, his eyelids drooping as the last of his blood burbled out, Dick saw a mirror over the back of the bar. Focusing on the reflection, he saw himself and the blood spurting out. Reality hit. He screamed in horror at the gaping wound. In the reflection, he saw Steph still dancing, oblivious to the world around her. There was Ellie. Fear and panic oozed from her like the blood from his neck. There was that asshole . . . But where was everyone else? Awareness faded as his life poured out onto the floor. Where was Vladimir? Dick looked down and saw Vladimir's bloody hands holding him upright. He looked at the reflection again. No Vladimir. No bartender. No locals. Dick's knees buckled; his head flopped back, forcing him to look up into Vladimir's triumphant eyes who was watching the life fade from his.

Vladimir spoke softly to the dying Dick. "Do not die too fast, my friend. You are the guest of honor." Then he turned to the bartender. "Sean, who says you never serve dinner here?" He held Dick's body out to the locals. "Better hurry before your food gets cold." He let go of Dick, and his body slumped to the floor; a marionette whose strings had been cut. In the background, the jukebox was playing the syncopated music of Cab Calloway's *Everybody Eats When They Come to My House* as the theme song for this dinner party.

The locals eagerly rushed towards the fresh blood seeping out of Dick's neck. The Samoan guarding the door saw the others going for the bloody mess and licked his lips. Intoxicated by the aroma of fresh blood, he bolted from his post to make sure he got his share.

Dick's body was descended upon by the bloodthirsty locals. A school of piranha would have been put to shame at their speed and ferocity. If any last screams came from his mouth, they were muted by the sounds of vampires gorging on his body.

It didn't take long for the vampires to part out the body. There seemed to be plenty to go around. Arms and legs, hands, no matter; every piece of Dick that had any blood in it would not go to waste. The initial frenzied scramble over, everyone focused on sucking the last drop of warm liquid from whatever scrap of Dick they could before it cooled. Warm, fresh blood was always the best and tasted the sweetest and, frankly, it had been an exceptionally long time since any of them had done this . . . with a human.

Apelu's late arrival in the fray netted him the greatest prize. The Samoan felt something at his feet before he dove into the frenzy and looked down to see Dick's surprised face looking up at him. Like it was a fumbled football, he scooped up the severed head and protectively carried the prize over to the wall where he sat and happily imbibed on the choicest blood from the kill.

Steph, unaware, uncaring, smiled in her hypnotic state, swaying to the music. The Cab Calloway record had clicked off, and the Sinatra version of *Strangers in the Night* played. Steph tracked sticky, red footprints across the barroom floor, dancing circles around the wallowing locals.

With a sense of panic so acute that she was frozen into silence, Ellie could only stare at the carnage. She had just watched Vladimir tear into Richard's throat. Fear kept her glued to the chair. She couldn't move even if she wanted to; her eyes were fixed on the feeding frenzy as the locals got their pieces and chunks of what remained of her boyfriend. There was no way to comprehend what she was witnessing.

———————————◦◦◦———————————

PAUL HAD WATCHED Dick acting like a jerk in disbelief. Vladimir obviously had the upper hand, and Dick shouldn't have gone after him on the man's own turf. What the hell was Dick doing, not staying with Ellie and protecting her? Steph had made her bed, but Dick seemed to have abandoned her. Too bad—*OH SHIT! What just happened? Vlad just bit into Dick's throat! Jesus!*

Paul looked over at Ellie, who was sitting next to him, frozen with shock. He looked around the barroom. All the locals were occupied. Apelu had left the door unguarded to join in with . . . Eating Dick, but there was now a clear path to the door. Paul's military training had taught him to seize the advantage when given the opportunity and think about it later. He hopped up and grabbed his walking stick.

"Ellie. Come on, we gotta get out of here!"

She didn't respond. Paul grabbed her by the arm and pulled her up out of the chair and towards the entrance. He turned the bolt with a loud thwack and threw the door open. But Ellie was incapacitated by what she had just seen and stood rooted to the floor.

"Ellie!"

Paul gave her a quick sharp slap to the cheek, bringing her back to the reality of the situation. Her eyes flared with anger at the hit.

"What the fuck . . .?" Then she recognized Paul, and the world came back into focus.

"We gotta get outta here!" Ellie latched onto Paul's arm, squeezing it with all her might, not wanting to be separated, and together they ran out of the slaughterhouse and into the night.

The door closed shut as they left, the bell happily wishing them to have a good night.

Vladimir eyed Paul and Ellie fleeing the bar, unconcerned about their escape. Instead, he focused his attention back on Steph—first things first. There would be time for a little hide and seek later. The bleeders won't get far. Vladimir placed a hand on Steph's hip and took her hand into his as they drifted across the floor.

The locals were heady with fresh blood from the first kill they had shared in many years. They writhed around, sucking and slurping all the precious red elixir that they could find, not content to let one drop be wasted. Their appetites sated for the moment, they luxuriated in the warm stickiness of the fresh human blood.

In a fog of exaltation, Steph faintly wondered what all these people were doing rolling on the floor. Why was there raspberry syrup everywhere? And what was this man doing to her? Vladimir's gaze mesmerized her. He raised his hand and caressed her cheek and brushed back her hair. *Oh, how that feels!* His mouth moved to her neck. He kissed it, and she moaned with expectation; her heart raced at a frantic pace. She closed her eyes in near ecstasy, then she felt it. The puncture. But there was no pain, only euphoria such as she had never felt before.

His fangs connected with her artery, and as he bit in deeper, she let out a gasp. His lips formed a seal on her skin, and he sucked in her blood. Then he stopped and gently withdrew his teeth from her neck. She opened her eyes, and Vladimir was looking through them, into her soul. He smiled, blood dripping down from his fangs and lips. Her blood.

Then Vladimir bit into his own wrist, opening a vein. The red force of his life flowed out, and he offered his bleeding wrist to her. Steph looked at the blood dripping from the bite and then into his eyes. Hesitantly, she placed her lips over the bleeding wound and, slowly, then with increasing vigor, drank in the warmth from Vladimir's beating heart.

Vladimir looked down at Steph, consuming his blood, and then around at his people. Bloodlust was in their eyes. Tonight, he knew, was the beginning of the end of this charade they had been playing for over one hundred years. Tonight, Vamp Town, as their keepers sarcastically called it, dies.

Chapter 16

THREAT RESPONSE

T HIRTY SECONDS AFTER the Action Team had loaded into the Osprey, they were airborne, heading off towards Central Oregon and Vamp Town.

The MV-22 Osprey is a highly sophisticated piece of engineering that can take off and land without a runway when configured like a helicopter. As a conventional airplane, it can reach a top speed of over 300 miles per hour at 15,000 feet, and it can travel 1000 miles before refueling. Those that know these aircraft like to say of them, "It's as if a CH-46 Sea Knight helicopter and an F-18 Hornet fighter jet had a baby."

The Action Team boarded the Osprey through the rear ramp and took their places in the none-too-luxurious canvas seats that lined either side of the fuselage. For all the technical sophistication required to design and build an aircraft with rotating engines and tilting wings, the interior of the Osprey was a study in utilitarian functionality. Exposed bundles of wires and cables cluttered the ceiling, and pipes ran along the surface of the walls.

The powerful engines turning 38-foot rotors screamed as they propelled the craft forward. The ride was far from smooth, often being compared to driving an old car over a rutted gravel road. This plane was designed to get some place fast and to get people on and off the ground as quickly as possible.

The Osprey lifted off the tarmac configured as a helicopter and corkscrewed up to its optimal flight altitude. After gaining sufficient forward speed to produce lift with its wings, the pilot touched the control on the stick, and the engine nacelles tilted down, out of hover mode, and faced forward allowing the Osprey to fly like a conventional twin-engine turboprop aircraft.

The pilot gave the crew chief a call from the "front office" and asked, "Ready to go fast?" The chief gave the 'go fast' hand sign to the passengers, who then all cinched down on their straps and held on, knowing what kind of G-forces the acceleration would cause. After the appropriate altitude and a cruising speed of 260 miles per hour had been achieved, the team loosened their straps and settled in for the approximately 300-mile trip between Mountain Home and Vamp Town, which would take a little over an hour depending on wind speed, weather, or the odd UFO encounter. This luxury of time provided them with the opportunity to check their gear and weapons again. One could never be overly prepared. The rote familiarity of the process left open the door for the friendly banter of pre-mission small talk, which filled the headsets.

"Hey, Okada, you get lucky last night?" asked St. Jean.

"Yeah, 'cause I didn't see you anywhere."

"Oh. Ouch! Burn."

"Ortega and I have a bet that you're going to root for OKC tomorrow night. I say, yes." Todd taunted Evers.

"No fuckin' way. I'm old-school Sonics fan. OKC? Who's that?"

"The Storm Clouds," Timmons said.

"Thunder," Ellingson noted.

"What're you guys talkin' about? Roller Derby?" Evers said, refusing to be baited.

Okada interjected, "So, my girlfriend says that we have to get married. Then she says she wants to come to my work and meet everyone."

"Bummer. My husband still thinks I work at the base commissary," Ellingson said.

Craig and Liz were seated up front with the crew chief, close to the com and tech gear. Fighting the roar of the engines, Liz asked Craig, "Sir, how many times have you had to do this?"

"What? Do What?"

"Um, go out to Vamp Town with an Action Team."

"Oh. Ah, none. This is the first time. My first time."

Liz was more than stunned by this reply. "Then how can you remain calm? I mean, if this is your first time dealing with vampires?"

"My first time doing this at Vamp Town. Not the first time with vamps. You'll find out. We do our fair share of hunting down holdout vamps, the free radicals. Remember our chat earlier? I've got plenty of experience with that."

"Oh. Yeah." Liz began connecting some dots. "Wait. You just said that you, we, hunt vampires. Really? Like hunting Nazi war criminals?"

"Something like that, but we give them a chance to be brought into the program first."

"First? If they don't?"

"We exterminate them."

Not sure how to take in all this new information, Liz sat back calmly, as if what she had just heard was old news. On the inside, however, she had other thoughts. *Holy shit! I'm going to hunt vampires!* Trying to maintain some composure, she asked Craig another question. "So, why aren't we wearing strings of garlic and crosses and stuff?"

"Well, those things work in close quarters, like when you go to bed. It starts the morning off on the wrong foot if you wake up with a set of fang marks on your neck. But, in action, if a vamp has gotten close enough for a crucifix to work, maybe, then you may as well say good night because those suckers can have you torn in two before you can shove it in their face. Let's just say, not good enough odds to count on them entirely."

The crew chief, at his control panel, handed a headset back to Craig. "Excuse me, sir. Control has a link established with the mayor."

"Thanks." Craig took the headset and put it on.

———◄○►———

THE LONE FIGURE of Alexei Rurik stood silhouetted against the last of the glowing sunset. After a day in his coffin/trailer, it felt good to stretch his legs. The sounds of the night were tuning up to perform a concert for him alone: the chirping crickets, screeching owls, the squeaking of bats. Off in the distance, coyotes were warming up for their solos and there was a slight breeze blowing through the branches of trees that probably were older than he, lay down a subtle, rhythmic bassline.

Alexei took in the incredible star field that was only visible this high up, away from the light pollution of populated areas. The waning moon had a slightly warm glow tonight. It took him back to those sun-filled days on the grassy slopes near the family dacha. The day when . . .. How long since he had felt the sun on his face?

He absorbed the light from the stars, pretending that it was the sun, and allowed nature's symphony to fill his mind with more pleasant thoughts. But not even this beauty could distract him for long from the weight of his position. As the Khan of all the vampires, Alexei had signed the treaty with Roosevelt without consulting any other of his kind. It was his decision, his responsibility, to make the move to save the remaining immortals from extinction.

Now, all these years later, he remained the leader of the reservation they inhabited. The CSC jokingly called it Vamp Town and him the mayor. Even now, he failed to understand American humor. Mayor? He was certainly no elected official. If elections were to be held, however, he wondered if he could realistically best his brother in such a contest. It was always easier to second-guess the choices one's leaders made than to wear their shoes, having to pick the best of two unacceptable options; death by hunting or slowly being strangled in pseudo captivity.

A cell phone rang, pulling Alexei back to the mountaintop.

The phone rang again. Still, in a fog of memories, it took a moment for Alexei to recognize the sound. He shook his head to bring him fully back to the present.

The phone rang a third time. Alexei reached into his pants pocket, then remembered that he had left the phone in his vest. Going back to the campfire, he grabbed the vest, pulled the phone out, and answered as it rang again for the fourth time.

"Hello?"

"This is CSC Control. Please hold for Agent Wright." The operator clicked off before Alexei could say another word.

"Hello, Alex. Do you know what's going on?" Craig asked.

"Ah, hello, Agent Wright. I am sorry for not answering right away. Some things I have been missing more after all the years are the simple moments in life, like watching the sunrise. Of course, the next best for me is to sit on the highest spot and watch the stars and the moon come out. I guess I became lost in thoughts about the past. No, I apologize. What is it I should know?"

"Sorry, bad timing. But there is no good timing for something like this."

Something like what? Oh, no! Alexei thought. "Tell me the worst."

Alexei could hear the urgency in Craig's voice. "There was an incursion into Vamp Town. Looks like nine bleeders entered your perimeter at approximately 4:30 pm. Drone flyover confirmed their position moving down the western hill and into town."

"I have been on my stargazing trip since yesterday, so I would not have known." *And no one came to find me to tell me,* Alexei reflected.

"I hope it's not too late, but I'm afraid that Vlad and his 'friends' may get their teeth into these people."

"Perhaps this is not the time for your horrible jokes but, yes, that would be a bad thing indeed. Vladimir has been growing stronger and asserting his position on others who have also become discontent. Access to fresh blood may make it hard for even me to control him and his sympathizers."

"What do you think he may do?"

"Do? Aside from having a feast. He opposed the treaty with Theodore. He sees the reservation as a prison. Without me stopping him, he is liable to leave. Vladimir on the loose in the world will not be pretty."

"Will he try to hook up with the free radicals?"

"Absolutely. My brother will try to find as many as he can and re-establish our house. No, this will not have a happy ending. I am heading back immediately. But it could be too late."

Alexei pocketed the phone and looked up to the beauty of the night sky.

⸺◆⸺

IN THE OSPREY, Craig removed the headset and handed it back to the crew chief. He sat in silence for a moment, mulling things about in his head. Liz watched as the gears in his brain worked. Wisely, she said nothing, waiting for him to do his job as team leader.

The crew chief turned back to Craig. "Sir. Vamp Town in thirty."

Agent Craig Wright sat up straight and took in a deep breath. This was shaping up to be a nastier situation than he had considered. Now it was time to get everyone ready for something considerably more dangerous than a rescue. They had to stop Vladimir from becoming the dominant vampire and going rogue.

———◆◇◆———

ON TOP OF the mountain, Alexei took one last look at the moon. He closed his eyes and wished that he was basking in the warmth of a rising sun. He took in a deep breath, opened his eyes, and returned to the reality that was his life, his immortal life, and got to work.

He closed the lid of the trailer, extinguished the campfire, and patted the hood of the vintage Army jeep. "Looks like I will be back for you later. Don't go anywhere."

Alexei raised an arm and drew it across himself and as he did, all the color erased from his body, which mutated into a dark, wispy shadow, darker than the night. The black tendrils swirled around the campsite once and then swiftly darted up into the air, disappearing against the night sky, and swept off for Vamp Town.

Chapter 17

A STROLL IN THE PARK

T HE CHEERFULLY RINGING bell on the door wished Paul and Ellie a good night as they ran out of the bar in a blind panic. In the middle of the empty street, they stopped and looked around, lost, not knowing what their next move should be. Across the street lay the unfamiliar terrain of the High Desert, now cloaked in darkness. From what Paul remembered of the landscape, there were no obvious hiding places for them beyond the limits of the town. Even if there were, finding them in the dark would be a challenge.

No, they had to find a refuge here, within the town, or try to get back to the bus, hoping to find some help along the way. Standing in the red glow of the neon open sign, they desperately looked up and down the street.

Ellie started blindly running as far from the bar as possible. Paul grabbed her arm. "No, we have to go back the way we came into this F-ed up town." Then he pulled her in the opposite direction she was headed. They ran down 4th Avenue—south—back towards the park where the passengers had entered Vamp Town. The two then turned the corner at B Street and stopped beside a near mint condition 1962 T-Bird parked across from the park. Paul eyed it appreciatively. "Nice ride." Then he reached out and touched the hood for support.

Ellie looked exasperated. "Really? We're running for our lives here, and you check out a car? No wonder that hottie rejected you."

"Sorry. Genetics." He squatted down next to the car and rubbed his bum knee. "And I just gotta stop for a moment."

Ellie lowered herself next to Paul. "You going to be okay?" she asked him.

"Wish I had that ibuprofen I left in my bag back there." He pointed his thumb back in the bar's direction. "But, yeah. I'll be fine."

The momentary pause in their situation allowed Ellie to process what had just happened. Perhaps not process so much as replaying the image, in vivid detail, of Richard's throat being torn to shreds by Vladimir. The more she watched it in her mind, the worse it got, and with it, her breathing turned into quick, shallow gulps.

Paul heard her panting for air and saw the fear on her face. He was familiar with the sound of hyperventilation and the look of panic, having been on both sides of that mask.

Paul placed a calming hand on her shoulder. He had his battle face on, grim and ready for action. She worked to calm down and get her breathing under control as she looked into his confident eyes, but after what she had just witnessed, it was too much to ask of her.

He could see that Ellie was on the brink of crashing, which would do neither of them any good, so he poked his head up from behind the T-Bird, looking for pursuers. Not seeing any, Paul lowered himself back down and wrapped an arm around the frightened woman's shoulder to reassure her he wasn't going to leave; perhaps transferring some battle earned confidence that they would survive this night.

Ellie took in a halting breath like she was stifling the urge to cry, trying to hold herself together, but then it was no longer possible, and the tears flowed. "Wha . . . what just happened? How could anyone just bite someone's neck off? God it was—"

"Horrible."

"No. It was *fucked up*! I mean . . . he, it . . . Vlad. He's not . . . human!" Ellie was starting to lose it.

Paul fingered the crucifix around his neck. With that idle gesture, a montage of images popped into his head: the dark shadow in the barn, the bloody hat, the jokes about having them for dinner, the dark red local drink, the hot local girl who was repulsed by his crucifix and, of course, Dick having his blood being slurped up by the local citizens.

"Ellie, listen to me. This is one of those lines that you will not believe but . . . These are . . . . Shit, I don't even believe it, but . . . everyone we have met in this town so far appears to be a vampire."

Ellie's eyes widened. "What the . . .? Are you *crazy*?"

"No, just listen to me. You wondered why that hottie left me alone?" Paul pulled the crucifix out away from his neck to show her. "My silver crucifix was visible around my neck. How about Steph acting hypnotized when that Vlad guy asked her to dance? Or the locals going into a frenzy when Vlad ripped out Dick's throat, and then they lapped up his blood. *VLAD RIPPING OUT DICK'S THROAT WITH HIS MOUTH!"*

Ellie closed her eyes and covered her ears like a child, attempting to block out things that made little sense. Paul grabbed her hands down.

"You're the one who just said Vlad wasn't human."

"Yeah, but that's not what I meant . . ."

"Yes, you did. I've seen some awfully inhuman shit being done by humans to humans. I can tell you that what happened to Dick was not a human act."

Ellie closed her eyes tighter, not wanting to consider this any further.

"Look at me. Whatever you call the people here, we still have to defend ourselves and help the others, if that is even possible anymore, and get out of this town." He gave Ellie a slight nudge and smiled weakly. "Hey. If they are vampires, we have only to survive until daybreak."

Ellie sniffed softly, but the shock of the situation was wearing off and awareness of their situation was sinking in. She wiped at her runny nose and looked at Paul. "Anyone ever tell you that your sense of humor sucks?"

"Not often enough."

"What are we going to do?"

"Okay. We need to make some weapons." Paul slipped his crucifix and chain over his head and handed them to Ellie. "But first I want you to wear this."

She closed his hand around the silver cross and pushed it back. "I can't. It's yours."

Paul gave Ellie a determined look and pushed his hand back to her, opened it, and dangled the chain from his fingers. The crucifix swung from it, reflecting flashes of the moonlight. "Please."

Ellie smiled and hesitantly took it.

"I stand a better chance of fighting these bloodsuckers than you do, and it might help you when all else fails."

A noise came from the park. Both Paul and Ellie reacted and peeked over the hood of the car. They saw Jenna and Kelvin with their new "friends" in the middle of the park by a gazebo.

The woman, Helena, was leading Jenna to a bench, who seemed to be in a trance as she sat down. The two women embraced. Helena stroked Jenna's hair and appeared to whisper into her ear. She unfastened Jenna's blouse, ran a hand down her neck, around her bare shoulders, and down to caress her breasts. Jenna shuddered and let out a warm breath, visible in the cool night air.

Kelvin and his "friend," Kurt, were leaning against a tree. Kelvin seemed mesmerized as Kurt stroked his cheek tenderly, unbuttoned his shirt, opened it up, and exposed his chest. Kurt lowered his head and kissed Kelvin at the base of his neck. Kelvin's chest heaved as he tried to catch his breath; his heart pounded, mainlining blood up to his head.

Both the vampires were unmistakably watching each other. One action by Helena towards Jenna elicited a responding effort from Kurt with Kelvin. They were enjoying watching each other toy with their victims as they engaged in a weird, sexually infused fantasy. The vampires worked their mouths up their prey's chests, tenderly kissing until they reached their arched necks. In unison, they placed their mouths on exposed throats . . .

Paul stood. "I have to warn them—"

The vampires both bit down simultaneously. Jenna and Kelvin gasped in ecstasy as the vampires began draining them of their blood.

"Shit!" Paul said, unable to say or do anything; a profound feeling of panic suddenly washed over him. *We are so fucked!*

The vampires watched, eyes fixed on the other, as they fed; drinking the warm, sweet elixir that had been kept from them. At first, they slowly extracted the life out of Jenna and Kelvin, savoring every mouthful.

Years of deprivation and subsisting on packaged blood or inferior animal blood vanished as they performed an ancient and essential function necessary for any living creature's survival. They were feeding, taking in nourishment. But the two were not just supping on hapless humans. They were engaging in the most intimate of rituals that vampires could share. The visual stimulation of watching the other was more than mere voyeurism. It was an act of complete gratification.

As they consumed their victim's blood, their actions became more frenzied and violent. Bloodlust overtook them. They bit, gnawed, and tore at their victim's throats. The feeding had become a savage slaughter, turning Jenna and Kelvin into bloody masses of torn flesh. The vampires wallowed in the remains of what once were two vibrant humans; gorging themselves like they had not done in a century.

Paul couldn't afford the luxury of being consumed by panic, so he pushed down the hysteria he could feel welling up. Snapping out of his shock, or just trying like hell to ignore it, he grabbed Ellie and pulled her away.

"Come on. We have to find the O'Neils."

"Where are they?"

"God, I don't know, but we gotta get off this street so we can think a bit." He turned and saw an alley between two buildings almost behind them. "Let's duck in here and regroup."

Paul and Ellie ran deep into the alley, hugging the dark shadows cast by the walls. They stopped behind a dumpster, which hid them from the entrance.

Ellie leaned against the brick structure and slid down to the ground. She shook her head and said in a shaky voice, "What the fuck?"

"Yeah, *What-The-Fuck*? I never saw this much blood in the Stan. Not even after an IED explosion. And believe me, I saw a lot of blood."

"Maybe they won't hurt the O'Neils because of their little girl. Maybe we just hold up somewhere until morning. The bus driver may have found help—"

"Ellie. Look at me." Paul said, grabbing her by the shoulders. "The driver is dead. Remember his hat with blood? I think Vlad got him. No help will be coming."

Ellie stared blankly across the alley to the opposite wall. It didn't even register in her brain that there were no old posters or graffiti visible on any surface or that this had to be the cleanest alley in America: no tires or piles of trash, no pallets or even smells of rotten food or urine.

"Okay." Paul said, "I'm not a big fan of these types of stories, so what do you know about vampires?" He did not know what they were going to do, but he had to distract Ellie from the grim thought that they would not live out the night.

Fighting down the terror that was building inside of her, Ellie tried to focus on the question. "Um, they can't see their reflections. They don't like garlic, holy water, or sunlight." She fingered the crucifix around her neck. "And crosses piss them off."

"K. Crosses are easy; we can make those with our fingers, but I doubt that there is a garlic patch around here, and the church certainly has to be fresh out of holy water." He was at a loss. "And daybreak is just too damned long from now."

"You can kill them with silver bullets."

Paul gestured with his empty hands. "Great, and I forgot to bring my gun . . ." Then he remembered and reached behind his back and withdrew the 9mm. "Well, you don't think the bus driver loaded this with silver ammo, do you?" He smiled weakly. "But this may slow them down. Right? Maybe?"

"Let's hope so." She paused, trying to dredge more weapon ideas up from the movies she had seen. "Oh! You can kill them with wooden stakes jammed through their hearts."

Paul grinned as he pulled out his Leatherman and opened the knife blade. "Now, that is something I can work with!" He picked up his walking stick and began carving one end down into a sharp point.

THE BARROOM FLOOR was a mess. It had a good coating of blood from the scattered body parts, which formerly constituted the person most knew as Dick. A handful of vampires lay about enjoying the satisfaction of having "dined" on the first warm, human blood that any had had in years. For the moment, they were content in the feast's afterglow.

Vladimir stood with Steph in the center of the bloody repast. She was still feeding off his wrist, and he forcefully removed her mouth, impressed with her suction. Once her fangs grew in completely, she would be a powerful member of his new family. He looked down at the others, wallowing in the remains of the bleeder. They felt the force of Vladimir's glare and stood, saturated in blood. Steph danced in and around them, licking the blood off their cheeks and lips as they all came to their feet.

"Come, my family. Others who have escaped, and they are yours!"

The vampires raced out the door but stopped, bunching up outside the entrance, the red of the neon emphasizing the blood that covered them. Without their leader, they were unsure of which direction to go to find the bleeders.

Vladimir exited the bar with Steph on his heels like a puppy. He lifted his nose to the air and sniffed in one direction and then the other. Then Vladimir took in a much deeper breath, and his eyes widened. He turned his gaze down the street in the park's direction and let out an eerie, screeching howl like a Great Horned Owl calling its mate. Then he pointed.

"There." He said gesturing to the south. "They are over there. Come!"

Chapter 18

ABDUCTION

THE O'NEILS FOLLOWED the local couple, Amanda and Charles, out the door of the Bucket of Blood. Marion was paying too much attention to Cindra and her whining about being hungry to have noticed, but Wilson saw that the monster of an Asian guy, Samoan, according to Paul, was standing at the door as if on guard. When Charles got close, the Samoan unlocked the door, which was weird. Why was the door locked and why hadn't he noticed when the door got locked in the first place? And what was it that Paul was doing? Was he trying to stop them from leaving? Why would he do that? But then Amanda came up from behind and ushered them all out the door and onto the sidewalk. Then the door was closed behind them, and aside from the jingle of that stupid doorbell, the other sound Wilson heard was the solid clack of the deadbolt as it was thrown back into the frame, locking the door yet again. Why? Things were not adding up. But then again, he was hungry and tired. The morning would bring a whole new perspective on the situation. Amanda and Charles led the way to their house but seemed to be in no hurry. They strolled down Fourth Avenue until they reached the park. The further they walked, the more comfortable Marion and Wilson became with the pair.

A husband and wife obviously in love with one another, Marion recognized with a bit of envy, watching the woman slip her hand into her husband's and then lean against his side, cuddling in, drawing warmth against the evening chill. Charles responded by wrapping his arm around his wife and kissing her gently on the top of her head.

They crossed B Street and paused at the edge of the park. Charles pointed diagonally across the dried grass to the middle of the residential block. "We're just over there. See it? The Mid-century modern sandwiched between the Cape Cod and the Victorian." Then the couple continued walking, cutting through the park, with the O'Neil family in tow.

Wilson looked around at the dying and wilting plants. "Must be having a heck of a drought."

Amanda looked back at the O'Neils. "Drought? No, why do you ask?"

"Well, this grass, for one thing and the brown foliage and other dried out plants all around your town. They're all in different stages of dying."

In a manner that showed that she couldn't be bothered with such considerations, Amanda responded, "There's plenty of water. God! Too much water."

Marion and Wilson gave each other a silent, questioning look.

They finished crossing the park and came to a stop in front of a perfect 1960s Mid-century modern ranch house. "Do you know what you would pay for one of these in Portland or San Francisco? This place is awesome." Wilson said.

Some muffled laughter came from behind them in the park. The O'Neils turned and saw Jenna and Kelvin with a couple of the locals on what appeared to be a romantic stroll. Marion frowned. "Didn't take them long, did it?"

"Now, honey. It takes all kinds. They seem like good kids."

"I guess." Marion kept Cindra from looking back and seeing Jenna with a woman and Kelvin with a man apparently connecting in unmasked intimacy. It was just too early for her daughter to learn about the sordid ways of the world.

Charles heard the laughter coming from the park behind them, turned, and saw Helena and Kurt with their conquests. "Sweetheart, I think we should get these nice people inside before it gets too cold," Charles said to Amanda.

His wife turned back to him and responded, "It doesn't seem chilly to me." Then Amanda also saw the two vampires, with Jenna and Kelvin. It would spoil their own dinner plans if the O'Neils were to watch their friends being reduced to shriveled, empty bags of bones. "Oh! Why, yes, it is. Come on in and warm up." She said as she hurriedly opened the front door.

"I'm hungry!" Insisted Cindra.

"We all are," said Charles, ushering them inside.

Amanda led the way into the house and turned on the lights. She was a bit surprised when the room became illuminated and uttered to herself, "They work!"

Marion, hearing her say something, asked, "What?"

"Oh, nothing. Sorry."

Charles gently finished pushing the humans all the way into the house behind his wife and closed the door.

This classic American home was as perfect an example of 1960s mid-century design on the interior as it was on the outside with an open, post and beam style of construction, clerestory windows and a ceiling line that continued out past the windows in the back to the overhang covering the patio.

Marion wandered around the house on a self-guided tour and came to a darkened hall. "The bedrooms down this way?" she asked.

"The bedrooms?" Amanda asked. "Well, I suppose so."

Marion caught Wilson's eye at that response as she continued to roam around the living room, which blended into the dining area that led to the kitchen door. She marveled at the furniture and decor which anyone who appreciated this period of design would drool over, and it was all in such good condition. Aside from the dust, and there was a lot, the upholstery had no visible signs of wear. The drapes looked like the pleats had just been pressed and hadn't been drawn open in years. Pulling them aside to peer out to the patio, Marion noticed that the back of the fabric was faded and showed signs of rot from sun exposure. "I bet you have some wonderful parties here in the summer. When that back door is open, the inside and outside become one big room."

"Oh, so it does," Charles said, as if noticing for the first time. "I'm afraid that we seldom have parties around here."

Marion's eyes continued to drift around the living room. The dust she noticed on the sofa was even more noticeable on the tabletops and books shelves. Where walls and ceiling met, there were some impressive cobwebs. The conspicuous lack of personal belongings also drew her attention. Where were the family photos, the knickknacks from vacations, the odd pieces of clothing like a sweater over the back of a chair or a coffee cup left out on a side table? This house was not a lived-in home. Marion recalled the police station from earlier; how it had furnishings, but nothing that showed life.

The five of them stood uncomfortably around the coffee table in the middle of the room in awkward silence. Amanda cleared her throat and clapped her hands together. "Well, let me get some food together. You must be starving. I know we are." She gave her husband a wink as she walked toward the kitchen.

"Is there anything I can do to help?" Marion asked.

Amanda stopped and turned. "Oh, no, you just sit there while my husband and I prep some appetizers, just a small bite or two before the main course. You just relax." As Amanda turned back towards the kitchen, she touched Cindra's hair and ran her fingers through it. Cindra hurried over to her mother and pushed against her thigh, looking for protection.

Wilson had seen the unkempt condition of the house as well and tried to brush off the sofa cushions, but only raised a plume of dust. Seeing that there was no winning, he stopped and turned a cushion upside down and indicated for his wife to sit, then he pointed to the armchair close to the kitchen door for Cindra to use. She hesitated, but Wilson pulled her away from Marion. "Come on. What is wrong with you tonight? This is a big girl's chair, and you get it all to yourself." He touched the back and gave it a turn. "Look, it swivels like a merry-go-round." Cindra slowly moved to the chair, and reluctantly did as she was asked, sitting in a very stiff and upright manner.

Marion picked up a magazine off the coffee table and blew off the dust. *LIFE, 1963*. A slightly creepy picture of Alfred Hitchcock and some crows were on the cover, which must have been pushing his film *The Birds*. She showed it to Wilson as she asked in a loud enough voice meant to be heard in the kitchen, "How long did you say you lived here?"

Amanda peeked her head out of the kitchen. "Oh, we didn't say."

Now Marion became uncomfortable with this whole situation and whispered to Wilson. He nodded in agreement, and they both stood to leave. "We don't want to be a bother. We'll just be heading back." Marion called out.

Wilson held out his hand to his daughter. "Come along, Cindra. We'll leave these nice people alone and stop bothering them."

Amanda and Charles exited the kitchen and stood on either side of Cindra. Charles placed his hand on top of her shoulder, and Amanda put her fingers in Cindra's hair and combed them through it. Cindra did not respond.

Wilson took a protective step toward Cindra. "Come on, honey. We have to be going now." Cindra showed no sign of acknowledgment. Amanda kept stroking her hair as though she was controlling the child through her hand.

Marion made a quick move to reach her daughter but found that she couldn't move. Wilson discovered he could not move either. Both were frozen, held in place by an unseen force.

Marion was shocked when she heard Charles' voice, not through her ears but emanating from inside her head; his lips remained motionless. The words he spoke were seductive and reassuring. *"Don't fight this. It will be so much more pleasant for you and Cindra if you just let go."*

Not understanding what was happening, Marion was, nevertheless, determined to resist, but she couldn't move or speak, seemingly a puppet under Charles' control. She shifted her eyes to Wilson, seeking help. However, the blank expression in Wilson's eyes told her that Amanda was constraining him as well. He had no fight left in him. Wilson was lost.

Amanda's seductive presence inside Wilson's mind had subdued him entirely. He understood what she wanted and was entirely ready to do anything for her; with her. Then, for a moment, he felt Marion looking at him, and the vampire's spell was partially broken. They both found that awareness of their surroundings had returned, but Marion and Wilson still could not move or speak. The O'Neils could only watch helplessly as the Wainwrights fondly stoked Cindra's hair. Their daughter's face remained blank and unemotional, exhibiting no recognition of her parents standing not eight feet in front of her. The vampires smiled, revealing their sharp fangs. Cindra stood up from the chair without prompting. She was an automaton, only moving as directed. The vampires laughed with triumph as they were about to experience their first kill in over one hundred years.

Amanda leaned down to Cindra's neck and brushed the girl's hair aside. She purposefully made eye contact with Marion, flashed a malicious smile as she opened her mouth wide, and then, ever so gently, bit into Cindra's neck and began sucking. There was no rending of flesh, no gushing blood, no screams of pain. It was a strangely tender and almost loving action. The looks of panic and terror on the faces of Marion and Wilson contrasted this perverse reversal of a mother nursing her child. And the vampire relished every moment of their mental anguish almost as much as the blood she was drawing from their daughter.

The terror that Amanda felt welling up inside Marion sent a charge through her, almost as intense and satisfying as that from her first kill. Energized by the sense of defeat that she felt from Marion, Amanda placed her full concentration on Cindra, *her* daughter now. She would not be without a child ever again. The sense of satisfaction overwhelmed Amanda as she lovingly continued to suckle at Cindra's neck.

Wilson and Marion were powerless as they watched Amanda, the vampire, bite into their daughter. Marion wanted to yell out, "Don't touch her, you bitch!" But no words formed on her tongue. Her mouth wouldn't move. She was furious that she couldn't do anything but watch Cindra under the woman's control. Nothing could compare to witnessing her precious child's neck being bitten by this abomination. The finality of the words she heard from the woman sent a feeling of despair through her paralyzed body. *"Your daughter is mine."*

Amanda stopped sucking on Cindra's neck, and immediately Charles took his turn. He, too, approached this act in the same tender, loving manner. When he finished, Charles looked at the O'Neils and deliberately bit into his wrist. Blood erupted from the wound. He lowered it down to Cindra but stopped. "Sorry, where are my manners?" He then held his bleeding wrist out to Wilson and Marion. "You must be famished. What? No? Well, okay, then. Children first."

Charles turned his attention back to Cindra and lowered his arm down so that Cindra's mouth was in line with his wrist. The first drop of his blood fell onto her closed lips. Then the second. The girl's tongue inched out, licking, tasting.

Marion and Wilson screamed for Cindra to stop, but the vampires muted their voices. Even if Cindra could hear her parents, their daughter had already ceased acknowledging their existence. She had a new mother and father now.

Then, without a moment's hesitation, Cindra grabbed Charles' arm with both hands and pulled it to her eager mouth. She locked her lips onto his wrist and drank from the wound. With a look of superiority, the man smiled at Marion and Wilson; a smile of pleasure as she greedily took in his blood.

"That's it, sweetheart. Slowly now, not too fast." Amanda said as she stroked Cindra's hair.

Marion and Wilson's screams turned into desperate cries of anguish that merely echoed in their heads as they watched their daughter drink a vampire's blood. Any hopes of their survival had just been put to rest with their fates, a foregone conclusion.

Amanda gently pried Cindra's mouth from Charles' wrist. "Not too much the first time, dearest. We don't want to hurt your father, do we?"

Wilson was bursting with rage but could do nothing with it. He was Cindra's father. He fought the power holding him, but there was no way to break free and get his daughter away.

Then Charles put his arm around Amanda's shoulder, and they posed for the O'Neils with Cindra standing in front of them, blood dripping from her mouth. It was the perfect portrait of an American vampire family.

Marion prayed that someone would help them, but no one came. They were alone. Their family lost.

Then the Wainwrights walked to Marion and Wilson. Cindra remained standing, like a pale porcelain doll.

Charles stepped next to Marion. He opened her blouse just enough to expose her throat, then lowered his head so that he could breathe in the scent at the nape of her neck. The fragrance of fear.

Amanda nuzzled in next to Wilson. She and Charles exchanged meaningful, lustful leers. The female vampire studied Wilson's throat. She ran her fingers up and down his neck and watched his jugular throb with the pounding flow of blood, his heart pumping madly.

The male vampire felt Marion's pulse point quicken. Marion's eyes revealed she was screaming, though all remained quiet inside the suburban ranch house.

Amanda addressed Marion, "You may be right about the 'bitch' part, but I wouldn't call myself an 'abomination." Then she spoke to her husband, "Would you, dear?"

"I most certainly would not, my darling." Then Charles looked at the feast they were about to consume, and politely asked his wife, "Shall we?"

The two vampires gazed longingly into each other's eyes, and on an unspoken cue, they simultaneously bit into the necks of Marion and Wilson.

Contrary to how they treated Cindra, this was an act of violence. Their fangs stabbed deep into their victims' necks. The vampires sucked and tore at the couple's exposed throats in a perverse act of ecstasy.

Amanda and Charles watched each other bite and suck. Their actions became more intense with every thrust of fang into warm flesh. Each movement incited the other into ever escalating acts of crazed feeding, doing more and greater damage to the bodies that were once Marion and Wilson O'Neil.

Amanda stepped back from Wilson's lifeless body and looked at Charles. "My dearest, you have a little on your collar."

Touching his shirt, Charles pulled away bloody fingers. "Why, so I do. And you should see yourself, sweetness. Wherever did our manners go?"

"Yes, we used to be such neat eaters."

The room that could have been a set for *The Dick Van Dyke Show* had become a bloody butcher shop. The vampires wallowed in the fresh blood. Nothing had tasted as good since they entered this hell of a town, this prison. While they feasted on the humans, Cindra remained standing, framed by the opening of the kitchen door, the ceiling light forming a perfect halo around this fallen angel's head.

Chapter 19

FEAR NO EVIL

T HE ACTION TEAM sat rocking back and forth in their seats, courtesy of the bumpy ride that the Osprey provided. A red glow from the nighttime running lights bathed the interior. The nervous banter among the team had died off, and the loud hum of the engines had taken over. Each of the seven was now lost in individual thoughts; mentally preparing for the encounter they would have with the vampires.

None of them knew if this operation would be a simple police action or end up as something more, maybe a life and death battle. Nothing good could come from having to rush to save innocent humans from being drained of their blood. Except for Liz, who didn't know any better, not one of the action team believed that tonight's activity would turn out well.

Several looked at their watches. Based on how long they had already been airborne, they knew that Vamp Town wasn't too far away. With the time they had remaining, they occupied themselves with busy work to take their minds off what might lie ahead in the night. Some inspected their weapons one last time while others cinched up their armor, tightened their gloves, or did radio checks. They all went through personal mental rituals as they prepared for the possibility of battle.

Okada fingered the beads of a rosary that hung around his neck. Finishing a silent prayer, he used the crucifix to make the sign of the cross—touching the forehead, heart, left shoulder, and right shoulder—ending his spiritual talk with God as he kissed the figure of Christ nailed to the cross.

Across from Okada sat Timmons. A wallet was open in his hands, looking at family photos. He traced the face of a woman with his finger, losing himself in the image, remembering the day it was taken.

Near the tail, by the rear door, Ortega sat with his back up against the fuselage. His eyes were closed, head rolling back and forth with the aircraft. He appeared to be asleep, but his teammates knew he was listening to his inner music; probably composing another of his piano pieces, perhaps adding to the symphony which he started a while ago—his magnum opus.

This action was their first encounter with more than a couple of vampires at a time. They had no eyes on the ground, so they were flying in blind, not understanding the numbers that they would potentially be confronting.

What they knew was that they were down five team members. Four were missing because of injury, reassignment, or retirement. The fifth member had just been lost in the mountains along the California/Oregon border to a lycan trying to escape out of Delta.

Until tonight, they had supposed that they could handle any situation unless you were speaking about a full-on vampire rebellion. Would they have to take on the entire reservation's population with only seven action team members—well, nine, if you counted Agent Wright and the newbie?

Sergeant Todd looked up through the interior of the Osprey to where Craig and Liz were sitting. She knew Agent Wright. He was good; thought fast on his feet. The entire team trusted him. But the wild card was the newbie. What was her name? Adams. *Shit, she just got the assignment a day ago. Now we gotta go in with an unknown,* she thought. Not good. Not her fault, though. Todd was only interested in keeping a change in her human status from happening or her lifespan from being cut short. If she died in action, how would the CSC spin her death to her husband? "A terrible cooking accident. Her knife slipped while she was dicing potatoes, and the blade found its way up to her throat and slashed it all to hell. Very messy. Sorry, we had to incinerate her body immediately. A grateful country thanks you. Here are her ashes." The morbid humor made her smile, and she laughed out loud.

The laugh drew the notice of Sergeants St. Jean and Evers who had been playing some game on a smartphone. They knew her sense of humor. "I wonder which of us got eaten this time?" Evers asked.

St. Jean got back to the game first. "Ha. Got you!" Raging zombies were swarming the game avatar that Evers was controlling and tearing it to shreds.

"Fuck you," Evers retorted.

"Well, at least we don't have zombies to contend with on this job," St. Jean said.

"No, just vampires and werewolves and other shit."

"Eh, it's a living."

"Shut up, you two. I'm trying to read," Ellingson yelled as she kicked St. Jean in the shin from across the aisle.

The crew chief flicked on a green light at the front of the craft, signaling that they were close to the target, then turned back to Craig and Liz. "We're fifteen minutes from touching down." The chief handed them a tablet. "I want you to see this live drone feed from Mountain Home." They were looking at an infrared video image of Vamp Town. The four-square blocks of the town glowed in diminishing intensities of red as structures and pavement shed accumulated heat from the day's sun; all surrounded by a lot of black nothingness.

Liz got a good look at Vamp Town for the first time. "That's a pretty compact place."

The chief pointed to spots on the screen. "A human has a core temp of ninety-eight point six degrees, which reads as light red-yellow areas. Like those two there." Several "hot spots" were visible, some brighter than others; many were moving. He was pointing to two of the human signatures in an alley in the northwest quadrant. They appeared to be stationary.

The chief continued. "Now, a vamp burns at a temperature lower than humans. They read as pale pink. But right after they feed, they get especially intense. The pink coloring will turn to a bright red depending upon the amount of blood ingested." He swiped the surface of the tablet, and the image zoomed in a bit, showing two super bright red spots.

"See the two bright red spots next to the two ice blue ones? There in the center of the park. My guess is we have two feeders and two dead bleeders. And . . . just a sec . . .." He grabbed the pad and tapped the image twice, calling up a wider view of the town. From the northwest, a group of bright red spots came out of a building that was the community "watering hole" and was moving south. He handed the pad back to Craig. "And there is a large group of feeders coming out of the bar. Must have had themselves a taste. See how bright they are?"

Craig studied the image. "Damn, this suggests that out of the nine people we know entered the town, we can only confirm that there are two left alive." He shook his head, acknowledging how bad this information meant for their mission.

The crew chief pointed to the pad. "Ah, sir, look."

On the screen, they saw a super bright red spot followed by a weak, pale pink spot that had just come out of the bar. These two joined the first group and paused a moment.

"Why are they stopping?" asked Liz.

As if responding to her question, the bright red spot led the group down the street south towards the park and the alley where the remaining humans were.

"Vlad," Craig said under his breath.

The chief watched the spots move. "Looks like they were stopping to get their bearings and now they know where our live ones are hiding."

"Like they're tracking their prey," Liz said, following the movement of the spots. "They've got the scent, and now they're going in for the kill."

"Chief, how close to here can we put down?" Craig asked, pointing at the alley.

The crew chief took the tablet and widened the image and pointed. "That empty area over there just to the southwest of the park."

"Well, then, looks like we have our LZ Chief. But before we land, I want Okada and Timmons to fast-rope down outside that bar, here in the northwest quadrant." Craig showed the Bucket of Blood in the overview of Vamp Town. "And I want to fast-rope two more here at the end of A Street. Then we set down, and the remaining force will proceed through the park. That doable?"

"Can do, sir."

"Good. Inform the pilot."

Craig stood and looked back to the action team and toggled his intercom switch. "Okay. We're going in hot. Remember, not all the vamps are hostile. Do not take one out unless you feel threatened. But if you have to kill, make sure you do it quickly and thoroughly. One mistake will be your last. Got your maps out?" The team nodded and waved their folded pieces of paper.

"Okada and Timmons, you'll fast-rope down to the bar where a large group of vamps has exited, about the middle of the northwest block. I need you to confirm that there isn't anyone still alive inside. Then join us in the park. Ortega and Ellingson, you'll fast-rope down to the east of the park at the southern base of A Street and work your way up in a flanking sweep. The rest of us will debark the bird just southwest of the park and enter the town at a diagonal.

"It looks like the vamps are massing along the north side of the park. If all goes well, we'll contain the rogues and end this nightmare. If not, I guess we'll see what seven action team members and two agents can do to stop something like twelve, maybe fifteen vampires. Hopefully, the other vamps will keep their heads down and away from the trouble. Knock on wood."

Craig scanned the faces of his team. "Sorry. I know this won't be easy. Be careful and good luck."

St. Jean spoke for the group. "Piece of cake, sir."

Craig smiled and turned back to Liz, and bent down. He released a few Velcro tabs around the top of her vest and pulled up a stainless-steel chain mail collar around her neck. "I told you I would help you with your collar and now's the time." He connected the collar snugly around her throat. "Hold out your wrists." Craig fished out some more chain mail from his bag. He wrapped it around Liz's upturned wrists, securing it tightly. "Now show me your knife." Liz handed him the hardwood knife he gave her back in the armory. He took it and held it by the blade, handle up. "See, a cross."

"I thought you told me . . ."

Craig held up a bottle of what looked like sunblock. "And squirt some of this on like they're doing."

Liz looked back at the Action Team, who were all smearing liberal amounts of the lotion over the exposed areas of their faces and arms. "What is this?" Craig squirted some in his hand and put it up to her nose. Liz's face wrinkled at the smell. "Garlic! You said . . ."

Smiling, Craig rubbed the lotion on his face. "Well, I didn't say crosses and garlic were completely ineffective. With vamps, you gotta use every advantage you can to stay in one piece."

"Well, the smell sure as hell grosses *me* out," Liz said as she copied Craig on applying the garlic lotion. "I can't see why it wouldn't work on a vampire."

"If it comes to close quarters fighting, which it more than likely will, any vamps getting a good whiff of this stuff should be distracted long enough for you to shove the knife blade into its damned heart as hard as you can."

Craig looked intently into Liz's eyes. "Copy?"

"Loud and clear, sir!"

He put a reassuring hand on her shoulder. "Good. Stick with me, and you'll get through this."

Liz looked at Craig and gave him a confident nod of the head.

I sure hope I don't let her down. Craig looked back at the other team members. Or let them down, either.

Chapter 20

CORNERED

CROUCHING BEHIND THE dumpster in the alley, Paul and Ellie focused on making some weapons that might help them survive until morning. Paul had used the Leatherman's saw to cut a piece off his walking stick and then whittled down an end into a pointed stake. Ellie took it and rubbed the tip against the pavement to sharpen it further as he shaped one end of the rest of his walking into a spear.

They had been working in silence, intent on making these minimal weapons, neither wanting to talk about watching Dick being savagely butchered in the bar or the carnage they saw as Jenna and Kelvin were slaughtered in the park. The experience was just so foreign to them. Even to Paul, who thought he had seen about every bad that there was to see.

Ellie held up her stake and touched the tip with her finger. Sharp enough, she pulled her finger quickly away and sucked on it, "I think mine's ready."

Paul held up his walking stick, turned the spear, and looked down its length, examining it like it was a pool cue. He pulled it back down into his lap and worked the tip a bit more with the knife blade. Then he held the tip out in front of him and sighed, "These aren't great."

Ellie reached out and placed her hand on his knee. "Paul, stop. I get it. We don't stand much of a chance. Even with a couple of sharp pieces of wood, we probably are going to die . . .." Ellie lowered her eyes and shut down the rest of what she was going to say. "But thank you."

"Listen. I've been in a few tight situations. The attack that gave me this fucked, God damned, limp was just the last one. I have witnessed a lot of bad things. What we just saw . . . That wasn't bad, that was pure evil, but as f-ed up as it was, it's no different from anything else I've experienced. Admittedly, we are dealing with vampires, which is hard to say and harder to believe . . .." Paul's voice drifted off as he tried to convince himself that what he had just said was anywhere near the truth of their situation.

Ellie looked around their hideout. "Have you noticed how clean this alley is? I mean, where's the trash? This dumpster's paint looks like it could be new if it weren't so dirty from the rain and dust."

"Yeah, I noticed a lot of things about this town."

"Your model train set idea."

"Right. It's just too ordered. Too predictable. And by the looks of things, totally unused."

"Well, there's at least one part that isn't unused. The bar."

"Yeah, The Bucket of Blood." A light went off in his head. "Bucket of Blood, Christ!"

"Someone certainly has a sense of humor." Ellie smiled, appreciating the joke, but wishing that they weren't the brunt of it. "So, using your train set idea, there is probably one of every type of building in this town. All different design styles and construction techniques."

"Yeah. And everything looks like it came from the middle sixties."

"Way before my time." Ellie joked. "But the interior of that bar sure looked like they took it straight out of *Mad Men*."

"This town has not grown up organically over the years. You know? It seems like someone dropped everything here all at once. For a purpose. I thought it was like a movie set, one of those perfect small-town USA locations that a studio built."

"I think I sorta just said that. But in the middle of Oregon? Not likely."

"You're probably right. And those cans of food. They're old army rations. No doubt. Which creates a whole bunch of new questions."

"What are you thinking?" she asked.

"Well, until I saw vampires with my own eyes, I would have thought any mention of them being real was crazy talk. So, here's some more crazy talk. What if the government built this place?"

"I'm not sure where you're going with this."

"Back during the early days of atom bomb testing, they built towns using proper materials and filled 'em full of everyday objects to see what the effect of a blast and the radiation would do to them. They even dressed mannequins in a variety of clothing types and colors to study the effects of the blast burns on people."

"You're saying they built this place to test nukes? Wasn't that all done in Arizona or Nevada?" Liz stopped to think a moment. "Unless this was one of those towns but not built to blow up." She paused. "That might explain those signs on the fence we had to crawl under."

"Signs?" Paul tried to visualize the fence. The razor wire he remembered, but signs?

"Yeah, Mr. Observant. They said something about this being an Indian Reservation or something like it called Res Site-Alpha."

"Sorry, I was too fascinated by what Dick was doing to notice them."

"So, what if this town was built—"

"To house vampires. Now *that* is crazy talk!"

"I know, but it's all I can think of."

For a moment, the hopelessness of their situation dissipated as Ellie and Paul found themselves lost in each other's gaze, but just for a second as the spell was broken by an eerie, screeching wail suddenly invading their refuge.

The high-pitched howl hurt their ears, and they could feel its vibrating urgency resonating through their bodies. It surrounded them, invading the alley from the park, from over the tops of the buildings, and even through the walls. It was a shriek that sounded like a mixture of an owl out on its nocturnal hunt and the howl of a wolf calling the pack for the kill.

Ellie's eyes grew wide. Paul nodded. "I guess they found us." He handed her the spear and took the stake.

"Your injury. You need that to walk with." Ellie asserted with concern.

"Point taken. Sorry. Bad puns aside, the spear is longer, so it might be better for you to fend them off. Hopefully, that won't happen, and you won't need to test my theory. Okay?" She reluctantly acknowledged the idea. "Besides, I've been trained in hand-to-hand combat. Come on, let's see where this alley leads. If we're lucky, we may avoid those bloodsuckers for a bit longer."

They stood and moved deeper into the alley, sticking to the darker shadows. Rounding a corner, they stared at a wall. The alley had come to an abrupt end. They were trapped.

Paul slammed his open hand against the wall in front of him out of frustration. "Damned dead end. So much for luck. It looks like we go back the way we came. Let's check any doors and windows we pass. Maybe vampires don't lock up at night."

Liz gave him a faint smile. "Yeah, just during the day."

They turned around and headed back towards the alley entrance. This time, they tried all the doors and windows that they had passed previously. Ellie found one window that was within reach by standing on her toes. She boosted herself up onto the ledge and partially into the opening. There was an awkward moment when she tried to wiggle through but found that it wasn't large enough for her, let alone Paul. Frustrated, she dropped to the ground and saw Paul watching her with a wry smile on his face. "Watch it!"

"What? I don't know what you're talkin' about."

"Whatever. Just don't say what you're thinking."

"It wasn't you. The window's obviously too small . . . but it was kinda fun watching you try."

Ellie squinted her eyes and gave him a disdainful look before continuing down the alley.

Paul shook his head again, not knowing what the hell he did wrong. *Wait, did she think I was checking out? Ah, hell! But maybe she's just playing with me? At least I hope so,* he thought as he limped after her.

When they arrived back at the dumpster, they crouched down behind it before they tried to make any further moves. Paul slowly peered around the corner, checking the opening of the alley to see if it was still clear. "Okay, the easy way wasn't an option. So we'll have to get around them the hard way which is out in the open. Follow me. Stay low behind the cars and stick to the shadows. You ready for this?"

Ellie grit her teeth and firmly looked back at Paul and shook her head. "No." Then she stood up, offered Paul her hand, and smiled gamely. "What are we waiting for?"

"Thanks," Paul said as he pulled himself up to his feet. Slowly, he crept to the entrance of the alley, peeked around the corner, and saw nothing. Then he inched out onto the sidewalk a bit and looked around. Still seeing nothing alarming, he motioned for Ellie to follow.

They took B Street back toward where they first entered the town, moving from one parked vehicle to the next. Paul stopped behind a car to rub his knee. When Ellie joined him, she tapped his back, so he knew she was right behind him. "You ready to continue?" he asked back to Ellie.

"I was just thinking the same about you. You are okay. Right?"

"Fabulous." Before moving on, Paul looked around the front bumper, then ducked quickly back.

"Shit! That Vlad is in the park with a bunch of vampires and Steph!"

Both Paul and Ellie slightly rose behind the car and peered through its windows, looking towards the park.

Vladimir was talking to the two vampires, who were soaked in the blood of Jenna and Kelvin. Steph was hovering nearby. A small trickle of red dripped down from her lips, and her neck sported two throbbing marks where Vladimir had bitten into her. The other blood-covered vampires from the bar gathered around them, waiting for instruction.

Helena and Kurt shook their heads at Vladimir's questions. He looked around the park, raised his nose to the air, and sniffed. Then he closed his eyes and inhaled deeply. Vladimir's body turned towards the very car that Ellie and Paul were crouched behind. His eyes flared open wide as he looked directly at them.

They quickly ducked down, but Paul and Ellie knew they had been spotted.

Vladimir let loose another of those eerie cries, calling his family closer to him. The bloodied locals clustered around and then followed his outstretched arm to where his finger was pointing. "They are right over there, my family. Enjoy!" The vampires moved toward Ellie and Paul in a focused, deliberate way, anticipating their next kill. They fanned out to encircle the car and cut off routes of escape.

Paul looked at Ellie. "Looks like we make a run for it. Damn it, I'm sorry."

Their faces were inches apart. Instinctively, Ellie leaned in and kissed Paul.

With determination, Paul broke away from the kiss and said, "We can do this."

Ellie nodded.

As Paul and Ellie made their move to run, black tendrils whisked around them. A shadow appeared, and Vladimir materialized, blocking their path, paralyzing Paul and Ellie in place. Neither of them could move.

Vladimir stared into their eyes. They could feel his mind reaching deep into theirs and pulling the strings which controlled them. "Normally, I would offer you up to my family, as I have just done. They have been deprived for so long."

Paul and Ellie looked around and discovered that blood-soaked vampires surrounded them. The lust for more blood was in their eyes.

"However, I see you may be useful to me." Vladimir released them from his mental grip, showing how reasonable he could be. "You see, my family has dwindled through the years, and it needs some new, uh, blood, shall we say? Join me and along with my beautiful Stephanie . . ." Vladimir gently caressed Steph's cheek. She responded as a cat would to being stroked. They could almost hear the purr leaving her throat. ". . . and I can make you so much more than you could imagine."

Vladimir reached out to Ellie while Steph sidled up to Paul, courting them.

Abruptly, there was a roar of propeller blades overhead.

Interrupted, Vladimir looked up and watched the Osprey fly over and land on the other side of the park. "Ah, the warden and the zookeepers have finally come." He turned back to Ellie and Paul. "It seems we will need to discuss this later." They felt their bodies tense up and found that they were incapacitated again.

Vladimir addressed the vampires. "After tonight, we shall have our freedom returned to us. But first, we will have to show the jailers the mistake they made and give them something to think about should they try to round us up again."

The vampires spread out, forming a skirmish line along B Street, ready to meet the Action Team head-on.

Chapter 21

VALLEY OF DEATH

THE OSPREY SWUNG around in an arc and approached Vamp Town from the north. The pilot rotated the wings vertically so that the rotors were facing up, setting it into hover mode as it approached the first Drop Zone. This maneuver altered the sound of the rotors and sent a vibration through the plane, which was enough of a signal to inform the Action Team that they were close to an insertion point and, possibly, a hostile environment.

The first to fast-rope down, Okada and Timmons, had put on their gloves and moved to the rear of the craft. The air pressure in the cabin changed dramatically as the crew chief lowered the rear loading ramp. Ellingson and Ortega, who were next up, stood to prep for their insertion. They checked that all their gear and weapons were firmly attached to their bodies. Going into the unknown without all the necessary equipment was not the best way to ensure one's survival. No one wanted to be the next to have their name erased from their locker, and, indeed, no one wanted to find themselves on the other "team" sucking the blood of one of their friends.

The crew chief gave a thumbs-up sign informing Okada and Timmons that they were in position. Timmons moved out onto the partially lowered ramp, holding a bag containing the fast-rope. He attached one end of it to a D-ring in the cabin's ceiling. Then he tossed the weighted bag containing the rest of the rope out of the hovering craft, watching the line extend as it uncoiled on its way to the ground.

Timmons lowered Night Vision Goggles (NVGs) over his eyes, grabbed the thick braided rope with his gloved hands, and stepped off the edge of the ramp out into the night, sliding out of sight.

Okada turned to the rest of the team and gave a stiff salute, then he too lowered his NVGs, grabbed hold of the black fast-rope, and slid down to join Timmons.

Ortega moved up to where his teammates had exited and looked down into the night to see if the two had made it to the ground. Satisfied, he then grabbed the end rope where it was attached and disconnected it, dropping it off into the darkness outside. Then Ellingson joined Ortega at the rear of the plane with another bag of rope and clipped the end onto the D-ring for their insertion just moments away.

The Osprey banked slightly to the right as it made the quick hop to the next DZ. "Check my Katana, will you Mateo?" Ellingson asked Ortega.

"Sure." He snapped at the straps. "All good. You got concerns?"

"No, man, but this is the real thing. No room for fuckups. Right?"

"Don't worry, Amiga." He patted the tactical crossbow slung over his shoulder. "I got you covered." She smiled, and they turned to the crew chief, looking for their signal to jump.

On the ground, Okada keyed his radio. "A1 to AC. On the ground across from target."

Craig heard the radio call from Ortega. "Command copies. Stand by until A2 is on the ground. Proceed on my mark."

"Copy," Okada replied and signaled to Timmons to take to the ground in the dark and wait.

Upon seeing the chief's signal, Ortega tossed the next weighted bag out of the rear and watched until the rope stopped uncoiling. He gave Ellingson a wink, flipped NVGs over his eyes, grabbed the rope, and quickly descended to the ground. Ellingson took a deep breath, reached out, grabbed the line, lowered her NVGs, and followed Ortega out into the night.

Sergeant Evers peered out over the edge of the ramp and, satisfied that Ellingson was on the ground, disconnected the fast rope and let it fall behind as the Osprey continued its sweep to the right and onto the LZ just a minute away.

Craig tapped Liz on the shoulder. "Showtime."

She stood up next to Craig, who gave her gear one last tug. The snugness of the straps holding her various weapons and ammo felt reassuring, but knowing it was all there was one thing. Remembering to use it in the heat of battle was something else altogether.

With little thought, Liz fingered the chain mail collar around her neck. Master Sergeant Terry would have an interesting thing or two to say about what he might consider a piece of elaborate stainless-steel costume jewelry. "Combat is no place for ornamentation, private! Next time I turn around, I do not want to see those things in your ears." It would be fun to see him wearing this around his neck with the matching bracelets.

"We're on top of the LZ," the crew chief called out.

The rest of the Action Team stood and faced the loading ramp. Through his earpiece, Craig heard from Ortega and Ellingson. "A2 in place and ready to proceed." Craig keyed his radio. "Copy. A1 and A2 proceed. We'll meet up in the park with or without a fight. Good luck."

"A1 copy. Over."

"A2 copy. Over."

The Osprey descended to the LZ like a conventional helicopter. Its powerful engine's rotor wash—a blinding plume of dust it kicked up around the landing zone (what the ground pounders called a brownout)—was so intense that it engulfed the vehicle and masked the Action Team as it charged out of the rear hatch down the ramp. Each of the five remaining team members emerged from the roiling cloud of dust, weapons at the ready, like Satan's Rejects being spat out of the fiery depths of hell. With determination, they headed into Vamp Town to do their jobs.

ORTEGA AND ELLINGSON moved slowly up A Street, mirroring the advance of the primary force as it entered the park. They kept down, staying behind the parked cars, or dodging from tree to shrub to fence. Their job was to be a right flanking surprise to corral the vamps that had gathered in the park. Not that their fast-roping into town had gone unnoticed, but the deafening roar of the Osprey's engines as it landed was probably enough of a distraction to draw focus away from them and towards the primary force, or so they hoped. If a stealth attack was ever necessary, the Osprey was not the way to keep things quiet. At any rate, Okada and Timmons were intended to be the actual surprise approaching the rear of the vamp's position from the north after first checking out the bar.

The Action Team emerged from the man-made sirocco—like so many dust bowl refugees—and took up well-rehearsed positions as they crossed First Avenue and entered the park. With the team off-loaded, the Osprey lifted off to hover out of harm's way: available for support, a strategic evacuation or to call in for more help. However, if they were calling for help, the odds were better than even. That meant the call was for body bags. The hard reality was that *they* were the help. There was no way another Action Team—if available—could arrive in time to do any good except clean up the mess.

⎯⎯⎯◄O►⎯⎯⎯

OKADA AND TIMMONS approached the open door of the Bucket of Blood. Music was playing somewhere inside. Then they saw the bloody footprints leading out of the door.

"Shit man," Timmons said as he felt the stickiness of the blood with his first steps.

"Yeah. Not good."

Timmons entered first, his HK with silver rounds at the ready. Cautiously, he stepped in, brushing the door. The bell dinged pleasantly above his head, which caused him to jump, propelling him quickly into the bar. Spinning around, he swept his weapon from one corner to the next. The room was in utter chaos. Tables were knocked over, chairs strewed about, and a considerable amount of blood was on the floor. He double-tapped his radio key, and Okada entered, gun at the ready, trying not to slip on the blood. They both swept the room for potential trouble. Eyes focused forward; weapons aimed at heart level.

Okada took another cautious step and slipped as though he had just stepped onto an ice rink. He looked down and saw that he had stepped onto a piece of torn fabric, which acted like a sled, sending his foot sliding along the lubricated floor. Rechecking his footing, Okada saw it wasn't fabric but a piece of torn and bloody skin that had made him slip.

"Holy fuck," Timmons said, watching Okada.

Now shifting their focus to the floor, they saw the bloody mess that was at one time a man named Dick.

"Oh, fuck me," Okada said in wonderment.

"It's like someone ate a grenade and it went off. Bam! Blood and parts everywhere." They circled the pieces of the butchered body.

Okada looked down and pointed with his weapon. "That's a hand."

"A shoe and what could be a leg over here." Timmons called out.

"Holy shit. There's a . . .." Dick's head laid tilted to one side. It looked like it had been torn from his shoulders.

Okada went behind the bar and through the door to the back room. He re-entered the room, shaking his head. No one.

"I say only one dead in here." He looked around one more time. "As far as I can tell."

Timmons radioed. "A1 to AC."

"Go A1."

"The bar is a fucking mess, sir. One body only, but it will take us some time to find all of it. The parts that haven't been eaten, that is."

"Copy A1. Exit and proceed to the park. Keep your eyes open." Craig directed. It had become clear that this story would not end in "happily ever after."

"I read you loud and clear."

Timmons turned to leave the bar while Okada made a final three-sixty and looked down at Dick's decapitated head one more time. His eyes stared blankly at the two Action Team members as if saying, "What the fuck you two looking at?"

Following Timmons out the door, Ortega slipped again and slid into the door, causing the bell to play its familiar, cheery tune.

"I'm not so sure I like this job anymore," Okada sardonically said as he wiped his boot on the doormat.

CRAIG LED THE principal element of the Action Team into the park. They could see the vampires lining up at the north end, ready for a fight.

Liz whispered, "I count thirteen. Maybe we got lucky."

"Thirteen ain't a lucky number, ma'am." Sergeant Evers pointed out, sweeping the field in front of them with his Milkor prepared to fire off canisters of aerosolized garlic at the first sign of trouble.

"You know the old saying," Craig tossed out. "Don't count your vampires before the sun rises."

St. Jean gave Craig a sideways glance. "That doesn't make any sense."

"Just trying to lighten the mood a bit."

"Appreciate it, sir." St. Jean looked at Liz silently, shaking his head at Craig's attempted humor. "But I'm the comic relief in this unit. No offense, sir." They continued to proceed toward the showdown.

* * *

AT THE SAME time, Ortega and Ellingson were across A Street, following the main body of the Action Team as they entered the park. Sticking to the shadows, they tried to stay out of sight, ready to jump in when needed. They halted at the sound of a door closing and ducked behind the trunk of a car. The Wainwrights were walking out of the house where they had taken the O'Neil family for "dinner."

Ellingson nudged Ortega and pointed to another, smaller figure a couple of paces behind the pair. Cindra was standing in a hypnotic trance, lips smeared with red bite marks from the Wainwrights on her neck still oozing. The fresh blood of Marion and Wilson was visibly smeared around their mouths and chins. Lost in the passion of bloodlust, they were oblivious to the sounds of the approaching Osprey.

Now that they had finished "dining," they were stepping out of the house like one happy family on an evening stroll, unaware of the confrontation that was about to take place in the park. They stopped and exchanged a passionate kiss. Tongues sought the last remainders of the O'Neils' life force like they were licking the bottom of a cake mixing bowl.

Amanda arched her head back, exposing her throat to her husband's wandering tongue, allowing him to lick her neck clean of any stray blood that may have escaped his scrutiny. She was flush with the warmth of her victim coursing throughout her body. Amanda opened her eyes to take in the dark sky on this momentous night, but instead of seeing the stars, she spotted the advancing Action Team with weapons at the ready. She tapped Charles on the top of his head, and he stopped, looked up, and saw the trouble.

Without hesitation, Charles charged toward the Action Team, moving in a super-fast run that made him appear to be taking flight. He let out the same high-pitched cry as Vladimir had, the vampire version of a rebel yell; an effort to propel fear into the souls of the enemy. Just as the vamp charged out into the street towards the Action Team Ortega, let loose a bolt from his crossbow. The wood spike connected with him dead center of the heart.

Charles stopped cold, surprised, and clutched the protruding bolt. His body shook. The vampire's skin rippled and convulsed as his insides strained to burst out of the thin membrane of skin that had held it all in place for over a hundred years. He dropped to his knees. Vaporous wisps leaked out from his ears, nose, mouth, and eyes. As he hit the ground, Charles looked like he was about to erupt and explode outward. But as his skin tore because of the stress from having stretched as far as it could, his body imploded, collapsing in on itself into a smoldering, gooey pile.

Amanda let a moment pass as she processed what she just witnessed. Charles was dead. As in, his continued existence was no longer a fait accompli. His immortal, unending life just found its terminus. Mad with rage, she screamed and charged at Ortega as he reloaded the crossbow. A very skilled bowman can draw the string back, load a new bolt, and be ready to fire in thirty seconds. And Ortega was more than skilled, but thirty seconds was time enough for one furious vampire to find her target. Without further thought, she charged Ortega in with a blind fury, passing Ellingson, who was still hiding behind the car.

Ellingson reached to her waist for the handle of her Katana. In a single smooth, swift motion, she sprung up from her crouching position, drew the sword out of its scabbard, stood, and swung the weapon. The hand-forged blade connected with Amanda's neck, removing her head. In the same motion, Ellingson pulled a wooden knife from a sheath on her thigh and wheeled around in an upward move, driving it deep into the vamp's heart, spinning away from the vampire. The headless body toppled towards Ortega, who leaped out of the way as it bloated outward and imploded into a steaming toxic mess, mixing with the goo from her husband's body, forever joined by their bodily fluids.

Ortega gave a grateful nod to Ellingson.

"Told you I had your back, Mateo."

"Not how I remember it . . . but thanks."

Chapter 22

ESCAPE

V LADIMIR STOOD LIKE a marble statue; a monument erected to shock and disbelief. He had just watched two of his precious family die. The possibility that innocuous humans could take out immortals, even ones whose strength had been dulled by a century of being caged like simple beasts, enraged him.

Vladimir closed his eyes, preferring to remember two of his favorites, not as steaming mounds of goo but as the vibrant beings he first met. Ripe for the reaping. They were a young American couple on the Grand Tour of Europe, escaping a cholera epidemic that had taken their newly born child. He was drawn to their mutual desire not to let grief drive a wedge between them and got caught up in the infectious strength which they gave to one another. The Wainwright's vitality in the face of adversity won him over, and he knew they were to be a part of his family, not sacks of blood to suck dry and left as empty husks slumped in a dark corner.

It was a glorious summer, traveling from Rome to Athens and then to Paris. He relished turning them at a slow pace, approaching them like a sculptor adding bits of clay, gradually building up the layers until, one day, the work finished, and he had created two more vampires. A masterpiece! Taking them out onto the streets of Stockholm on their first feed was one of his most cherished memories. Simpler times.

Vladimir unquestionably believed himself the savior of that young man. In a few short years, the United States was to be embroiled in a civil war in which hundreds of thousands of men would die. The man was bound to be on one of the opposing sides and fall to a lead ball or worse, be maimed and live as a cripple for the rest of his life, unable to truly express his love for the woman he married. No, Vladimir did him a favor and now—now Charles was dead as well as his beautiful Amanda. Dead! Immortals! Such a waste. The jailers were going to pay for that and their long years of confinement.

Now was the time to liberate themselves from their artificial bondage and set out into the world as free beings. Alexei had grown weak and could no longer maintain a hold on him. His older brother, the cautious one, had led them to this agreement to keep vampires "safe" and away from the feeble bleeders. What had that accomplished? Vampires doomed to an eternity of confinement, suppressing their instincts to hunt, unable to explore the world and taste new experiences. The treaty had been wrong then, and it remained wrong today.

But today Vladimir had taken in fresh, living blood. Vladimir could feel the potency of Dick's essence pumping into his mouth. Combined with the living blood from the old bus driver—though not as vibrant—this surge of power now flowing through him was what he needed, at last, to best his brother. Alexei was no longer the stronger and could not control Vladimir or his followers.

Vladimir ended his moment of self-indulgence and opened his eyes, shifting his focus back to the coming battle. Five of the CSC "overlords" were approaching from the south through the park, and the two who had killed Amanda and Charles were swinging around to his left flank, trying to encircle him and his twelve followers. Vladimir tilted his head back and let out the call, signaling the vampires to attack. The battle for their freedom was at hand.

———————◆◆◆———————

THE DISTRACTION OF losing two of his favorites had caused Vladimir to loosen his mental grip on Paul and Ellie. Paul first noticed that he could move and gave Ellie an arched eyebrow, turning his eyes down to his hand, and then wiggled one of his fingers.

Her eyes widened with understanding, and she tried to move a finger as well, then a hand. They made eye contact again, and he mouthed the words, "one, two, three." When he mouthed "three," they made a run for it. Ellie bent down and grabbed the walking stick and handed it to Paul.

"Thanks," Paul said, hammering it to the ground for needed support. Without looking back, they fled west, away from the park—to where they had no clue. All they knew was that they were heading out of this town of vampires, and that was all they needed to know. His injured knee hampered Paul's ability to keep pace with Ellie. The stress that had been placed on it over the past day had caused it to stiffen and the pain to intensify. If it weren't for the walking stick turned spear, he doubted he could even move at all. Without his dead weight holding her back, he was sure that Ellie would be further down the street and closer to freedom than she was. Paul felt bad that he might be the cause of her not escaping, but was also grateful that she didn't abandon him.

The wild shriek emanating from Vladimir calling the vampires to battle instantly set their nerves on edge. The audible frequency of the cry far surpassed Paul and Ellie's brain's ability to register as sound at all, but they could feel it in their guts, and what they felt was the need to speed things up!

Then the sound of weapons firing came at them from the park, a sound that Paul was all too familiar with. Ellie turned back when she heard the loud report of the guns. It was an unconscious response, but the need to satisfy her curiosity was overpowering. Knowing there were people in the park who seemed to be here to help made her want to learn if she and Paul would be safe or not, confirming the continued need to flee.

In turning back, Ellie saw Paul struggling to catch up to her, and then, beyond him, she saw the muzzle flashes from the weapons. Between the battle and Paul, she also saw the Samoan vampire who had guarded the door in the bar. He was running after them, his size hampering his speed, but with Paul's injured knee, the Samoan was going to catch him. "Run faster!" She yelled.

Paul could tell that Ellie saw something which motivated her to yell for him to hurry. He turned and saw Apelu loping down the street right towards him. Even in the face of imminent danger, Paul mused, *I thought he used to be faster than that.* Then he shook himself out of it, reached for the 9mm, and fired it into the former running back. Each slug hitting the Samoan caused him to stagger, but he was not stopped. Paul fired again; this bullet tore off the big man's left ear, yet he kept running on course.

Paul finished the magazine and threw the gun at the charging Apelu, then quickly pivoted back towards Ellie, but the violence of the action caused his knee to buckle. He hit the pavement in such searing pain that he felt he might have done irreparable damage to his injured joint.

Ellie watched Paul hit the ground with the vampire almost on top of him. "Oh, shit!" She ran back to Paul and reached down to help him stand up. "Come on!" she yelled.

Paul grabbed his leg. The pain brought tears to his eyes. "Fuck! My knee. Oh, God!" He rubbed the spot. "Get out of here!"

"Not that cliché. We stick together!" Ellie reached down and grabbed Paul under his arm, helping him back up to his feet. Using the walking stick to steady himself, he stood, placing his weight on his uninjured leg.

"Okay, I'm good. Let's go."

Ellie looked back and saw that the vamp was within arm's reach. As if she had done this a million times, Ellie pulled the stick out from under Paul, causing him to fall back to the ground, and she turned the walking stick so that the point was facing toward the charging vampire. The laws of physics being what they are, the vamp could not stop his inertial forward motion, and driven by the force of Ellie's fierce resolve the spear tip—turned wooden stake—connected with his chest, and plunged straight into the vampire's heart and out his back.

A look of surprise appeared on Apelu's face, eyes wide, mouth open like a perverse china doll. He looked at Ellie and saw that she still held the spear. He reached out to her, wrapped his fingers around her throat, and pulled her to his open mouth and deadly, sharp fangs. Instantly, from the depths of his gut, streams of gaseous vapor rolled out of his open mouth, causing Ellie to gag at the putrid odor. The whites of his eyes clouded over in a smoky gray film. His skin rippled and convulsed. Panic set in as he realized what was happening to him. He let go of Ellie and grabbed the spear, trying to free it from his dying body in a desperate attempt at reversing the inevitable.

Ellie backed away from the shuddering vamp and crouched to help Paul. They watched in morbid fascination as the former football player's body bloated, strained to explode, and then fell in on itself, imploding into a smoldering pile of viscera.

"Better than the Fourth of July." Paul smiled.

Ellie placed a hand on Paul's shoulder, squeezed it, then helped him up to a standing position. She left him balancing on his good leg while she went over to the gooey pile of smoldering vampire innards to reach for the spear. "You still want this to help you walk?"

Paul hopped to the steaming mound and looked at the walking stick, which was covered in the viscous mess. "Um, I think I'll take my chances. Just leave it stuck in his heart. His heart's in there somewhere, right?" He put an arm around Ellie's neck. "But I could use your shoulder for a bit of help." They took a few paces before Paul had to call for a halt and sat down. "Shit! That hurts." He complained as he rubbed his bum knee again. "Maybe I should reconsider."

Ellie walked back to where the spear was sticking up out of the mound of steaming muck of a once fearsome Samoan vampire. She extracted it and brought it back to Paul, the sharp end dripping.

Studying the slime, Paul got to his feet. "Thanks. I guess."
He accepted the walking stick, then wiped a hand against the
back of Ellie's blouse, suggesting that he may have touched
some. "Gross."

"Hey!"

"Just a joke."

"A bad one," Ellie said, thinking back to when Richard used
her other blouse to wipe the bus driver's blood off his face.

"Sorry." Paul apologized as he instantly understood what
was on her mind. *Fuck me! I'll never learn.* "Let's get the hell
out of here." And they continued their escape.

"Didn't know I had it in me, did you?" Ellie asked a few
moments later.

"What?"

"Bet you didn't think I could take down that big vampire."

"Oh . . . No, guess not. But I don't think that anything could
surprise me anymore."

"Well, so that you know . . . I didn't know I had it in me."

The sound of automatic weapons brought them back to the
continued need to keep moving and get out of the town.
Then Ellie came to a stop. Two figures were running towards
them. She tensed up and drew out her small stake, preparing
to take on the next two vampires.

"Hold it." Paul cautioned Ellie. "Those look like our guys. If
I knew who our guys were."

Okada and Timmons came running down the street towards them. They had just watched Ellie kill the vampire.

"Shit, that was good work. You two, okay?" Okada asked as they come to a stop.

"Think so," Paul responded.

"Lie low, and we'll come back for you when this is done." The sound of more weapons fire came from the park. Timmons pulled out his backup handgun and offered it to Paul. "That was nice shootin', but lead doesn't work on the bastards."

Paul reached for the gun.

"But these do. Silver. Aim for the heart."

"Got it."

"How about me?" Ellie asked. Okada produced his other sidearm from a leg holster and handed it to her. "Sorry, didn't know you could shoot."

"I can't, but I'm a quick learner." She said, taking the gun.

The sound of gunfire intensified.

"Gotta go."

— ◄O► —

OKADA AND TIMMONS ran down the street towards the park, leaving the two bus passengers to fend for themselves. They stopped at the corner of a building and peered around it. In the park, humans and vampires were fully engaged, fighting for their continued existence. They could see that their guys were outnumbered and had been backed up to the gazebo. To the left stood a tall, imposing figure, with a few vamps beside him. He appeared to be the "commander" of the vampires, which meant that he must be Vladimir. Then they saw Agent Wright emerging from the melee, pulling that new partner of his towards Vladimir.

Timmons spoke quietly out of the side of his mouth to Okada. "So, what do we do? Help the boss or reinforce the team?"

"Wright's job is to deal with the leaders. He's the brains. We're the muscle, and we need more muscle over there." Okada pointed to the park and the mostly surrounded Action Team.

"Then let's do it." They ran into the fray towards their brethren. Okada made eye contact with Craig just long enough for him to see what they were doing. Then the two continued to the gazebo, unloading silver rounds into the vampires who engulfed it.

Instead of continuing to run for safety, Paul and Ellie followed the two fighters to the corner of the building and stopped. They peered around the structure and had a good view of the battle raging in the park.

"Who are these guys?" Ellie asked Paul.

"Don't know. But they're military for sure. And they came loaded for bear like they knew what they were up against. But those fuckin' vampires appear to have the upper hand." He grabbed the slide of his handgun and chambered a round. "It looks like they might need some help. You up for that?" Paul asked.

She smiled resolutely. Images of the O'Neils and Jenna and Kelvin and even Richard appeared in her mind. "About to ask you the same thing." Her grin was genuine, but it masked the tight feeling in her gut. This situation far surpassed her comfort level, but she knew she had to try.

Chapter 23

CONFLICT

A S SOON AS the last operative stepped off the loading ramp, the Osprey lifted off the ground to go into mission-support mode and hover over the town until needed. *If* needed, it would set down and be available for immediate evac. *If* needed, they would call in for further support and lay down, covering fire. *If* needed, they would land when the dust of battle had settled and return the bodies of the team home for burial, which was a concept that did not precisely apply since the remains brought back would not be the body in a bag but ashes in a can.

If killed by a vamp, CSC protocol required that a wooden stake would be driven into your heart, your body decapitated, burned, and the ashes sprinkled with holy water. If you were merely wounded, everyone in the CSC also knew that protocol called for a silver bullet to the heart, after which would follow the staking, decapitation, burning, and holy water routine.

Wounded or dead, you were returned to base in a canister big enough to hold your ashes. "A grateful country thanks you for your sacrifice"—though none of your family would ever be told why or how that sacrifice was made.

Craig and Liz looked across the park at Vladimir and his rogues, who were lined up, ready to fight. The distraction of A2 taking out those two vamps drew both sides' attention. And Liz saw for the first time the Action Team at work.

Ortega and Ellingson were impressive in their surprise encounter with the vamps. The smoothness and efficiency of their actions made it look like killing vampires was easy. It encouraged Liz, giving her a bit of strength in a situation that was rapidly looking like she might have been selected for the wrong job. She had thought that maybe she would get assigned to some sort of secret organization, like perhaps special forces, CIA, FBI, maybe even Secret Service or something black-ops-like but herding vampires? That was not on the radar. And the way their bodies imploded when killed—not expecting that at all.

Craig marveled at how his two team members killed the vamps in a no-nonsense, business-like manner. "Wow," he said in admiration. Craig had been with this team for several years and knew their capabilities, but fortune had been with them, and they never had to show off their skills, not to this extent and at least not in front of him.

Vamp Town had been a relatively quiet assignment, not like sites Delta and Epsilon. The lycans were a reasonable lot, but full moons brought out the animal in them. All joking aside, Action Teams had spent more time dealing with those wolves than they ever had with the vamps. The lycans often required force to subdue them and not always were the Action Teams left unharmed. Craig's mind flashed on the images of Swanson getting his ticket punched while he was sitting comfortably back in Control-West whining about how bored he was. That was a real professional moment. *Shit!*

Next to him, St. Jean muttered in awe at the performance, "Pretty slick."

"Yeah, gotta get her to teach me how to use a Katana when we get back." Sue Todd said in a matter-of-fact tone.

Craig returned to the issue at hand. The vamps were lined up ready to take on the Action Team, and they appeared to have the numbers on their side to do it. "Sergeant St. Jean, what do you see?" (He never messed with the night vision equipment, which he felt was just too cumbersome. Instead, he relied on others for their input.)

Sergeant St. Jean redirected his NVGs over to the vamp line. "Well, they're kind of like us, sir. Frozen. How Ortega and Ellingson handled those two must have surprised them more than us, but they sure as hell look ready for a fight."

"This will not be good," Evers commented in a business-like tone, making sure that he had a chambered gas canister ready to fire from his Milkor riot gun.

"Well, they are stronger," Craig replied out of the side of his mouth.

"Just a bit, sir. And Vlad has a look of rage on his face. He's talking, and his bloodsucking pals are listening," St. Jean commented.

Abruptly, Vlad threw his head back. The tendons in his jaw loosened as his mouth opened to an inhuman size, and he let out an eerie, high-pitched, screeching howl that the entire world could hear.

"Ah, Sir . . .," Todd said.

"Shit, I heard."

"They heard it in Portland, for God's sake." St. Jean had to add.

"No, not that," Todd continued. "Vlad has two of the passengers, but he's ignoring them because of us. They're escaping."

"I hope they find a safe place." To the rest of the team, Craig said, "Time to do our jobs. Adams, you're with me. We need to cross the park and get to Vlad."

Liz had one hand on her 9mm. The other was firmly around the handle of the wooden knife that Craig gave her. If this had been a cartoon, she would take a loud gulp, Adam's apple overly exaggerated, rising and lowering in her throat as she went into the park with Craig. But this was life, and her mouth was too dry even to swallow. Gulping would come later, preferably with a bourbon on the rocks, water optional.

Craig took the first step into the park. Liz followed slightly behind to his right. To Craig's left was Sergeant St. Jean, while Todd and Evers walked next to Liz. They were a determined group of fighters heading towards their appointment with destiny. Liz could not help but notice a similarity with her father's favorite western, *My Darling Clementine*, which portrayed the Earps and Doc Holliday slowly walking down that dusty street in Tombstone to meet the Clantons at the O.K. Corral. She hoped that the outcome for them was as positive as it was for those characters in that film. Ahead, the vampires entered the park and approached the Action Team. Between the two groups stood a gazebo and an expanse of dried-out grass.

About halfway into the park, Ortega and Ellingson joined up with the rest of the team. Then all hell broke loose.

The vampires did not hold back any further, and they flew toward the Action Team with venom.

Craig did not join his team in the battle. He knew that eliminating Vlad from the equation was critical to the success of this action. So he steered a path around the advancing vampires and made straight for the insurgents' leader. If Vlad got away, it wouldn't matter much if he and his team survived or not. The delicate balance between humans and vamps created by the treaty would forever be altered. And an unsuspecting world would have to live in fear of the night again.

Craig had hoped that Alexei would have already arrived and put an end to all this before it turned ugly, but the gunfire coming from his people's weapons wiped that thought out of his mind. But it no longer mattered how quickly Alex would arrive, because it wouldn't be soon enough to stop the killing. Now he had to act. Just what he was going to do was a question yet unanswered, but he had to do something. So, he marched on towards Vlad, tuning out the battle, staying focused on the responsibility that was his alone.

———— ◄O► ————

THE BATTLE EXPLODED around the two agents as though an accelerant had been poured onto an open flame. For Liz, the fight was a whirlwind of motion. From her perspective, the vamps seemed to have an unfair advantage. They could defy gravity by turning into black wisps of vapor and then materializing in a different location to resume their attack. But Liz was quickly learning on the job that the Action Team was not without its strengths.

Silver bullets were highly effective in stopping a charging vamp when hit anywhere on the body like the intent of the Colt .45 automatic when it was first developed. Place a slug from that gun anywhere into a charging, machete-wielding Filipino freedom fighter, and he'd go down every time. Unlike the lead of a .45, however, silver would not knock down a fanged assailant, but it would stall his charge, and if one was fast, there was just enough time to put another slug into its heart before the vamp reached you. Then it was lights out, implosion time. Liz saw one vampire go down that way.

Keeping up with Craig was hard. He moved through the battle with little regard for what was going on around him. It was as if his intense focus on getting to Vladimir gave him a cloak of invisibility or supernatural protective armor. The fighting did not distract him from his end goal.

Liz, on the other hand, could not keep from looking at the fight. She had never been in battle. All simulations and war games she had taken part in were not real and, in any case, would not have prepared her for watching a human being torn apart by three vampires. What was her name? Not the one with the sword, but the other. Liz never really got to meet anyone, and there she was, torn to shreds, with three vamps crowing over their kill, tantamount to some weird victory cry. Was it Todd who had just gotten taken down? *Todd. Oh my God!* Liz realized in horror. She looked for Craig, but he had already cleared the battlefield and was far ahead of her, beyond the gazebo.

"Shit!" Liz yelled, feeling the wisp of a vamp brush through her hair as it flew over her head. She ducked out of instinct and then looked to see it materialize next to one of the Action Team. Her eyes fast focused on his name patch, Timmons. The vamp landed too close for him to use his AR, so he quickly dropped the rifle and pulled two Bowie knives out of sheathes attached to his legs. The sharp, silver-alloy blades flashed as he swung around, parrying the vamp's initial attack with its long, sharp nails. Then Timmons used the knife in his left hand, point facing out in front of him like a fencer, and lunged. The vampire darted away from the thrust but did not see the other blade as Timmons brought up his right hand in a sweeping upward arc, slashing across the vamp's forearm. He screamed in agony as the blade deeply sliced through the skin, opening a vaporous wound. The vamp did his wispy thing, dematerializing, then popped up behind Timmons, who anticipated the move, spinning around in a one-eighty to his right with the knife in his left hand pointing out, leading the turn.

Vampires might be extraordinarily strong and centuries-old with teeth able to rip a throat open, but trained fighters they were not, and Timmons' move surprised this one as the tip of the leading blade embedded into the vamp's gut. At the same time, he brought up the other knife and drove the point straight into the vamp's heart. Surprise washed over the vampire's face as his body convulsed and erupted towards an explosion, only to implode on itself into a heap of burbling stew.

Then everything turned into a blur as Liz saw the surrounding fight become a super-fast speed mix of colors and motion, all blending into a Jackson Pollock painting of lines and streaks interspersed with red splashes of blood. She found herself immobilized, standing in the middle of the calm eye of a shit storm. Her heart rate quickened; breath came in short, shallow gasps. Increased blood flow brought a warm flush to her face. *Is this what panic feels like?* she wondered.

Liz had lost all comprehension of the flow of time, with the action roiling around her, moving at an alarming pace. She slipped on something and looked down. Her boot was in a muck of some still vaporous vampire entrails.

Then the swirling blur of activity solidified, and the fight resumed at normal speed. She could not tell how many of the Action Team remained standing. Trying to judge the number of vampires still in the fray was equally hidden from her, but it was abundantly clear that the humans were surrounded and about to be overrun.

Liz turned her head to a sound. *Wump. Wump. Wump.* It was the guy with the Milkor, firing the aerosolized garlic canisters into the crowd of vamps. The garlic vapor had a debilitating effect on many of them, allowing the Action Team to fall back to the gazebo, the only defensible position around.

The smell of garlic had a crippling effect on Liz, too. She gagged, trying to catch her breath, and doubled over from the urge to vomit. Then the tangy sweet smell dissipated as a breeze blew across the park. Liz's eyes cleared, and she saw the guy with the Milkor fumbling for his sidearm. He had remained behind the team, firing off the canisters, allowing the rest to make it to the gazebo. Now he was alone in a sea of bloodsuckers, and one was attacking him. He squeezed off a couple of rounds, hitting a vamp, causing her to stumble back, but not killing her.

The wounded vampire ignored the bullet hits and moved to attack him again. He fired another round, but it missed. Then, as if the vampire had no injuries at all, it morphed into its wispy, vaporous mode and materialized right onto the poor guy's neck. The vamp opened her mouth; her fangs looked impossibly long to fit in such a petite space. Moving at lightning-fast speed, she took a large bite. A gush of blood erupted from the gaping wound, and the vamp was off to the gazebo to continue the fight.

Liz could only watch as the vampire pounced on the CSC fighter. Even though it happened so quickly that she had no time to react, she saw the attack in slow motion, with every gruesome detail playing out before her. She turned to flee the carnage, but found the raging battle had become a barrier of blurred bodies in action—a freeze-frame tableau—keeping her from escaping. In every direction she turned, there was a wall of frozen humans and vamps, in the throes of killing one another, surrounding her, creating a hollow spot in a sea of pain and spurting blood, leaving Liz and the dying man as the only ones moving in real-time.

⸻◆⸻

AFTER MAKING IT beyond the center of the battle, Craig turned to see if Liz was still with him. *Fuck! Where is she?* he asked himself when he didn't see her. Now was not the time for a newbie to get lost. He glanced left, then right, to double check. She definitely wasn't with him. Then he turned around and looked back towards the middle of the park, where his team was locked in fierce fighting with the vampires.

It was there that he saw Liz through the fast-paced blur of the action. She was kneeling next to a fallen team member. *Who was that?* Craig couldn't tell from his vantage point. All he could see was Liz and the wounded team member. He saw them moving in real time while the battle swirled around them as though the combatants were all on a super dose of speed. Their frantic movements of attack and defense became a smear of color and motion that turned transparent, enabling Craig to watch her and the fallen teammate.

LIZ LOOKED DOWN at the wounded man lying on the ground at her feet. The speed of the attack and the severity of his neck wound left her feeling unsteady. When the man coughed, blood gurgled up out of his mouth and spurted out the gash in his neck at the same time. She blinked. The reality of the situation came rushing back. All this was real. Liz kneeled next to the man and tried to close the wound with her hands, but she could not stop the gushing blood. Each heartbeat sent out a new spray of red. *What do I do? Come on! What should I do?* Treat for shock? Direct pressure? Tourniquet? *No stupid a neck wound.* An artery. "Shit!"

And this was when she realized that a severed artery in the neck had no treatment, no solution, no way to fix it. This man was going to die. She rested back on her haunches and wiped the sweat from her forehead with her sleeve. A feeling of helpless despair flooded her mind. Then she heard the voice of Master Sergeant Terry. *"Adams! What in the hell are you doing? Feeling sorry for yourself? You have a man down. What are you going to do, soldier?"*

Liz's focus returned to her fallen comrade, and with renewed vigor, she attempted to staunch the bleeding wound in his neck. The man turned his head and looked up into her eyes. He coughed; blood bubbled out of his mouth. He coughed again. "Stop. N . . . nothing you can do to save . . .," the man tried to say. With extreme effort, he grabbed her wrist, pulled her hand away from his neck, and stared into Liz's eyes, pleading. "Don't let me become one of them!" he said, coughing up more blood. "Finish me. Please!"

What was he asking her to do? Does he want me to kill him? The thought shocked her. She looked into his eyes, and they widened, begging for her to end his misery and to release him from the potential of becoming a blood-drinking creature of the night.

The man coughed again. "Please . . .."

Liz stood and pulled out her 9mm. The man grabbed the barrel and directed it over his heart. He looked at Liz, eyes thanking her, and he nodded. Now.

Liz began to perspire. Her heart rate picked up. She held out her arm towards the injured man; his hand still guiding her to the target. And she pulled the trigger.

———————◆◆◆———————

CRAIG WATCHED LIZ aim her gun at the fallen man and pull the trigger. The man's body lurched from the impact of the bullet. Then the frenzied action of battle resumed in real-time, and Craig lost Liz in the heated blur of the fight.

He didn't hesitate. Craig charged back into the raging storm of battle to get Liz. A vamp in a John Deere hat charged him. Without hesitation, Craig pumped him with a silver slug in the heart like an enraged James Bond and continued with determination towards his partner. When he reached Liz, she was still standing over the team member's body, gun in hand, hanging to her side, oblivious to the desperate fight around her.

"I didn't know his name . . . "

"Evers. Sergeant Eugene Evers. I'll tell you about him later, but—" Craig grabbed her shoulder. "—I need you. *NOW!* Copy?"

Liz blinked, "Copy." She looked around at the mayhem as though she was seeing the battle for the first time. Nothing registered. Then a switch went on in her head, and she saw what was going on and stared wide-eyed at the battle.

For the first time, Craig also looked around and took in the ensuing fight. The vampires had his team backed into the gazebo in a last-stand style of defense. He grabbed Liz and dragged her out of the fray towards their target, Vladimir.

Craig keyed his radio, calling the hovering Osprey. "Big Bird, this is Kermit. We have a potential situation here. Prepare to execute the last option. We may need to erase Vamp Town."

"Uh, copy, Kermit. Contacting Control now. The fly-boys with the package left Mountain Home a little after we did, so they should be here shortly and ready to drop on your mark."

"Roger. Make sure that they understand not to be too trigger-happy. We're not done down here just yet."

"I get your drift, Kermit. Not to worry."

Liz snapped out of her stupor at the words she had just heard. "Wait, what did you just call in?" She demanded of Craig. "What is the last option?"

Still dragging her out of the park, Craig explained over his shoulder, "A MOAB. If we can't contain the vamps, we sterilize the reservation."

"A Mother of All Bombs? On the town? With the team still in it? How about the people we came to save?"

"Expendable, all of us. The vampires must be contained, and if they are busting out, we have to stop 'em. There's Vlad over there. If we do our job, then it won't be necessary."

Liz saw Okada and Timmons peek around the corner of the building north of them, slightly behind where Vladimir and his few vamps were watching the fight. "Sir, look."

Craig looked to where she was pointing and made eye contact with Okada. "They're going to help the team. We might have some hope left." Craig pulled out his .357, checked the rounds, and ran towards Vladimir. Liz followed, checking the magazine of her 9mm as she did so.

From the north, new gunfire was heard, adding to the mix of the battle racket. Okada and Timmons were charging towards the gazebo, bringing needed help to their teammates. Like a Hawaiian cowboy, Okada whooped and hollered as he and Timmons both fired their weapons, spraying the vampires with silver-clad rounds.

Craig breathed easier and pulled Liz with him towards Vladimir.

Chapter 24

FAMILY FEUD

T HE PIERCING WAIL calling for Vladimir's people to attack the humans also served as a summons for all the other vampires remaining in Vamp Town to assemble. They did not know why. They only responded to the inexorable strength in Vladimir's voice, and the urge to follow was too potent. Now they had assembled at the fringes of the park, awaiting his bidding.

Each vampire entered the life of immortality in a like manner. Another vampire had selected and turned them. However, each one's experiences were as different as the flavor of blood from one human to the next. Some vampires were hundreds of years old. Others were young by comparison, having just turned before the treaty. The residents of Vamp Town represented all the human races, though race meant nothing among the immortals. Once transformed, vampires found old prejudices dissipated as they learned all humans bleed red no matter their skin color: black, white, yellow, or polka dot. Vampires were "equal opportunity suckers." But no matter how long they had trod the face of the earth, an immortal was bound by specific natural laws, and the chief among them was their deference to their leader, the strongest of the group. Usually, that would have been Alexei, who was absent, but there was something in Vladimir's call that they responded to. He was projecting strength and confidence that the vampires could feel. Was this the power shift that many believed would eventually happen?

For over a hundred years, this group of vamps had been "locked up" on one tiny reservation after another until landing here, all thanks to the agreement Alexei made with the American president. That human no longer lived, however, but the immortals remained, as good as prisoners held by Alexei's mental strength, a hold that some believed was weakening.

They remained fixed on the sidelines, watching Vladimir and his followers make this defiant action of challenging the status quo, taking on the humans in open rebellion. And from what they could see, Vladimir's faction had the upper hand. The humans were making a last stand at the gazebo and did not appear to have a chance left in the world without more help. Even the addition of just a couple more vampires to the fight would assure a victory over the bleeders, but none made a move. They waited to see the result of the mutineers' actions, letting others do the dirty work. Then, when the outcome was clear, they would throw their lot in with Vladimir or remain loyal to Alexei. It was a matter of playing the odds.

The various looks of lust, envy, and hunger that were visible on these vampires' faces showed how most of them felt as they stood on the sidelines and watched humans bleeding and dying. The heady copper smell of fresh blood made them salivate. Some licked their lips as they watched the precious red elixir soak into the dry ground. Others were just a hair's breadth from tossing their caution to the wind and joining the insurrection.

Suddenly, the show before them became clouded as black, smoke-like tendrils spread out across their view and then merged into a shadow and solidified into the form of a body. Alexei had arrived. There was a look of intensity in his eyes. All previous feelings of indecision and blood lust dissolved under the iron gaze of their master. The Khan. For an instant, they felt his mind penetrating theirs, and they knew that his strength had not waned, but in fact, he seemed to be stronger than ever, and they remained his to control.

The "good" vamps had gotten their marching orders and charged into battle in one shadowy blur. Their directive was to insert themselves into the brutal fight and separate the militants from the humans without further death on either side. A tall order, but their sheer force of numbers would easily overpower the relatively few followers of Vladimir.

Satisfied that he had regained control, Alexei's attention turned to his brother Vladimir and saw Craig and Liz approaching him. *What are they thinking?* Alexei asked himself. *Vladimir will destroy them.*

He saw Vladimir grab Liz by her chin, lift her, and toss her to the side with one hand as if she were a piece of lint picked from his coat. Then his brother grabbed Craig by the throat with his other hand and lifted him off the ground.

Alexei knew he must act immediately to save Agent Wright—his friend. In that instant, Alexei reaffirmed his commitment to another friend, Theodore Roosevelt. He drew an arm across his body and quickly dissolved, morphing into black tendrils, and then filtered himself in, around, and through the battle towards Craig and Vladimir.

CRAIG HUNG SUSPENDED off the ground from the iron grip that Vlad had on his throat. Breathing became more difficult as Vlad's hand slowly tightened, crushing his trachea. He fought for his feet to find some purchase so that he could break the choke hold, but his feet merely waggled, uselessly, in the air. A portion of his oxygen-starved brain thought how silly he must look with feet dangling, kicking back and forth over the surface of the sidewalk like some kid sitting on an oversized chair. "And that's the truth. Thzzzt!"

Vladimir stared into Craig's bulging eyes. "How long did you think you could hold us, keep us from our needs, our desires? You support an individual's rights here in America? Yes? How about our rights?" He let out an almost crazed laugh. "Now, I lead. I am stronger than Alexei. My people do what I say from this point on. My declaration of independence."

Craig just gurgled, unable to say anything, as he uselessly kicked his feet, trying to free himself from Vlad's firm grasp.

Behind all this, Ellie and Paul had worked their way over to Liz, who was sprawled out on the ground next to the brick wall Vladimir had thrown her. A line of blood ran down her cheek from a cut on her scalp. Head swimming, Liz struggled to get to her feet, desperate to help Craig, but she had no weapons. Her gun had to have fallen from her hand when Vladimir had hurled her, and she had no idea where the wooden knife was but probably in the gut of some vamp. She awkwardly tried to stand, but a wave of vertigo washed over her, and she collapsed back to the ground, vomiting.

With the focus on the man that Vlad was choking to death, no one saw Ellie and Paul rush in to help Liz, who was wiping her mouth with her sleeve as she stood again to go at Vladimir. They grabbed Liz and tried to hold her back.

Still stunned, Liz thought they were vampires. She flailed her arms, desperate to keep them away. In the tussle, Liz's hand got caught on the chain around Ellie's neck and ripped it to the ground. She found herself looking through a nearby window and into the room beyond. Some coherent part of Liz's brain spotted her own reflection in a mirror that hung inside the house. She suddenly stopped fighting when she also saw the reflections of Ellie and Paul. Then she saw Craig's image levitating in the air because Vladimir was not visible holding him up. It was all too much to comprehend. Her head whirled, knees buckled, and she crumpled to the ground against the wall. Next to her hand was the silver chain and cross. She picked it up and handed it to Ellie.

No words were exchanged. Ellie merely smiled, accepting the chain from Liz. As her fingers ran over the worn silver body of Christ, Ellie knew she had to help these strangers who were trying to rescue them. She grasped the cross in her hand and rushed up to the imposing vampire, who was intent on squeezing the life out of Craig.

With hate and vengeance coursing through his very being, Vladimir could think of nothing but the red face of the agent that he was choking to death and didn't see Ellie as she charged in and shoved the crucifix into his face. There was a flash as the silver cross burned the vampire's cheek. A smell of cauterized dead flesh wafted up from the wound. Vladimir faltered, dropping Craig to the ground, and staggered backward. Ellie crouched down at Craig's side as he gasped for breath.

Paul joined the attack on the vampire with his sharpened walking stick and rushed Vladimir as he regained his footing. Targeting Vlad's heart, Paul charged forward to skewer the monster.

The bartender, Sean, who had stayed with Vladimir as the others went on the attack, saw the threat to his master and inserted himself between the advancing spear and Vladimir's body—the vamp equivalent of throwing himself on a hand grenade.

Paul couldn't avoid the altered target; his forward motion drove the spear deep into the bartender's chest, just missing the heart by fractions of an inch. The vamp's eyes flashed wide with surprise and pain. He grabbed the stake with both of his hands and tried to pull it out, but Paul applied more pressure, driving it deeper into Sean's body until the point was sticking out of his back.

The bartender collapsed to his knees, still struggling to remove the spear. His frantic actions only motivated the implement of death closer to his heart. Fine threads of vapor escaped from his nose and ears. "Vladimir . . . help me!"

Vladimir looked down at Sean and reached out. The bartender smiled, grateful for the master's help. Vladimir opened his hand and wrapped it around the wounded vamp's throat.

"Master!"

"You are too weak to take with me." Vladimir's hand tightened.

"Nooo . . .!"

Vladimir's fingers closed tightly around the bartender's throat, and with his claw-like nails, he ripped out the vampire's jugular veins and windpipe. The bartender convulsed. Internal organs boiled out of the opening in the neck as his body distended, ballooning outward, stretching the skin to the point of tearing before collapsing in on itself and into the vaporous heap of viscera that all dead vampires became.

Vladimir touched the burn on his cheek from the silver cross, then looked at the humans and laughed. "You think your superstitious totems and wooden sticks are strong enough to stop me?"

Defiantly, Liz rose to her feet and approached the smug vampire. "No, asshole. But I can think of one thing that can. Good morning, Vlad."

The triumphant smile faded from Vladimir's face. His eyebrows rose. How could he have been caught so off guard? He turned and looked. There, in the east, the tops of the mountains were glowing. Vladimir turned back and flashed his fangs in a rage, ready to lash out and finish these insignificant humans. He decided he would take out this new female first. She looked tasty.

As Vladimir stepped toward Liz, black threads of vapor flashed onto the scene and converged between her and Vladimir. Alexei materialized, giving his brother a withering scowl.

Behind them, the battle was slowing. The addition of the "good" vamps had swung the tide of battle. The exhausted Action Team readily accepted the help from these vampires and fell into the role of support, helping subdue Vladimir's fellow rebels.

The glow in the east continued to grow brighter as the rebellious vampires were brought to stand with Vladimir. The "good" vamps and Action Team surrounded the entire group.

Alexei and Vladimir stood face to face in the ultimate sibling showdown, neither showing any emotion nor moving a muscle. The intensity of the moment silenced vampire and human alike. No one moved. The civil war had begun. Brother against brother.

Then Vladimir backed up to his fellow mutineers, pulling Steph along with him. "There is no point in trying to stop me, Alexei. I am now as strong as you." He inhaled; his newfound power coursed through his veins. "I am going to leave this failed social experiment, and I will take whomever else wants to follow."

"We signed an agreement . . ."

"You signed an agreement. I had no say in the matter. No one did. You, Alexei, always stronger, always smarter. Even as mortals, you were the older brother who always knew better."

"The treaty saved our lives. Without it, they would have hunted us to extinction."

"So you say. You are naïve, my brother, and Roosevelt was an idealist. You think you are somehow mortal again because you drive that old jeep, wear flannel shirts and blue jeans, and go camping? That you don't have to sleep in a box during the day? How long did you expect me to play at a life that is as unreal as this toy town?"

"There has to be a way we can make this work."

The morning sunlight began to spread across the valley floor, creeping like a moving wall towards Vamp Town and those that stood gathered in the park.

"No, brother. I am . . ." Vladimir gestured to the others and Steph. "No. *We* are leaving." He turned to all the assembled vampires who had followed Alexei and helped put an end to the fighting. "Follow me. If you stay, you are nothing more than zoo animals, an orca in a tank. What new tricks will they teach you to perform, I wonder? Your lives continue only at the whim of your keepers."

For the first time since they were mortals, these vampires felt out of their element; inherent tendencies momentarily stifled, as though an ancient spell had been lifted. Two leaders of equal strength stood before them, and neither Vladimir nor Alexei could compel them to do anything. With no clear leader, the vampires were free to choose whom to follow and which path to take. But with the brightening day swiftly approaching, life-altering decisions had to be made quickly.

Faced with such a monumental decision, some of the assembled were torn but remained frozen in uncertainty. Many of them stepped behind Alexei while several others moved over and joined the group of rogues that wanted to follow Vladimir.

Alexei pleaded with these vampires, "Please, can't you see Vladimir will only bring you to your demise? You will be hunted and killed. Is that what you want?"

The silence that followed answered his question.

"I shall reunite the fragments of our race that would not go along with this ridiculous farce of an existence," Vladimir declared. "I will rebuild our once noble house. We will be stronger than ever."

The drone of aircraft engines cut off further debate. It was the C-130 with the MOAB making its initial approach. Everyone looked up and saw the approaching warplane.

Craig got a call from the circling Osprey, which he heard in his earbud. "Big Bird to Kermit."

"Go for Kermit." Craig got a couple of questioning looks from the Action Team and vampires alike. Kermit?

"Sir, the C-130 is making its approach to drop the payload. Do they execute or stand down?"

Craig looked around at all assembled. Glancing up, he saw the transport with its rear ramp open, ready to drop the explosive device. He could stop Vladimir now with one word. Then he looked into the eyes of his team. They knew what was about to happen, but they accepted it as a part of the job which they signed up to perform. Then he looked at Liz. This was her first day on the job and he realized she accepted it, too.

Finally, Craig looked at Alexei. His expression was one of betrayal, not believing that the CSC had a plan to exterminate everyone to keep the vampires in line.

"Theodore would not have proposed such a thing." Alexei lamented.

Craig and Alexei stared into the other's eyes. Not a battle of wills but a fight for understanding. After a moment that seemed like eons to those watching, Craig keyed his radio. "Stand down. Repeat. Stand down."

The Hercules had been circling over the top of Vamp Town. The bright orange casing of the MOAB could be seen ready for deployment. A crewman waved as the rear ramp closed.

Vladimir raised his voice for all to hear. "You see? They are ready, even now, to destroy you!"

A few more vampires stepped out and joined Vladimir.

Looking sadly at Alexei, Vladimir continued, "Farewell, my brother. You will not stop us. And do not follow. I will destroy you if you force me."

Paul broke through the crowd. "Steph! Don't! You don't have to do this . . ."

Steph looked at Paul and spread her lips in a mock smile, showing the beginnings of her new fangs protruding as a response.

Craig put his hand on Paul's shoulder, partially as a comforting gesture but mostly to hold him back.

Alexei stepped in. "There is nothing that can be done for her. She is not entirely turned, but the process is not reversible. Stopping the process will kill her."

The bright spot of the sun was becoming visible over the top of the hill.

Vladimir smiled. "Now we must be off. Come, my family, we are headed to a new life."

With that, the vampires who chose to flee Vamp Town dissolved into black wisps and headed west, away from the rising sun.

Vladimir turned back and held out his hand to Steph. "Come."

Steph took his hand, and he wrapped his arms around her body. Then Vladimir dissolved into wispy, black tendrils that engulfed her, and they too were off, heading into an unsuspecting world.

Chapter 25

END OF AN ERA

ALEXEI LOWERED HIS head in defeat. After such an extended number of years of keeping his people, his family, safe and alive, this failure to continue doing so stabbed him like a stake driven into his heart. What would happen to those who had left to follow Vladimir on his mad quest to reunite the disparate elements of the vampire houses? Would the hunters return and resume their relentless pursuit of vampires, killing all they found? Would the CSC become that group? No doubt some variation of that would occur.

But what had Vladimir and his followers done other than seek the freedom to be what nature drove them to be? Of course, that was a crazy thought. Was it nature that turned people into vampires? What human, given the option, would choose to become a blood-drinking pariah?

Did he, himself, not have the same feelings as the rogues? Were those that fled so very wrong?

Did he, Alexei Rurik, Khan of the vampires, "Mayor" of Vamp Town, in signing the treaty, bring about precisely that one thing he tried to avoid, the inevitable destruction of those he had known and loved for centuries? Perhaps. That they fled meant that they would be hunted and killed. Was this his fault?

And what of those who stayed here with him? What would happen to them? Would the government coerce him into cooperating so they would be safe? Would the CSC hold their lives over his head as a tool to get his cooperation? Were they not now all hostages, and was he the quisling who had sold them down the river?

Many more questions flooded Alexei's mind as he watched the blazing light move unrelentingly towards him. The group of vampires that had remained in Vamp Town had retreated into their dark places to escape the treacherous sun. Alexei watched them flee destruction, and yet he could not find the strength to save himself. Perhaps it would be better for the sun to end this for him now and leave the whole mess to everyone else. He was so very weary of immortality.

The burning ball of light was now completely visible in the sky. The shadow of the eastern mountains had quickly vanished, and the line of light demarcating Alexei's continued existence or his death drew threateningly close. Wisps of vapor rose from the exposed portions of his body.

Craig rushed up with a thick thermal blanket and wrapped it around Alexei. "You can't let yourself go like this, Alex. You can't give up. Not now, after all these years."

Alexei tried to wriggle out of the blanket but sighed as he realized the truth.

Craig continued, "You would be letting your friend Theodore down, as well as your remaining people. They need you."

While Craig argued for Alexei to come to his senses, the O'Neil girl, Cindra, emerged from behind a tree. She stood in a trance, lost, oblivious to all that had transpired. She was still safely in the tree's shadow, but not for very much longer. Ellie ran up to Craig and Liz. "That girl was a passenger. Where are her parents?"

Paul rushed over to her. "Cindra. Is that your name? Where—" His question was cut short when Cindra flashed the beginnings of a new set of fangs with a cat-like hiss. Paul hopped back, alarmed.

Craig looked at her. He shook his head and pulled a silver knife from the sheath on his belt and walked over to Cindra, ready to put her down. Alexei reached for Craig's arm. His hand sizzled in the sunlight as he did so. "Stop, my friend. This is not how to resolve this tragedy."

Craig stopped.

"I made a promise to Theodore that the killing would end. I can't take back what has been done to this child, but I can teach her that there is a way to live without hurting others."

Liz's mind was still swimming from all that she had experienced in the past twenty-four hours and couldn't hold in her feelings. "What next? Are you going to . . .? What? Become her what? Does she become your puppet, like Steph with Vlad? This is sick!"

"I will be her guardian . . . Unless you want to end things for her right now? It matters not if you put a silver bullet through her heart, let the sun destroy her, or hold her back from the change that is already advancing through her body. Death will be the result for her, no matter which path you choose."

Liz looked first at the Action Team members who were standing around them and then at Craig. No one moved. "All right, I'll do it myself." Liz picked her gun up off the ground, chambered a round, and headed for Cindra. Cindra flashed her fangs and hissed like an angry cat. When Liz got within arms-length, she aimed at the little girl's heart and paused. She remained motionless, pointing the gun, but didn't pull the trigger.

The look on her face showed a determination to shoot, but an internal struggle was moving her to inaction. Liz had never actually killed anyone, any human. (Was Timmons still a human when she pulled the trigger, ending his suffering?) And this little girl was still mostly human. Right? Liz's hand shook as she tried to pull the trigger with all her might, but she could not.

Craig had moved behind Liz and put a hand gently on her shoulder. Liz still held the gun out, pointing towards Cindra, gripping it in frustration. He stepped around to face her, placed a hand on the weapon, and slowly pushed the barrel towards the ground.

"Seriously? You think this is a good idea?" Liz asked in a voice drained of emotion.

"I'm not sure what to think. But what I know is that this situation is . . . .. Shall I say, a bit fucked up," Craig replied.

"I'm new on the job, and there are still a lot of things I have to learn, but aren't we supposed to keep the vampires contained? And wouldn't that mean keeping their numbers from growing? Not to mention condemning this poor girl to the life of a blood-sucking monster!"

"I will admit that this scenario is not one that I had seen coming," Craig confessed. "I don't think the CSC higher-ups had thought any of this through, either. I am sure after all that has just happened, my position within the Center will be ended. But what I can tell you is that I trust Alex. He's no monster. If he says that he can help this girl, then he will."

The sunlight had finally reached Cindra. Threads of vapor began to rise from the girl's body. The exposed skin on her hands and face started sizzling like meat on a griddle.

From under the protective blanket, Alexei called out, "Please!"

Liz exhaled, releasing all her pent-up tension. "Yes. *Yes!*"

Alexei rushed to Cindra just as the sun was about to wash over her. He scooped her up, turned into wisps of darkness, and vanished.

The morning sun now filled the valley, bathing Vamp Town in its warmth. It was a glorious High Desert morning. The sky was a brilliant cerulean blue with a few fluffy white clouds.

Liz became weak, and she all but collapsed onto the curb, experiencing the let-down after the insane adrenaline rush of the past twenty-four hours. For the first time, she could look at the little town around her. *I wonder if I could live here for even a month, let alone for a lifetime?* she thought.

Craig turned and walked over to Paul and Ellie. Action Team members had gradually positioned themselves behind them. Craig nodded, and the Action Team handcuffed the two remaining bus passengers.

Paul turned in surprise, trying to resist. "What the fuck!"

Ellie struggled furiously as she, too, was restrained. "Hey!"

All night there had been one surprise after the other for Liz and now this. She jumped up from the curb, not sure what to do, but she was as shocked as Paul and Ellie at this turn of events.

Craig shook his head apologetically. "Look, I'm sorry about this. The sad irony is we saved your lives, but because you survived, we cannot allow you to tell anyone about what you have been through."

"What? What are you going to do to us?" Paul asked as he successfully twisted his body out of Okada's grip.

Eyes wide with this new threat, Ellie looked at Craig. "You aren't going to kill us? You can't. Not after we saved *your* lives!"

Liz didn't know what was happening, but she knew a massive injustice was about to take place, and she wanted no part of it. Liz elevated her gun and looked threateningly at Craig. The Action Team raised their weapons at this aggressive move, prepared to act if needed. With venom in her voice, she asked, "Yes, Agent Wright. Just what are you going to do?"

Craig stepped directly into Liz's line of fire and stared into her eyes. "The same thing that I would have to do with you if you ever thought you would quit. The same thing that will more than likely happen to me after letting Vlad go." Letting that sink in, he continued, "Remember yesterday, in the lecture hall? You are the property of the Federal Government. We all are." He pointed to the Action Team. "And now so are they."

Things had kept getting weirder for Liz. What she believed was black and white had become a lava lamp of ebbing and flowing blobs of color that morphed and changed. Thirty-six hours ago, she thought vampires were ingredients for scary movies or overly sexed teen-focused TV shows. Learning about monsters, the CSC, discovering that her job was to contain vampires, and now to take part in exterminating witnesses . . .

"Unless you would like to join them . . .?" Craig asked.

Liz gave a deep sigh and dropped her head in defeat. Reluctantly, she holstered her gun and walked over to a parked car, and leaned against it for support. Drained, she stood and stared blankly out into the bleak landscape.

"Now for you two." Craig took a deep breath. "This arrangement is not just with vampires." He waved his hand across the town before them. "The country . . . The world cannot discover that these beings exist. The instability it would create is unfathomable. And beyond what you have just witnessed, there are other 'creatures' that we also 'supervise' and monitor and, sometimes, imprison."

Ellie was even more confused than Liz. "I'm not sure I understand what you are . . ."

"We are members of the CSC, the Center for Specter Control. The short story is that we contain and monitor the monsters that live on this planet. Monsters you have heard about since the day you first saw Dracula on late-night TV."

Paul shook his head, trying to understand. "But why?"

"How safe would you have felt growing up knowing that bloodsuckers actually existed or that when the moon was full, werewolves ran through the streets?"

The visible fear showing on their faces answered the question.

"Exactly. The modern world would cease to function. Look, unless you have the knowledge, the training, and the complete understanding of what is going on, you will have to be quarantined . . . kept away from society."

Liz had turned back to Craig and the two prisoners when she realized no one was going to be killed here. "Like in a Federal prison?" she asked.

"Agent Adams, I wonder if you even read any of the material you were given? I mean, beyond the Catholic Church part?"

Liz fidgeted. "Well, I was . . . and then you got the call . . . and . . ."

"Right." Now he continued with Paul and Ellie. "There is a 'town,' like Vamp Town, for those who cannot be allowed out in the world knowing about such things. In that you can never leave without an escort makes it a prison of sorts. I'll give Vlad that."

Then the roar of an Osprey's engines was heard as it approached and prepared to land.

Craig spoke louder to be heard over the approaching plane. "Okay. You do have an option. You two showed a considerable amount of ability and courage in this messed up situation. The CSC constantly needs new members, especially field agents. We seem to lose one or two a year due to . . ." He paused. For an instant, his former partner Kathie, red hair ablaze in the morning sun, was standing next to him as if conjured up by the swirling dust from the landing Osprey. He blinked; Kathie's face faded away with the settling dust, and he was looking at Liz. "... extenuating circumstances."

Liz did not know how to read the unsettling look on Craig's face as he stopped in mid-sentence and looked directly at her, but not at her, at someone else. She saw his Adam's apple move up and down as he seemed to swallow back some powerful emotions. When he blinked, it was as though he had returned from a mental journey into an uncomfortable past. Self-conscious, Craig quickly looked back at Ellie and Paul when he realized he had been staring at her. Then she remembered back in the locker room, and she fingered the vest that he said was his former partner's. *Was he seeing her just now? Did she die in the field? Did he have to end her life like I just ...?*

Craig had to clear his throat before he continued speaking to them. "Last night was a severe loss." Now he was fully back in the present. "You, sir, look like a vet? Iraq? Afghanistan?" Craig asked Paul.

"Afghanistan. Active duty. On an extended leave to visit my folks and heal my knee."

"And maybe to work out in your head why it was you who survived and not your men?"

"Sort of, except that the question is why I got hurt and everyone else walked away."

"You said your knee needed healing? So it's not a permanent thing."

"Had the surgery. All good. It's just that I was supposed to stay off it for a while. Yesterday kind of set me back a bit in that department," he said, lowering himself to the curb and finally giving in to the pain that had returned with a vengeance.

Craig nodded to Paul, accepting his answer, then he turned to Ellie. "And you? What's your story?"

Ellie thought for a moment. "I learned tonight that I am stronger than I allowed myself to believe."

"I'll vouch for that. You should have seen her skewer that Samoan running back," Paul said.

Ellie smiled, a little embarrassed by the praise.

Craig took a moment to plan what he was going to say next. "So, aside from being formally interviewed, passing a few tests, and getting through basic training . . . either of you interested in joining a super-secret organization that deals with monsters and other scary shit that has no retirement program and could send you across the country at a moment's notice?"

"Don't forget the dangerous part, boss," Ellingson chimed in.

Craig looked around at the battlefield. "I think one goes without saying."

Paul closed his eyes as he thought about the offer. "You're asking us to join with the C . . ."

"CSC."

"So, joining this CSC is really no different from being locked up in some fake town for the rest of our lives, except that we'd have something interesting to do and we can get out into the world?" Paul asked. "Okay. I'd rather protect the country from vampires than what I have been doing."

Ellie hesitated. "Would we be together?" She smiled at Paul.

Ortega rolled his eyes.

Ellingson smiled.

"I can't promise you anything. Agents are in thin supply. But if you work hard and show your value to the organization, there's no telling how things could work out. And I'll be the first to request that we add both of you to our little family."

Ellie looked at Paul.

"I can't emphasize enough how much your lives will change. This job is not an easy one, and it comes with significant risks and few rewards." Craig looked at Ellie and Paul, making sure they understood what he was saying. He could see a bit of apprehension in Paul's face and just a touch of fear in Ellie's eyes, but they both nodded their understanding.

"Count me in. I'm ready to take on new challenges," Ellie said.

"Let's see, house arrest or protector of humanity? Tough choice. I'm in too," Paul added.

Craig gave the nod to release Paul and Ellie. "I'm going to let you out of those restraints. I think you both are what we need in agents. It will be a bit before we get this mess sorted out and cleaned up, so in the meantime, get some rest and a bite to eat. Adams, please escort our guests to the Osprey, introduce them to the crew, and get yourself back here ASAP. We have a lot of work to do today."

"Copy, Sir."

Paul turned back to Craig. "If I don't show up in Tacoma on Sunday, I'm AWOL. The MPs will be out looking for me."

"If we can create a place like Vamp Town, I think we can make a few adjustments to your record. Now, if you'll excuse me?"

Craig turned to the other team members, and together they headed over to the carnage in the park. A clean-up unit was disembarking the second Osprey and was beginning the gruesome task of cleaning the aftermath of the battle. Team members donned hazmat gear and started scooping up vamp remains into buckets and pouring them onto a pile where flame throwers were used to burn the lot. What couldn't be easily shoveled up was burned until it was just a stain on the earth. No vampire remains would be allowed to exist beyond ashes.

Other members of the CSC separated the remains of their fallen comrades and laid them out away from the vamp fires. Liz somberly crossed to the grassy spot where the fallen team members had been placed. Craig silently joined her. The first body had the name Timmons on a patch above his left breast pocket. Liz turned to Craig with a question on her face.

"James. They liked to call him Jimmy to piss him off."

Sergeant St. Jean quietly added, "And boy, did it ever."

"He got us back more than a few times, though. Rest well, Jim," Ellingson said.

At the next teammate's body, Craig identified her as Susan Todd. "Not going to enjoy telling her husband about this. He's a good guy. But it's the lie about how she died that's the hardest."

The last body was that of Evers, the bitten team member she had to shoot. "Eugene Evers. You don't have to tell me." Liz squatted down and touched his cheek, fighting back her tears. "I'm sorry, my friend." And then she stood and joined the rest of the team.

There was a moment of silence and a final salute of farewell. Craig turned to Liz, and they walked back towards the Osprey.

"How come they're staying?" Liz asked of the team.

"They have work to finish with their comrades," Craig replied.

"What do they have to do? I should help." And Liz turned back as each of the dead bodies had a wooden stake driven into their hearts. Liz stopped breathing as she watched the violent acts being performed on the fallen warriors' bodies.

In shocked silence, she saw St. Jean raise an ax over Timmons' neck but turned away as he brought it down, severing the head from the body with a dull thunk.

"Procedure," Craig said. "We have to make sure they will not return as vamps."

Liz forced herself to turn back to watch as the ax blade fell on Evers' neck. She grit her teeth at the sight but did not close her eyes or turn away. She would never turn away again.

Ortega opened a plastic jug and poured a clear liquid over the bodies. Ellingson struck a flare and dropped it into a puddle of the liquid, igniting it. The team stepped back and silently watched the bodies of their brothers and sister being consumed by fire.

"We only bring back the ashes of our dead," Craig said softly.

Chapter 26

UNCERTAIN FUTURE

"HELLO CALLER, THIS is Dr. Gwen. You're on the air. How can I help?"

"Hi. My name is Mike."

"Hi, Mike."

"I think I'm seeing things."

"Yes?"

"For the past three nights, there have been these lights hovering over the field behind the house. And they change color and stuff. My dog goes bananas when they're outside like he can hear them—"

"Mike, I'm sorry, but I think you are looking to call a different program. I help people with personal problems."

"And aliens in my backyard is not a prob—"

A loud banging startled Craig just as his eyes shut for the third time. He heard the banging again; he closed his mouth and snapped his head upright. He was caught sleeping in the control room again. Craig reached for the mouse and clicked off the late-night radio show streaming on the computer.

Another knock and his sleep-clouded brain recognized it coming from behind him. Wiping away any bit of moisture that may have slipped out of the corner of his mouth, he swiveled his chair around to see who had interrupted his quiet time. The banging happened again. He saw Liz standing behind the glass window at the back of the control room. She held up a cup of coffee and arched her eyebrows in a manner that said, "Open the door if you want this." Craig nodded an enthusiastic "Yes" and turned back to the desktop and pushed the button that buzzed the door open, allowing Liz to enter.

He heard the door open and close and Liz's footsteps as she approached, but he didn't turn back to her. Something was wrong. Scanning the desktop, Craig's brow furrowed. He lifted some paperwork, looked behind the monitor, and opened several desk drawers. When he slammed the third drawer, Liz had arrived and set his coffee down but had to pull it away quickly when Craig almost knocked it over as he turned one way, then another, looking under and around the desk.

"Just what are you doing?"

He got up and looked behind the desk.

"Craig?"

"Is nothing sacred around here?" Craig asked in an accusatory tone.

"What are you talking about?"

"That asshole moved, my duck! First, he trampled it with his blue bronco. Now he's taken it." Craig grabbed the toy horse and hurled it across the empty control room. It bounced off a couple of workstations before it landed at the front of the Control Center under the large monitor.

"Oh, I see. So why do you think it's a guy doing it?" Liz shoved the cup at Craig.

He took the lid off and inhaled the steaming aroma. "What?"

"You said *he* trampled your duck. How do you know it was a he?"

"Well, I just assumed. There's a pimple-faced kid who runs this station during the day. I know it's him, dicking with me. And who said it was my duck?"

"You just did."

"Yeah? I guess I did."

"Anyway, I know Commander Cole is a huge Boise State fan."

Craig took in a large mouthful of coffee and let it trickle down his throat. "Thanks for the caffeine. I owe you. So how do you know? She say anything?"

"Well, if you cared to ask." Liz gave a mischievous smile. "She wondered if I would like to go to a game or two next season. You know, Boise is just a hop away from here."

"Yeah, I know," Craig said while walking down to retrieve the toy horse. Bending down to pick it up, he found it with a broken leg. "Shit." At the first desk, he found a tape dispenser. appropriated some, then did a half-assed fix on the toy. He returned to the workstation and tossed the blue horse on it. "There. All good. Don't go tattling to your new friend. Okay?"

"Your secret is safe with me. Besides, I'm more of a Banana Slug fan myself." Liz confessed.

"Oh, God."

"So, how about visiting our new 'volunteers' when they're done training later?"

Craig looked at his watch. "I'll be asleep at five. Sorry."

"Well, Commander Cole wants a report on them and since you were the one . . ."

"Jeez! Alright. Give me a call an hour before so that I won't sleep through it."

"Not a problem. Besides, aren't you a little curious? I mean, Ellie has been back from her basic training at Fort Benning for over a week now and should be catching up with Paul on the CSC way of doing things."

"I suppose you're right. Don't know why I'm being such an ass. It's probably because I've had to pull night—"

"We."

"Yeah, we've had to pull a week of working the night shift that is throwing me out of sorts."

"That and your missing ducky."

"Watch it. That's serious."

"Listen, I hear you got lucky. A couple of weeks of graveyard is nothing. In my after-action interview, I got the sense that they were seriously thinking about sending you into exile. And me along with you. Apparently, you were right in how the higher-ups would take Vlad getting away."

"Well, the brass seemed to conclude that I had nothing to do with the bus breaking down and the passengers stumbling through a chain-linked fence into a secured area. That and they could only blame themselves too in the budget cuts, which ended live guards on-site. Also, there is no budget left to replace a highly trained asset such as myself." Craig took in some of the coffee. "Sometimes it's good to be me. Still, I'm sorry that you had to be taken down with me on this."

"Hey, I'm your partner. And I didn't have much to say in the matter, anyway," Liz offered.

They both sat drinking their coffee and checking the readouts from the reservations. All indicators showed green—a quiet night.

Liz broke the silence. "It's not like I didn't deserve a bit of punishment of my own. Thanks for not saying anything, by the way."

Craig gave Liz a blank stare. "What are you talking about?"

"Come on. I pulled my weapon twice and not on a threatening vampire. First on an eight-year-old girl—"

"Who had just been turned . . .,"

Now Liz became a little sheepish as she continued, "And then on you and the team, well, not on you guys directly, but I had it drawn."

"To protect Paul and Ellie from the evil 'Man.' I get it. You weren't entirely up to speed with the program. Twenty-four hours before you got thrown into a battle with vampires, you didn't know that they even existed. Having to shoot Evers didn't help either."

"And being thrown against a brick wall . . ."

"Yes," Paul nodded in agreement. "Why would I report that?"

"Well, thank you." Liz stood and went over to a file cabinet and pulled open the middle drawer. She reached way in the back and gently pulled out the rubber duck.

"Hey!" Craig was now excited.

"I saw pimple face stash it in there."

"So, it wasn't Cole."

"No, but I couldn't resist." Grinning with satisfaction, she tossed the duck Craig.

———◦———

IN A YARD tucked behind the armory, the Action Team was going through some hand-to-hand combat drills. The sun was low in the sky, which meant it was time to end the day's workout.

The old hands were sparring with one another, taking turns being a vampire or werewolf or possibly a mutant, while the other had to fight them off without getting bitten or otherwise infected. Of course, this infection was only simulated. But if a sparring partner playing a monster could get close enough and wipe the fingers of their gloved hands across exposed skin, then one could find him or herself with a pesky, itching rash from the ointment applied to the fingertips, nothing serious but something that wouldn't go away for several days. An annoying and relatively painless reminder to keep your head down or be turned into a howling-at-the-moon animal.

The team was paired off in twos, practicing on top of mats scattered around the yard. Paul and Ellie were working on the center mat, Paul playing the vampire. Paul made a lunge and took a swipe at Ellie's neck. She ducked, spun around, and circled behind him. Recovering, Paul turned a one-eighty to the right and approached her again. He leaped and went for her neck again, but when he did, she somersaulted under him, between his legs, just as he lifted off the ground in his charge. Ellie recovered and bounced back onto her feet, ready for another assault. The other team members broke away from their fights and watched the two newbies as they circled one another.

Side wagers were made, with Paul being the odds-on favorite, based on his military service and active duty in a combat zone. But there were some wishing that they had bet on Ellie instead as they watched her effectively countering Paul's attacks. He lunged again. This time, Ellie grabbed him by the collar and tossed him over her head. Paul landed on his back, looking up into the sky, dazed, not expecting the move. He shook his head and stood when Ellie drew out a metallic device and brought it down to Paul's heart. The device buzzed. Score for Ellie.

"You're now a pile of steaming goo, you bloodsucking piece of shit!" Ellie declared.

The team applauded her win while Paul stood a bit slowly. "I have to say that you learned more than I thought you would during basic. Ouch!" He rubbed the small of his back.

"Did I hurt you or your pride?"

"A bit of both," he said, rubbing the injured knee.

"Oh! So now you're going to say that I re-injured your knee."

"Now you two play nice," Ellingson said, walking over to Paul. She put a hand on his shoulder and made a play out of brushing the dust off his back, and when her hand got lower, she grabbed his butt and gave it a goose. The others laughed, and Paul jumped away, rubbing the seat of his pants from Ellingson's sneak attack.

Ellingson rested her arms akimbo on her hips. "That makes two times you let your guard down, newbie. The first time was when you let Ellie throw you, guessing that you had the strength and experience to best her no matter what. The second time was when I got a handful of that tight ass of yours. We aren't fighting the Taliban here, Army."

"Oh? And where did you serve before this?" Paul asked with a tad bit of resentment in his voice.

"Coast Guard. Long story."

The other members laughed, knowing her complete story, and, yes, the Coasties were not the typical path to becoming a monster keeper.

St. Jean interjected, "Taliban, Nazis, bank robbers, they're all human, so we think like them. Monsters! Now monsters think differently than we do because they are no longer people. They're not like humans. They're altered. When we fight them, we fight to stay alive, to remain human. You know? When they fight us, we are seen as a fresh, warm meal."

Ortega checked his watch. "Okay, kids. Hit the showers and grab chow. More of this tomorrow."

"Shit, Mateo, who made you the boss?" Ellingson asked.

"One of them." He pointed to Craig and Liz, who had been standing against the armory wall. "Well, actually, that one," he said, pointing directly at Craig.

"Oh, yeah, I think I remember something like that," Ellingson replied with a grin.

With training over for the day, the operatives headed for the shower room. As they entered the building, they all acknowledged Liz and Craig, who were standing near the door. When Paul and Ellie passed, Craig held up a hand and stopped them. "Paul, why don't you and Ellie hold up just a sec?"

The sun was setting, causing the buildings to cast long shadows on the ground.

"You two are handling the CSC side of training very well," Craig said. "Of course, Paul, you should have had little trouble with the physical stuff since you've been through it before. I'm sure you must've been surprised to discover that not all your prior training could apply directly to fighting monsters."

Paul used the back of his hand to wipe some sweat off his face. "Well, training to fight the Taliban is not quite the same as learning to fight Big Foot, that's for sure."

Craig laughed, "Big Foot, that's a good one." Then his face went deadly serious. "Who told you about Sasquatch?"

Now Paul got a bit concerned. "Ah, no one, sir. Just made it up."

"Sorry, just fuckin' with you. Everyone knows there's no such thing as Big Foot."

"Um, okay," Paul responded hesitantly, not sure what to believe anymore.

Liz spoke to Ellie. "And your test scores show a natural aptitude towards the psychology of the whole thing."

Paul rubbed his back. "Oh, I think she has the physical stuff worked out pretty well, too."

Ellie reached for Craig's arm. "Let me show you."

"Maybe next time," Craig said, pulling away.

"Actually, sir," Ellie started, "I'm glad I was, um, 'drafted' into this outfit. I enjoy the work, and it's good to know that I will be able to defend myself from all the monsters that are out there."

Paul gave Ellie a silent look, showing that he knew who she meant.

Suddenly, black fingers of mist materialized in the middle of the group. The wisps threaded together and formed into the shape of a body, then solidified, revealing Alexei. He stood in front of the four. A slight amount of vapor was rising from the back of his neck as the setting sun tried unsuccessfully to destroy him, its scorching power having decreased for the day.

Craig was shocked to see the mayor. "Alex! What the hell? I mean shit! What are you doing here?" Craig looked around to see if anyone had spotted him.

"I have been thinking about what has transpired, what my family has brought to this world and my promise I made to Theodore. Being the mayor of Vamp Town is no longer enough."

Craig was still looking around. If anyone had seen a vampire appear inside the CSC compound, all holy hell would break loose, and with good reason. "Um, wow, Alex, we can't talk here. Now. Do you know how much trouble we can get into with you here? Do you know how much trouble you could get into? Like stake-in-the-heart trouble? And then to show up in front of trainees!"

"No, my friend. Now is precisely the time to talk *and* in front of these two. They know far more than you did when you signed up to work with me. Do I need to remind you about your bladder issues the first time I materialized in front of you?"

Liz, Ellie, and Paul tried to conceal their smiles.

"Stop! You convinced me. And for the record, you startled me, and I spilled my coffee."

"As you say . . ."

Craig still looked around for prying eyes. "Okay. What's on your mind? Is it about Cindra?"

"No. Cindra is fine," Alexei reassured them. "She is having difficulties with the idea of immortality, losing her parents, the whole tragedy of the situation. There have been a few issues which I believe we can work through."

Alexei took a long moment, gathering his thoughts. "I want to join the CSC. I want to work as an agent."

The surprise of the statement took everyone back.

Craig almost had to lift his jaw off the ground. "Not that I don't live in the heart of a crazy F-ed up world already, but that has to be the most insane idea I have ever heard. Sorry man, not going to happen."

"Stop. Let me finish," Alexei urged. "I believe I am uniquely qualified to help in the search for my brother. And I believe that some of my, as you might say, 'skill-set' can easily translate over to the management of the other 'exotic creatures' that walk the earth." Alexei searched in the eyes of Craig and Liz. "I can now understand what my brother has felt after all these years of being maintained and caged, not unlike animals in a zoo."

Craig protested. "Wait, a sec—"

"What do you call yourselves?" Pressing his point, Alexei continued, "Monster Keepers? Sounds like a play on zookeeper, doesn't it?"

"I um . . .,"

"After so many years of being kept, locked up, managed."

"I prefer to call it protective custody," Craig interjected.

"However, you choose to call it. Having no sense of purpose where even one's natural tendencies are suppressed . . . Is it any wonder that Vladimir got bored? I share his boredom."

"But you can't leave. You're the mayor of Vamp Town."

"Come on, my friend, that too is one of your silly human jokes. I am no more mayor of a fake town populated by vampires than you are president of the United States. Yes, I have been the strongest, which is how our kind rule, but Vladimir showed me that my strength has been waning.

I need a new challenge. I want to honor my promise to Theodore, and joining your organization will be the best way I can accomplish that."

Craig heard Alex and didn't disagree with him in principle, but to allow a vampire into the CSC? Well, that was unimaginable, and the higher-ups would never agree. "This will not happen, Alex. I don't even have to ask to know the answer."

"You don't know Vladimir. He is formidable, and his appetite is voracious. It will take someone with equal power to stop him. That someone is me, but for how much longer? My brother is still recouping his strength. But after he has consumed enough fresh blood . . . then even I may not be able to stop him, and the earth will not be safe after that." Alexei looked Craig straight in the eyes, which unnerved him a bit. "Agent Wright. Now is the time to take action against him."

Alexei could see the gears working in Craig's head, and he continued with his well-rehearsed argument. "It's a new era. Locking away your monsters may not be all that easy anymore."

"Wait, how do you know that?" Craig demanded.

"I have been communicating with the other 'mayors' on many of the reserves."

Surprise spread across Craig's face.

"Please. Do not be obtuse. You know that I have always had the ability to travel the three hundred miles from Vamp Town to stand here in front of you. As for the fences . . . Some of your so-called 'specters' are easier to keep inside established boundaries, others not so much. You know my people stay where they are because I will it so.

"What leaders of the other reservations and I have been talking about is the general unrest of the inhabitants, our citizens. There is a real danger that your organization and your complacent world are about to be overwhelmed by vampires, lycans, mutants, and the other unnatural entities you have been collecting and locking away."

Craig was reluctantly seeing where Alexei's point of view. Still, he hesitated to accept the idea of a vampire, even a "good" one, on the team, and he was positive that management would reject the idea outright.

"You will need someone like me with my abilities, strength, and powers. I am an asset, not a liability."

Liz found an opening to ask a question. "I'm still not understanding what's happened with Cindra."

"There is nothing more that can be done for her. She started turning when she was bitten and swallowed the blood of her attacker. She needs to continue the process. Otherwise, she will die. Believe me; I know of what I speak. I haven't always been the bloodsucking vampire you see before you today." Alexei saw the furrowed brows of the humans. "LOL, as you say today. Yes?"

The four humans smiled weakly at the potentially awkward joke, though not dissimilar to one that any of them might tell. Who would have thought that a vampire could have a self-deprecating sense of humor?

"Believe me; I am as concerned about her as you. I am easing her into the life she was not asked to be a part of, making her transition as slow as possible so that she ages a few more human years before becoming entirely immortal." He shook his head. "I have seen many vampires who were turned as children go insane because they carried a child's mentality in an immortal body."

"We saw how Vlad behaved. If that wasn't insanity at work, then I'm afraid to see a real stark-raving vampire," Paul interjected.

Alexei gave Paul a cautionary look. "Do not confuse insanity with cunning."

"But back to that whole 'vampire as CSC agent' thing," Craig inserted.

"Please. Even the *Enterprise* had Worf, a Klingon as a crew member," Alexei said with a warm smile.

Everyone looked at him in astonishment.

"What? Is television only for mortals? Try living forever to learn what idle time truly means."

Alexei could see that Liz, Ellie, and Paul were convinced, but it was Craig that had to be fully on board with the idea. And even then, he still had to convince the ones above him that this was good. "Know what I say is true. I am uniquely qualified to hunt my brother and rein him in before Vamp Town becomes irrelevant, if it hasn't already."

Craig could only shake his head. A substantial part of him wanted to send Alexei back to the reservation and figure out how to lock it down completely, but he wasn't sure how. The other part of him knew Alexei was telling him the facts. All those recent breakout attempts from Site-Delta had sent up the red flags screaming of something serious happening.

"Alex, you know it's not my call. Others run this agency, but I will make sure your request is noted."

Alexei smiled. "Thank you, my friends. I honestly believe that this is the best thing for all."

Craig shook Alexei's hand.

"Until this moment, I did not know what being a politician was like," Alexei mused. "Looking back, I can see why my friend Theodore was so good at it. Walking softly while carrying a big stick is exhausting. I have more respect for him now than I ever have had."

"I'm, ah, not sure that was what Roosevelt meant . . ."

"Perhaps I misquote Agent Wright, but who knew him? You or me?"

Craig held up his hands in surrender. "I concede."

Though Craig could see Alexei's perspective and even agree that he might be an asset, he still had an uneasy feeling. Maybe it was the idea that the CSC system, as designed, was in danger of falling apart. But what could they do to fix it?

Alexei stood between Liz and Craig and draped his arms around their shoulders.

"My friends, I know that the times ahead are going to bring troubles none of us are prepared for. But to quote from one of my favorite movies, 'I think this is the beginning of a beautiful friendship.'"

Chapter 27

EPILOGUE

Seattle, Washington Six Months Later

T HE RAIN HAD been pouring down all day, typical for autumn in the Puget Sound. The bar had seen little business in the last hour, which was not common at such a late hour, but most of the regular customers were at home studying for mid-terms. If, however, you had a desire to be out in this type of weather, this would be the ideal place, small, dark, and cozy, a brick-walled basement hideaway with a retro 70s décor that the college kids liked.

The bartender wiped down the countertop for the umpteenth time, waiting for the couple sitting by the fake electric fire to finish staring into each other's eyes and get the hell out so he could close for the night.

The front door opened. The little bell mounted to the top rang with a happy, light, dinging sound. A man and woman entered. They shook off the water from the deluge before they stepped all the way into the bar, then hung up their coats on the hooks mounted in a dark niche.

Vladimir and Steph stepped out of the shadows and up to the counter. The bartender arched his eyebrows and nodded his head up over to the couple by the fire. Vladimir slowly turned and saw the man and woman as they softly spoke, smiled, giggled a bit, and then continued to gaze into the other's eyes, oblivious to the world around them.

Vladimir turned back and ordered two drinks. The bartender pulled down a bottle that was hidden from view and wiped off the dust. "Sorry, haven't had many orders for this vintage." He opened it, poured out a thick red liquid into a glass, and set the bottle on the bar. Vladimir picked it up and studied the label. He sniffed the cork and nodded his approval. Then he picked up the glass by the stem and swirled the liquid around, held it up to the light, inspecting the color and clarity of the drink as it clung to the side, and watched as it slowly slipped back down into the bowl. Vladimir took a quick sharp sip and swished it around in his mouth, then swallowed with a smile. "Yes, that will do nicely." He handed the glass to Steph. "You will like this. It's earthy with hints of copper and finishes with a slight sweetness."

"A blend?"

"No, it's a single source private reserve." The bartender chimed in. "A nouveau."

Steph took a sip and swished it around in her mouth, coating her entire pallet. "Oh, yes, I think this will do nicely, for starters." Her eyes glanced over to the couple, who were now becoming quite intimate.

The bartender looked at the two. "It's what college students do nowadays. Can't they get a room?"

Vladimir looked back at the two lovebirds. "Now, what would be the fun of that?" He moved the empty glass towards the bartender, indicating that he wanted it filled again. "And my companion will have another one as well."

Vladimir and Steph took their time as they enjoyed their glasses of the finest intoxicant that wasn't straight from the source. But these drinks were only a precursor to the upcoming event.

Vladimir looked at the bartender and nodded his head over to the entrance. He got Vladimir's drift and went over to the door, pulled the string on the neon OPEN sign, switched it off, and quietly turned the deadbolt.

Vladimir whispered into Steph's ear. She giggled as he spoke to her. Smiling with mischievous eyes, Steph crossed over to the table next to the couple and sat next to the man. As Steph sat, she brushed her knee against the man's leg. He looked down at the touch and saw a shapely leg leading up into a noticeably short skirt. The skirt was so short as to invite one's imagination to figure out what else Steph might be wearing under it. The man followed Steph's legs further up and saw an open blouse revealing more of Steph's breasts than would be considered "in good taste." But tasteful dress was in the eye of the beholder, wasn't it?

The man slowly looked up from Steph's decolletage and fell into her eyes. Milk-white orbs with black pupils that reflected no light. The man gulped. He was hopelessly lost in Steph: her body, her eyes, her very being.

His girlfriend watched in a state of shock at how brazen Steph had been. She was left speechless at how her boyfriend had just turned from her and now was a drooling idiot. Everyone in her sorority told her all men were alike, and she believed it up to a point, but Bret? She thought differently of him, but apparently, she was wrong. Again.

The woman stood, disgusted at the display she was witnessing. Bret was so absorbed in the woman sitting next to him he had forgotten all about her. She waited just a moment to see if he even saw that she was about to leave. A pause. A cough. Then another. She grabbed her coat off the back of the chair and turned. Vladimir appeared as a wall in front of her, blocking her immediate escape. He looked across the room at the bartender and winked. The bartender walked over to the jukebox and pressed a button.

The woman wanted to say something to her boyfriend, but she could not work her mouth. She turned back, but Vladimir was still a looming presence between her and the door. The sound of a needle dropping on a record was heard and then *Only You*, sung by the Platters, played. Vladimir held out his hand to the woman. He looked into her eyes.

"My name is Vladimir. Would you care to dance?"

The woman was drawn to him instantly. Vladimir took her into his arms and twirled her around on the floor. He whispered to the woman, "You are my destiny." She became a puppet in his arms. They dipped to the music and swirled around the floor effortlessly. She had never moved this gracefully in her life. Holding Vladimir's hand, she knew she was falling for his magic, didn't understand—or care.

The woman looked over at Bret. Steph had him in her thrall. He was all but drooling as she lowered his head down to her breast with a satisfied smile. Steph stroked the man's cheek and leaned into his ear, whispering something.

Vladimir looked at Steph as he moved his head towards the woman's arched neck. He whispered into the woman's ear, "You are my dream. You are mine."

Vladimir and Steph looked into each other's eyes as they bit into the necks of the man and woman at the same time. They shared a moment of ecstasy. Then they sucked the lifeblood from their victims.

———◆◇◆———

THE VOICE AT the other end of the phone signal had an angry, irritated tone.

"Where the hell are you? Remember the weekly staff meeting? Or did your grandmother die again?"

"Come on! You know I only miss those 'staff infections' if I'm following a story."

"Seems like that's one of your excuses every week. That and the dying relative, but I don't recall the last time I saw a story resulting from your absences."

"This time it's for real. My police buddy called me around five this morning. They found two more bodies, university students, blood completely drained. They both have what appears to be puncture wounds on their necks."

"That makes how many this month?"

T.C. checked his notes. "From what I can tell, these two make a total of six, and we are only into the second week of the month. Over the past five months, there has been an average of three a week."

"Serial killers are not our standard content. I hired you to cover city government and the occasional beer tasting event."

"That whole tunnel digging machine stuck for months kind of turned me off to the scandals of Seattle government. Listen, Walt, after they found the third body, I did some

Googling, looking for similar deaths. You know, to find a pattern or link of some kind. It looks like, before this rash of murders here, there hasn't been another similar series of deaths going back as far as 1890, in New York City, when Teddy Roosevelt was commissioner of police. I didn't know that he was the commissioner, did you? Jesus, and he was only 36."

"So, your big story is a history piece on Theodore Roosevelt? Did you know he was president too?"

"Funny. New York had an identical series of deaths, blood-drained bodies, neck wounds, the works. The papers back then called it the Night Stalker Murders."

"Wasn't that the Ramirez guy?"

"No! I mean, yes, but he was in the 1980s. I'm talkin' about the 1890s, New York. Not Southern California."

"K?"

"Roosevelt set up one of the first detective units dedicated to catching a serial killer."

"They ever find the guy?"

"No, but the string of killings stopped after about a year. Every so often, though, a single murder happens somewhere in the world that has all the same telltale signs."

"A cult?"

"Maybe. But why the concentrated killings a hundred years ago and then nothing much to speak of and then another concentration today here in Seattle?"

"Okay." Walt considered what he had just heard. Real or a load of crap from the one reporter on his payroll who had a genuine gut instinct for this type of thing. "I want to see something in my email by the end of the day."

"Got it."

"And don't miss any more of our Monday staff meetings. We're a weekly paper. The meetings are the only way we can all stay focused on the upcoming issue. Got it T.C.?"

"Heard you loud and clear. You'll have my first installment by the end of the day. And thank you."

The publisher of the *Emerald City Weekly* looked at the screen on his cell. The signal had been disconnected. The screen went dark, and he wondered just what T.C. might be getting the paper and himself into.

Author's Note

Thank you for giving **Vamp Town** a shot. I am not the first new author who has said this, but writing a novel is not for the easily discouraged. From the time I thought that it was a good idea to take a screenplay and turn it into a novel (hey I had it mostly written already, right?) to the point of self-publishing, over two years have come and gone. A fair amount of my time was spent just trying to learn how to format the damn thing.

A big thank you to my Beta readers. I had no idea what I was asking you to do at the time, but your individual input helped me shoehorn the first draft into ever-narrowing parameters, which enabled me to be more concise in my storytelling. Thanks to my editor, Janet Tapper. Your questions, protestations, and "gentle" suggestions were listened to, though not always heeded. I did employ a lot of what you suggested. Honest! And thanks to my buddy Steve Cridland for taking promotional photos of me.

Finally, a special thank you to my graphic designer brother, Brian Seats, who designed the cover.

You can learn more about me and my second book, ***Blood City***, at www.jeffseats.com. Please consider leaving a review with Amazon.

About the Author

Jeff Seats lives in Portland, Oregon, where he has worked in the entertainment industry as a scenic designer, set decorator, and production designer for stage and motion pictures. You can visit **www.jeffseats.com** to see some of his past work as a designer and photographer.

Bonus Material

Scan the QR Code or visit **www.jeffseats.com/vt-bonus** for maps, photos, and links to articles I used to develop the world of *Vamp Town.*

www.ingramcontent.com/pod-product-compliance
Lightning Source LLC
Chambersburg PA
CBHW051316250626
47155CB00007B/2339